THE
Lindens

One House.
All the People Who Called It Home.

BARNEY JEFFRIES

THE LINDENS

Prologue   1
1885

Reading Keats to Cows   5
1894

Odds   41
1916

Loss   68
1930

Henry Cook's Diary   98
1939-41

Rabbit Pie   155
1954

The Well   192
1976

Dulce Domum   220
1982

Wayfarers All!   242
1987

Gathering   271
1995

The Blake Midwinter   306
2008

Floorboards   360
2016

Offering   392
2021

Epilogue   439
2035

Acknowledgments   441

To Mum and Dad

"...he seemed to have lost all interest for the time in the things that went to make up his daily life, as well as in all pleasant forecastings of the altered days and doings that the changing season was surely bringing.

"Casually, then, and with seeming indifference, the Mole turned his talk to the harvest that was being gathered in, the towering wagons and their straining teams, the growing ricks, and the large moon rising over bare acres dotted with sheaves. He talked of the reddening apples around, of the browning nuts, of jams and preserves and the distilling of cordials; till by easy stages such as these he reached midwinter, its hearty joys and its snug home life, and then he became simply lyrical."

Kenneth Graeme, The Wind in the Willows

PROLOGUE
1885

It was to be the best house he had ever built, and Arnold Cann had built hundreds of houses.

At nine years old he'd spent ten-hour days feeding the kilns where cakes of clay were baked into bricks. Aged thirteen, he was laying the bricks in rows, layering the rows on top of each other until they became walls, until the walls became houses. By seventeen he was taking charge of the sites where he worked. He was a strong man, with broad shoulders, big, skilful hands and a booming voice that could stop you in your tracks from a hundred yards. But he had a sharp mind too. He knew the price of bricks and the price of labour. He knew what land sold for, and what a house sold for, and though he'd had little enough in the way of schooling, he could see that in the difference between those figures was powerful conjuring. A man could break his back for six shillings a day laying bricks and trowelling mortar, and the pounds would stack up in the bank account of another who'd never done an honest day's labour in his life. Some men might have turned bitter, or radical; Arnold Cann wanted to be one of the conjurers.

The trick to making money was to have money in the first place. Failing that, the next best thing was to find someone who was willing to lend it. Then you could take a patch of scrub, clear the trees and level the earth, lay the foundations and build great piles of money. And when you'd done that, they wanted to lend you more. A larger patch of scrub. More houses, bigger piles. Magic.

He learnt new tricks. Labour was cheap, but bricks were a cost. Why should someone else be taking a cut? He could make his own bricks. He bought an old smallholding with ten acres on the edge of a nondescript village in the south of the county, where the flood plain of the Avon wrinkled into woods and chalk downland. Rough and marshy, it was poor farmland, but the perfect site for brickmaking: red clay, amber sand, coppiced willow and hazel to feed the kiln. Digging money from the earth.

Aged forty, Arnold Cann was a wealthy man, with a wife and three children, in need of a house befitting their status. The family seat that would secure their place among the gentry.

Arnold Cann had grown fond of the country around his brickworks: the oak trees that stood sentinel along the road, the bluebells draped across the wood in spring, the lapwings that rose like smoke off the fields. Practical man of business that he was, Arnold Cann was not immune to such charms.

He had the old cob cottage pulled down, and set about building the house of his imagining. Not fancy, not ostentatious, but a proper house, square and solid, made of his own red bricks dug from the earth where it stood. It had gabled roofs and bay windows, four tall chimneys and seven steps up to the front door. There were four bedrooms and an indoor bathroom for the family, two smaller rooms for the maid, the cook and the housekeeper. Each of the two drawing rooms was larger than the damp hovel where Arnold Cann had been dragged up with three brothers and three sisters, seven of them sleeping on a bed the size of the newly installed grand piano.

He dug a cellar where he could lay down wines for guests who needed to be impressed, and a well a hundred feet deep. The back of the house faced south: he rolled out a lawn and built a walled garden that trapped the sun. He built stables and a coach house, and beyond them he laid out an orchard. At the far end of the lawn, atop a flight of steps looking over the brickworks, he built an octagonal folly with a steepling roof. A whimsical flourish, perhaps, but a chance for his lads to hone their skills, and to make use of bricks that didn't make the grade. Arnold Cann didn't like things going to waste. If you knew where to look, you could find patched-up cracks and tell-tale paw prints from a batch the cat had run across before they set.

Either side of the driveway he planted a row of lime trees. One day those wispy saplings would become a verdant avenue, admired by every passer-by, in whose shade his son's sons would drive in horseless carriages. That was the image in his mind when he christened his family home: The Lindens.

Though he was not much given to flights of fancy, when he looked on the houses he had built, he could be brought up short by the thought of all the unknown, unknowable lives that would play out beneath those roofs, the loves and the laughter and the tears, the intrigues and agonies, the dramas and daily rituals. One day, a hundred years hence, long after he had returned to sand and clay, this house would stand, and somebody whose parents' parents were not yet born would look upon what he had built and call it home.

READING KEATS TO COWS
1894

Late afternoon, late summer. Roger Cann sat in the folly, a copy of Ovid's *Metamorphosis* open in front of him. It was stiflingly hot. He had read the same page three times and hadn't retained a word. Translating the tale of Philemon and Baucis into alexandrines had seemed like a good idea at the time, the sort of thing that a Man of Letters might spend his time doing. So far today, he had managed a total of six lines, and one of those was missing a foot.

A bluebottle was droning above his head, beating itself repeatedly against the window pane, confounded each time by the existence of glass. It was a surprisingly beautiful thing, iridescent green like a peacock's feather. A spider's web hung from the rafter above the window. Several times the fly brushed close to its treacherous threads. Roger picked up the empty wine glass from the desk; he had been drinking his father's claret, purloined in secret from the cellar. Trapping the fly against the window, he slipped Ovid under the bottom of the glass, then carried it carefully to the doorway. He lifted off the book and let the bluebottle take flight for freedom. It circled once above his head, then buzzed back through the door to resume its attack on the window pane. Roger sighed. He wasn't sure whether to curse its stupidity or admire its perseverance.

On the far side of the lawn, his mother was plucking the faded heads off the rose bush, which appeared to be one of her favourite pastimes; Roger was sure she spent more time complaining about the garden's untidiness than admiring its beauty. Beyond the wall, wisps of smoke from the kiln eddied in the air. Roger wondered whether he envied the labourers in the brickyard: digging out the clay and the sand, piling it into the wagons the horses hauled along iron tracks, mixing it and moulding it and baking it like bread. Or so he imagined: he knew little about brickmaking. Or breadmaking for that matter. He had never paid much attention to his father droning on about bricks and mortar and all that. Still, there was meaning in it, wasn't there? A life of industry, honest labour, manly companionship, making things that people needed. On the other hand, it must be hideously hot.

He let his gaze wander the other way, over the hay meadow towards the clay pits. There was no sign of her yet, but in the distance the five brown cows were lined up by the gate. That meant she would be coming soon. This afternoon he would speak to her. He ducked back inside and swallowed another glass of the claret to fortify himself. Then he slipped out the folly, around the rockery and up the hill towards the meadow, ducking behind the juniper trees to keep out of his mother's line of sight. Though he was doing nothing illicit. Simply taking a stroll up to Marshmead, the boggy acre of land at the far end of the property.

The cows had appeared there a month ago. This happened from time to time. Roger had never given them much thought. He remembered his father saying something about leasing the field.

"To whom do the cows belong?" he had asked the other day.

"Cuth Hobson. Dairyman, lives up the lane."

It wasn't the dairyman Roger was interested in. It was the maid. Every afternoon, when the shadows began to lengthen and the light took on a golden hue, she would come to milk the cows. (She came at dawn too, but Roger was not awake to witness this.) She was everything one imagined in a milkmaid: fair headed and rosy cheeked, with strong hips and generous breasts. Roger was hopelessly in love. He had contrived several times to cross her path, but he had no idea what to say to her when he did. Thirteen years at public school, three years at Oxford, and women were a mystery to him. So were country people in general, though The Lindens had been his home for nigh on ten years.

The meadow was abuzz with insects. Swifts wheeled overhead. The sweet smell of newly cut hay wafted on the air. Perhaps he would abandon his education and become a cowherd. His parents would disapprove, of course, but then his father already disapproved of him. It must be an idyllic existence. Poets waxed lyrical about the pastoral life, although thinking about it this seemed mostly to concern shepherds and shepherdesses. Cattle figured less prominently in literature. Roger could only think of *Tess of the d'Urbervilles*, a book he had read recently, which painted a less than bucolic picture.

He strolled over to the gate where the cows were waiting. They were pretty things, with their chestnut hair and the long lashes round their big dark eyes. They scattered as he approached, but then sidled back, inquisitive. He held out a hand towards them. One took another few tentative steps in his direction, then pressed her neat black nose against the backs of his fingers. It was surprisingly wet. He snatched his hand away.

"She won't bite."

Roger whipped around. She was standing just a few feet away, a look of amusement on her face. Close to, she was more beautiful than ever. Nineteen or twenty perhaps. Her hair was loosely tied in a white bonnet, a few ringlets escaping over her forehead. Her eyes were not unlike the cows', he thought, though that didn't seem like a line a poet would use.

"Wilt thou, Mabel?" The cow came forward to nuzzle the girl's hand, and she gave it a scratch between the ears.

"She's very pretty," Roger said. He had friends at Oxford who could so easily have followed it up with *Though not half so pretty as you, miss* or some such line, but the words stuck on his tongue. His mouth felt dry.

"Yes sir. Jerseys are. And good milkers too." Her voice was musical, lilting, with a light Wiltshire burr. "You're from the house," she said when he didn't reply.

He nodded. "Roger Cann." He held out a hand, then quickly withdrew it, realising it was the same gesture he'd just employed with Mabel the cow.

"Mr Hobson's daughter, sir. Tessa." She gave a small curtsey. "You seem amused, sir?"

"Oh, it's nothing," said Roger hurriedly. "A coincidence. You see, I had just been thinking of *Tess of the D'Urbervilles*. It's a book," he added. Rather a scandalous one, not at all the thing to mention in the presence of an innocent young girl.

"I know 'tis a book sir. I read it myself."

"Oh." Roger was taken aback. "And how did you enjoy it?"

"I don't know if enjoy is the word. But it made me cry, and it made me angry. Also, it's a valuable warning to beware of the rich squire's son, sir."

Despite the deference in the *sirs* and the curtsey, she was looking him straight in the eye; challenging or teasing, he wasn't sure.

"I hope you don't take me for an Alec D'Urberville."

"Ah, then perhaps you're more of an Angel Clare, sir? Romanticising the innocence of country life." She gave him a pitying look. "I'm not sure which of 'em was worse." Then she softened. "But he writes well, Mr Hardy. And he's learnt a thing or two about cows."

"You read a lot then?"

"I like to. When I have time."

The big black Bible was the only book in the Hobson household when Tessa was growing up. But she had been quick to learn her letters, and her numbers too: two and two are four, four and four are eight. Sixteen, thirty-two, sixty-four. She pictured them in her head, stacking like haybales, doubling in size: 512, 1024, 2048, 4096, 8192. She had attended the village school till she was thirteen, when it was decided, against the protests of Miss Carlisle the schoolmistress, that her time would be better employed milking the cows and helping her mother with the household chores. Tessa had been outraged. She had tried to reason with her parents. She had prepared a speech arguing that not only was learning worthy for its own sake, but that her parents themselves would benefit in the long run because with an education she would be able to earn more money for the family. She had thought it persuasive. Her father had not.

"Earning money for the family? With thy book-learning? I'll tell thee what to learn, missy: learn thy place."

She had lost her temper then, and received a clip round the ear for her troubles. But eventually they negotiated a compromise. Miss Carlisle would continue to lend her books, and for two wonderful hours a day, after she returned from the morning milking, after she cleared away the breakfast things, after she fetched water from the pump on Chapel Green, after she washed the bowls and scrubbed the pans, and before she had to start thinking about preparing luncheon, she would read.

Over the next five years, she devoured books as fast as Miss Carlisle could provide them. Shakespeare of course, Homer, Tennyson and Keats, Coleridge and Wordsworth. She read Plato and Marcus Aurelius and Voltaire. She read Darwin's *Voyage of the Beagle* and *On the Origin of Species*, and tried to explain to her family how the tree of life had grown over hundreds of millions of years, how it had branched out in different directions, how it kept dividing and putting out new shoots, and how she found that idea more wonderful and glorious than the story of God making everything in half a dozen days. She had earned another clip round the ear for that.

Then there were the novels. Dickens, Thackeray, Eliot, Austen, Trollope. She loved them not just for the pleasure of the stories and the company of the characters, but for the knowledge they gave her of a world beyond the boundaries of the parish. Though she herself had never been further than the cattle market in Salisbury, Tessa felt she understood the world better than most.

It wasn't that she wanted to leave. The village was her

home, and the novels tended to be in agreement that this was something that mattered. She loved the woods and the fields, the birds and her cows, the ever-changing light and the circling seasons. Her days were full. Milking was always a pleasure when the sun shone; when the cold turned bitter and the rain soaked her to the marrow, well, then it was a relief to come indoors and warm herself by the kitchen fire. In between, she churned butter and baked bread, collected the eggs the hens had left in half a dozen nests dotted around the yard. She hoed the spring soil, earthed up potatoes, pulled weeds in Dawson's cornfield with her sister Eliza for a shilling a day – money given to their mother for the housekeeping, and drunk away by their father in the Red Lion.

One day soon she'd marry someone like him, most likely. And become like her mother. Lord, she hoped not. Her mother, who sighed and grumbled her way through every day, who, finding no joy in anything, found fault in everything. When had her mother last taken a stroll through the woods in August and tasted the sweet white kernels of the cobnuts? When had she last listened to the turtle dove's burr as the sun rose on a misty May morning? When did she last add a dainty sprig of parsley to each plate when she served up dinner? When had she last read a poem that tore a hole in her soul? Had she ever? Dora Hobson complained of headaches from the birds singing too loudly, and took the crowing of the cockerels as a personal affront.

It wasn't inevitable, Tessa told herself. Whatever happened, she would never forget the small joys of life, would never lose touch with the infinite worlds without and within. She didn't need a husband to make her happy, but a good one surely wouldn't hurt. There were precious few men to choose from in the village. Clem Shipham, the only boy she'd ever kissed, had been the pick of them. Now he was married to Ada Chapman and they had a baby on the way. He had been sweet on her when they were younger, could have settled down together maybe. But there was a double meaning in the word *settle*. Settling meant accepting less than you wanted. She wasn't ready to settle. "Ideas above her station, that one," her mother used to tell people. It wasn't a compliment. But why shouldn't she aspire to higher ideas? Why should her station be stationary?

Tessa hitched the milking pails onto the yoke and tucked her stool under her arm, then set off down the lane toward Marshmead. She walked a little quicker than usual. Would he be there again? Roger Cann. The Canns weren't real gentry, even if they didn't mix much with the ordinary folk of the village. "Got no right to make out they be our betters," her father would grumble. "Her might be all hoity-toity, but he come from nothing, just like we." She had never given much thought to their pale, gangly son, though she had seen him from time to time on her way back from the milking, or slouching in the family pew at the front of the church. When they spoke yesterday she had thought him haughty at first – surprised that she knew what a book was – but awkward was more like it. He had just "come down", he said; she knew this meant from Oxford University. He had read classics, he told her, and when she asked why, he laughed and said that was a good question.

She spotted him from across the field, leaning against the oak tree by the gate, apparently absorbed in a book. As she approached, he looked up in feigned surprise. "Oh, hello there. Miss Hobson!"

Tessa had to stop herself laughing; he was not a good actor. "Fancy seeing you here, sir."

"Ah, well, I wanted to find somewhere to read."

"A strange place to pick then, unless you were reading to the cows?"

His sallow face reddened. He was easy to tease, this boy. "And what is it that you read, sir?"

"What? Oh." He showed her the book. "Keats. Poetry."

"Oh, I think they would like that. Usually I sing when I milk them. It soothes them, helps bring the milk down. But perhaps you could recite something instead?"

"I think you're teasing me."

"Not at all, sir. Read, do."

"Well. How about *Ode on a Grecian Urn*?" He cleared his throat and began. "*Thou still unravish'd bride...*" He broke off, coughed, and continued.

"*Thou still unravish'd bride of quietness.*
Thou foster-child of silence and slow time,
Sylvan historian, who canst thus express
A flowery tale more sweetly than our rhyme..."

As he spoke, an image came into Tessa's mind. Herself in an impossibly distant future, sitting in a rocking chair in an elegant room, grandchildren draped around her. *I fell in love with your grandfather,* she would tell them, *when he read* Ode on a Grecian Urn *to Mabel, Maureen, Dorcas, Dinah and Lavender*. The thought made her smile, though it was a silly one. Fall in love with him indeed!

Still, he had a soft, musical voice. And he read well. He was self-conscious at first, but seemed to relax into the absurdity of the moment, and addressed the final lines looking Mabel directly in the eye: "*Beauty is truth, truth beauty,– that is all / Ye know on earth, and all ye need to know.*" Mabel stared back at him, then snorted and turned away. Tessa laughed.

He gave a tentative smile. "Do you think they liked it?"

"Oh yes, sir. But I think they preferred it when the

rector's son read them some Wordsworth the other day." He looked stricken. "I'm only joking, sir. As if they would prefer Wordsworth to Keats."

He laughed properly then, and so did she. A man who could laugh at himself was worth something.

"What do you do with the milk?" Roger asked. She probably thought him a fool, but he wanted her to keep talking. "You make it into butter perhaps?"

"Just what we eat ourselves. Most of it we sell to the creamery in Alderbourne. A man comes and collects it from all of us round here as has cattle."

Like brickmaking, Roger was painfully aware that he knew next to nothing about dairy farming. Knew nothing, in fact, of how a family like Tessa's lived. It struck him that this might be more valuable knowledge than the conjugation of Latin verbs.

He sighed. "It must be a charming life."

"Oh yes, sir. I spend all my days lounging in the meadows listening to poetry, as you see. And cows are like to walking goldmines."

She really did think him a fool. "I sense you are speaking ironically."

"Perhaps a little. 'Tis pleasant on a day like this. But the milk don't sell for much. The creamery's the only place that'll buy it. They keep the price so low it barely pays the rent on the grazing."

It seemed jolly unfair that her family had to pay rent to his. It wasn't as if his father needed the land for anything else.

"Couldn't you ask them to give you more money?" Roger

asked. "I'm sure they're decent chaps. If you explained the situation..."

"You have a touching faith in your fellow man, sir."

He listened, rapt, as she talked about how they struggled, the small farmers, and what she'd do about it, if she had the means to.

"If we could build our own creamery here in the village... Then we could sell directly to the big dairy in Salisbury, without them in Alderbourne taking a cut. Or even send it by train. Southampton. London, even...."

He had never met a woman like her. True, he knew precious few women, but even if he had met thousands, he knew with utter conviction that he would feel just the same.

After dinner that night, he sat with his father drinking port and smoking cigars. This was usually a strained affair. While Roger was used to it with his Oxford set, Arnold Cann still had the air of a man who would rather be drinking mild in the tap room of a public house. Roger was not comfortable around such people. His father would complain about people Roger had never met, give incomprehensible accounts of tedious business matters, hold forth on what the government should be doing and wasn't, or vice versa. Roger would try to listen, but then lose himself staring into the flame of the oil lamp and the shadows on the wall behind, giving occasional nods and all-purpose vocalisations which he hoped conveyed agreement with whatever his father was saying. It usually worked, except when he came up against a direct question.

"Well, boy?"

"Sorry... what was that?"

Arnold sighed. "I asked, have you given it any more thought? What you plan to do, now that you've finished with your Greeks and Romans?"

Roger hated this question. The fact was, he hadn't the faintest idea. For many of the friends he mixed with, this wasn't even a consideration. They didn't have to decide to *do* anything – just to continue living the life they were born to.

This was anathema to Arnold Cann, he knew that. His father had told him often enough.

"I started out with nothing, don't you forget that, and look where I am. If I'd had the start you've had in life, I'd be the Lord bloody Chancellor by now."

His mother had been so proud when Roger won his place at Oxford. She had hugged him and even cried a few tears, which she tried to pass off as hay fever. It was a personal accolade, public recognition that she had successfully raised a child of the first rank.

His father was more ambivalent. "Latin and Greek. Reading books written in languages no ordinary person spoke for a thousand years. What's the point, I'd like to know." Although he didn't want to know. He never listened when Roger tried to explain, about classical civilisations and the roots of modern language, about philosophy and theology, poetry and myth. His father had no interest in such things.

"I don't rightly know, pa."

Roger knew this wasn't a satisfactory answer. His father was disappointed in him, he was aware of that. "I had been wondering..." he began, then trailed off. His father would think him foolish. But then, his father thought him foolish already. And *she* hadn't sounded foolish, that afternoon, when she talked about it with such clear-headed passion. She had sounded entirely convincing. "I had been wondering about the dairy business."

His father barked with laughter. "The dairy business? And what in the world do you know about that?"

"Well…" Roger tried to remember the things Tessa had said. "The small farmers around here, they all sell their milk for a pittance to some little man in Alderbourne. It's highly inefficient. He goes round to them all in a cart. And there are times in the winter when those tracks are barely passable."

"The road to Alderbourne too," Arnold agreed. "Gets flooded sometimes down by the ford." He waited for his son to continue.

"So, well, I had been thinking. What if there were some large barn in the village – a local creamery or what have you where everyone could bring their cows to be milked, or bring the milk over themselves. Then it could all be collected from one central location. Somewhere near the main road."

To Roger's relief, his father nodded. "Economies of scale, lower production costs, take a cut off the top. Go on."

Emboldened, Roger continued. "That's not all though. Forget Alderbourne. You can make far more selling to the city dairies. We're half a mile from the railway here. The morning milk could be in London by luncheon."

Arnold Cann was looking at his son with a strange expression – interest, surprise, even a hint of respect. "So where might you be thinking of building this here creamery?"

"Well… The Lindens would seem to be a convenient location. And, well, you have lots of bricks."

His father laughed again. "I can tell you the price of bricks, aye. Then you can do your costings, work out what volume you can turn over, set your margins, forecast your net profit… Don't understand a word I'm saying, do you?"

Roger gave a sheepish grin. "I would say it's all Greek to me, but I'm afraid I find Greek a deal more comprehensible."

"It's a not a joke, boy. If you want to succeed, you need to be serious. If you're not serious, then don't waste any more of my time with your daydreams."

"No, I am serious. So I should be, um, working out how much things cost..." Roger tailed off. It struck him that he had no idea what even a pint of milk might cost.

Arnold poured more port. "All right. Listen. I might consider investing – that means putting my money into – this venture of yours, if you can convince me I'll make a profit. That means I get out more money than I put in."

"Right. And how would I...? Well, how do I know that?"

"You tell me. You know how much I invested in that education of yours? About time it started paying out."

The next day he met her in the lane that ran along the back of the brickworks. She had two pails yoked over her neck, a three-legged stool hooked under her arm. She smiled when she saw him, and Roger felt a quiver pass through him. "Out for a walk, sir? There's a coincidence."

"Well, I thought I might take a little stroll. Can I help you carry any of that?"

She laughed. "Tain't heavy now. After milking maybe. Though I don't suppose you could manage it then."

"Well, perhaps you wouldn't mind my company, as long as we're walking the same way?"

"'Twould be an honour, sir."

They ambled along side by side. Roger plucked a stem of grass and twined it round his finger.

"I spoke to my father last night," he said. Tessa turned to him, immediately alert. "About the things you were talking about. Just floated the idea of building a whatsit... a creamery. Transporting the milk on the railway and so forth."

"And what did he think?"

"Well, I think he rather liked the idea. But of course he wants to know about the, um, turning over the margins, forecasting the nets, all that. So that more money comes out at the end than goes in at the beginning."

Tessa nodded. "He'll want to make a profit, naturally."

"I have to say, I'm not exactly an expert in these things..."

"We need numbers," she interrupted. "We need to know the price they pay for milk up in London... I can find that out from them at Alderbourne. Then we need to work out how much milk we can produce... well, there must be at least a dozen that keeps a dairy herd in the village. So there's Fred Brewster, has a score of Ayrshires, so call that twenty gallons a day..."

Roger listened, entranced, as she reeled off lists of names. She seemed to know every dairy farmer in the parish, how many cows they kept, how much milk the different breeds produced, balancing stacks of figures in her head. "Of course, if we had the capital, we could buy more. And I could manage twice as many myself if I didn't have to carry the milk on my shoulders for half a mile."

She had quickened her pace as she talked, as if her feet were keeping time with the whirring cogs of her brain.

"Could we perhaps walk round via the claypits?" Roger suggested. He would rather not walk past the house, in case his mother saw them and asked awkward questions. Having successfully overseen his education, finding her son a suitable wife was now Lydia Cann's principal aim in life. His sisters had already married, and married well. Elspeth had wedded the eldest son of a baronet with a crumbling manor in the Wylye valley, and already borne him a son and heir. Grace had, more rashly, fallen in love with a naval lieutenant, but he was a respectable man and had since become a captain. In company, Lydia Cann missed no opportunity to talk up her son's achievements. "Such an eligible bachelor he even has a degree to prove it," she would say, laughing as if she had never made the joke before while Roger silently squirmed. Since he had come down that summer, she had kept up a constant barrage of dinners, tea parties and card evenings at which he had been introduced to a succession of young ladies. They simpered artificially or looked bored as Roger attempted to engage them in conversation. He couldn't imagine any of them talking as Tessa was now, her face alight with purpose.

"We need to find out the cost of freight. George Foster works on the railways, I'll talk to him..."

"Might you be able to write this down?"

She nodded. "I'll do it when I get home. And you need to find out from your father how much the building would come to."

"Right. Um, I suppose that depends how big it is?"

"True. I can work out the rough dimensions. Twelve stalls, say, eight by five..."

They turned off the lane and followed the path round the back of the claypits, where alders and willows grew. Waterlogged in winter, now the ground was cracked and dry. Blackthorn and brambles tangled together, the sloes and blackberries beginning to ripen. Roger reached up to pick a handful of plump dark blackberries and offered them to her. With a toss of her head, Tessa indicated her lack of free hands, and opened her mouth. Trying not to let his hand shake, Roger placed the largest, softest berry on her tongue, willing himself to look her in the eye as he did so. Did she know the effect she was having on him as she licked the juice from her lips? He suspected she did.

The cows were waiting by the gate on the other side of

Marshmead, but they came trotting over when they saw her. Roger recognised Mabel, who seemed to recognise him. He reached out to scratch the tuft of hair between her ears.

"Will you recite to them again, or shall I sing?"

"I would dearly love to hear you sing."

She set the stool on the ground and squatted down beside Mabel. The cow backed herself into place and stood placidly. Tessa sang "The Sweet Nightingale", accompanied by the steady tinkle of the milk against the pail, her voice soft and melodious. Roger averted his eyes from the cows' swollen udders.

He should tell her that she sang more sweetly than any nightingale. It felt false, though. Had he even heard a nightingale singing? Not that he was aware of. He tried to remember his Keats. *My heart aches, and a drowsy numbness pains / My sense, as though of hemlock I had drunk...* then something about *being too happy in thine happiness.*

"There are nightingales in Ashridge copse," she said, as if she could read his thoughts. "Have you heard them?"

"I don't believe I have. I should like to."

"I walk up there to listen sometimes."

"I walk there too," Roger said. The track to the wood began just along the lane from The Lindens. "Perhaps I might accompany you."

She smiled. "'Twould be a pleasure. But you'll have to wait till next spring if you want to hear a nightingale. They don't sing now. They'll disappear soon for the winter."

How little he knew about nature, Roger thought. How little he knew about anything.

"I suppose you country folk must be very knowledgeable when it comes to birds and plants and whatnot?"

"Oh yes. You should hear the talk in the Red Lion whenever there's a new issue of the *Proceedings of the Royal Society* on the biological sciences."

Roger had the feeling he was being teased, but pressed on. "One can't help feeling that modern man has rather lost his connection with the natural world. And I think there's a lot one can learn from this simple country life, untouched by our industrial age."

She gave him a quizzical look. "Well, maybe. But I reckons we might learn us a thing or two from this industrial age of yourn."

Was she exaggerating the Wiltshire accent? Once more, Roger suspected, he was being teased.

"Will you sing some more?"

As she milked Dinah, Tessa sang "The Bold Grenadier". *They went arm in arm along the road till they came to a stream / then they both sat down together to hear the nightingales sing.* She liked the idea, although the song didn't end well. At the same time, she was juggling figures in her head. What she could make with ten cows, and an extra half a shilling per gallon – and surely that was a conservative estimate? Imagine having that spare money. To not worry about going short on food in February. To buy linen for the beds, cloth to make dresses for Eliza and herself... And if they could spend more on winter fodder, then yields would be higher... call it five shillings a week. She could go to London and see a play. She could take the train to Bournemouth or Southsea for the day, even stay a night or two in a boarding house, or take a boat to the Isle of Wight...

Later that evening, by the light of a tallow candle, she put figures down on paper. The simplest thing would be to divide the costs and the profits evenly between everyone. Or, fairer, according to how many cows they had. No, how much milk they gave; you could record that after every milking. But that would never work. She couldn't imagine any of the dairy farmers round here putting up the money towards building the dairy or paying the freight costs. That was where Arnold Cann came in. He'd make his profit all right, just by skimming the cream off the top. *For whosoever hath, to him shall be given.* That was how the world worked. It was absurdly unfair, but she couldn't change it. She just had to do her best to work around it. What would it be like, to be one of those people who money had favoured? To live in a house like The Lindens, with feather beds and oil lamps and your meals brought to you by servants. To drink tea and coffee in china cups, and wine. To have a whole room just for books.

The image came to her again, the opulent room, the grandchildren round her knee. *I fell in love with your grandfather when he read* Ode on a Grecian Urn *to the cows.* Roger Cann was sweet and silly and utterly clueless about the world. He had golden curls and dreamy hazel eyes, and when they looked at her, she saw delight in them.

Oh, but it was an absurd idea. Marrying Roger Cann! Having grandchildren together. Even Eliza would laugh at that, Eliza who had been sweet on every man in the village between fourteen and forty at one time or another and never neglected to tell her about it. Milkmaids didn't marry men like that, with his lardy-dardy voice and his gentry manners and more money in his trust fund than her family had ever known. It was quite out of the question.

"Tessa Cann," she murmured to herself. It sounded well. She repeated it a little louder: "Tessa Cann. Tessa can."

.   .   .

23

"And this is my son, Roger. Roger, Mrs Tavistock, Miss Millicent."

Roger inclined his head with a "How do you do?"

"Charmed, I'm sure," Mrs Tavistock replied. Her daughter, who appeared to be studying the carpet, gave the slightest inclination of her head.

His mother really was becoming desperate. She had met the Tavistocks at a party his sister Elspeth had hosted some weeks before, which Roger had steadfastly refused to attend. "Millicent is a delightful girl," his mother had trilled. "She plays the piano exquisitely. And her father is a high court judge."

The Hon. Mr Justice Tavistock's judicial prominence notwithstanding, Roger saw little to delight him. Miss Tavistock had a long face and a protruding chin, with bushy brown hair pinned up in an elaborate coiffure that brought to mind a trussed chicken. She was old, too, surely closer to thirty than twenty. Despite his mother's machinations, there was no hurry for Roger at twenty-three to get married, but he could understand why the Tavistocks might feel time was running out to deliver their daughter from a life of spinsterhood. He felt a swelling of pity for her.

"Roger came down this summer. From Oxford."

"You mentioned that already, mother," said Elspeth, who was making up the party with her husband, Mr James Woodford. "At least twice."

One could not fail to notice the condescending tone she had adopted towards her parents since her marriage. Her father-in-law, Sir Walter Woodford, Bt., was approaching seventy and riddled with gout; Elspeth would before long be Lady Woodford, and was already rehearsing the role. Roger had never been close to his eldest sister. Seven years his senior, she had paid him little attention during the weeks when he was home from school. What on earth would she make of Tessa Hobson?

"Magdalen, wasn't it?" asked Mr Woodford.

"Merton, actually," Roger corrected. He spent the next few minutes discussing with his brother-in-law the merits and otherwise of various colleges, avoiding any further contact with Miss Tavistock. But inevitably they were seated next to each other at dinner, and Roger felt obliged to at least attempt conversation.

"Do you like to read?" he asked.

"Oh yes," she nodded. Roger waited for her to say something more. When she didn't, he asked her what she liked to read. After some hesitation, she offered a faint "books", and turned her attention to the duck pâté.

"I like to read Keats' odes," Roger said matter-of-factly. "Aloud to cows."

Miss Tavistock showed no reaction, but Roger's father caught the end of the sentence.

"What's that, boy?" Arnold Cann called from the head of the table. "Talking about cows again?" He addressed the room at large: "Roger plans to go into the dairy business."

Lydia and Elspeth visibly stiffened, but Arnold Cann continued. "Quite the entrepreneur, this lad. He's going to centralise the milk collection in the area and send it by train to London. Isn't that right, son?"

Everyone turned to Roger, who realised he was expected to speak. "It's a simple idea really," he said. "Here, there are lots of cows and not many people, and in London, there are lots of people and not many cows. And if we deliver lots of milk from here to there, then, well..."

"Then we make lots of money," finished his father. "I'm waiting for him to show me his forecasts before I decide whether to invest. When are you going to have those done, eh?"

"Very soon, sir." *As soon as Tessa gives them to me,* Roger didn't add. She was nearly finished, she had told him that afternoon. She still had to speak to George Foster about the railway costs. Somehow, what had begun as little more than an attempt to keep a pretty young thing engaged in conversation was turning into something real, with actual implications for his life, and the lives of others. Did he want to work in the dairy business? He had no idea: he knew nothing at all about it. Could he imagine himself as a businessman, like his father? He didn't think so: he had nothing of his father's forcefulness, nor his worldly wisdom. Was he ready to do anything to impress Tessa and be close to her? Yes, yes he was!

When dinner was over, the younger generation played whist. Roger liked cards, but Miss Tavistock made a poor partner, reacting with excited surprise when she won a trick, but seemingly oblivious to what cards her opponents held or when she should give Roger the lead. He thought again of Tessa, adding up figures in her head, the look in her eyes, as if she knew something you didn't and was weighing up whether or not to tell you. She would be a fine card player.

To be fair, Millicent Tavistock played the piano respectably – a Chopin nocturne, a technically correct "Moonlight Sonata". Unfortunately, she spoiled the effect when she gave in to her mother's exhortations to sing. Her pitch was flat, her expression flatter still. Roger thought of the easy purity of Tessa's voice, and ached to hear her sing again.

What did it matter if her father was a drunken dairyman, not a high court judge? It wasn't her father he was in love with! And what was the use of money, education, a position in society if you couldn't follow your own heart's desires? A wave of despair washed over him and pulled him under. How could he possibly marry Tessa? He imagined announcing the news to his family: his father's wrath, his mother's anguish, his sisters' scorn. Besides, would she even want to marry him? Perhaps her only interest in him was as a means to earn more money for her milk. What if he were to confess his love to her, and she were to laugh? Or take offence? Everything would be ruined.

The Woodfords and Tavistocks departed at eleven. The evening had been a torturous one. It was clear even to Lydia Cann that there was not a glimmer of a spark between her son and Millicent Tavistock. Still, she insisted that he should walk the ladies out to their carriage.

The night air felt unseasonably warm. Or perhaps Roger was simply inured to the cold. There had been sherry, claret with the meal, port, then more claret: he was some way from sober. All of a sudden he was full of sentimentality. Poor Miss Tavistock! How many painful evenings had she had to endure, held up to a parade of bachelors of diminishing eligibility, rejected by each in turn? And how many more would there be? Could anybody fall in love with a Millicent Tavistock, with her long face, her slow-witted nature?

"Thank you for your piano playing," Roger said gallantly as he handed her into the carriage. "I thought the Chopin simply beautiful."

It had, in truth, been accomplished but unremarkable. But Roger was pleased he said it: he wasn't sure if she took it as a compliment or recognised it as a gesture of kindness, but either way, Millicent smiled, the first genuine smile he had seen her give all night.

He watched the carriage pull down the driveway. The moon was almost full, silhouetting the row of young linden trees, now nearly the height of the upstairs windows. Roger felt that a walk to clear the fug from his head might be a good idea.

An owl hooted from the brickworks. Roger cupped his hands together and blew a hoot in reply. He was proud of his owl hooting, a skill he had honed in school. Having the best hoot in the dorm, he had played an important role in organising illicit night walks and midnight feasts, which had earned him a certain cachet.

A moment later, another owl replied, this time from the direction of Ashridge. Roger hooted again, and once more he heard the hoot from Ashridge. Roger laughed with delight. He was having a conversation with an owl! Frankly, it was the most rewarding conversation he'd had all evening. He strode off up the track towards the wood, then stopped and gave another hoot. Again the reply. The other owl didn't appear to have moved.

Reaching the end of the track, Roger vaulted over the five-bar gate into the wood. It was darker under the trees, the branches casting shadows in strange looming shapes. The owl hooted again – close now. Following its call, Roger took the left-hand path that wound slowly uphill through the hazel coppice. He blew another *tuwhit-tuwho.*

Tuwhit-tuwho answered from the clearing at the top of the rise. Then Roger heard another sound, coming from the same place. A girl's laughter. A figure was sitting on a fallen tree trunk, her profile clear in the moonlight. Roger's heart lurched, though surely it was nothing more than an apparition conjured by his own intoxicated imaginings.

"'Tis you, Master Cann!" Tessa gave a giggle. "I wondered who I'd been talking to."

"Tessa? I took you for an owl!"

"And I you, to begin with."

"Was I not convincing?"

"Not bad. But I don't think you'd have fooled a real owl."

"What are you doing here?"

"'Tis one of the places I like to sit," she said simply.

Since she was a little child, Tessa had always found herself wakeful when the moon was full. Tonight, thoughts had been buzzing round her brain like a swarm of bees in a chimney. The dairy. Figures, complex multiplications to estimate yields per month and convert pints and gallons into shillings and pounds. Lines from Keats. Roger Cann.

She had tried to slip out unnoticed. Her mother had nodded off in front of the fire and her father would be at the Red Lion for some time yet, but Eliza had asked where she was going, and hadn't believed Tessa when she said she just wanted to take a walk to cool her mind.

"Meeting a young man, I bet. Tell us who 'tis, Tess!"

"Bain't no one. I just need some fresh air, is all."

"Give him a kiss from me, whoever he be."

Tessa shook her head as she stepped out of the cottage. All the same, her feet took her in the direction of The Lindens. She'd lingered near the end of the driveway. She could see two coaches in the yard, and could hear the heavy breathing of horses from the stables. At the front of the house, a beam of bright light shone from a gap in the curtains. Roger had told her he was in for a ghastly evening. Still, a part of her imagined the lighted room behind the curtains and felt a queasy jealousy. Turning away from the house, she headed up the lane to Ashridge. It was a beautiful night, and it felt better to be outside than at home in the cottage. It would soon be closing time. Cuth Hobson could be many things, generally best avoided, after a Friday night down the Red Lion – tediously philosophical, maudlin, amorous, angry, violent. Sometimes all of them in quick succession. If she stayed out another hour or two, he should be asleep by the time she got home.

She shuffled along the trunk to make room. Attempting to sit, Roger lost his balance. His hand brushed her thigh as he steadied himself. He snatched it away as if scalded, then perched awkwardly beside her. He willed her not to move away. She didn't. He had never been so close to her before. He could smell her scent – warm milk, wood smoke and lavender. Her head was uncovered, and her hair hung loose around her shoulders.

"I come up here and watch the fox cubs sometimes, in the spring." She gestured to the hollow in front of them. There were several large holes dug into the bank.

"Ah, this is old Reynard's den, is it?"

Roger winced. Why couldn't he just talk normally?

"Tis the foxes' earth, if that's what you mean."

"I didn't think you liked foxes. You country people, I mean. Aren't they pests?"

"That they are. I respect them though. They have to live by their wits, foxes. And the kits are little charmers. Chasing each other in and out of the holes, rolling around on top of each other. They make me laugh. And they bain't scared at all at that age. They come up right close."

Once more, an owl hooted. Tessa laughed.

"That one was real. See if he'll talk to you."

Roger cupped his hands together and gave his best hoot. In the long silence that followed, he could hear Tessa's breathing, just inches from his ear. Her sleeve brushed against his as she brought her own hands to her lips and hooted. He had to admit, hers was the more convincing. A few seconds later, the owl hooted back. Absurdly, Roger felt jealous. Tessa laughed. They sat together, listening to the silence.

"A penny for your thoughts," Roger said eventually.

"I wouldn't sell them so cheap. But you may have them as a gift, if you wish."

"With all my heart!"

"Well, I was thinking about how many stalls we'd need in the dairy. How many will be bringing milk in a churn and how many milk that's still inside the cow. And then I was thinking that when it's built we should add another few head to our herd, but my old man's not going to pay for that, even though it's clearly a good investment..." She broke off and laughed. "Well, you did ask. And your thoughts? Fair exchange."

He had to tell her. If not now – here on this most beautiful of nights, in the dark of the wood, with the courage of a pint of claret inside him – then when?

"My thoughts? Oh Tessa, my thoughts are all of you." Roger pulled her into a clumsy embrace. His lips sought hers. To his joyous amazement, she responded – tentative at first, then hungrily. Roger could hear her shallow breathing, and his own fluttering heart beating against the bars of his chest. He tasted blackberry juice on her lips. Then she pulled away.

"'Tis late," she said, getting to her feet and drawing her shawl around her shoulders.

Roger was seized with torment. Everything was ruined. Now she would think him an Alec d'Urberville for sure. She would never speak to him again. "Tessa, please, forgive me,

I..." he began. But she reached out a finger and touched it against his lips.

"'Bain't nothing to forgive. A gentleman shouldn't rush a maid, is all." Her face was in shadow, but he could hear a smile in her voice. "Still, a gentleman might offer to walk a maid home."

Overcome with relief and gratitude, Roger offered his arm. But it was she who led him through the wood, picking her way quickly over tree roots and brambles and ducking overhanging branches. When they emerged back into the lane, the moon brilliant overhead, it seemed as light as day.

"We mustn't be seen," Tessa said as they approached The Lindens. The house was dark save for a candle burning in one of the servants' windows. "If your family sees us together, they'd never let me in your sight again."

Roger feared she was right. Yet at that moment he felt ready to defy his father, his mother, his sisters, anybody who would dare come between him and Tessa. "I love you, Tessa," he blurted out. "With all my heart."

She stopped and looked him straight in the eye. "I might be growing fond of 'ee too. But I don't think that'll impress your father."

Her pupils were dark moonlit pools. Roger wanted to dive into them, deep, deep down.

"I don't care what my father thinks!"

She laughed, but not unkindly. "I care what your father thinks. 'Tis important, this investment of his. Or is it a game to you?"

"No, I swear. I'll do anything for you, oh Tessa, beautiful Tessa."

"Then bide a while." She reached her hand to his face, then kissed him once, lightly on the lips. "'Twill warrant the waiting."

As they passed the drive, in a moment of romantic inspiration, Roger plucked a leaf from the nearest linden tree. He pressed the heart-shaped leaf into her hand.

"Take this, as a token of my love. Of my true heart forever!"

"I think you're a little drunk, sir."

"Drunk on love, Tessa! Drunk on your love."

She stifled a giggle. "And also wine." But she kept the leaf clenched between her fingers.

They parted where the lane joined the road through the village. Roger watched her walk briskly up the road beneath the oak trees. At the turning to the track that led to her cottage she stopped, turned and waved once, then he lost sight of her behind the hedge.

As Roger floated back to the house, he gazed up at the stars. Space was incomprehensibly vast! This was not, he was aware, an observation of startling originality. And yet he had found the one thing he wanted more than anything in the whole universe right here, in his own village! Perhaps this was not an original observation either. Yet it was no less true and no less staggering for all that.

The cottage was dark when Tessa got home. She lit a candle and tiptoed into her room. Eliza was asleep, breathing evenly. Her father was snoring on the other side of the wall. Tessa reached under her bed and took out the volume of Keats that Miss Carlisle had given her. She pressed the linden leaf between the pages.

Just as the bells stopped ringing, Roger saw Tessa slip into the back pew. All through the service, he was aware of her presence behind him. Listening for her voice during the hymns, wishing he could turn around and look at her. During communion, he watched her as she knelt at the altar and held out her hands for the bread and the wine; during the intercessions, he prayed for forgiveness for the sinful thoughts that had come into his mind as he did so.

Afterwards, he spotted her deep in conversation with a young man beside the lychgate. As Roger passed, they turned to look at him. The man said something, and they both laughed. Roger hurried away. He felt crushed. What a fool he had been! She was laughing at him. And no wonder. He had been drunk – his aching head this morning was testament to that. He must have seemed ridiculous, declaring his love for her, clumsily trying to kiss her. No doubt she had been telling that man all about it, and they were laughing at the silly squire's son who thought he was in love with her when all she was interested in was his father's money.

And yet... she had kissed him back...

That afternoon, Roger paced up and down while the cows waited placidly at the gate to Marshfield. When she appeared at the end of the meadow, he almost turned tail, but she raised a hand and waved. He stopped still. There was an agonising wait as she approached through the meadow, the yoke slung over her shoulders. What was he to say to her? He couldn't even pretend to be reading. Why hadn't he brought Keats with him?

But before she reached the gate, she hailed him.

"Master Cann. I was hoping I'd find you here."

"Tessa! About last night. If I made a fool of myself..."

"Never, sir! I told you, your owl hooting is not bad at all. And there's no shame in mistaking mine for a real owl."

A surge of relief washed over him. Then she reached into one of the empty pails and drew out a sheaf of paper.

"'Tis all here. Costs, volumes, profits and so on. I spoke to George Foster about sending freight on the railways this morning – ah, but I'm forgetting you know that already, you saw us talking outside the church. I've written it all down. Have a look and see what you think."

She handed him the papers. Roger took them as if they were a love letter.

Now his heart beat fast again as he knocked on the door of his father's study. "Come," barked the voice from inside. Roger opened the door to a cloud of bitter pipe smoke. His father sat at the mahogany desk, perusing a pile of papers.

"Yes?"

"Sir, what we talked about the other night, with the creamery."

"Well?"

"You said I should bring you some figures. The, erm, turnover, profits and whatnot." He held out the file. He had copied it down straight from the pages Tessa had given him. She had beautiful handwriting, far neater than his, but Roger thought it best to make it look like his own work.

Arnold glanced over it. "You did all this?"

"Yes sir."

His father motioned towards a chair by the window. Roger sat in silence, trying to read his expression. Arnold Cann slowly turned the pages. It was a long time before he spoke.

"This looks sound," he said eventually.

Roger wanted to dance with delight. "Thank you sir."

"I had no idea you were an expert on the dairy industry."

"Well, I'd hardly claim to be that." His father seemed to want him to say more. "I spoke to a few people."

"Oh yes? Who?"

"Some of the farmers in the village." Roger had a stroke of inspiration: "I spoke to a few of them in the Red Lion."

Arnold looked at the papers again. "I like the numbers." He nodded. "It's ambitious, but it doesn't look unrealistic. Thorough. Room for improvement in these margins, I would say. Seems your dairymen are making a deal more than they were before, but it's us who are taking the risk. And it's risk that brings reward, boy. Remember that."

"Yes sir." Roger wanted to protest. If anyone deserved reward, it was Tessa. His father seemed to be suggesting that she should be taking less: that, he had deduced, was what margins meant.

"So who exactly did you speak to?"

"Um, there was Fred Brewster..." That was the only name Roger could remember. "And Cuth Hobson."

Arnold Cann gave a derisive laugh. "That old sot? I wouldn't trust his information further than I could throw it. He leases Marshmead, up by the claypits. Has his cows there at the moment. But I expect he told you that."

"Yes sir. I spoke to his daughter too. She seems... well, I think you could trust her information," Roger finished lamely.

"Oh yes. Bess or Jess or something."

"Tessa."

"That's it. Pretty girl."

Roger could feel his face flushing. "I suppose so."

"Prettier than that filly the other night, anyway. Miss Tavistock. Are you going to marry her?"

"Tessa?" Roger asked, alarmed. Could his father read him so plainly?

"No, dolt. Millicent Tavistock."

"Oh yes, of course. I mean, no! That is, I can't say I was especially enamoured."

"Can't blame you. Face like a horse. You know, her father said they'd pay to have her teeth removed. Wedding present. Would save a lot of money over the years."

Roger had noticed Miss Tavistock's teeth: they were mottled, and several were missing. Tessa's teeth were white as the milk in the pail.

"Your mother will be disappointed. Still, no doubt she has other options available."

"I'm not sure I want to find a wife that way," Roger said. "It seems rather like a bridal cattle market."

To Roger's surprise, his father laughed. "You really are an expert on cows now, aren't you?"

Autumn was coming. There was a heavy dew and a chill in the air, as if the morning were practising for the frosts that were now only weeks away. Exhausted from the opulence of the summer, the trees had lost their lustre. Leaves were rusting. Watery sunlight seeped through the morning mist.

Tessa had finished the milking. Walking back through Marshmead, she saw a figure standing by the gate. Her heartbeat quickened: Roger, who rarely rose before nine, was not in the habit of meeting her in the mornings. As she came closer, she realised with a start that it wasn't Roger but his father.

"Good morning, sir," she said, curtseying as best she could with two full pails yoked over her shoulders.

He nodded a curt good morning. She needed to open the gate and he was in the way. He appeared to have no intention of moving. "Tessa, isn't it?"

"Yes sir. Cuth Hobson's daughter."

"How much milk d'you have there?" His voice was abrupt, with nothing of his son's bashful manners.

"Close to eight gallons if you please, sir."

"Is that good?"

"Not bad sir. There's five cows, and I'd hope for three gallons a day from each of them this time of year. More after they been in calf. Less in winter."

He nodded, apparently satisfied with the answer. Then: "You've been talking to my son." It wasn't a question.

She took a step back, and a few drops of milk slopped over the side of the pails. What had Roger told him?

"Putting ideas into his head about dairies. You needn't look so alarmed, girl. God knows he needs something to fill that empty skull of his."

"We spoke about a few things, sir."

"Did you now?" Arnold Cann looked thoughtful. Then he began firing questions at her. Who did she sell the milk to? What was the price? What about butter and cheese? And what did she do for winter fodder? What was the cost, and how did that affect the yield? Tessa answered politely but confidently. The answers were all there at the front of her mind: she could picture the figures she'd written on the papers. She tried to ignore the way he was staring at her.

"It's a funny thing," Arnold Cann said eventually. "Here's my son, no interest at all in anything but his dead poets and dead languages. Doesn't know the first thing about business, let alone the dairy business. Suddenly he fancies himself as an entrepreneur. And he presents me with a rock solid business plan. Seems to know all his costs. Even starts projecting how he could increase the yield with better winter fodder. Remarkable really, wouldn't you say?"

"Yes sir."

"Did you write it for him?"

She was taken aback by the directness of the question. "Beg pardon, sir?"

"You heard me, girl. I'm just wondering if my son has any acumen in him at all, or if it all comes from a milkmaid."

"I told him what I know, sir."

"All your ideas? Centralising operations, transporting the milk to London?"

"It makes sense sir. If we could command a better price..."

"I won't say I'm not impressed. Any of it from him at all?"

Tessa thought. "He did suggest, sir, that you might build a dairy here at The Lindens." This wasn't exactly a lie, though truth be told it had taken a lot of prompting before he had made the suggestion.

"Suppose I did that. Suppose I built a dairy here at The Lindens. I'd be taking a risk. And even if my son's proposal looks good on paper, I can't be certain that he's a sound investment. I hope I'm wrong, but I'm yet to be convinced."

He shook his head slowly, then continued: "But I think if he had somebody local on board, somebody who knows dairy farming, that would be different. Somebody who knows his or her numbers too. Then I might be persuaded."

"If I find such a person, sir, I will be sure to mention it."

He gave her a hard, appraising look. Then he stood aside and, with a slight bow, held the gate open for her. "A good morning to you, Miss Hobson."

"And to you, sir."

Tessa felt his eyes following her until she turned into the lane. Then she stopped to rest. As she took the heavy yoke from her shoulders, she felt she might lift off into the air. She looked to the sky above her. Swallows were gathering, readying themselves to leave for the winter. She was always sorry to see the swallows leave. They brought good luck, some said. Kill a swallow and the milk would turn to blood. She watched them wheeling above the alders. They flew to Africa, Tessa knew. What was that like for a fledgling, that first flight? To discover that the world didn't end at Stourton Down, but went on and on, was infinitely larger than you had ever imagined it. To fly off into the blue, beyond the horizon, into an unknown tomorrow where anything was possible.

ODDS
1916

"Oh my dear! It's too, too awful!" Lydia Cann said again. "Poor, poor George. Poor, poor you."

Elspeth graciously accepted her mother's condolences, dabbing her eyes with a lace handkerchief. She let herself be guided towards the best armchair, and sank into it with a dramatic sigh. Tessa knew it was an unkind thought, but she couldn't help thinking Lady Woodford was relishing the situation. She was the centre of attention, as she always wished to be. She was entitled to all the sympathy she wanted, and she knew it.

They had received the letter earlier that week. Elspeth's son, George, had lost three fingers on his left hand in an explosion. It was a terrible, tragic thing. And yet: George was already back in England, recuperating in a stately home-turned-hospital in the Dorset countryside, less than an hour away by train. For him, the war was over, honourably discharged as no longer medically fit for service. A future assured, for the price of half a handful of fingers. Wasn't that a deal worth making?

What a world, that she found herself envious of a

mother whose son had been maimed merely. That she could wish such a fate for her own sons.

"He is safe home now," Tessa said. "That must be a comfort to you all."

Lady Woodford gave her a gloating smile. "Yes. God has spared our son's life, in His mercy. The Lord moves in mysterious ways."

"He does," Lydia Cann echoed.

He does indeed, thought Tessa. Lieutenant Woodford would be forever a war hero. He had Done His Bit. The fact that he had sustained his injuries in an accident a mile behind the front line would be conveniently forgotten. Meanwhile, every minute of every hour of every day, a British soldier was killed, the Lord, in His mercy, deciding not to spare his life. Perhaps He only took an interest in the sons of baronets and higher-ranking members of the aristocracy. Tessa's own niece Jenny, Eliza's eldest, had lost her fiancé last year at Gallipoli, one of a hundred thousand lives the Lord had mysteriously deemed expendable.

Still, Tessa prayed every day for her own sons' safe return – first thing in the morning, last thing at night, and at those moments in between when the daily cares and diversions fell away and she was left staring into the abyss of their absence. Thomas and Cecil still had all their digits intact as far as she knew. But for how much longer? They were out there in France, only two hundred miles as the swallow flies, but another world, impossibly distant. It was no time at all since she had tended their grazed knees and salved their nettle stings with dock leaves, listened to Tom's worries and soothed Cecil's night terrors when he had been woken by the wind rattling the sash windows or the roe deer's eldritch shriek. Now they were facing fears and dangers unimaginable, and there was nothing she could do to protect them.

To distract herself from the horror, her brain would turn to numbers. Objective, unemotional numbers. They offered some comfort. Too many boys had died, far too many, but still only a small fraction of the total who had marched to war. Much more likely than not, her sons would come home safe and sound. But she couldn't leave it at that, and the more she poked at the numbers, the less secure they became. The chances of one son surviving might seem manageable. But the chances of both surviving were half that. And what happened the longer they stayed out there? Did the odds of disaster diminish as each day passed and the end of the war, however distant, drew nearer? Or did they increase with every spin of the wheel? With the right figures and the right formula, Tessa supposed, one could work it out. She wasn't sure, though, if she wanted to know the answers.

The maid, Peggy, brought in the tea tray, with the best teapot and three china cups and saucers, then returned bearing a plate of scones with a pot of cream and jam. The last of last year's strawberry. Thomas had been home on leave in strawberry season: she could picture him now, sitting on the garden bench in his uniform, scoffing the reddest berries straight from the basket just like he had when he was a toddler. She hadn't seen him since.

"Shall I be mother?" said Lydia Cann, inevitably. Tessa wished she would leave the tea to steep for longer. Tea was becoming harder to get hold of as it was; it was a waste to drink it so insipid. At least Peggy and the other servants could get a proper brew out of the pot later.

"And where is my brother this afternoon?" Elspeth asked.

"He's over Stourton way. One of our suppliers there has some milking cows to sell."

Ivan Martyn had been called up last month. He had half a dozen Ayrshires, and his wife Rosie, eight months pregnant with their first child, couldn't manage them alone. But they were healthy, steady milkers, and would make a worthwhile addition to the Marshmead herd.

"Ah of course," Lady Woodford sniffed. "The cows."

Though they had been related by marriage for nigh on twenty years, Tessa knew that, to her sister-in-law, she would always be a milkmaid. She might ape the manners and the talk of a respectable lady, but something would betray her – a country phrase, her laugh, a finger out of place as she held a teacup. It had bothered her, once. She had craved the approval of the family she had married into, thought for a while that she could be one of them. These days, she was long past caring. She leant over the table and topped up her own cup, the tea now a little less anaemic.

Her life had changed overnight as magically as any fairy tale, though marriage was not the happy-ever-after but only the beginning of the story. From a two-roomed cottage, where every remark, every snore, every piss in the night could be heard by the whole family, to this grand new house: The Lindens. She had a room of her own complete with Wilton carpet, velvet curtains, a horsehair mattress, a walnut dressing table with a looking glass, a vast wardrobe to hang the many dresses that Elspeth had insisted on passing onto her – not so much from generosity as to avoid potential social embarrassment on her own behalf – along with the absurd array of undergarments that made dressing such a palaver. Instead of bread and dripping and stews cooked in the soot-blackened pot over the fire, she ate three-course meals brought by servants – servants! – in a dining room with oil lamps and a velvet tablecloth, with china plates and wine in crystal glasses, and a baffling arrangement of silver cutlery. There was an indoor water closet and a whole room for the bath. Where once her days had been a parade of chores from sunrise till she blew out her candle, now Tessa could spend her evenings sitting in a cushioned armchair reading by gaslight.

She was lucky, she knew it, though sometimes she had had to remind herself. Throughout those early years of her marriage, she had felt she was constantly being watched, being judged and found wanting. Living under the same roof as one's in-laws was a trial, however large and elegantly gabled the roof. She respected Arnold Cann, who was astute, unaffected and listened to the answer when he asked her a question. At the same time, he was brash and opinionated, and prone to tyrannical outbursts should someone or something upset his plans or routines. As for Lydia, Tessa had tried to like her, for Roger's sake if nothing else, but it was a one-sided effort. Tessa had ruined the life Lydia had planned for her son: for that crime, she would never be forgiven. To throw himself away on some country trollop without a penny to her name! After all they had done to raise him up in the world. How could he be so foolish, so ungrateful? What would the Woodfords say?

Roger had sworn he would never give her up, even if his family disowned and disinherited him. On balance, Tessa believed him; she knew he believed it himself. In the event, they found an ally in Arnold Cann. When Lydia had protested that Roger and Tessa would be married *over her dead body*, he had shrugged and said it would save some money to hold the funeral and the wedding together.

Perhaps the elder Mr and Mrs Cann had once loved each other, though Tessa found it hard to imagine. A state of ill-tempered tolerance seemed to be the best they could manage. She appeared oblivious to his snide comments; he largely ignored her nagging. Tessa suspected that Arnold's devotion to his work – the trips away from home, the long evenings in his study, his daily rounds of the brickworks, the claypits, the dairy – was at least in part a way of avoiding spending time with his wife; perhaps Lydia had been hurt by it, once upon a time.

She and Roger would never be like that. For all she loved The Lindens – and she did: the garden full of flowers, a lawn to bask on in the summer sun, the blossoming orchard, the thrush and the great tit singing in the trees outside her window – sometimes she wondered whether she and Roger wouldn't be happier if they moved into a place of their own somewhere. No servants, no fancy furnishings, no in-laws. Just the two of them, just being themselves.

"Just be yourself, my angel." That was what Roger told her, but who that was Tessa wasn't quite sure any more. She felt like an imposter around the servants. Enid, the cook, was a cousin of her mother's, and Gertie, the maid at the time, had known Tessa since she was a babe in arms. They bristled if she gave orders but took umbrage when she tried to speak to them as an equal. In the early days of their marriage, she liked to make breakfast for Roger – porridge with milk and brown sugar, which seemed the height of luxury, or scrambled eggs and bacon with toast and marmalade – and take it up to him in bed, until Enid said she would tender her notice if certain people wasn't going to show no respect for her cooking.

From her mother-in-law, there was a daily catalogue of petty grievances and catty criticisms, punctuated by moments of forced friendliness.

"You may pick flowers from the garden any time, dear,"

Lydia had condescended when Tessa had admired the stiff display of delphiniums on the mantelpiece. "I do so love to have flowers in the house."

The next day, Tessa gathered armfuls of cow parsley, yarrow and flowering grasses and arranged them in an old milk churn. Lydia looked on aghast.

"What on earth are you doing?"

"You said you loved to have flowers in the house."

"Flowers, yes. Not weeds!"

When Lydia had company, Tessa's presence was both expected and unwelcome. Social occasions were a trial she could never pass. "My, my, you do prattle on, don't you dear?", Lydia might say if she tried to be friendly. If she remained quiet, there would be some barb about timid little church mice, or how unfortunate it was that some people had so little to say for themselves. Elspeth on her visits spoke to Tessa as if she were handling each word with sugar tongs, and it was all Tessa could do to stop herself from telling her to take the poker out of her bloody arse. It would have been almost worth it to see their faces.

She was grateful for Arnold Cann's rough and ready presence. Like her, he had come from humble beginnings, and set little store by social airs and graces. Yet he commanded respect. That was easier for a man. Nobody would deny that Arnold Cann had made his own fortune; Tessa, in the eyes of the world, had married into hers. The only question was whether she was the simple wench who had struck lucky as a result of Roger Cann sowing his wild oats too close to home, or the cunning vixen who had ensnared him. Public opinion, she suspected, leant towards the latter. Well, let it – better cunning than simple.

She listened now with half an ear as Lady Woodford droned on about the house where George was convalescing,

Lord Somebody-or-Other's place near Blandford, a second cousin of Sir James's apparently.

"I couldn't bear to have our house over-run like that. Imagine!"

"By all accounts, the common soldiers can be terribly coarse," Lydia agreed.

"Still, we must all do our bit," Elspeth said. "Though I must say it's a mercy that Woodford Hall is too small to be of use to the War Office."

Woodford Hall was not small. It was to The Lindens what The Lindens was to the Hobsons' cottage. Still, Tessa thought, there must be houses that were twice as large again. Then twice as large as that. How many more times could you double it before you reached the largest house in the world?

Tessa's own family had reacted to the news of her marriage with less than unbridled delight. "Who's going to milk the bloomin' cows now then?" was Cuth's first reaction. "What's a toff like that want with a girl like 'ee? That's what don't make sense to me," her mother added.

"He loves me, ma. We love each other."

"Huh. He'll tire of 'ee soon enough, shouldn't wonder."

It might have been easier if she had moved away, instead of six minutes' walk along the lane. "Suppose madam thinks she's too high and mighty to come see us now," her mother would complain if Tessa went more than a few days without calling on her. If she came by more often, then it would be, "What's the matter, ain't got a home of your own to go to?" Dora Hobson and Lydia Cann were more alike than either of them would care to admit, though when, not long after the wedding, her mother had raised the idea of inviting the new in-laws round for dinner, Tessa had firmly quashed it.

The prospect was appalling, though she was aware how limp her excuses sounded.

"T'ain't what they be used to. Besides, we'd hardly all fit around the table."

"Oh, I understand," Dora pouted. "We bain't good enough for them and their hoity-toity ways. And bain't good enough for 'ee neither, your ladyship."

"Oh Ma, don't say that," Tessa protested. "'Tain't that at all." She corrected herself in her head: *it isn't* that. Was it?

But it was the change in her relationship with Eliza that stung. They had been so close throughout their childhood, just eighteen months and no secrets between them. She had wanted to confide in her sister about Roger when they began stepping out together, but she'd hesitated: it felt as if telling somebody else might break the spell, and besides, it wasn't her secret alone to share. And then Eliza had come to her with news of her own: Seth Cotter, the pigman's son who she'd been taking up to the hayloft in Brewster's barn these last few months, had proposed to her. She'd accepted, naturally. He was going to ask their father any day now.

"I told him I were still a maid, the first time, and I reckon as he believed it. Don't say aught, Tess, will 'ee?"

"Of course I won't," she promised, though whether her sister's previous conquests would be equally discreet, she wasn't sure. "And art in love with him?"

"Reckon so, aye," Eliza smiled. "Fancy! I'll be married afore my big sister."

That might have been the time to tell her, but Tessa didn't want to steal her sister's thunder. And the longer she left it, as Eliza's chatter filled up with wedding plans and how Seth had called her his angel and the house he going to build for them on Chapel Lane, the harder it became. When she couldn't put it off any longer, it felt like a betrayal.

"Him from the big house?" Eliza repeated. "And he's really going to marry thee?"

"I wanted to tell 'ee before, Liza. 'Tweren't never the right time."

"Lawks! I dunno what to say."

"Wish me joy, maybe?"

"Oh ah. I couldn't be happier for 'ee," Eliza said, forcing a smile. But the look that flitted across her eyes said something else, words they had thrown at each other a thousand times as children: *'Tain't fair.*

And it wasn't. It wasn't fair that Tessa should have her storybook romance instead of a tumble in the hayloft. It wasn't fair that she would have a big wedding just a week after Eliza's, and have lace and ribbons on her dress and a real diamond necklace her husband had given her. It wasn't fair that she was marrying a gentleman, and a gentle man too, when Seth Cotter turned out to be neither. Like Cuth Hobson, Seth was given to violent rages, though he only ever struck his wife when he had drunk too much; like Cuth Hobson, he drank too much too often. Tessa would see the signs she knew from her own mother: the tugged-down bonnet that didn't quite cover the violet bruise on her temple, the overly cheerful protestations of her clumsiness in the matter of broken plates and minor injuries, the slow dimming of the light behind her eyes. More than once, Tessa resolved to say something, but her attempts were shooed away or hit a wall of silence. It hurt to see her sister suffer, and it hurt that she wouldn't confide in her. Though it must hurt far worse to be Eliza. No, life wasn't fair.

Tessa and Roger had been married in the village church in August, a year to the day after he had first read Keats to the cows. Tessa had suggested that Mabel and co should come to the wedding – "Think how pretty they would look, all garlanded with flowers" – but Roger, still not always sure when she was joking, had said this would be too much for his mother. Poor Lydia: seething under her huge hat with its absurd artificial fruits, boiling with shame as Lord and Lady Woodford took their seats across the aisle from Tessa's tribe of cousins who gaped and giggled in their ill-fitting Sunday suits and frocks.

Tessa floated above it all, lighter than air, effervescent as the real French champagne they drank at the wedding breakfast on the lawn of The Lindens. Later that night, there had been music and dancing in the dairy. They had hung hops and garden pinks from the rafters, scenting the air with a heady sweetness. Feet pounded the freshly swept flagstones as her cousin Martin on the fiddle and Clem Shipham on his squeezebox spun jigs and reels and horn-pipes. Roger was a hopeless dancer, all flailing limbs and treading on toes, peeling off in the wrong direction in the strip the willow, bumping into her as he tried to do-si-do. But then Clem would call out "Swing your partners!", and Roger held her tight as they swung, faster and faster till she felt like her heart would burst through her ribcage and spin off into space.

And if a few sharper-eyed guests noticed an extra glow about her, the bloom of her cheeks a little redder, her breasts a little plumper, they kept their suspicions quiet. She was three months pregnant by then. Thomas had been conceived one beautiful night in May, not long after their secret had finally become a matter of public gossip. They had taken an evening walk up to Ashridge.

"You promised me nightingales," Roger said. "I haven't forgotten, you know."

At the fox earth, they sat on the tree trunk where he had first kissed her, watching the new year's cubs as they frisked in the moonlight, pouncing and tumbling like kittens.

"Hark!" Tessa whispered. "There."

Somewhere overhead, a nightingale was tuning up. It tested its range of sounds, slowly building the notes into longer phrases.

"Is that it?" Roger asked after a while.

"You sound disappointed."

"It's not conventionally musical. I think I'd expected something... more melodic."

She laughed. "'Tis their persistence that's most remark-able. And their imagination. He could go on for hours and never repeat himself."

They lay on a bank among the red campion and the wild marjoram, listening. After some minutes, Roger whispered, "Actually, it's the most beautiful thing I've ever heard."

Then they kissed, and then... if it was a sin, then God forgive her but she would do it again and again.

She might have wished for more of those nights, more of those days on the crest of an endless summer, the world so fresh and rich and green. But time circled on and life marched forwards. If their love no longer blazed with flaming passion, it remained a steady flame that radiated warmth through their home and their lives. Sometimes she found her husband exasperating – the oft-repeated anec-dotes, his feeble grasp on numbers, the way he let his mother talk to him as if he were still a child, though his hair was receding and he needed spectacles to read by. She knew, too, that two children and forty summers had taken their toll on her body, and his desire. But still he was kind and gentle, still he made her laugh and read her poetry, and still there were nights when, after the lamp was switched off, they would reach for each other and twine their bodies together, familiar and new each time.

Miraculously, together they had created two brand new human beings that were partly him and partly her and entirely themselves. Thomas had his father's hazel eyes, his gangly form and golden hair; Cecil could have been Tessa as a boy. She loved her firstborn with such a fierce intensity that, when Cecil arrived two years later, she didn't think it possible that she could experience such love again. But her heart expanded effortlessly to accommodate the younger brother. She sometimes wondered how many more children it could have taken in. But a daughter, Mary, had died at three days old, and another unknown life was lost before it had even begun in one night of agony, weeping and far too much blood, Roger clutching her hand and pleading with her not to die: "Life without you wouldn't be worth living, Tessa."

"That's a daft thing to say," she told him. "Life's always worth living."

But she didn't want to live without him either. Roger wasn't likely to be called up, thank heaven; not now he was over forty, and short-sighted to boot. Besides, keeping the population of London supplied with milk and butter was seen as a worthy contribution to the war effort. Enough of a Bit for Roger to be doing.

Arnold Cann began work on the dairy a matter of weeks after he had first spoken to her, a long brick building adjoining the stable with stalls for a dozen cattle and a large loft running along its length where they stored fodder for the winter. By the time of the wedding, milk from nine-tenths of the cattle in the parish was being whisked off to London on the early morning train. The enterprise had grown just as Tessa had known it could; her figures turned out to be uncannily accurate. Within a year, they had bought up the creamery in Alderbourne at a knock-down price, and before long they were selling butter, cream and hard white cheese along with the raw milk.

It was Roger who proposed the name Marshmead Dairies. As the face of the business, he had proved more capable than his father had ever imagined possible. In negotiations, he stuck closely to the script Tessa sketched out for him, but his ingenuous manner often led the other party to believe they were getting the better of the deal. He treated the local farmers with respect, and they in turn respected him, despite his habit of slipping involuntarily into a laughable imitation of a Wiltshire accent.

Money came back to the village. Families who had struggled through the hard years of the eighties and nineties mended their sheds and rethatched their cottages. Their children built new houses. Lydia Cann bought new curtains and wallpaper. Production at the brickworks increased; Arnold Cann took on more labour, and the wages circulated through the Red Lion and the general stores, the butcher's and the grocer's and the newly opened haberdasher's. Even Cuth Hobson, who refused to accept any charity from his daughter, found he was earning more than he could drink his way through, and amazed everyone, Mrs Hobson more than anybody, by taking his wife off to Weymouth for a week.

Tessa's own horizons had stretched far beyond Weymouth, though it had seemed so exotic on their honeymoon. She and Roger had promenaded along the seafront there, bathed off Chesil Beach, found fossils at Lyme Regis and taken the night sleeper back from Exeter. Since then, they had travelled to Italy – Florence, Pisa, Siena, Rome – and to the south of France, dazzled by light, art and antiquity, fresh oranges and peaches. She had been transfixed and transported by Ellen Terry and Nelly Melba on the London stage. She had even, to the consternation of her mother-in-law and to Roger's concerned bemusement, gone to Hyde Park to demand votes for women and heard Emmeline Pankhurst inflame a crowd a thousand times the population of the parish. She had come back full of righteous indignation, raring to change the world. But she had little time to do so. Besides, her own vote, if she had one, would only be swallowed up among the hundreds of dutifully cast ballots that would inevitably return the same old shire Tory as the Member of Parliament for their own constituency. For all Arnold Cann liked to sound off over the dinner table, politics rarely intruded on daily life at The Lindens.

Until one day a Serbian anarchist shot an Austrian aristocrat, and the bullet ricocheted through millions of lives all over the world.

"And how is Sir James's young cousin?" Lydia Cann was asking her daughter.

"Georgiana?" Lady Woodford sighed. "This was supposed to be her coming out season, poor thing. Such a shame this dratted war had to spoil it."

They would go on and on like this. Conversation for Lydia was an endless series of questions about relatives and acquaintances, relatives' acquaintances and acquaintances' relatives, many of whom she had never met but whose lives she followed through regular updates from her daughters. Elspeth for her part was happy to feed her mother titbits of gossip from the social season, embellishing them as she fancied. Lydia gobbled it all up; if she couldn't have that life herself, living it vicariously through her daughter was the next best thing. Tessa, having little to contribute and little desire to, finished her tea and wondered what excuse she could make for leaving when she heard the back door open. A few moments later Peggy came into the room.

"If 'ee please ma'am, Mrs Cotter is here."

"Well, show her in Peggy, please," Tessa told her. Then she smiled sweetly at her in-laws. "I hope you don't mind if my sister joins us."

She knew very well that they did mind. While they had grudgingly come to accept that Tessa could conduct herself decently among respectable people, the rest of her family were looked upon like pets that were not housetrained and should certainly not be allowed on the furniture. Eliza seldom entered the drawing room, which was the domain of the elder Mrs Cann. When she did come round, which was less than Tessa might have wished, they usually drank tea in the kitchen or chatted outside, where the divide gaping between them seemed easier to bridge.

"Eliza, you remember Roger's sister, Lady Woodford," Tessa said.

Eliza gave an awkward curtsey. "Pleased to meet you again, your ladyship." Elspeth returned a regal nod.

"Shall I bring more tea, ma'am?" Peggy asked.

"Not on my account, Pegs," Eliza cut in, sounding more like herself. "I weren't planning to stay long."

"Well, take a seat anyway." Tessa motioned to the space beside her on the settee. Her sister sat down gingerly. "I got a letter from Reggie this morning."

Tessa's heart quickened.

"Says he's well, and your lads too."

Reginald, Eliza's one son amongst three daughters, was in the same battalion of the Hampshire Regiment as Tom and Cecil, though they had taken different routes to get there. From the officer training corps at school, the Canns had both gone on to Sandhurst; Private Cotter had enlisted in the ranks while still some months shy of his eighteenth birthday. It was comforting to think of them all together, even if they were no longer as close as they had once been. Reggie was a year younger than Thomas, a year older than Cecil. When they were little they had played together effortlessly, climbing trees, prospecting for gold in the sandy banks of the brickworks, riotous variations of croquet on the lawn, acting out the stories Tessa loved to read to her sons – *Treasure Island*, King Arthur, *Tom Sawyer*.

"Sends his love to thee, of course," Eliza said.

Tessa noticed that the maid was still lingering by the door. "And to you as well, Peggy, I'm sure."

Peggy turned scarlet, bobbed quickly and scurried out of the room. Tessa scolded herself. She shouldn't tease the girl. If she were suffering just a fraction of the fear and longing that Tessa experienced every day, then Tessa felt for her. Peggy had been with them since she was thirteen; she was seventeen now. Tessa knew that Reggie and Peg were sweethearts. She wasn't sure how serious it was on his side – he wrote to her, though not more than every two or three months – but the girl was clearly besotted.

It was hard to imagine Reginald Cotter as someone a girl would fall in love with, though there was little enough choice in the village, as Tessa remembered only too well. He had been an unprepossessing boy, heavy-set and clumsy with a shock of untameable red hair. Lord knows Tessa had tried to get through to her nephew, buying him little gifts, taking an interest in what he did and what he thought. He would reply in grunts and mumbles, rarely smiling or looking her in the eye. Still, he was a regular visitor to The Lindens, coming and going around the grounds as he pleased. Tessa knew how much his presence irked Lydia Cann – this village urchin trespassing on her property – which was partly why she encouraged it. Reginald kept out of the way mostly. Sometimes Higgs the gardener would catch him sneaking strawberries or peapods, and once Tessa herself had clipped his ear for shooting at the wood pigeons with his catapult. He preferred the company of the horses to people, though when Tessa had asked him if he wanted to ride Dapple, the boys' New Forest pony, he shook his head and stomped away.

Funny really – she used to see him more often than her own children for eight months of the year. It was never to be questioned that the boys should go to boarding school; it was simply what happened. Tessa regretted it at the time, and regretted it all the more now: those precious childhoods had been and gone, and she had missed the half of it. She envied Eliza having her son with her throughout the year. *'Tain't fair.*

At least it helped prepare her for their absence now. She had got used to her sons spending months away from home, cut off from her in a strange, cruel, male world. She would wait hungrily for their letters, counting down the days till she would see them again. Though now the letters came less regularly, and the school holidays, too short then, seemed like an eternity compared to the scant few days of leave her sons were granted. Thomas had been home twice in two years, for four or five days at a time. Cecil had come home for visits during his training, but since he shipped out to France at the beginning of the year, she had not seen him at all.

"Says he's been appointed sergeant now," Eliza said, pride in her voice, though Tessa doubted her sister knew any more about the arcane workings of the army than she did. Thomas's letters were full of Divisions, Units and Platoons, COs and NCOs, CSMs and RTOs, Lt. Cols and the BG. He himself, not yet twenty-one, was now a captain. Tessa had only an approximate idea of where this slotted into the military hierarchy, but the meaning of the word was clear enough, and it sounded like a role for Thomas. In school, he had been a senior prefect and had captained the first XV at rugger and the first XI at cricket. He had the confidence, the charisma of a leader of men; somebody that people would follow into battle. Or perhaps that was how every mother thought about her firstborn son.

He was Arnold's favourite grandchild (grandparents were allowed to have favourites, he told her). Shortly after Thomas was born, Arnold had presented Tessa with a wooden cot he had made, with birds carved into the head-board, and he had doted on his grandson ever since. The cot had been followed by a toy train, wooden chairs for the boys' den in the laurel hedge, a marvellous rocking horse brought home from a trip to London. Arnold would take Thomas along on visits to his building sites, stopping off on the way home for cake or an ice. They spent rainy afternoons in his study, melting sealing wax and stamping imaginary letters.

"He was never like that with me," Roger complained. "But then I was a great disappointment to him, until you came along."

"Grandpa says I'm going to run the family firm one day."

"And would you like that?"

The boy nodded. "I'll run it firm but fair."

She imagined it often, Thomas living with them at The Lindens with his wife (Tessa would be an exemplary mother-in-law) and children, taking charge of the business. Apart from anything, she would need the help. Though

Arnold at seventy remained sharp as a tack, he increasingly left the running of the enterprise to her. Enterprises, rather: dealing with two dozen milk suppliers and daily deliveries to London, making sure the right quality and quantity of bricks were dispatched to the right building sites at the right time, balancing the books, discussing Arnold's various property developments with Mr Dix the lawyer. She could imagine those things coming as naturally to Thomas as they assuredly did not to his father. Nevertheless, she had wanted him to go to university, to choose his own path in life – though nothing would make her happier than if that path led him back home again. He had been offered a place at Oxford, at his father's old college; he should have been there now, about to start the last year of his degree, but of course the war had come along. He had been enthusiastic about joining up. It was a lark, it was what all the young men were doing, but it was something magnificent too: a shot at glory, a quest, a chance to be part of something great. That was Thomas to a tee.

Cecil was different. His own choice to fight was a reluctant one, and Tessa was all the more proud of him for that. He had explained his reasoning in a letter from school; it still made Tessa weep every time she read it.

Dearest Father, Dearest Mother,

I have decided to join up as soon as I finish school. There. I've written it.

It is not a decision I have taken lightly. I abhor the whole idea of war. It leaves me flabbergasted that a Christian country should embrace it so enthusiastically, when after all the Bible is pretty clear about "Thou shalt not kill", "Love thine enemy" and all the rest of it.

I even thought about being a Conscientious Objector, though please don't mention this to Grandfather or Grandmama as I am sure they would disinherit me forthwith. Do you remember Ralph Fuller? (In the year above me at school – played the flute in the orchestra.) He's a pacifist and refused to fight, and he's in Dartmoor Prison now. I respect him for not wanting any part in the madness that has taken over Europe.

I have nothing but contempt for the jingoism we see in the newspapers and that I hear from the boys and the masters (or most of them – Mr Mullins, who teaches history, is a Socialist and insists the whole war is a struggle for control over markets and that the working classes should have no part in it – I suppose it's safe enough for him to preach this at our school since there are no members of the working classes within earshot!). I hate their talk of "sticking it to the Bosch", "the Huns" – I cannot hate the Germans. Wasn't Beethoven German, and Goethe, and Mendelsohn, and Schubert, who wrote such a divine song about a linden tree?

It can never be right to fight out of hatred. But it is right to fight for what you love – and I love my country. Oh, not the flag and the King, Britannia rules the waves, God make thee mightier yet, &c. &c. But the land. The Lindens. The skylarks singing above the chalk downs, the cuckoo calling from Ashridge in April, the cows chewing the cud on a drowsy August afternoon down in Marshmead. These are things I would fight to defend. I would be a coward if I didn't.

Are they really under threat from Prussian militarism? Is it likely the Germans would or could invade our island nation? It seems impossible to contemplate. But I do know there are men and women and children in Belgium and France who love their land too, and who have seen the fields and woods of home ripped apart, scarred by trenches and barbed wire, and have heard the birdsong replaced by the sound of whizzbangs and machine gun fire. If I would fight for my home, isn't it right that I should fight for theirs too? After all, the birds and the trees and the fields in France can't be so different from here.

I know you will worry (especially you, my dear mother). But I know you will be proud of me too.

I can't wait to see you in the Easter hols – only two weeks now!

Your loving son,
Cecil

He had always been the quiet, thoughtful one. He questioned everything, all the inequities and iniquities of life, even as a small child. "Why don't Enid and Gertie dine in the dining room?" he had asked one suppertime.

"Because they're servants, of course," Tom answered. "Servants eat in the kitchen."

He pondered this. "Does everyone have servants?"

"No, only the more well-off," Tessa told him. "My family had no servants when I was growing up. We lived in a tiny little house."

"As small as Reggie's house?"

"Smaller than that."

"Does Reggie have servants?"

"Reggie's an oik."

"Thomas, that's enough." Tom had just come home from his first term at prep school, and had already been infected by some of the attitudes that Tessa had hoped he would be immune to.

"Why do we have a king?" Cecil was asking now. "Why do we pray to God to save the king?"

"Now, which of all those questions do you want me to answer?"

"Does it make any difference whether I join in? Is there a certain number of people who have to pray for something for God to do it? If I don't sing God save the king and the king dies, will it be my fault?"

She had worried that the school, in trying to make him fit the mould, would squash him, but he had continued to deal with the world on his own terms. He had little interest in sport – a severe handicap at his school – but made up for it by singing in the choir, playing first oboe in the orchestra, acting in school productions – Edgar in *King Lear* in his upper fifth, Prospero the following year. An extraordinary performance for a schoolboy, and that wasn't just the doting parents' opinion – the English master had said so himself. He was a gifted scholar too, though where Thomas was studious and serious, Cecil's academic excellence appeared effortless. *"Despite his exam grades, Cann Minor appears to spend more time daydreaming than studying,"* one report had complained. *"One can only imagine what he might achieve if he paid as much attention to the writing on the blackboard as he does to the view outside the window."*

"He doesn't work half as hard as I do, and he still comes top of the class," Tom had complained to his mother. "It's not fair."

"Life's not fair," she told him.

And it wasn't. It wasn't fair that this bloody war had come along when her boys' lives should be coming into flower. Cecil was nineteen – the age Tessa had been when she met Roger. She remembered the sense of the world opening up to her: falling in love, the plans for the dairy, wild dreams dawning into a bright new reality. What an age that was to be: a time to be living, not to be killing and evading death.

Or, for some, failing to evade death. Because life wasn't

fair. Sometimes you simply had to accept the fact, and hope to God that you would be one of the lucky ones.

The room felt stuffy and oppressive. Tessa needed to get outside. She turned to Eliza. "It's a beautiful day. Will you walk with me a little?"

Eliza accepted the invitation, grateful to escape from her sister's in-laws. They walked across the lawn and up the steps past the folly. The bank was ablaze with late-flowering poppies, dancing like ballerinas in the welcome breeze. Tessa's heart swelled. Poppies were such jolly flowers.

"What other news?" Tessa asked. "In Reggie's letter?"

"He said they were heading south, but he couldn't say no more than that. Somewhere in France. He thinks he'll be back on the front line soon," Eliza added. "Says he hasn't seen any action for ages."

"Long may it stay that way," Tessa sighed.

They passed the apple tree she had planted on the top lawn at the turn of the century, laden with perfect apples striped green and scarlet. A Laxton Fortune. They were Thomas's favourite apple. Two more weeks and they would be ripe. And he wouldn't get to taste this year's crop. Tessa felt, suddenly and intensely, a memory of the boys in the orchard, filling the wheelbarrow with apples for making cider and throwing the rotten ones at each other. Laughing, always laughing.

"Reggie used to get into fights when he was at home," Eliza said. "He had a temper on him. Like his old man. I used to worry about him, that he'd start on someone he didn't ought to and get himself in trouble. 'Twould keep me awake at night." She gave a small, sad laugh. "Seems silly now, don't it? Worrying about a broken nose or a black eye."

"Oh Liza." Tessa held her arms out to her sister, and they embraced. She felt Eliza's shoulders slowly untensing. The last twenty years seemed to melt away as they held each other. Eliza was sobbing softly.

"'Twill be alright, won't it? They'll come safe home, all of them."

"You'll be back to worrying about Reggie fighting outside the Red Lion again in no time," Tessa said. It was kinder to joke than to give voice to her own fears.

They walked up the sloping path that led to the meadow. Tessa used to call it Juniper Hill for the juniper trees that separated it from the top garden, but Cecil had misheard it as Jupiter and the name had stuck. Become a part of family folklore, like the elm tree at the top of the bank that Tom had named the Ace of Clubs for its clover-leaf aspect. Another memory came over her: Jupiter Hill in the snow, all the boys on the sledge – Reggie was there too – hurtling down the slope and crashing into a snowdrift against the garden wall. The surge of fear she'd felt, and the relief when all three of them emerged from the snow laughing and pulled the sledge straight back up the hill again.

"How's Jenny bearing up?" Tessa asked.

"Not so good, not so bad. She don't like to talk about him much. Seems like everything's normal enough and then something can set her off just like that. Like Christmas Day when Seth brung in the turkey, and she just rushed out of the house – because of the country Turkey, you see?"

Had she and Eliza really not talked properly since Christmas? Surely she would have shared that story if they had. Tessa didn't want to let herself feel sad.

"Goose this Christmas then," she said.

Eliza stared at her, appalled. Then they both burst out laughing.

. . .

Peggy took the kettle off the range and topped up the teapot. The leaves had been stewing for two hours, and made a good strong mug. Lady Woodford had just left, which was a relief, though it was sad about her son. Peggy finished off the last of the scones, mopping up a smirch of strawberry jam from the plate, then washed the cups and saucers. When would Reggie write to her next? It had been more than three months now, and she'd written him ten letters in that time. Not long letters. Peggy didn't find writing easy – not just shaping the letters and spelling the words, but what to say. She wanted to tell him everything, which made it hard to think of anything at all. Still, he had writ to his mother so all was well. That was the main thing. She wished Mrs Tessa hadn't teased her about it in front of everyone though.

He'd never mentioned marriage or anything of the sort in his letters. It hadn't been serious when they'd talked about it, she knew that. The day before he left it was, nigh on two years ago. He had called round at the house to say goodbye to his aunt, but Mrs Tessa knew she wanted to see him and had said she could have the afternoon off. They had walked through the meadow up to Marshmead. Butterflies there'd been, clouds of them. She hoped he might pick a flower for her, but he didn't. She plucked a pink corncockle and tucked it behind her ear.

"Will you miss me?" she asked.

"Ah," he nodded.

"I'll wait for you."

"Good."

"What will we do when you come home again?"

"What'd thou have us do?"

She had spoken lightly because she didn't want him to see how heartsick she was. "Run away together? Get married? Or at least do the thing that married people do," she added daringly.

"Alright."

"Which one?"

"Whichever thou lik'st."

"We could move into a little cottage of our own somewhere."

"A cottage? No. I'm going to live in a house like this one."

"Like The Lindens?"

"Ah. But not as a servant."

She believed him. Reggie was smart and strong. Masterful. If he wanted to live in a house like The Lindens, he would do it.

"Can I live with you?" she ventured.

"Course. Said I'd marry 'ee, didn't I?"

She knew not to push it any further: those words were something she could hold onto while he was away, a treasure she could take out and polish from time to time.

After she had finished a second cup, she took the teapot outside to slosh the dregs into the geranium pots outside the back door. As she turned, she saw Jim Braithwaite from the post office crossing the yard. She liked Jim, who had a booming laugh and flirted with female customers of all ages even though he was well into his sixties.

"You're just too late for a cuppa, Jim," she said, expecting him to make some gallant reply. But then she saw his expression, and the telegram he was carrying.

"Is Mrs Cann here?" he asked. "Mrs Tessa, I mean."

The teapot slipped out of her hands. It hit the paving stones and exploded like a grenade.

LOSS

1930

"I'm sorry for your loss."

If she heard that one more time, she was going to scream. How many was that now? She should have kept count. Like the way she and Roger would count the *hallelujahs* in the Easter service, or the number of times Lord Woodford said *rather, what?* over the course of an evening. One of the little games they shared. Well, she'd lost that now.

"Thank you." She shook the proffered hand – an old university friend of Roger's whom she hardly knew. It wasn't his fault. What else could you say to the bereaved? No words could carry the weight of it.

There was dirt under her fingernails. From the earth she had thrown onto the coffin. It was March, chill and drizzly. Perfect funeral weather. The soil was muddy from the rain, but she hadn't wanted to wash it off. It was a connection, of a sort. It was awful to bury the body of someone you loved.

Though having no body to bury had been worse.

She was sick of funerals. Fifteen years ago, the name Cann appeared on a single grave in the village churchyard:

the small cross over the tiny coffin of her daughter, Mary. Now they were taking over. Well, only one Cann to go now. And at least when that funeral came she wouldn't have to host the reception. Why couldn't these people just go home? The drawing room – light and airy in happier times – felt claustrophobic, the air thick with cigarette smoke and the smell of damp coats and unfamiliar perfumes. The last thing she felt like doing was making small talk with extended family and friends, and receiving their stilted condolences.

Sorry for your loss.

So much she had lost over the years. So much that had drained away since that summer's afternoon in 1916, when a telegram had blown a hole through her life.

Deeply regret to inform you that Captain Thomas Cann died in battle July 2nd. Lord Kitchener expresses his sympathy.

A world shattered in fourteen words. The "deeply" had been written in by hand – specified by the sender, or added by a sympathetic operator at the other end? She would never know.

The worst that could happen, had happened. Her Thomas. Her prince. Her blue-eyed boy. Gone forever, and never even the chance to say goodbye. Everything that he might have been, every moment they might have shared together, lost.

Except it wasn't the worst. *The worst is not, so long as we can say "This is the worst."* Edgar in King Lear. One of the parts Cecil had played in school. She remembered those words when, not a week later, the other telegram arrived.

Deeply regret to inform you that Lt. Cecil Cann died of wounds July 7th. Lord Kitchener expresses his sympathy.

What were the odds? Not so very long, when you thought about it (and she had, for hours and hours for years afterwards): two junior officers in the same regiment, both on the front line in the first bloody days of the Somme.

The next day, the sun rose and the birds sang. She could not, would not believe it. A few days later, three letters arrived with the afternoon post. One from Thomas, full of hope and glory, proud to be playing his part in what he believed (*"though I can't say too much about it here"*) was going to be a decisive turning point in the war. One from Cecil, describing how on the march down they had camped by a copse and he had spent his guard duty listening to a nightingale and a pair of tawny owls, wistfully reflecting that he wouldn't get to taste a fresh strawberry from the garden this year, and sending his love to the dogs. The third letter was from Lieutenant Colonel Granville Winterburn, expressing his deepest sympathies. Captain Cann was a marvellous chap and would be greatly missed. He regretted that he didn't know Cecil so well but he was popular with the lads and would also be greatly missed. He was sorry for their loss.

Sorry for your loss. Food lost its taste. She lost her appetite. She lost two stone. Lost her looks. Lost the sparkle in her eye and the colour from her hair. She lost the desire to get out of bed in the mornings. She had lost her future. Lost the daughters-in-law she had never met and the grand-children who would never be born, who would never grow tired of her telling them again how she had fallen in love with their grandfather when he read *Ode on a Grecian Urn* to Mabel, Maureen, Dorcas, Dinah and Lavender. She had lost February 23rd and September 8th, Tom and Cecil's birthdays: days of joy and thanksgiving lost, now dates she could hardly bear to contemplate. All that love she had poured into them: lost now.

She dreamt of the boys most nights. They were small

children again, and something undefined but awful had happened to them. Or she would receive a letter explaining that it had all been a mistake and they hadn't died, and she would know that she was dreaming but try desperately to convince herself that she wasn't. Sometimes she dreamt that Thomas was dead but Cecil had survived, and sometimes the reverse. It felt as if she were being tested, as if her mind were trying to trick her into revealing a greater grief for one or the other; she passed the test, however. There were hideous nightmares too of battlefields and bombs and mutilated bodies. Worse than these, though, were the enchanted dreams where both boys were simply there, home at The Lindens doing ordinary everyday things, playing catch on the lawn or sprawled on the hearthrug, a chessboard between them. She would feel a sense of perfect peace wash over her. And when she woke, for a few moments she would bathe in that feeling as the sunlight flowed through the curtains, before reality broke again.

Sorry for your loss. The war had been won, but everywhere people had lost. And Tessa more than most.

They lost money. Tessa barely noticed the businesses slipping away. Though housebuilding had dwindled to nothing during the war, the years that followed should have been a boom time. Lloyd George had promised to build a land fit for the returning heroes. But the sand and claypits were depleted, and small kilns like theirs were dying anyway, unable to compete with the city factories. Arnold Cann no longer took any active part in building projects. The loss of his grandsons, Thomas in particular, had affected him more than he cared to let on. The family firm lost its purpose, no longer a legacy to pass down through the generations. He sold what assets remained, and put most of his money into shares. By then, his judgement was becoming erratic. He lost nine-tenths of his fortune in a series of investments based on poor advice and rash decisions. Tessa, later, would blame herself. He had come to rely on her sound, shrewd sense over the years. If she had not been so distracted with her own grief, she would never have let it happen.

It was the same with the dairy business. Things were changing. Fewer people in the village kept cows. Fred Brewster's widow had sold his remaining Ayrshires to the tannery in Downton. John Bracken's sons had moved to Southampton to work in the dockyards. Bert Frost and the Hardcastle boys never returned from the war. Marshmead Dairies had to cart in milk from further afield to keep up the volume. At the same time, farms elsewhere were consolidating and new, larger dairies were pushing prices down. Even Roger could see that this was eating into their margins. Ten years before, Tessa might have risen to the challenge: seen the trends, adapted, gambled. Now, she didn't have the energy. They folded, sold what assets they could, keeping just half a dozen Jerseys. Tessa couldn't bring herself to part with the cows completely.

Sorry for your loss. Lydia Cann, bit by bit, lost her mind. She became forgetful, losing people's names and mixing up household objects, asking someone to pass her the custard to pour on her roast and complaining that the gravy on her apple crumble was lumpy. There was the time that she planned an extravagant dinner party, ordering guineafowl and turbot and insisting Enid make a trifle, but neglected to invite any guests – though this was less embarrassing than the occasion when the Tavistocks pulled up with their daughter Millicent and her husband in his motorcar, expecting a dinner of which the rest of the household was entirely unaware. Sometimes Lydia took Tessa for a servant.

"You girl, what are you doing in my daughter's room? Get down to the kitchen this instant."

"That's Tessa, mother. She's my wife," Roger would say again.

"Your wife? Stuff and nonsense. But you can't stay a bachelor forever, you know."

In uncharitable moments, Tessa suspected her of doing it on purpose. Mostly she felt pity, though mixed with irritation. Tessa largely ran the household, but sometimes Lydia would insist on taking charge, creating confusion among the servants by issuing instructions that contradicted something Tessa had said the day before, or were simply baffling. At times she could be perfectly lucid, but then the next day she would be hysterical, demanding to know where Elspeth and Grace were, accusing her husband of hiding her daughters from her. Though when they did visit, often as not she failed to recognise them. The visits became increasingly rare: Elspeth claimed to find her mother's condition too distressing, while Grace, who had always found her mother trying, now felt both resentful and guilty. She blamed Elspeth for not doing enough to look after their mother; Elspeth said at least she had done *something* and where pray tell had Grace been all these years. In the end, it was mostly Roger who looked after her – gently, patiently giving her the care and attention that Tessa could have used herself. Everyone agreed it was a mercy when, one September night in 1922, Lydia Cann slipped away in her sleep.

Tessa lost her own parents not long after. Her father's liver finally failed on him in his seventy-sixth year. His wife followed him only three weeks later. To those who didn't know better, it sounded romantic. That was what Eliza let herself believe: "Ma died of a broken heart." Technically this was true: her heart had stopped suddenly. She had not, however, been weeping over her husband's grave at the time: she had been eating cake. Tessa couldn't remember her mother as happy and relaxed as she seemed in the days leading up to her death.

They nearly lost Arnold Cann the following summer. Tessa found him slumped against the chair in his study, his jowls drooping and his speech slurred and nonsensical. At first she thought he was drunk, but she sent Peggy to fetch Doctor Askew.

By the time the doctor arrived, Arnold was sitting up, but had lost the power of speech. "Stroke," the doctor told them. "He'll live. He may never recover fully. But he's strong as an ox, this one. It will take more than a blood clot to down him."

Over the weeks and months that followed, Tessa spent much of her time with her father-in-law. They hired a live-in nurse to take care of washing, dressing and other necessities, but it was Tessa who supported him round and round the garden until he could walk with the aid of just a stick. Walking was one thing; talking was another. Arnold seemed to understand what she was saying, seemed to want to say things himself, but the words eluded him.

"Aphasia," Doctor Askew explained. "It's quite common. Be patient. Encourage him. But don't expect miracles."

He could no longer read. Tessa stayed at his side for hours as he sat in his favourite armchair in the lounge or, on sunny days, on the bench beneath the rose arch. She liked to read aloud (another thing she had lost now – excepting the cows, who did she have to read to?). She read to him from the *Times* and, when that became tedious, from Dickens. They started with *Oliver Twist*. Arnold Cann had never read a novel in his life, but he seemed to enjoy it.

"More," he said one day when she stopped reading.

Then he laughed, proud of himself. "Asked for more... like the boy. Like Twist."

They went on to *David Copperfield*, then *Great Expectations* and *Bleak House*. She was sure he could follow the story, though sometimes he would nod off as she read, and he still struggled to find the words he had lost and to string them into sentences.

"Forgotten names... flying animals..." he told her one day. They had walked to the orchard – as far as he could manage these days. It was a May morning. The trees were heavy with blossom, white petals kissed with pink ("tree flowers," Arnold managed).

"Birds, you mean?"

He nodded. "Birds. Names of birds."

A pair of sparrows were flitting around in the Bramley tree. "Sparrows," she said. He repeated it back. She pointed to a robin.

"The gentleman in the red waistcoat is a robin."

"Robin," he repeated. "Robin Hood."

"And those two singing there are great tits."

"Great tits," he said. Then he giggled like a schoolboy.

Tessa quickly pointed to the swallow wheeling overhead. "That one's called a swallow."

"Swallow," he repeated. Then with some effort, he added: "Swallow. Like food."

A memory hit her, of feeding spoonsful of boiled egg to Cecil when he was two or three: "Open... shut... swallow..."

Cecil swallowed the mouthful, then said, "Like the bird."

"Exactly! Clever you. Now, open... shut... swift!"

Giggling with a mouthful of egg.

"Open... shut... house martin!"

Every time he had a boiled egg for the next two years they had to keep up the same ritual. *Open... shut... treecreeper!*

Open... shut... dabchick! Open... shut... greater spotted woodpecker!

She didn't have to feed Arnold, but in many ways it felt like raising a child again. It was good for Tessa. It gave her a purpose, drew her out of the dark place she had retreated into. She shared in his small triumphs: correctly identifying a nuthatch, walking all the way to the church to visit his wife's grave, coming out with increasingly complex sentences.

Two years after the first stroke he had a second, and this time there was no coming back.

So then it was just the two of them. Roger and Tessa Cann, sole owners and occupiers of The Lindens. They no longer even had domestic servants. Enid had retired the year before, and they hadn't replaced her. It wasn't as if they needed to impress anyone, and Tessa could cook perfectly well herself. Peggy still came six days a week to help with the cleaning and in the kitchen, but she had moved out of the house when she got married back in '22.

Tessa had longed for it, once: she and her husband having The Lindens to themselves, their home where they could do exactly as they pleased. But the life they had been left with was not the one she had pictured: she had lost all that. Lost the daughters-in-law that she used to imagine, those charming young women who loved her sons almost as much as she did. It was strange to think that they were out there somewhere, the women Tom and Cecil would have married if they had lived: two real women, but married in this life to other men, raising someone else's grandchildren. Her own grandchildren were lost forever, the little tribe she had dreamt of, spending glorious long summer holidays full of adventure, hanging their stockings around the fireplace at Christmas, playing cricket on the lawn, their parents joining in, the children's glee as Tom smashed the inevitable six-and-out into the brickworks.

It was a shrunken life they lived. Tessa still milked the cows twice a day, churned butter, sold a little excess milk to the Red Lion. They kept chickens, grew vegetables. Funny really: it wasn't so different from the life she'd been raised to. Like the fisherman and his wife in the fairy tale, losing everything and ending up back in their hovel after one wish too many. Though she still had the house. And she still had a good husband. Roger had been her constant companion for over thirty years. The first person she spoke to in the morning, the person she still kissed every night. He had shared in her losses and borne his grief with a grace she found exasperating but took strength from. They had spent all their adult life together, and they would grow old together, and that was something.

She hadn't paid much attention when he began to complain of headaches. Who didn't have headaches? The years after the loss of Tom and Cecil, she had had them all the time. But then he began getting strange moods. Roger, so placid, so patient, became irritable in a way she had never known before. Sometimes it would flare into shocking rage, set off by the smallest thing – a misplaced paper, a blackbird in the fruit cage, a noisy crowing match between Wellington the cock-of-the-roost and some young pretender. Afterwards, he would express surprise and remorse: "I'm not quite sure what came over me."

One evening late last summer, they had taken a stroll across the meadow in the golden light. The grasses hummed with insects, and butterflies rose from the nettles and brambles as they passed: commas and peacocks, small tortoiseshells and silver-washed fritillaries. When they reached the gate to Marshmead, he stopped, breathing heavily. It was the very spot where she had first spoken to him. She was about to mention it, when suddenly his whole body went rigid. He braced himself against the gatepost. "Roger? Are you alright?" she asked, but he only stared at her, his mouth open and oddly contorted. She immediately thought of Arnold Cann after his stroke. Then almost as suddenly as it had begun, the fit passed. Roger stepped back from the gateway, slowly bending then straightening his arms.

"I'm sorry... not quite sure what happened there. I think I must have had – a funny turn."

They sat down on the grass. She put an arm around his shoulder and rested her head on his chest, his heartbeat against her ear gradually returning to normal. Ten minutes later, Roger was saying he felt right as rain, and though she suggested that they call Doctor Askew just in case, he pooh-poohed the idea. Nothing to worry about. He just needed a big mug of sugary tea – that had always sorted him out when he fainted at school.

But when he had a second seizure three months later, she did send for Doctor Askew. He sent Roger for tests in Salisbury, then to a specialist in Southampton.

A tumour was growing on his brain. The odds weren't even worth calculating. A year, if they were exceedingly lucky. Months, more likely. Too late to do anything about it.

"The best we can do," the doctor told her, "is make him comfortable. And try to appreciate what time you have together."

She wished they had been able to do more of that. That they could have made those last months a precious time, devoted to sharing everything that was important in life: listened to the nightingales singing in Ashridge, strolled the garden in summer smelling every flower, read aloud from the greatest poets and dined on only their favourite food.

They might have travelled too, experienced a little more of the world together. But it wasn't like that, not when someone was dying from a debilitating illness. Roger had little appetite, he was weak and tired all the time and suffered from crushing headaches. In such a state, it wasn't easy to appreciate the shadows of the trees in the orchard in the evening sunlight, or savour the taste of the year's first fresh strawberry for the last time.

"I'm the lucky one, you know," he told her one day. "If you had died before me, I don't know what I would have done. I can't imagine life without you."

She squeezed his hand.

"I remember the first day I ever spoke to you," he went on. "I'd been up in the folly, trying to translate Ovid. *Metamorphoses.* The story of... No, the name's gone. A poor old couple, who offer hospitality to some gods in disguise. Jupiter and Mercury. After they die, the gods turn them into trees. An oak and a linden, entwined."

"Did you ever finish it?"

"No... I suppose I got distracted."

"You should."

Over the next two weeks, when he had the energy, Roger shut himself away in Arnold Cann's old study and wrote. When Tessa asked if she could read it, he shook his head and said no, not yet. Finally, he gave her a sealed envelope.

"Philemon and Baucis. Read it after I'm gone," he told her. "It will be like a final farewell from me. And that way you won't have to pretend to like it. I'm afraid I always was a rather mediocre writer. Really, I don't know what would have become of me without you."

She still hadn't opened the envelope.

At least the end, when it came, came quickly. Another seizure, the worst so far, then an awful forty-eight hours where he had struggled back to lucidity for the briefest intervals. Once, near the end, he had sat up in bed and quoted from Hamlet. *There is a special providence in the fall of a sparrow. If it be now, 'tis not to come. If it be not to come, it will be now. If it be not now, yet it will come. The readiness is all.* Then he had sunk back down on the pillow again. She told him she loved him. That she could never have wished for a better husband. She hoped he had heard.

And now she had lost him too. And here she was in the same black dress she had worn to his father's funeral, accepting the sympathies of friends and distant relatives and bare acquaintances, and they were all so sorry, sorry for her loss, and they had no idea, no idea what her loss was like at all.

Reginald Cotter was taken aback to hear his aunt scream. It was a small scream, almost a polite one, but a scream nonetheless. All he had said was that he was sorry for her loss, and wasn't that what people expected you to say at funerals? Heads had turned to look at them. She had tried to make a joke of it: "Sorry, Reggie. It's just you're about the ninety-eighth person to say that to me today."

Was he supposed to apologise?

"Tell me something nice about Roger. I'd much rather people did that. Or a happy memory you have of him."

Reginald thought. He remembered Uncle Roger asking dreary questions about school and performing predictable uncle tricks, making a thruppenny bit appear from behind his ear then vanish again.

"I remember how he used to do magic tricks when I was a boy. I thought he really had magic powers."

That wasn't true – he had noticed the coin folded into

his uncle's palm the second time he did it – but it made his aunt smile, so it was the right thing to say. Reginald, who did not like many women, liked his Aunt Tessa. He'd got into a fight over her once, at the Red Lion. He'd overheard Bob Carter calling her a cunning vixen, and it had taken three men to pull Reginald off him.

She had always been kind, hadn't minded having him hanging around the garden and the dairy all the time. The Lindens had been a part of his life since before he could remember. It was strange to be back – it must be ten years since he had last been here. The drawing room, though crowded now with his extended family and people he didn't know, felt less austere than he remembered. He had been in awe of the big house, with its dark wooden furniture and towering ceilings. Unused to people who had servants and houses with formal rooms that you weren't supposed to go into, he was terrified of old Mr and Mrs Cann. He remembered her shouting at him for kicking a football into her roses, even though all he had done was knock down a few petals. The thorns on her roses had punctured his new ball.

Though he had steered clear of the house itself, The Lindens had been his domain. Not a bad childhood, when he looked back on it. Tunnelling among the haybales in the loft above the dairy, jumping off the steps of the folly, climbing the trees in the orchard to reach the biggest, reddest apples on the furthest branches. Sliding down the sandy banks of the brickworks, feasting on gooseberries and currants in the fruit cage, chasing the cows in Marshmead. He liked playing with his cousins, but he was just as happy when they were away at school and he had the place to himself. Happier maybe. It wasn't the same with Thomas and Cecil after they started boarding school. Coming home full of tales of sporting triumphs and midnight escapades, endless impressions of teachers – "masters" – and boys he'd never met. Reginald had felt left out. Why couldn't he go to boarding school? There were about thirty of them at the school in the village, all in the one room, from the tots who still wet themselves to the burly young men with their first moustaches and the girls who already looked alarmingly like women. He might have liked to go to a school with boys his own age, to play rugger and cricket and learn about history. At the least, he'd be away from his father and his violent moods for eight months of the year.

"Can I go away to school like Tom?" he had asked his mother. She had snorted with laughter.

"Go away to school? Hark at 'ee. What an idea!"

"Why not?"

"Because them schools costs hundreds of pounds a year and they bain't for the likes of us, that's why."

"But Tom goes. And Cecil will too when he's old enough."

"Ah. And the Canns is rich. And we bain't."

"That's not fair."

"No, it ain't. But that's how it be."

And that was how it was. He was not somebody who would go to boarding school. He would never have servants. And he would never live in a house like The Lindens.

That was something that could gnaw away at you. Reginald had no time for socialism, but there was something to be said for social mobility. It wasn't right that your life should be determined by the rank into which you were born. Maybe it had always been in his cousins or maybe he just became more aware of it, but after they went away to school he had begun to notice an arrogance about them. Like they thought they were better than him. Though Tom, by virtue of being eleven months older, had more often than not been the leader, he now assumed total authority. Cricket games changed from a reasonably fair system of turn-taking into long sessions where Tom batted, Cecil did most of the bowling, and Reginald was expected to run around the garden retrieving the ball from among the flowerbeds and under bushes. At their camp in the laurel hedge, Tom and Cecil sat in oak chairs that their grandfather had made for them while Reginald perched on an old chimney pot. Tom had a compass, a microscope, a pocket watch and a tinder box and he never let his cousin use any of them.

Petty really, to remember those things a quarter of a century later. His cousins weren't the worst of their kind by any means – God knows he'd met far worse in the army, the Eton types who would have looked down with disdain on boys like the Canns who went to minor public schools, and who had not the foggiest notion of the lives of ordinary people like him. But it had wounded him then.

Sometimes he used to indulge in a daydream where Tom and Cecil were dead – he invented a tragic or grisly demise, depending on his mood – and he was left to inherit The Lindens. He was ashamed to think of it now.

Though they had joined the same regiment, he saw little of his cousins in the war, even when they were in France together. They were friendly enough when he did, and he had spent one memorable afternoon with Cecil when they'd met quite by chance in a village some miles behind the front line and ended up sharing a bottle of calvados from a local farm. Even so, the class differences persisted, codified into ranks. By virtue of the school they went to, Tom and Cecil were entitled to give orders to those beneath them, and Reginald and his ilk were obliged to obey.

Still, war was a great leveller. When you'd stared into the eyes of a dying stranger, when you'd dragged a fallen comrade's body across no-man's-land with shells screaming above you, then the school you went to, your parents, the house you grew up in, none of that meant a thing. And death didn't discriminate. It was fairer than life: life was fixed. Death was a game of chance.

It was down to chance that Tom and Cecil's battalion had been on the front line in that first push while he had been ten miles away in the town brothel. Down to chance, though sometimes against heavy odds, that he had survived four years of warfare. And yes, war was hell and peace was a heavenly blessing. And yet, when the Armistice was signed, among the laughter and the singing and the drinking, he had felt a sense of let-down. War had given him purpose. It had given his life structure and meaning, and charged it with an intensity that civilian life could never match. The army was all he knew. He didn't have an education, hadn't learnt a trade. But he was now Warrant Officer (Class II) Cotter. Not much higher you could go in the non-commissioned ranks.

Two weeks after returning home, he volunteered himself to the Colonial Office, and was posted into the West African Frontier Force. That summer, he sailed for Nigeria.

In between there was the matter of Peggy. The girl had carried on writing to him throughout the war. It was not a correspondence for the ages. *You must forgive me I am not a good writer and I just writes like I speaks*, she had written. He had little interest in most of what she wrote *(Today Lady Woodford come for tea and Mrs Lydia got all in a state coz I used orange pekoe instead of Darjeeling, stuck up cow, I bet she wouldn't of noticed if Lady Woodford hadn't of said. Talking of cows I don't think I ever told you there was two calves born last week...)*. He wrote back, though infrequently. He had a sense of duty. There was little sentiment in his letters; when she let it slip into hers, it made him uneasy *(I miss you... I still think about that time before you went away when we walked up to Marshmead and we talked about living in our own house together, that was a beautiful day... I pray you will be safe because I don't know what I'd do if anything happened to you.)* She often put *xxxxx* after her name. He understood this was supposed to represent kisses, but he hadn't reciprocated. Once or twice he had signed himself *"Your Reggie"* and written *SWAK* on the envelope, but he hadn't actually sealed it with a kiss, and it felt forced and false. Other soldiers talked longingly and lovingly of their sweethearts. Reginald envied that feeling.

Two days after getting back he had gone round to The Lindens to tell her it was over. He understood that this would hurt her, but it needed to be done. It was a smaller thing than killing somebody, and he hadn't shirked that when he needed to.

She had cried a bit, which was tiresome.

"Did you ever love me?"

"I dunno. I thought I did, maybe."

"If you had, you'd know it. Ain't no maybe about it."

He supposed she was right. Whatever love felt like, what he had felt for Peggy wasn't it. His fellow soldiers provoked stronger feelings: people literally ready to lay down their life for you, and you for them. That stirred something in him. In amongst the bravado and the jokes and the boredom, sometimes people would let their guard down. There had been times when Reginald had shared conversations of an intimacy and an openness he had never known before. Those people had made him want to fight like a hero. To win their approval and protect them from harm. But that was different, wasn't it?

He had seen her when he arrived, carrying in a tray of

tea cups. She had grown older, which wasn't surprising, and plump, to put it kindly. He had felt nothing much.

"So are you back in dear old Blighty for long?" Aunt Tessa was speaking to him.

"A few months."

"And then where? Off to Africa again?"

"Burma, probably."

"'O the road to Mandalay, Where the flyin'-fishes play.'"

His aunt had a habit of quoting poetry, Reginald remembered. She had read a poem during the funeral service. Something about a nightingale that she said was Uncle Roger's favourite, though Reginald couldn't make much sense of it.

"I do envy you," she sighed. "You'll see elephants."

He had seen elephants in Africa. Had shot at least a dozen. They were better to shoot in Africa, he'd been told. The Asian ones didn't have tusks.

"My husband always wanted to see an elephant. And a rhinoceros. Though I don't suppose we ever would have had the chance."

She looked suddenly like she was going to cry. Luckily at that moment two ladies who Reginald vaguely recognised as his uncle's relatives appeared, and he was able to go and help himself to sherry and cheese straws.

"A lovely service, wasn't it?" Lady Woodford said. "Though I must say your choice of reading was a little unconventional."

"It was what Roger wanted," Tessa said, bristling. In fact, she had wanted him to read it at her funeral. She had marked the poem in the book with the linden leaf he had given her all those years ago.

"Oh, of course. He was always a funny sort. Dear Roger."

"Dear Roger," echoed Grace.

It was an impressive feat to look ostentatious at a funeral, but with her ostrich feather hat and lace veil, the large jet brooch and matching earrings, Elspeth managed it. Nearly forty years Tessa had known her. Their relationship had never become anything approaching sisterly, but over the years they had learnt to rub along. She liked Grace better, but saw her less; she and her husband had moved to Devon after his retirement, and visited only rarely. Tessa wondered when she would see her again. Elspeth, who still lived locally, might continue to visit out of duty, or pity, or curiosity. Tessa hoped she would. It wasn't that she would miss the company. But she didn't want to lose the last connection she had to Roger. They were his closest living relatives. She could see something of Roger in Elspeth's mouth and jaw; Grace's hair was grey now, but when she was younger she had had the same golden curls as her brother. And her brother's elder son.

"I suppose we need to talk about the will," Elspeth said.

An hour after they had buried Roger's body? Honestly? "Oh. Yes, of course. There were some small bequests to your children, and grandchildren. Including Meredith." Grace's youngest granddaughter had been born only two months before. Roger had never met her. "He wrote her in especially."

"Dear Roger," Grace said again.

"Yes, dear Roger." Elspeth frowned. "And the house…" She left the words hanging.

"The house?" Of course he had left her the house. The thought that he might do anything else! "The house is mine."

Lady Woodford gave a tight smile. "Of course. And

nobody expects you to leave, as long as you want to live here."

"Well, I'm glad to hear it!"

"But was there any... what's the word? ... provision for what would happen to the ownership..."

"In the event of my death? I suppose that will be up to me to decide. As the owner of the property."

Praise be to Lord Birkenhead and his Law of Property Act! Tessa remembered Sir James Woodford railing against it at the time. Women inheriting property – whatever next? If Roger had died five years earlier, his family would be trying to evict her by now.

"I'm sure Roger, and Father, would have wanted The Lindens to stay in the family," Grace said.

"Father built this house," Elspeth added. "Though you know that of course."

"I was aware. Having lived here since the last century."

"Yes. Though I imagine you will find it rather lonely now, you poor thing. I fear it must seem like rather a large house when you're all alone."

"Perhaps I shall let the chickens roost inside," Tessa said. "In fact, I may leave it to the chickens in my will."

"Now, now, there's no need for – your sense of humour."

"We just want what's best for everybody," said Grace.

"And if you ever did decide you might prefer to take somewhere smaller..."

"Lady Woodford, Grace, please let me be clear. This is my home. I have no intention of leaving. I do not believe my husband's funeral is an opportune time to talk about the contents of his will, let alone mine. And I do not need to be reminded that I have lost my husband and my children and am all alone in a house that I too would have wanted to stay in *the family*."

Lady Woodford smiled with her teeth. "You're right, my dear. We'll talk about it at a more suitable time."

"Oh, I don't think we will," Tessa said. "I don't think there's anything more to be said on the matter. Though of course," she added sweetly. "You're very welcome to visit any time."

Peggy watched Reginald Cotter from outside the doorway. He was standing on his own by the far window next to the piano. Eating one of the cheese straws she'd made. Red Leicester, Mr Roger's favourite. That same scowl on his face. She had found it romantic once. Brooding. It was a dozen years since he'd last been here, and it was silly but her heart had given a little leap when she saw him. He looked old before his time, white streaks in his sandy hair which was thinning on top. He'd never been exactly handsome in your conventional way, but he'd looked fine in his uniform. When he came back from France he had medals on his chest. Her heart had truly leapt when she'd seen him then. After they signed the Armistice she had thought he would be home before Christmas, but it had taken six months that seemed as long as the war itself. It was a sweet May morning, the birds singing and blossom on the trees. They walked up to Marshmead among the cowslips and the cow parsley, she and her sweetheart safely back from the war. Heaven itself couldn't have felt half so good.

The feeling lasted all of ten minutes. He had just come straight out and said it. "I'm going to stay in the army. I'm not coming back here, so there's no point you waiting for me any longer."

He might as well have stabbed her with a butcher's knife.

"But I've waited for you all this time. You said we'd live together. I said in a cottage, and you said it would be in a house like this one."

"Well. I ent going to be living in no house."

"I could come with you."

"No you couldn't. Going to Africa. Tain't no place for a woman."

She couldn't begin to imagine Africa. It was hot, she knew that. Dusty. She was aware suddenly of the buzzing of the insects in the grass. The droning and the chattering made her head hurt. Pollen in her eyes and nostrils. It made her sneeze, twice, and her swollen eyes watered.

"Don't cry," he said. Not comforting – he sounded more annoyed than anything.

"It's not that. I get hay fever sometimes."

It gave her an excuse to let the tears fall. She asked him if he had ever loved her. He said he didn't know, and that was enough for her to know he never had.

She watched him drain his glass of sherry. After that first little judder had passed, she felt relief more than anything. Make no mistake about it, she'd had a lucky escape. It didn't matter how much you loved someone, you could never be happy together if they didn't love you back.

Her Charlie loved her. She knew it, and so did he. They'd met at a dance in Brewster's barn. He'd walked her back to The Lindens afterwards, and kissed her outside the gate to the driveway. She'd given him a leaf from one of the linden trees. Shaped like a heart it was. Mrs Tessa said they were a symbol of everlasting love. That a vow made under a linden tree would never be broken.

Charlie Morgan was a hurdler, like his father. He came from over Stourton way, but he often worked in the hazel coppice in Ashridge. He took to calling in on his way home.

He'd take a cup of tea in the kitchen, and she would give him bread and jam or cake from the pantry if Enid wasn't around. Sometimes if she'd got her chores done she would walk back with him across Stourton Down. It was on one of those walks, approaching a year after Brewster's barn dance, that he had got down on one knee among the bluebells in Stourton Hangar and asked her to marry him.

She had said yes, of course she had. He was a good man. A kind, quiet man. He never talked much, but that was the only way he was like Reggie. He was open and honest and she knew she could trust him. The only thing closed off from her was the two years he had spent in the army. He didn't like to talk about the war. Well, you couldn't blame him for that.

They had married in the village church, and Mrs Tessa had insisted they have the wedding breakfast at The Lindens. They cleared the dairy for dancing in the evening – just as they had for her own wedding, Mrs Tessa said. As her husband held her in his strong arms and twirled her round the floor, Peggy thought back to the night they had met, and was amazed again to think that life could work out the way it did. They had moved into a cottage at the far edge of Ashridge. Peggy had lived at the Lindens since she was thirteen years old, and now she was twenty-three. It had been her home nearly half her life. But it felt good to have a place of her own. The cottage was a little damp and with trees on all sides the sun rarely made it through the windows, but it was just the sort of home she had imagined. They had three children. Martha, Nancy and Christopher. Seven, six and four now, all at the village school. Where did the time go? She had kept on working at The Lindens. Charlie didn't make a lot selling hurdles so it was good to have a steady wage coming in, but that was only part of it.

She felt a sense of duty, not just to the Canns but to the house itself. Like they both needed her. She still felt that. Probably always would. She kept the place running. And now that poor Mrs Tessa was on her own, she would be needed more than ever.

There was a tray of empty tea cups and sherry glasses on the table where Reginald was standing. She marched right over.

"Reginald Cotter. How do?"

For a moment, he seemed to consider pretending not to recognise her. Then he gave a nod.

"Peggy Yates."

His voice was different. An army man, not the country boy she'd known.

"Peggy Morgan now."

"Ah. Congratulations."

"Thankee." She knew he hadn't married – she'd have heard – but she stole a glance at his naked ring finger all the same. "Shame it's such a sad occasion brings you here."

"Yes."

The years hadn't made him any more talkative.

"I just wanted to tell you. That were a good thing, saying not to wait for you no longer. I done well not marrying you, Reg Cotter." She looked him straight in his eggshell blue eyes. "I hope you'll be happy. Because I am."

She swept up the tray and walked back across the room, her heart taking flight and singing like a lark.

"Thou can't stay, just for the night?" his mother asked again.

"I'm not on leave. I only got an afternoon's pass."

"An' how's 'ee going to get back to Warminster tonight?"

"I told you. I came in a motor car."

"But we barely seen 'ee. Why, didst even talk to Jenny and the littlun?"

"A bit." His sister and her baby girl bored him. Jenny appeared to be pregnant again. She mainly talked about children, a subject that Reginald had little interest in.

"Well, come and see us soon in that motor car of yourn."

"It's not mine. I only borrowed it."

"Well, come see us anyroads. Suppose thou'lt be going off to foreign parts again soon?"

"Ah. Burma."

She nodded, though she clearly had no idea where that was. For all she knew it was a town in France. Why couldn't he have had a mother like Aunt Tessa? A mother who knew about places like Burma and quoted poems about them? A mother who lived in a big house with books and servants? A house that he would one day inherit.

It wasn't fair. Never had been. Never would be.

After he had shaken off his mother, Reginald felt a little maudlin. Sherry glasses were small, but he had drunk a lot of them. He found his aunt Tessa to say goodbye. She thanked him for coming.

"You know, if you ever need somewhere, when you're ready for a rest from your travelling, there's always a home for you here."

He was moved by that, but wasn't sure how to tell her. So he just said thank you and said again that he was sorry for her loss. Then he went out to the yard, where the car was parked in front of the dairy. A chicken had shat on the bonnet. He wiped it off with the oil cloth and started the engine.

He was looking forward to the drive. It wasn't often he had the chance to drive a car for pleasure. Forty miles, straight up the Bristol road, with a headful of fortified wine and nothing but the roar of the engine for company. He set off down the drive between the bare skeletons of the lindens, scattering a crowd of chickens. He rounded the corner and the house disappeared in the rear-view mirror. He wondered when he would see it again.

It was after six by the time the final stragglers had departed. Lady Woodford had taken her leave coolly, Grace trailing in her wake, mumbling something about poor dear Roger and how sorry she was for Tessa's loss. Roger's nephews and nieces had slipped off without saying goodbye.

Eliza was the last of the guests to leave. "'Twill be a job washing all them cups and plates. I can give 'ee a hand."

"Thank you, but no need to trouble yourself. Peggy's here, and she has the Forster girls to help her."

"Art sure thou don't want to stop at ours for the night?" her sister asked. "'Twould give me the creeps, being all alone in a big house like this."

"Honestly Liza, I'll be fine. There are no ghosts in this house that I don't know and love."

It was a comfort, in fact, to think of them there. Roger. Tom and Cecil, and baby Mary. Arnold Cann, even old Lydia. Something of our souls stayed in the places we lived, the places we loved, surely. She could do with the company.

After Eliza had gone, Tessa went to check on Peggy and the girls in the kitchen. Portia, their old rough collie, followed her.

"Yes, there might be some chicken left," she told the dog. "Maybe some sausage rolls, if Peggy hasn't finished them all."

Peggy hadn't finished the sausage rolls, though she had polished off the remains of several glasses of sherry. She looked happy, Tessa thought. The washing up was all done. Bettie Forster was wiping down the last of the glasses, while her sister Nan sorted the crockery into sets.

"Thank you, girls," Tessa said, and the Forster sisters curtsied. "And thank you, Peggy. I don't know how I'd manage without you."

"Thankee ma'am. And won't never have to, I hope. Would you like me to fix something for supper, ma'am?"

"No, thank you Peggy. I don't have much of an appetite."

"Yes ma'am."

"I spoke with your old sweetheart earlier."

"Reginald, ma'am? That were a long time ago."

The girl had been heartbroken, she remembered. Four years of waiting, hoping, wishing, praying for his safe return, and when he came back he'd given her the brush-off just like that. But young hearts healed quickly. Tessa had been so pleased for Peggy when Charlie Morgan came along. She was fond of Peggy, felt almost motherly towards her. She would never know what it was like to see one's children married – though she had thought of it so often that her imaginings had taken on the hue of memory – but watching Peggy and Charlie exchanging vows in the village church, there on the chancel step where she and Roger had spoken those same words, she had felt her heart swell.

"He's heading to Burma next. Imagine that."

"I spoke to him too, ma'am."

"Did you? And how was that?"

"It were good, ma'am. I wished him happiness, and told him I were happy myself." She blushed. "Excepting the present sad circumstances, ma'am, begging your pardon."

"Peggy, please, don't apologise. I'm sure Roger would want you to be happy."

"Mr Roger were a good man, ma'am. He were always very kind to me. I'll miss him, ma'am."

"Oh Peggy." She had cried a few tears at the committal, but had kept them back since. Now they came in great convulsive sobs. Bettie picked up the tray of crockery and ushered her sister out of the room. Peggy put an arm around her, and Tessa let herself be held till the sobbing subsided.

"I'll miss him too."

She stood on the steps of the back porch, looking out. The rain had stopped, though the tiles were wet, soaking into her slippers. Over behind Ashridge, the clouds had ripped open and the sky was bleeding crimson. The pair of oak trees at the edge of the meadow stood silhouetted before it, their branches, still bare of leaf, like gigantic blood vessels. *Come and look at the sunset*, she wanted to say. How many hundreds of times she and Roger had shared a sunset together – standing on this porch, or gazing out of the dining room window, or leaning on the gate to the meadow. How many nights he had paused before closing the bedroom curtains to remark on the colours still lingering in the sky, or to point out the full moon, or the crescent moon, or the new moon with the old in her arms.

Red sky at night... She imagined him coming up behind her, folding his arms across her belly, pulling her into him. *"There'll be some delighted shepherds tonight,"* he'd say.

It would be a beautiful day tomorrow. There would be tulips and narcissi in the garden, and the birds carolling in the spring. April was almost here – her favourite time of year. The swallows were on their way back from Africa. In a couple of weeks she would hear the first cuckoo, and have nobody to tell. The turtle dove would purr for his mate, and the nightingales would sing in Ashridge as melodious as ever. And so the years would spin by. She was fifty-five years old. Call it another twenty. She cast her mind back to twenty years ago. 1910. Before everything. The boys still in school, Roger not yet forty, she only thirty-five; it had seemed so old at the time. Arnold Cann was still full of life, milk and money flowed from the dairy, rumours of war were no more than idle gossip in the newspaper.

Twenty years was a long time.

Dusk was draining the colour from the sky. Over the treetops, Venus blinked on. The childhood rhyme came into her head. *Star light, star bright, first star I see tonight, I wish I may, I wish I might, have the wish I wish tonight.* She didn't know what to wish for. Bringing people back from the dead was beyond the powers of a star.

A tawny owl hooted. She cupped her hands and hooted back.

Portia whined from the doorway, then trotted out and sat beside her. Tessa offered her hand for the dog to sniff. She still had some soil under her fingernails.

I don't wish for anything, she thought. *I just wish I can find a way to be happy with what I have.*

HENRY COOK'S DIARY
1939-41

16th September 1939

*The old woman has given me this ~~dairy~~ diary to
write things down in. She says it must all be
a bit overwhelming and she can understand I
might not want to talk about it but that it
would be good for me to write down my
thoughts and feelings because it must all be
very different. It is all very different. I just
want to go home.*

23rd September 1939

*I have been here for one month now. I am staying
with the old woman whose name is Mrs
Cann in a house whose name is The Lindens.
The Lindens is a huge house. There are at
least 10 rooms and I have one to myself. At
home we only have 3 rooms, the bedroom, the
living room and the kitchen, plus the privy
outside. Here there is a bathroom and a lava-
tory inside. Mrs Cann is old, she is a widow.*

*There are 2 dogs that bark a lot and try to lick
you, they are called Byron and Shelley, and
there are lots of chickens which can't fly but
will run away flapping if you try to pick them
up. As well as chickens there are 4 cows, there
used to be lots more cows because there was a
diary but there isn't anymore. Also there is a
housekeeper called Peggy who is old too
though not as old as Mrs Cann, a man called
Mr Harris who works in the garden and a cat
called Hubert. Sometimes I talk to Hubert but
I don't feel like talking to the other people yet.*

25th September 1939

*The first morning here I got woken up by a cock-
erel crowing. It was early but it was already
light. I didn't know where I was at first and
then I remembered and I wished I could go
back to sleep again. We left London the
morning before, there were hundreds of children at the station and most people were
being noisy because they were excited, and all
the adults kept saying we were going on a
lovely holiday. Ma said that too but I could
tell she didn't really mean it because otherwise why would she start crying when she
waved me off? We had a badge pinned to us
saying our name, our school and where we
came from in case we got lost. After the train
we got put on a bus, it stopped in lots of
villages and children got taken off. Some children were crying and some of them had got
separated from their brothers or sisters but I*

*don't have any brothers or sisters so I didn't.
We got dropped off outside the church and
there were lots of people choosing which of us
they were going to have. It was a bit like
getting picked for football and I thought I was
going to be the last to get picked, then Mrs
Cann stepped up. She said she thought I
looked a little sad and that she knew what
that felt like. She asked what my name was
and I pointed to my badge, then she said,
Henry Cook, would you like to come and stay
with me? So that's why I'm here.*

28th September 1939

*They say it isn't safe for children to be in London
in case the Germans drop bombs or invade
but if they do that then what will happen to
Ma? If it's not safe for me then why should it
be safe for her? One of the other boys asked
about it at school. Miss Forrest said not to
worry, that the Germans weren't going to
invade and that our mothers would be safe,
but that seems stupid because if that's the
case then why do I have to come here at all?
Nothing is happening in the war anyway
even though it started almost a month ago.
Dad has joined the army but he isn't doing
any fighting, he has gone to Scotland to do
training even though that's in the wrong
direction. He sent a letter to me, he said they
make them run up hills with heavy packs on
their backs so he's fitter than he's been for
years but the food isn't very good and nor is*

the weather. He said he's going to learn to drive a tank, he said it can't be harder than driving a bus. He also said he misses me. Ma writes to me twice a week. She is training to be a nurse. I miss her.

4ᵗʰ October 1939

One reason I don't like talking at school is because the people here speak differently, they have country accents and if they spoke like that at home people would tease them but here they tease us for talking normally. I don't like school much because I don't know anyone except one other boy called John from my old school but he's only 7. There are about 40 children in the school, Miss Forrest teaches the top class and Mrs Moss takes the babies. There are 5 other evacuees but I don't know them. Sometimes the children from the village seem friendly but sometimes they aren't. One morning somebody had written VACCIES GO HOME in chalk on the school wall, Miss Forrest got really cross and made everybody stay behind until somebody owned up but nobody did so we all had to stay behind for ages. One boy called Stuart came up to me and said I bet you think you're something special don't you staying at The Lindens. I didn't say anything and he said what's the matter can't talk or something? Then he said he could go to The Lindens anytime he likes because his Great Aunt Tessa lives there so there.

5th October 1939

*It's so dark here at night because of the blackout
but also because there are no streetlights here
like at home. The house makes noises all
night. The pipes ring and the floorboards
creak and when it's windy you hear it whistle
through the chimney pots and the trees
outside. One night I heard this shrieking
sound from outside that sounded just like a
ghost. I might have cried a bit because Mrs
Cann came and knocked on my door. She
asked if I was all right then the thing shrieked
again and Mrs Cann said that's a barn owl.
She said there were lots of creatures that
made noises at night but that they wouldn't
do me any harm. She tried to give me a
cuddle even though I wasn't really scared, but
she's quite bony and she smells like an old
person and it made me miss being cuddled
by Ma.*

9th October 1939

*The other children at school are all playing a
game called conkers, the conker is a big nut on
the end of a string and you take it in turns to
hit each other's conkers and try to break
them. It looks fun but I don't know where you
get the conkers from.*

10th October 1939

*I got another letter from Ma, Mrs Cann brought
it to me. She said you must really miss your
mother and your home. She said she under-*

stood that, she said her boys used to miss home when they were away at boarding school, and she used to miss them too. She asked if I'd like to go to boarding school and I shook my head and she said I don't blame you. She said that all the people in the government and all the generals in the army went to boarding school. Then she said that explained a lot actually and laughed although she didn't seem to think it was funny.

14*th* October 1939

There are lots of trees here with apples, Mrs Cann says I can help myself to the ones on the ground which are called windfalls but lots of them have bruises or worms or bits where birds have pecked at them so I don't. Today Mrs Cann asked if I wanted to help her and Harris make cider which is a drink made from apples. I watched for a bit. There's a machine called a press that you put the apples in and Harris turns a handle and it squeezes the juice out. Harris asked if I wanted to try the juice but it looked brown so I didn't.

18*th* October 1939

I woke up in the night last night because I heard the owl. It doesn't seem so scary now I know it's a bird.

22*nd* October 1939

Today Mrs Cann's sister and her sister's daughter and grandchildren came round for lunch, one of the grandchildren is Stuart the boy from school. He can be quite mean at school but after lunch Mrs Cann said why don't you take Henry to play outside, I'm sure you've got lots of great hideouts to show him, and he said come on then so I went with him though I don't think either of us really wanted to. But it was actually fun. He took me to his best den, you have to crawl through a hole in the hedge to get to it, there are two old wooden chairs and a chimney pot for seats and a fireplace made of bricks that Stuart says he found in the Brickworks. We fetched lots of little twigs and Stuart got some matches and dried moss which he keeps in an old tobacco tin in a hole in one of the tree stumps and we made a fire. Stuart asked if I had a den of my own. I shook my head and he asked if I wanted to share this one. He said it used to be his uncle's den years and years ago.

23rd *October 1939*
When Stuart saw me at school today he called out alright Henry and I waved back at him. He was with his friend Max and after I'd gone past I heard Max say he's weird but Stuart said no he isn't he just doesn't say much.

25th *October 1939*
Today at break Stuart came up to me and said did

*I want to play football, usually I just stand
by the tree in the corner of the yard and
watch but I do quite want to play, he said I
could be on his team. We played at breaktime
and at lunchtime, when the bell went the
other team said next goal wins which wasn't
fair because we were winning 6-5 but luckily
Max scored for us. I didn't score a goal but I
did do one good kick that was going towards
the goal until someone stopped it. Stuart said
I wasn't bad and did I want to play again
tomorrow. I said yes without thinking then
everyone started clapping and saying Henry
spoke but as if they were laughing at me, they
said say something else but I didn't want to
after that.*

3rd November 1939
*This evening Mrs Cann said she wondered if I
    would do her a favour. She said she would
    love to read aloud to me, she said reading
    aloud was one of her favourite things and it
    was the only way you got to read children's
    books when you were a grown up. She asked
    what sorts of books I like and she said lots of
    names but I hadn't heard of any of them so
    she said why don't we read* Treasure Island?
    *She read the first 3 chapters, it's about a boy
    called Jim who lives in an inn and an old man
    called Billy Bones comes to stay there and
    other pirates are looking for him. Jim's father
    dies and then Billy Bones dies because he gets
    the black spot. We were sitting by the fire and*

Mrs Cann said it was a good story to read next to a roaring fire.

7th November 1939

Treasure Island is really exciting! Jim was hiding in the apple barrel and he overheard Long John Silver talking to the crew, he is a pirate and he's going to try to steal the treasure. Then they see land and it's the Treasure Island, but we had to stop there because Mrs Cann's eyes were getting tired. She said don't you dare read on without me. Mrs Cann does a special voice for Long John Silver and sometimes she does the same voice when she talks to me just for fun.

12th November 1939

Today is Remembrance Sunday. We went to church in the morning. At 11 o'clock an old soldier played the Last Post on the bugle and there was the 2 minutes silence. Mrs Cann sat very still but I could hear some people sobbing. After the service we paraded behind about 10 soldiers in uniform who fought in the last war but are too old to fight in this one. They had medals. They stopped at the war memorial by the church gate. I hadn't read the names on it before but this time I did. There are 8 names and 2 of the names are Thomas Cann and Cecil Cann. I wondered if they were Mrs Cann's sons but then I looked at her and she had tears streaming down her face so then I knew.

16th November 1939

We finished Treasure Island. *It's one of the best books in the world. They got the treasure but lots of people died. I hoped that Long John Silver would turn out to be good in the end because he kept changing sides and I liked him even though he was a pirate. In the War the Germans are the baddies and we're the goodies but I wonder if there are some Germans who want to be good? Or maybe they don't see it like that at all and they think that they're the goodies.*

21st November 1939

I got another letter from Dad today, it's only the second time he's written. He's still in Scotland but he says he's going to Egypt soon, he says he probably won't get to see the pyramids but at least the weather will be better. It was quite a short letter.

23rd November 1939

Today I was in the garden with Mrs Cann and she asked me how many birds do you know Henry, she pointed at a robin and said do you know that one and I nodded, then she said what about him and I shook my head and she said that's a blue tit. She taught me a great tit and a blackbird and a house sparrow then she said that's probably enough for today. I hadn't really noticed it before I came here but there are lots of different types of birds in all

shapes and sizes. I'm going to learn all their
names.

24th November 1939
I was in the lounge with Mrs Cann and a bird
flew up to the window, it was one of the ones
she showed me yesterday. I pointed at it and
said blue tit. I didn't even know I'd said it
aloud but Mrs Cann just smiled and said very
good.

25th November 1939
Mrs Cann was in the kitchen when I came down
for breakfast. She pointed out of the window
at the bird table and asked if I remembered
what bird that was and I said it was a great
tit and she said that's right well done. Then
another bird landed on the bird table and the
great tit flew off. It was blue and yellow with
a long black beak and Mrs Cann said it was
called a nuthatch. I said nuthatch a few
times. It's a good word to say. Nuthatch
nuthatch nuthatch.

29th November 1939
In school we have been reading Just So Stories
by Rudyard Kipling and today Miss Forrest
made us write our own Just So stories. I wrote
one about a bird that found a little brown egg
and tried to hatch it, it sat on it for weeks and
weeks only it didn't hatch because it wasn't
an egg it was actually a nut and that's how
the nuthatch got its name. Miss Forrest read

*my story and said it was outstanding. At the
end of the lesson she got some people to read
their stories out loud and then she said Henry
what about you? I didn't think I could but
then I did and at the end people clapped and
after school Stuart and Max said it was a
really good story.*

2nd December 1939

*Today I asked Mrs Cann if she would teach me
the names of more birds. She looked really
pleased when I asked her. She said why don't
we go out for a walk and write down the
names of all the birds we see. So we walked
all round the garden then up through the
meadow to Marshmead and back past the
Claypits and the Brickworks, Mrs Cann
pointed out the different birds and I wrote
their names down. I couldn't tell all of them
apart but this is the list:*

Robin
Blue tit
Great tit
Coal tit
Long-tailed tit
Wood pigeon
Blackbird
Sparrow
Wren
Dunnock
Nuthatch
Chaffinch

Greenfinch
Rook
Crow
Jackdaw
Magpie
Jay
Starling
Mistle thrush
Fieldfare

It was the best day I've had since I came here.

6th December 1939
*I got a letter from Ma today, she said she hoped I
could go back home for a few days at Christmas. It makes me happy when I get letters
from her but it makes me sad at the same
time.*

9th December 1939
*Today Stuart came over again and Max came
with him. Stuart had brought his trolley-car
and we raced it down Jupiter Hill. Then we
played sardines for hours. There are so many
good hiding places in this house e.g. in the
cellar and in the big wooden chest on the
landing and a big wardrobe in one of the
bedrooms that nobody sleeps in. And there's
the other buildings too like the Folly, the Coal
Shed, the Coach House, the Stable, the Dairy
(my best hiding place was in the hayloft
above the Dairy). Also when I was hiding in
the Folly I was looking at the bricks and some*

*of them have animal pawprints in them, a cat
I think. We went to the den too and had
another fire, Max and Stuart sat on the chairs
and I had to sit on the chimney pot but I can
go up there on my own anytime and I get to
sit in the chairs then.*

16th December 1939
*Mrs Cann has given me the job of collecting eggs
    from the chickens, she says we all need to do
    our bit for the War Effort. There are lots of
    chickens, I counted over 40 but it's difficult to
    tell because a lot of them look alike. Mrs Cann
    says they are called Cuckoo Marans because
    their feathers look like a cuckoo. I've never
    seen a cuckoo but it looks a bit like they're
    wearing chain mail like a knight. There is a
    big male one with a red crown and dangly
    scales below his beak that look like a dragon,
    his name is Coriolanus and he is the Cock of
    the Roost, which is the king of the chickens.
    Some of the chickens are smaller, they are
    called Bantams and they have funny
    topknots and feathers on their legs. There are
    3 nesting boxes in the chicken house where
    the hens make nests in the straw to lay their
    eggs. Usually there are 1 or 2 hens sitting on
    the nests and you have to stick your hand
    underneath them to take out the eggs, they
    make cross* brrrawk *noises and sometimes
    they try to peck you but their feathers feel soft
    and the eggs are cosy and warm underneath
    them. They are going broody which means*

they want to sit on the eggs to turn them into chicks but Mrs Cann says she wants to keep them in lay but we can have chicks in the spring. The hens don't just lay in the nesting boxes because they roam about everywhere so I have to look for eggs in other places too like the manger in the Dairy, hay bales in the Stable, wood basket outside the back door, etc. One hen called Imogen had a nest in the hedge on the lane up to Ashridge and wanted to go broody but Mrs Cann said the fox would get her. The fox killed one of the hens the other day, we saw a big pile of feathers by the hedge. Byron and Shelley raced away barking madly but they didn't catch it. Mrs Cann said it was sad but foxes had to eat too.

22nd December 1939

I discovered that you can lift up one of the floor-boards under the rug in my room. It's like a secret compartment. I'm going to keep this ~~dairy~~ diary under there so nobody else can read it. I'm going back home tomorrow!

3rd January 1940

I haven't written for a while because I went home for Christmas. I got the train up to Waterloo on my own the day before Christmas Eve. Ma met me at the station, it had been almost 4 months since I had seen her and it felt even longer than that. She was wearing her nurse's uniform and she has had her hair cut shorter. Until I saw her again I'd almost forgotten

*how much I miss her. Home isn't much
different but it feels small compared to The
Lindens. I missed having a garden to play in,
we used to play in the street but there aren't
many other children around now. Mr Roberts
came for Christmas Dinner. He works for the
Government and Ma said he had nobody to
spend Christmas with so she'd invited him
(she calls him Ben). He was quite nice but it's
a shame Dad didn't have leave over
Christmas although I suppose it's too far to
come home from Egypt anyway. He did send
a card though and said he would buy me a
really good present when he next saw me. It
was strange not having him around. Ma
asked if I was happy and if Mrs Cann was
nice and I said I was and she was and Ma
said she was glad to hear it but she sounded
sad when she said it. When I got evacuated I
felt really homesick but when I was at home
part of me felt homesick for The Lindens.*

10th January 1940

We are reading The Wind in the Willows. *Mrs
Cann says it's one of her favourite books, she
says she read it to her own sons (the ones who
died in the last war). It's about a Mole who
meets a water rat called Ratty and goes on an
adventure in the Wild Wood, and there's also
Mr Toad who lives in a big house called Toad
Hall (when I picture it in my mind it looks
like The Lindens). Mole leaves his house to
live with Ratty but in one chapter he goes*

*back to his old home at Christmas and it
makes him feel sad because he misses it even
though Ratty has a better house by the river.
That made me feel a bit sad too.*

13th January 1940

*I asked Mrs Cann if we could go and spot birds
again, she said she would love to. I found the
list from before and we spotted all of them
except the mistle thrush and the greenfinch
but we saw a goldfinch instead. We also saw
a treecreeper, a redwing and a lapwing.
When we got back in we made a big chart
with a list of birds down the side and the
months across the top so I can tick off the
birds I see each month. Mrs Cann says it
could be a valuable scientific record.*

17th January 1940

*We are reading a book about King Arthur and the
Knights of the Round Table. Mrs Cann said
they were her son Tom's favourite stories and
she has given me a box of his old knights.
They are little figures made of lead and they
have swords and shields painted in different
colours and some of them have horses. She
says Tom wouldn't mind if I play with them.*

20th January 1940

*Max and Stuart came round again today. I
suggested we play King Arthur and the
Knights of the Round Table, Stuart didn't
know who that was but Max did. He wanted*

*to be King Arthur and I was Merlin and
Stuart didn't want to be any of the knights I
suggested so he was just Sir Stuart. We found
some old dried up cow parsley stalks that
were good for sword fighting, you can whack
them against each other until one of them
breaks. The Folly was Camelot and we went
on a quest all around the grounds, through
the Forest (the Brickworks), across the Waste-
land (the orchard and the meadow) as far as
Marshmead and the Claypits. It's been
raining so much that there's a proper pond
there now. We called it Lancelot's Lake. I like
living somewhere where you can go on quests.*

27*th* January 1940
*It's turned really cold this week. It hasn't snowed
but it's been frosty every morning and when I
woke up there were ice crystals on the inside
of the window. There's ice in the puddles in
the lane and it's fun to slide on it and try to
crack it on the way to school. Today I went
up to Lancelot's Lake and the ice is strong
enough that you can properly skate on it. Ma
would never let me skate on the pond in the
park when it froze because the ice might crack
and I could drown and freeze to death but I
know it's safe here because the water isn't
very deep anyway. Still, I don't think I'll
mention it when I write to her.*

3*rd* February 1940
I asked today why the house is called The

*Lindens. Mrs Cann says it's because the trees
along the drive are linden trees. She says her
husband's father planted them more than 50
years ago, and she's known them since they
were saplings. That makes it sound a bit like
they are people. I have decided to give them
names. On the right side they are Larry,
Luke, Lennie, Lancelot and Long John Silver
and on the left side they are Lucy, Louise,
Lily, Lizzie and Lottie. Mrs Cann also showed
me another linden tree which she planted
herself along with an oak tree, by the gate to
Marshmead. She said she planted them there
in memory of her husband because that's
where they first met. They have names too,
they are called Philemon and Baucis.*

9th February 1940
*Today I went to play at Max's house after school.
They have an Anderson Shelter in the garden
for when there's an air raid. They haven't
used it yet but it makes a good den, it was
dark and we had 2 candles in jars. We played
a game where a bomb had fallen on the house
and we were trapped under the rubble and
we had to live down there until finally our
parents came to rescue us. I asked Mrs Cann
what we'd do if there was an air raid at The
Lindens and she said we'd go down the cellar.
She said we'd be safe as houses there, then she
said that was a poor choice of simile.*

15th February 1940

We have 2 new people living in the house. They
are Heather and Celia and they are Land
Girls. They are going to do their bit for the
War Effort by helping Harris in the garden
because we need to grow our own food and
help Mrs Cann with the cows. They are both
quite young for grown-ups. It's certainly
noisier at supper time. Mrs Cann says it's
wonderful to have us all in the house, she
says it makes her feel young again although
you'd have thought it would make her feel
even older because all of our ages put together
would probably still be less than she is.
Heather laughs a lot and is from the East
End, Celia is quite posh and wants to be an
actress in the West End. Heather had never
seen a cow before and she's terrified of them
which makes Mrs Cann laugh. She looks
younger when she laughs. Old people don't
usually laugh very much. Heather says Mrs
Cann must have been very beautiful when
she was younger. It's hard to imagine that, it
would have been way back in the last century
when Queen Victoria was king.

20th February 1940
The stars are really bright here. Mrs Cann
pointed out a constellation called the Great
Bear or the Plough, it doesn't look like a bear
but it does look a bit like a plough (I know
what a plough looks like because there's one
in Mr Jenkins' barn by the school). Mrs Cann
showed me that if you make a line up from

the 2 stars on the right then you come to the Pole Star and if you go straight down from the Pole Star that's always where north is. I don't think I'd ever seen the night sky properly before. It's better than in London.

23rd February 1940

Today Mrs Cann met me when I came out of school which she doesn't normally, I just walk home on my own or sometimes play with friends. She didn't seem like her usual self, she was a bit quiet and I asked if anything was wrong. She said she was on her way back from the churchyard so she thought she'd see if I wanted any company. Then she told me that today was Tom's birthday, and he would have been 44 years old.

2nd March 1940

Imogen (the chicken) has gone broody in the manger in the stable. Mrs Cann says that's a sensible place and we can let her sit on the eggs and hatch out chicks. She says it takes 3 weeks so they should hatch around Easter. It's good to have chicks for Easter, she says.

4th March 1940

Mrs Cann says spring is here because the daffodils are out. Daffodils are bright yellow flowers. There are also paler yellow flowers called primroses that grow on the bank by Jupiter Hill and Mrs Cann showed me which are pin-eyed and which are thrum-eyed. She said I could look at them with her magnifying glass if I wanted so I picked one of each type. They were very interesting to look at, I asked why they are different and Mrs Cann said it was to do with pollination. She said there was still an old microscope knocking around some-where and she would look it out for me if I was interested and I said I was. The other reason you can tell spring is here is because the birds are singing more. Mrs Cann says that when we hear the cuckoo we'll know spring has arrived for good.

8th March 1940
I like the look of the house from the front. It is square and it looks a bit like a face. The windows are eyes, the front door is a nose and there are round steps going up to the porch like a smiling mouth.

12th March 1940
There are lots and lots of books here, there's a room that Mrs Cann calls the library which has bookshelves going all the way along one of the walls from the floor to the ceiling. I've read The Jungle Book, Five Children and It *and a book about Robin Hood, plus* Trea-sure Island *again to myself and another book by Robert Louis Stevenson called* Kidnapped. *Mrs Cann said she was sorry all the books were old but she doesn't know much about children's literature these days. Celia has promised to send for some of the books she*

*and her brothers had when they were
growing up, which won't be quite as old. I like
reading to myself but I still like it best when
Mrs Cann reads to me aloud when we're
sitting by the fire after supper. We've just
finished* The Adventures of Tom Sawyer
and now we're reading The Adventures of
Huckleberry Finn. *I like to imagine floating
down the Mississippi River in a raft, and the
jungles of India, and the Scottish Highlands.
We hardly have any books at home.*

17ᵗʰ March 1940

*Desdemona and Esmerelda (2 other hens) have
    gone broody with Imogen in the manger. We
    haven't let them have any more eggs but Mrs
    Cann says they can be foster mothers. Imogen
    is a pecker but Desdemona and Esmerelda
    just ruffle up their feathers and go* brawk *if
    you stroke them. It seems unfair that Imogen
    has to sit for 3 weeks and they've just come
    along with a week to go, but Mrs Cann says
    Imogen is a scatterbrain and she's never had
    chicks before but Desdemona and Esmerelda
    are sensible experienced mothers. Mrs Cann
    knows the names of all of the chickens. She
    says they all have different personalities.*

25ᵗʰ March 1940

*Yesterday was Easter Day. I went out to the
    Dairy before breakfast to see if any of the
    chicks had hatched and 3 of them had. One
    was still wet from the gooey stuff inside the*

*egg but the other 2 were all fluffy, one was
yellow and one was black. For breakfast
Peggy made coloured boiled eggs, she put dye
in the water so some of the shells were blue
and some were red. It felt a bit funny to be
eating eggs though, knowing that if you just
left them under a chicken for 3 weeks they'd
turn into chicks. We went to church in the
morning. Mrs Cann said I should count how
many times we sang "Alleluia" in the hymns.
I counted 22. She said that wasn't bad but her
record was 34. We checked the chickens again
in the afternoon and there were 7 chicks in
total. The last egg was just cracking but
when we came back later it still hadn't
hatched so Mrs Cann peeled off the shell by
hand. The chick wasn't really moving and
she said she didn't think it would make it. She
gave it to me to hold while she moved the
empty shells out of the nest. It was a bit slimy
and it had blood on it but after a few minutes
it started to move its legs and soon it was
standing up. Mrs Cann said it was an Easter
miracle.*

26th *March* 1940
*Imogen and co brought their chicks out into the
yard this morning, they were all running
round on their little legs. Desdemona and
Esmerelda have 4 black ones and 3 yellow
ones. Imogen has the one that was born last
which is grey but otherwise you wouldn't
know it was any different from the others.*

30th March 1940

I finally got a letter from Dad. He says Egypt is
    very hot and there are palm trees with dates,
    he has driven a tank and ridden on a camel.
    He hasn't done any fighting yet but he says
    he's there to help protect the Suez Canal
    which is important because lots of ships go
    through it bringing us things we need. I am
    still collecting eggs for the War Effort. I don't
    think I want to be a soldier though so I hope
    the War will end before I have to.

14th April 1940

Yesterday Mrs Cann said she heard the first
    cuckoo of the year and today I heard it! It
    was really easy to identify, it just said
    "cuckoo" lots of times. It was somewhere in
    the Brickworks. I didn't see it but Mrs Cann
    says you hear them all the time but seldom
    see them. I suppose people who really know
    about birds can tell them apart by their songs.
    In the garden Mrs Cann pointed out a bird
    saying "teacher, teacher" and that was a
    great tit and then later we heard a bird
    singing really loud and she said that was a
    great tit too. She said if in doubt it's usually a
    great tit. I can recognise a tawny owl hooting
    too. Mrs Cann can hoot like an owl, she says
    she's going to teach me.

18th April 1940

We saw the first swallows today, they were flying
    around outside the Dairy in big circles and

*catching flies. I counted 4 of them. Mrs Cann
says they are a sign of summer but one
swallow doesn't make a summer. She says
lots of birds go away to hot countries like
Africa for the winter but come back here to
have their chicks. They fly thousands of miles
but they always come back to the same place.
Birds are much cleverer than people think.*

23rd *April 1940*

*I asked Mrs Cann what her favourite bird was
this evening and she said a nightingale. She
sounded very certain about it. I asked her if
we could see one and she said they came to
Ashridge in the spring. She said they weren't
much to look at but it was the way they sing,
it's bewitching she said. Heather asked if they
really sing at night and Mrs Cann said yes
they did, then she said to me that I could stay
up late one night and go to listen if I wanted
to and I said I did. Heather said when she
was in London she had heard a new song
called A Nightingale Sang In Berkeley Square
and tried to sing a bit of it to us but she kept
getting the giggles. But she said it was such a
romantic song and Mrs Cann sighed and said
oh yes, nightingales were romantic.*

29th *April 1940*

*Birds go broody just like chickens do. They build
nests and lay eggs and the hen bird sits on
them until they hatch. It's obvious when you
think about it but it's not something I'd*

*thought about before. Imogen has abandoned
her chick. She's back in lay and she doesn't
sound broody anymore. The chick tried to
follow her around for a couple of days but she
just pecked it. The poor thing looked so sad
but Desdemona and Esmerelda have adopted
it now and it seems much happier. Mrs Cann
has named it Perdita.*

10th May 1940

*My birthday! I am 10. Mrs Cann gave me a book
called* British Birds in their Haunts *by C.A.
Johns. It has colour paintings of all of the
birds in Britain and there are so many of
them! They are really beautiful pictures.
Stuart gave me a bag of aniseed balls, Celia
gave me a box of watercolour paints and
Heather gave me a handkerchief which she'd
embroidered with my initials H.C. on it. They
gave me the bumps at school and threw me
REALLY high on the one for luck and they
sang For He's A Jolly Good Fellow. Max and
Stuart came back for tea and Peggy had made
a cake and everybody sang Happy Birthday
to me. When I blew out the candles I wished
that Ma and Dad were here. Ma sent a card
with a picture of a boat which she'd signed
from Dad as well. I hope he remembered it's
my birthday.*

18th May 1940

*The weather is nice now, it feels like summer is
coming and it's good for playing outside.*

There's lots of stuff to do here even if you're not really doing anything. From the Folly you can climb onto the wall that goes along the side of the garden, I used to be scared at first but now I can walk all the way along it, and then jump off onto the lawn or climb down the drainpipe by the greenhouse. I like going in the greenhouse too. It goes all the way along one side of the house. Harris has lots of plants in there, he is growing cucumbers and tomatoes and Mrs Cann is growing lots of flowers in flowerpots which I helped her fill up with compost. There's also a water trough made of bricks that's covered in duckweed but you can sometimes see goldfish underneath. On the other side of the wall is the Brickworks. There are sandy banks that you can roll down and there are still some rails that Mrs Cann says trucks used to run along but pulled by a horse not an engine. Nobody makes bricks there anymore and lots of it's overgrown with brambles and nettles. Mrs Cann says it will turn into a wood eventually. She says it all used to be woods around here and if you left it alone then eventually a forest would grow up all around the house like in Sleeping Beauty.

1ˢᵗ June 1940

There are swallows nesting in the rafters of some of the buildings here, I counted 4 pairs in the dairy and 2 pairs in the stable. As well as swallows there are birds called house martins which look a bit like swallows but smaller and white underneath. One pair is nesting in the front porch, they have a nest made out of mud and Mrs Cann says they nest there every year. She says they often nest in houses which is why they're called house martins. I asked where they nested before there were houses, and Mrs Cann laughed and said that was a good question. Then she put on a voice like she was a house martin, saying "Look, the people have built houses – finally!" She does silly things like that sometimes, she can be really funny.

9th June 1940
Today I helped Mrs Cann and Heather in the garden, we picked broad beans and peas and podded them. The broad bean pods are soft and furry inside. Mrs Cann said I could try some of the peas and they were the best peas ever, much tastier than when they're cooked. Heather's uncle is a market gardener and she says that after the war is over that's what she's going to do, only she says she's going to grow lots of exotic things and sell them to posh hotels and restaurants. Mrs Cann was very interested and started asking her lots of questions, I thought it was quite boring and I didn't really listen but they both got quite excited, and after a while Mrs Cann went and got a notebook and started writing down numbers and lists.

17th June 1940

Today I had the first strawberry of the year.
There was only one proper red one and Mrs
Cann said I should have it, she said there's
nothing like the first ripe strawberry of the
year fresh from the garden and that I should
savour the experience. It was definitely the
best strawberry I have ever tasted. I said it
was like biting into summer and Mrs Cann
said that was exactly what it was like.

19th June 1940

The swallows' chicks have hatched and so have
the house martins. You can hear squeaking
from the nests and see these wide open beaks
sticking out when their parents fly back
giving them food.

28th June 1940

We have been eating lots and lots of strawberries.
We have them with fresh cream from the
cows but I like them even better when you
just pick them straight from the strawberry
bed. Mrs Cann made it my job to pick them,
she says as my fee I can eat a maximum of 1
out of 20 while I'm picking them plus any
that have bad bits in. There are 3 beds and I
pick them every other day. There are also red
currants, white currants and black currants
but not like the currants you get in buns.
They grow in bunches called strigs, you can
pick them off one by one or run your finger
along the stalk to make them all fall off into

the bowl which is called strigging them. The red currants are quite sharp and Mrs Cann uses them to make cordial and vinegar, the white ones are sweeter. Black currants are really sour but Mrs Cann says they make the best jam. There are also gooseberries in the fruit cage, the bushes have sharp thorns and there are red and green ones with thick hairy skins but there's also a bush with little yellow ones that squirt into your mouth and are sweet and delicious. There are going to be raspberries soon too.

12*th* July 1940
Peggy and Mrs Cann have been making jam and I've been helping, weighing the fruit and sugar, stirring it, putting it into jars etc. plus tasting it of course! They'd saved up the sugar ration and we can get extra sugar instead of our jam ration because it's fruit season so we had nearly 10 pounds which Peggy said we could stretch out to 40 jars. We've made 10 jars of strawberry, 10 raspberry, 12 blackcurrant and 8 gooseberry. Mrs Cann says later in the summer we'll make plum and blackberry jam and maybe quince and crab-apple jelly.

16*th* June 1940
The swallow chicks are now fledglings which means they are learning to fly. Hubert sits in the yard watching them and sometimes the parents sweep down really close to him like Spitfires but he just pretends to ignore them.

Sometimes the fledglings get stuck on the windowsills in the Dairy flapping against the glass because they don't understand that they can't go through it. Yesterday I managed to pick one up, it flapped at first but I cupped it gently in my hands and then it went very still. I carried it to the door and opened my hands and it flew away.

20th July 1940
School holidays! No more school until September! I don't hate school but I don't like having to stay indoors all day, particularly when it's sunny outside. Except of course for the first 3 days of the holidays it rained all the time so I did stay indoors. I read British Birds in their Haunts *and tried to copy some of the pictures.*

30th July 1940
Today we played cricket on the lawn. Max and Stuart had come round and we were playing with a tennis ball and a bat we had found in the shed under the Folly. We were taking it in turns to bat, bowl and be the wickie/fielder. Then Heather came along and said she'd be a fielder but soon she asked if she could bat. She turned out to be quite good, hitting the ball all over the garden. Even Stuart said she wasn't a bad batsman for a woman. Then Celia joined in and believe it or not she was even better. She could bowl overarm and make it spin in different directions, she said she had 3

*brothers and they had taught her. And THEN
Mrs Cann came out to see what we were
doing and Heather said come on Tessa, come
and have a bat and she said oh alright then. I
was bowling and I thought I should give her
an easy ball so I looped it up underarm, and
she swung the bat and it went way up over
the wall and landed in a big patch of brambles and stinging nettles in the Brickworks.
Mrs Cann said that was 6 and out. It took us
ages to find the ball and I got stung but it was
worth it. Mrs Cann said that she used to play
cricket with her boys. Tom was always
hitting a 6 and out, she said.*

15th *August 1940*
*I went picking blackberries along the lane from
Marshmead. I picked a whole bucket full and
my fingers turned all purple. We had them for
pudding with cream. You can stir the cream
into the blackberry juice which is purply red
and makes swirly patterns, like a marble. The
strawberries and currants are finished now
but there are still some raspberries. The
plums on the trees are beginning to ripen too,
there are some purple ones and greengages
and little dark blue ones called damsons. Mrs
Cann says we'll be able to pick apples and
pears soon as well.*

24th *August 1940*
*We have been helping with the harvest on Mr
Lightfoot's farm. We had to get up really*

*early and worked all day. My job was to help
gather up the corn after it had been cut and
build it into stooks, I got to use a pitchfork but
it was tiring. I saw lots and lots of birds:
hundreds of sparrows, plus all the finches,
yellowhammers, linnets and masses of
pigeons and rooks, which all come down to
feed on the corn. But it's sad too because there
are birds and animals living inside the field
and as the cutting machine comes round their
home gets smaller and smaller and they start
making a dash for it across the field –
partridges, hares, tiny little harvest mice.
There were kestrels and buzzards overhead
too. I wanted to stop for a bit to see if I could
watch one catch a mouse but I got shouted at
to get back to work. The wheat is going to be
used to make flour to make bread. Every time
I've eaten a loaf of bread the wheat must have
been grown in a field somewhere. I'd never
really thought about that before, I suppose
you don't when you live in the city. I would
like to live in the countryside when I grow up.
Sometimes I pretend that after the War we all
come and live here at The Lindens, with Mrs
Cann and Heather and Celia too. Dad could
learn to drive a tractor and Ma could be the
village nurse.*

30th August 1940

*I found a giant puffball! I walked up to Marsh-
mead with Byron and Shelley and I saw this
big white ball in the grass. I didn't know what*

it was but I picked it up and brought it back to the house. Mrs Cann said it's a type of giant mushroom. Peggy cooked it for supper, it tasted a bit sweaty but I wanted to eat it because I'd found it.

1ˢᵗ September 1940

Last night we had an air raid! The siren went off just before I was going to bed. We got blankets and cushions and all went down to the cellar. We had candles and Mrs Cann made hot chocolate over a paraffin stove. Heather said at least there was plenty of wine. Mrs Cann laughed and said she still had some bottles that had belonged to her father-in-law that she'd been saving for a special occasion, so why not? She let me have a sip but it tasted horrid, probably because it was so old. We played whist and rummy then Mrs Cann said I should try to sleep. She told me a story about a boy who discovers a cave and finds King Arthur and his knights sleeping there, and Celia sang "Keep the Home Fires Burning" which made Mrs Cann cry. I must have fallen asleep because when I woke up in the morning I was in my own bed. I hope we have another air raid soon.

8ᵗʰ September 1940

I wish I hadn't written that I hope we have another air raid. We haven't had one here but yesterday the Germans launched an attack on London, they dropped lots of bombs and it said on the wireless that hundreds of people were killed. Peggy said it was a mercy I was here, she meant it nicely but it just makes me more scared for Ma.

14th September 1940

The Germans have been dropping bombs on London every night, it is called the Blitz. We got a telegram from Ma saying she was safe and not to worry but I do worry. We listen to the news on the wireless in the evening, Mrs Cann doesn't usually listen to the news but Heather's family lives near the docks and she is worried about them. Mrs Cann said that the odds were overwhelmingly in our favour, that there were 8 million people in London and that the chances of being killed by a bomb were very small. Heather said that's not much comfort if you're one of the unlucky sods that is though, and Mrs Cann said no it wasn't.

22nd September 1940

Today was the Harvest Festival. All the village seemed to be in church and people had brought lots of vegetables and fruit, there were enormous marrows and apples and things by the altar and on all the windowsills. On the altar there was a big loaf of bread baked into the shape of a sheaf of wheat, it looked really good but Mrs Cann said it was made of salt dough and you couldn't eat it.

23rd September 1940

*At school today we had to go to the church and
collect all the food from the harvest festival
then take it to poor people and old people
around the village. It was better fun than
being in lessons. We went in pairs, I was in a
pair with Stuart. One of the people we had to
go to was his Granny Liza (Mrs Cann's sister)
who is a widow and lives in a tiny cottage. I
asked Mrs Cann why she didn't live at The
Lindens too because there's lots of room here
but she just sighed and said some people could
be very stubborn.*

25th September 1940

*The swallows are leaving for Africa. I wonder if
they'll fly over Dad? Most of them have gone
already but there are still a few hanging
around. They meet up on the telegraph wire
that I can see from my bedroom window, it
looks like they are still waiting for the last of
their friends to show up. I suppose the swallows must have been leaving this time last
year but I didn't notice them then. To think I
didn't even know what a swallow was!*

27th September 1940

*Last night the Germans bombed Southampton.
We could see a red glow in the sky and Mrs
Cann said the city was on fire, it was beautiful in a way but horrible too. It said on the
wireless that more than 100 people died.*

29ᵗʰ September 1940

*Tonight after the sun set the sky was all red. I
thought Southampton was on fire again but
Mrs Cann said it was just from the sun. She
said there'd be some delighted shepherds
tonight. I didn't know what she meant and
she said it's an old saying, red sky at night,
shepherd's delight. She says it means that if
there's a red sky after sunset it will be fine the
next day which is good if you're a shepherd
who's got to stand outside with his sheep all
day. But a red sky in the morning is the shepherd's warning because then it means it's
going to rain.*

30ᵗʰ September 1940

*It was a beautiful sunny day today. I said to Mrs
Cann that the shepherds must be delighted.
She laughed but it almost looked like she was
crying too.*

4ᵗʰ October 1940

*After school today we all went to get conkers from
the tree in front of the Vicarage. Most of the
best ones are in the Vicar's garden but
Reverend Simms doesn't mind as long as you
don't tread on his flowers. When you find
your first conker you have to say "Obbly
obbly onker my first conker." We got some
beauties but Stuart said we'd get better ones
from the tree up in Marshmead because
nobody else knew about it. He's going to come*

round tomorrow and he's going to show me
how to play conkers.

5th October 1940

Stuart and I got 40 conkers, we picked up more
than that but we decided just to pick our 20
best each. Peggy let us borrow a skewer from
the kitchen to make holes in them, then you
tie a string through them and you take turns
to hit each other's conker until one of them
breaks. We had lots of games and at the end
of the day I had a 9er because it had just
beaten Stuart's 8er. I don't want to use all my
best ones for fighting though so I'll go and get
some more tomorrow.

7th October 1940

My conker is now an 89er! I won 2 games at
break and 2 more at lunchtime, then after
school Billy Grayson challenged me. He said
his conker was undefeated in 50 matches and
was an 88er. I think he was lying but I'm not
complaining if it makes mine an 89er!
Everyone says he soaks his conkers in vinegar
although he denies it. Anyway, it was an epic
battle but in the end I managed to crack the
shell of his right down the middle, then it
came off the string next turn. Grayson
stormed off and people cheered me!

8th October 1940

Billy Grayson challenged me to a rematch. It was
completely unfair. I thought his conker looked

*suspiciously shiny, but he just said it was
fresh and claimed I was scared to play him
again, so of course I had to play him.
Anyway, my conker got smashed but it turns
out he'd painted it all over with his sister's
nail varnish, which is DEFINITELY cheating. A few more people took him on at break
but after a while nobody wanted to play him,
so he didn't get to be a 100er, he was stuck on
99. When I told Mrs Cann about it she said
that served him right. She said her son Tom
was a champion conker player, he used to put
his conkers in the oven overnight to harden
them up and why didn't I do that, so I've put
3 conkers in the bottom oven. She also said to
look for weaknesses in the other player's
conker and keep a short string so you can aim
better. She said if in doubt aim for any gaps
around their string.*

9th October 1940

*Victory! Billy won the first 2 matches easily, but
in the third I managed to hit his right on top
of the hole and open up a great big crack. He
didn't want to play again but by that time
most of the class was watching so he couldn't
back out of it. And in the next game I split his
conker down the middle with my very first go
and stamped on it. Everyone was cheering
and saying "well done, Chef!" (which is my
nickname because a Chef is a type of Cook).
Anyway, my conker is now a 105er and I've
decided it's going to retire undefeated.*

12th October 1940

Today we made cider. We all picked lots of apples
in the orchard and took them down to the
yard in a wheelbarrow (Harris let me ride in
the wheelbarrow on the way back up). Then I
helped to chop up the apples and put them
into the crusher. You tip them down a chute
then you turn a handle and it mashes up the
apples into pulp. Then Harris pours it all into
the press, he turns a wheel and it squeezes all
the juice out, the juice pours into a big bucket,
then we put the dried up apple pulp into
buckets to feed to the cows. Mrs Cann said to
try the juice because it doesn't become cider
for a while. It's dark brown and looks murky
but it tastes <u>delicious</u>, like apples (obviously!)
only more so. She kept a jug of it for us to
drink at supper time and she says I can try
the cider at Christmas.

22nd October 1940

I discovered an old well at the bottom of the
orchard. I hadn't seen it before because it's all
overgrown with nettles. It's got a big stone
slab over the top of it but I managed to move
it out the way so I could look down. It was
really dark, but I could just see the water,
way down. I dropped some stones in. I heard
the splash when they hit the water but I
couldn't hear them hit the bottom. I wonder
how deep it is.

26th November 1940

*The Germans have been bombing Southampton
     again. Last night the air-raid siren went off
     here and we went down to the cellar but the
     all clear went after less than an hour. We
     hadn't even finished our game of rummy.*

1ˢᵗ December 1940

*They are still bombing Southampton, the sky is
     red every night like there's a volcano on the
     horizon. The siren in the village has gone off a
     few times but we haven't had a proper air
     raid here. Stuart says the Germans don't
     want to bomb Salisbury because they use the
     Cathedral spire to navigate by, he says his
     uncle told him and he's in the army. An aero-
     plane dropped a bomb in a field near Stourton
     the other night. Some boys from school went
     to see it and they say there's a huge crater.
     Mrs Cann says they weren't trying to hit
     anything but that sometimes the German
     aeroplanes don't manage to bomb their
     targets so then they just let go of their bombs
     above the countryside so they can fly home
     quicker. She says most pilots, even Germans,
     don't want to kill people if they can help it.
     But they do kill people all the same.*

8ᵗʰ December 1940

*Ma wrote to me to say that I shouldn't go home
     for Christmas this year. She says it's too risky
     for me to come to London with the bombing.
     That means I won't have seen her for a whole
     year. I wish she could come here but she says*

*she's going to be on duty. I hope she won't be
lonely with Dad away. I think Dad will still
be in Egypt for Christmas although he hasn't
written for a while. I haven't seen him for
even longer.*

14th December 1940

*I've decided to make Mrs Cann a Christmas
present. I'm making a book called* Birds of
The Lindens *and it has a page for each of
the birds I've seen here this year, with the
name of the bird, the months when I've
observed it and some other facts, and for some
of them I'm going to draw pictures (I can
copy the facts and the pictures from* British
Birds in their Haunts*). Mrs Cann took me
into Salisbury and gave me some money so I
could buy a present for Ma and I found a
brooch with a swallow on it. It's the most
expensive present I've ever given anyone. She
also gave me some money to buy presents for
Heather and Celia, I got Heather a hat and
Celia a copy of* The Winter's Tale *by
William Shakespeare because she likes him
and that sounded like a good one for
Christmas.*

22nd December 1940

*Tonight it was the carol service. The church was
all lit up with candles and it was even fuller
than for Easter or Harvest. Carols are better
than the usual hymns. The first one was
"Once in Royal" and the choir all processed up*

the aisle carrying candles. Max and Stuart are both in the choir, they have to wear dark blue dresses called cassocks with white robes over the top called surpluses which they both hate. Anyway somehow Stuart managed to set fire to Max's surplus with his candle (he says it was an accident) and Reverend Simms grabbed a vase of flowers and threw the water over him to put it out. Then he made the rest of the choir blow their candles out. Heather giggled and said that was a bit unfortunate, because he had said at the beginning of the service that the candles represented the light of Christ.

26th December 1940

Christmas was wonderful! The house looks lovely. Harris cut down a big Christmas tree which Mrs Cann put real candles on. We hung up lots of holly and ivy and Mrs Cann cut some mistletoe off one of the trees in the orchard and hung it up by the back door (I have to avoid seeing Heather and Celia there otherwise they try to kiss me which they think is hilarious). On Christmas Eve after supper Mrs Cann made mulled cider with cinnamon and cloves and I was allowed a mug, it made me feel all warm and glowing. Celia played some carols on the piano and we sang along. Then we all sat round the fire and Mrs Cann read a poem called "The Oxen" about how all the animals can speak on Christmas Eve and we read the first half of A

Christmas Carol *by Charles Dickens. Mrs Cann read most of it but Celia did the voice for Scrooge, she sounded nothing like herself. Mrs Cann gave me a stocking to hang up by the fireplace even though I don't believe in Father Christmas, and in the morning it was full of sweets and nuts and there was an orange at the bottom. We opened the presents under the tree. Mrs Cann said* Birds of The Lindens *was one of the best presents anyone has ever given her. She gave me a new fountain pen (the one I'm writing with now) and a painting of a family of long-tailed tits in a frame which I'm going to hang on my wall. Heather gave me a football and Celia gave me a twin pack of playing cards with a picture of a robin on the back (she taught me to play a game called Racing Demon where you have a pack of cards each, it's fast and furious!). Ma sent me some metal soldiers which are like the ones Stuart has. After that we walked to church then we came back here for Christmas dinner. Stuart's family came too, there was him and his sister Rosemary, his mum and dad plus his Grandma Liza, so there were 9 of us in all. It almost made me forget that Ma wasn't there, even though this was the first Christmas I've spent without her. After Christmas dinner we went for a walk around the village then we came home and played Charades and In the Manner of the Word, and we read the second half of* A Christmas Carol, *where Scrooge decides to be nice and*

celebrate Christmas after all. Only 363 days
to go until next Christmas!

8th January 1941
I asked if we could read A Christmas Carol
again but Mrs Cann says it's a book you can
only read at Christmas, the same way you
can only sing carols at Christmas. She said to
everything there is a season and a time for
every purpose under heaven. But she says
Charles Dickens wrote lots of other books, so
we are going to read one called David
Copperfield. *It's over 900 pages so that*
should keep us going for a while!

16th January 1941
It snowed last night. A few flakes started falling
when we were going to bed and before I went
to sleep I undid the corner of the blackouts to
peep out and there were fluffy white feathers
everywhere in the moonlight. Then this
morning everything was covered in snow,
even the branches of Lancelot, Long John
Silver & co. I got to be the first to make foot-
prints on the lawn along with Byron and
Shelley who were going berserk and chasing
each other in figures of eight. I started making
a snowman, then Heather joined in too and
said it should be a snowwoman, she was
quite bossy but it was funny too because she
went and got some of her own things e.g. a
big red hat, a flowery shawl, a handbag etc.
and it looked really good. Then Max and

*Stuart came round to go sledging. Mrs Cann
said we could use Tom and Cecil's sledge, it's a
proper wooden one with metal runners (Max
and Stuart only had tea trays). We went
sledging down Jupiter Hill. One time I went
REALLY fast and I fell off into a snowdrift
which luckily stopped me from slamming into
the wall. I saw Mrs Cann on the Folly steps,
she was there for ages just watching us.*

1ˢᵗ February 1941

*Lancelot's Lake looks like a lake again. It dried up
in the summer but after the snow melted we
had lots of rain and half of Marshmead is
flooded. It's good for watching birds, I've seen
mallards, moorhens, coots, dabchicks and a
tufted duck. Yesterday I saw a pair of snipe in
the reeds. I recognised them from the picture
in* British Birds in their Haunts. *The bird
I'd really like to see is a kingfisher but there
aren't any fish so I don't suppose I will.*

9ᵗʰ February 1941

*Stuart came round for Sunday lunch with all his
family plus his Uncle Reg who is visiting
because he is about to go off to India. He is a
Colonel and I didn't like him. He has been to
Africa too. Stuart asked him if he'd seen an
elephant and he said better than that, he'd
shot one, and a rhinoceros, a lion, a giraffe
and lots of other animals. I don't know why
anyone would want to shoot an animal. We
had roast mutton which was nice but all the*

same I probably wouldn't want to eat it if I had to kill the sheep myself.

15th February 1941

I had a fight with Stuart today. His Uncle Reg had given him an air rifle and he brought it round this afternoon. At first it was quite fun, you put a little metal pellet in the barrel then you cock the gun and line up the sights on the thing you want to fire at then you pull the trigger. We shot at some tin cans in the orchard and I was quite good. Then he said why don't we try and shoot some birds. I said I didn't want to but he said don't be wet and went on about all the animals his uncle had shot. There was a blackbird on the top of one of the trees so I said go on then, try and shoot that. I just wanted to shut him up. I didn't think he actually would because he's not a very good shot but he must have got lucky because he hit it first time. It fell right out of the tree. I ran over to it and it was lying on the ground, it looked stunned but there was no blood and it was still alive. I was going to pick it up but Stuart had already reloaded the gun and he shot it again from point blank range. I punched him in the face and made his nose bleed. I've never hit anybody like that before but I just felt like I really hated him then and it felt good. I picked up the black-bird's body and went up to the Folly and locked myself in. I stayed there for hours until Mrs Cann came and found me. I thought she'd be angry because Stuart is her grand-nephew and because she doesn't like fighting. But she just asked me what had happened and I told her about the blackbird. She said she could see why I was upset but it was still wrong to resort to violence. Then she said we should have a funeral for the blackbird, so we buried it in the vegetable patch. Mrs Cann recited some lines from Shakespeare about the fall of a sparrow. I was going to point out that it was actually a blackbird but she had that look where she looks like she's about to cry so I didn't.

23rd February 1941

Today would have been Tom's birthday, I remembered because I wrote about it last year. I told Heather yesterday and she said we should do something to mark it. We made a sponge cake together, it fell apart a bit but we managed to glue it together with strawberry jam, and I picked some crocuses and primroses from the garden. Mrs Cann cried and I thought maybe we'd done the wrong thing but she said no, it was really lovely.

1st March 1941

It is the first day of spring and there are daffodils out on the lawn. Some of the birds are getting ready to leave, like the redwings and the fieldfares. I saw a flock of 27 fieldfares gathering in the field. But others will be arriving soon, like the swallows, swifts, martins, flycatchers

*etc. And the cuckoo and the nightingale. I
hope I get to hear a nightingale this year.*

15th *March 1941*

*I got a postcard from Dad. It's the first time I've
    heard from him since Christmas. It had a
    picture of the pyramids on it but he says he
    still hasn't seen them. He says we've been
    giving the Eyeties a good kicking and that
    driving a tank in the desert is more fun than
    driving a bus through the streets of London.
    He also said he missed me and couldn't wait
    for us to all be at home together as a family. It
    seems like such a long time since we were.*

30th *March 1941*

*Today was Mothering Sunday. We went to
    church in the morning. Usually the sermons
    are really boring and I just stare at the
    stained glass window and the patterns in
    the woodwork but today I listened. Reverend
    Simms talked about how in wartime many
    mothers are apart from their children. He
    said he knew there were mothers there
    whose children were fighting overseas and
    children whose mothers had sent them away
    for their own safety (he looked at me when
    he said it although some of the other evac-
    uees were there too) but that even when we
    were far away, we could always be sure
    that our mothers loved us. Then he said it
    was like that with God too. But I'm not sure
    if I believe in God so that spoilt it a bit.*

There were posies for children to give to their mothers and I wished Ma was there so I could give one to her. There were also some spare ones for people who didn't have mothers/children so I gave one to Mrs Cann. She took one herself and after the service she went and put it on her mother's grave. Then she went and stood by the cross that says IN LOVING MEMORY OF THOMAS JOHN CANN (1895-1916) AND CECIL PETER CANN (1897-1916) UPON ANOTHER SHORE AND IN A GREATER LIGHT which is next to the one that says ROGER ARNOLD CANN (1872-1930) BELOVED HUSBAND. There's also a little stone which I hadn't noticed before that just says MARY CANN 1901. I think she must have had a baby that died but I didn't want to ask. Mrs Cann stood there for a long time. I waited in case she might want company on the way home. I watched the lambs skipping around in the field behind and listened to a blackbird singing in the yew tree. I like the graveyard. It's a sad place but it's peaceful too.

13th April 1941

Today was Easter Sunday. There were 24 Alleluias in church, 2 more than last year. We have lots of chicks already this year, Desdemona and Esmerelda are co-broodying again, Miranda has a family of 5 and Perdita has 4, they are grey like her.

15th April 1941

*I heard my first cuckoo of the year! I didn't see it
but it was singing loud and clear in a thicket
by the Brickworks.*

20th April 1941

*The swallows are back! I saw 5 of them. I wonder
how they feel when they get here? Is it like
going on holiday or like coming home?*

10th May 1941

*My birthday! I'm 11! Mrs Cann got me the best
present ever: a pair of binoculars! They are
amazing. From my bedroom window I can
see the chickens in the yard as if they're only
a few feet away and of course I can use them
for birdwatching. Heather gave me a notebook on a string with a pencil attached, for
birdspotting she said, and Celia gave me a
book called* The Hobbit. *Ma sent a card that
she signed from Dad too and a stripy jumper
that she'd knitted which is nice but a bit
small. This year it was a Saturday so I didn't
have to go to school although that meant I
didn't get the bumps. We went for a walk
across the fields to the river and had a picnic
with nettle beer and a birthday cake with real
chocolate. Heather and Celia came too and
the dogs, it felt like we were a funny kind of
family even though Ma and Dad weren't
there. And the best thing of all was that we
saw a kingfisher! I'd been wanting to see one
ever since I first saw it in* British Birds *in*

their Haunts – *a year ago today! We saw a flash of blue and then it settled on a branch just beyond the bend in the river. It was quite a long way away but I could see it with my binoculars. It was smaller than I imagined but the colours were even brighter than in the painting. Mrs Cann said that was the second part of my birthday present and it had been quite a job to arrange it but I'm pretty sure she was joking.*

11*th* May 1941
After I went to sleep last night the Germans launched a huge raid on London. It said on the wireless that more than 1000 people were killed. Sometimes I forget that there's a war on. It seems so strange that I could be having my birthday and watching a kingfisher here while less than 100 miles away there are bombs and fires and people dying.

19*th* May 1941
There haven't been any bombs for more than a week. On the wireless they are saying the Blitz is over. The Germans want their planes to attack the Soviet Union instead. At school people are talking about how evacuees might go home soon. I want to go home but I want to spend the summer here too. I haven't heard a nightingale yet.

25*th* May 1941
Now I have! I asked Mrs Cann if it was the right

*time of year to hear them and she said it was
(which I already knew) and then she said we
could go up to Ashridge and listen if I didn't
mind a late bedtime (which of course I didn't).
We went out long after supper when the sun
was just going down behind the wood. Byron
and Shelley wanted to come but Mrs Cann
said they couldn't because they might scare
the birds off, and they were the wrong poets
anyway. I didn't understand what she meant
but on the way up to Ashridge she explained
that someone called John Keats had written a
poem called "Owed to a Nightingale" and she
recited some of it. I didn't really understand
what the words meant but I liked the music of
them. She said that when she first met her
husband he had read the poem to her cows
and that was how she had fallen in love with
him. She said they had come here together to
listen to the nightingales sing every year for
more than thirty years. But this was the first
time she had come since he died. We didn't
hear the nightingale for a long time. We sat
on a fallen tree trunk in a clearing and drank
tea from a flask and ate Digestives until it
was almost completely dark. We heard a
tawny owl going* tuwit-tuwoo. *I did the owl
hoot like Mrs Cann had taught me, and it
hooted back! We saw 4 deer, a fox and a
badger. Mrs Cann had just said that if we
didn't hear the nightingale in the next few
minutes then we should probably call it a
night when suddenly she said "hark!" and I*

heard it. Sometimes when birds sing it's just their way of calling to each other but the nightingale sounds like it's singing for fun. It makes so many different funny noises and you never know what the next one will be like. I closed my eyes to listen and I listened for a long time but I must have dropped off to sleep because the next thing I knew it had stopped. Mrs Cann said it was time to be getting back. When I woke up this morning it all seemed like a dream.

11*th* June 1941
Martin and Tony weren't in school yesterday and today Miss Forrest told us that they had gone back home to London. That probably means I'll never see them again and even though they weren't particularly my friends that feels strange. It made me think that that's what it must be like when somebody dies, except then you know for sure that you'll never see them again ever.

15*th* June 1941
I had the first strawberry of the year. It was only a small one and it had a peck in it because a blackbird had got under the net but it was the best strawberry I've eaten since the first one last year. Mrs Cann says it's always like that.

20*th* June 1941
Yesterday I got a letter from Ma saying I can come home soon. She says it's safe to come

back to London, she says there are more chil-
dren around and my old school is open again.
I prefer the school here with Miss Forrest, it's
much smaller than the school in London and
I know everyone. I want to go home but at
the same time I don't.

2nd July 1941

I'm going home on July 31st. Mum says her friend
Ben can drive down with her and pick me up
in his car and won't that be fun?

3rd July 1941

I asked Mrs Cann if I can come and stay even if
we don't have to be evacuated again and she
said of course I can. She said I'll always have
a home here. I don't want the Germans to
start bombing London again but I hope I
come back here at least part of the time. I'm
already thinking about all the things I'm
going to miss, like the harvest and the
damsons and the apples, the swallows leav-
ing, conkers and making cider.

10th July 1941

I just want to stay here. It doesn't feel like I'll be
going home. It feels like I'll be leaving home.

30th July 1941

Today was my last full day here. Ma will be here
tomorrow lunchtime. It was a beautiful
sunny day and I decided I would walk all
around The Lindens so I could say goodbye

properly to everywhere and do all the things I wanted to do for the last time, like walking along the wall, picking raspberries from the fruit cage, sliding down the banks in the Claypits and climbing the conker tree etc. although I didn't get to do everything. I also decided to record every bird I saw today. I saw wood pigeon, robin, blackbird, dunnock, house sparrow, great tit, blue tit, coal tit, nuthatch, crow, rook, jackdaw, magpie, wren, chaffinch, greenfinch, goldfinch, starling, green woodpecker, swallow, house martin, swift, pied wagtail, spotted flycatcher, black-cap, kestrel and moorhen. Plus I heard the cuckoo and a chiffchaff and just now I heard a tawny owl so that makes 30 different birds in total. Not bad for one day. Mrs Cann says she will keep filling in the bird chart for me. I asked her if this would still be my room and she said of course, so I'm going to leave this diary in its usual place under the floorboard for when I come back.

RABBIT PIE
1954

From the dining room window, Irene watched the car disappear around the corner. Then she strode upstairs to the bedroom. She opened the top drawer of her dresser, reached behind her unmentionables and took out the scrap of paper. Then she went back down to the hall to the telephone. She lifted the receiver and listened. Just the dial tone: nobody else on the party line that served their end of the village. Her finger shaking, she dialled the number on the paper. A woman's voice answered on the fourth ring. "Mill House?"

"Can I speak to Mrs Roberts please? I believe she's staying with you."

"Who shall I say is calling?"

"It's Irene. Her sister."

"Just a moment, my love."

It was more than a moment. Irene could feel panic rising. *Stop it*, she told herself. *There's plenty of time.* Then Clara's voice, brisk and business-like.

"Rene? Has he gone?"

"He just left."

"Good. I'll come straightaway. Give me half an hour, tops."

Half an hour seemed like an age, and no time at all. "What should I do?"

Clara let out a small sigh. "Pack what you can carry. Don't overdo it. Don't get sentimental. Make sure Eric is ready. I'm on my way already."

Irene heard the click of the receiver and the line went dead. She replaced the phone in its cradle and went back to the bedroom. She took out the trunk from the walk-in wardrobe and opened it on the bed. The same trunk she had taken to India. She remembered packing it before the voyage out, almost twenty years ago. She didn't remember packing it to come home. The servants must have done that. She began stuffing clothes in the trunk automatically, trying simply to do and not think.

Looking back now it seemed so young, but when Irene was twenty-seven she was already resigned to the probability that she would die an old maid. Mrs Harmison's invitation to come to India as her *companion* only seemed to confirm it. Still, it was an opportunity for a fresh start, and a fresh start was what she needed, after what had happened with Teddy. And India! She pictured herself riding an elephant to the Taj Mahal, drinking fresh tea on the veranda while tigers stalked the jungle at the end of the lawn. Of course she had known even then that reality was unlikely to measure up to her imagination (when did it ever?), though she would go on to do plenty of sightseeing, see elephants if not tigers, and drink a great deal of tea.

She had hated it to begin with. The feverish heat, the dirt and the dust, the shameful poverty. She didn't warm to the Indians she met, whom she found by turns obsequious or rude, but the British were worse. Pompous but boorish men who drank too much and spoke too loudly; waspish memsahibs trading gossip, slights and judgements; lecherous husbands flirting with other men's wives, but quick to anger when it was their own wife doing the flirting. And then the war had come, and she had been trapped there with them all, and it had become her life. When the war ended and Mrs Harmison had returned home, Irene stayed in Patna. She had a small inheritance (a deceased aunt who had never married and reminded Irene of herself to an uncomfortable degree), and nothing to go back to.

It soon became apparent, though, that she would have to go back. Talk of independence and partition was growing louder; there was an edge to the obsequiousness, the rudeness more open. Mr Gandhi in his absurd loin-cloth was preaching non-violence, but his people didn't seem to be listening. Riots and massacres in Calcutta spread into Bihar, though at least the Hindus and Muslims seemed more intent on killing each other than turning on the Europeans.

Colonel Cotter and his unit were stationed there in August 1946 to keep a lid on the situation. He wasn't a dashing young military man out of a Jane Austen novel, not even a Captain Wentworth. He was approaching fifty with a bald head that he almost compensated for with his thick copper moustache and bushy eyebrows. She had met him at a cocktail party at the governor's residence that she had been dragged along to by the Manwarings, old friends of Mrs Harmison's whom she suspected felt sorry for her; Claudia Manwaring, at least, seemed to believe it was still possible that Irene might one day find a husband, and was keen to introduce them when she discovered that Colonel Cotter had never married.

"Never had time for it," was the gruff reply when Claudia asked him why not. "Been in the army all my life."

"Well, perhaps you'll take a wife when you retire," Claudia suggested. Colonel Cotter grunted. Irene felt herself blushing.

The Manwarings arranged a dinner party the following week, and she found herself seated beside him. He was stiff and taciturn, leaving Irene to talk more than she usually did. But he was happy to listen to her, or at least appeared to be. Eventually the wine began to loosen his tongue.

"Where will you go?" he asked her. "When it's all over?"

"When what's all over?"

"This. The Raj. It's coming to end. The wogs won't want us here once they have their blessed independence. Can't say I blame 'em."

"I don't know. Go home, I suppose."

"Still have somewhere you can call home then? You're lucky. Some of these poor buggers don't. This is all they know. Rude awakening coming. Though I'm a fine one to talk. Joined the army at the start of the Great War – had to lie about my age too. Spent most of my life overseas. France. Egypt, Nigeria, Rhodesia. Burma. And India of course."

"So you don't have a home in England?"

He paused, and for the first time something resembling a smile played over his face. "Well. It's not my own. But there's my aunt's house. I was brought up there, sort of. Big place in the country." He drained his glass of wine. "When I think of home, that's the place that comes to mind."

Over the next few months, they saw each other often. Irene could tell that Colonel Cotter –"Call me Reginald" – was, like her, not an enthusiastic participant in social gatherings. Something about him didn't fit; his manners were awkward, his accent unnatural. Still, he disliked many of the same people that she did, and she liked him for that. It didn't escape her notice that they both found it easier to talk after a couple of drinks, but at least there was somebody she enjoyed talking to. Somebody who noticed her.

They were married the following year. His proposal was more business-like than romantic. He could do with a wife once he was back in England, she needed somewhere to live, and of the available women he had come across, she was the least objectionable. At the time, she had taken this as wry humour. She wasn't romantic herself; at least not anymore. She needed to leave India. Her inheritance wouldn't last long. She was too old for a career, too old for motherhood probably. She could return home, live with her parents, succumb to her destiny as a maiden aunt. Or she could accept a marriage proposal. Of the objectionable men she had come across, he was at least available.

He said it shouldn't be a big wedding. Cuthbertson, the regimental chaplain, officiated and Lieutenant McDonald – Macca, a giant Glaswegian whose accent she could barely understand – was Reginald's best man. Mr Manwaring gave her away. It would have been silly to ask any of her family to come all the way from England, even if there had been time to arrange it.

She had approached the wedding night with trepidation. She had never been with a man before. Reginald was the first person she had so much as kissed since Teddy. In the event, he drank too much and was snoring loudly by the time she emerged from the bathroom in the new silk night-dress she had bought for the occasion. Her relief was coloured with a tinge of disappointment.

They visited the Taj Mahal for their honeymoon, but she had seen it before and he appeared unmoved. They cut the trip short because he wanted to join a hunting party. It was the one area of colonial life that appealed to him, though this time he returned in a morose mood, having failed to bag a tiger.

They sailed back to England in '47, leaving just before the monsoon. To begin with, the move to The Lindens was supposed to be temporary. They would stay there until Reginald found a suitable house nearby. She had raised the idea that they could look a little further north – Berkshire, perhaps – to be closer to her own family. But he had said that he had family responsibilities too and made her feel selfish for suggesting it. He wanted to stay in Wiltshire, and it was his hard-earned money. Though money wasn't the problem: he had a colonel's pension and the army salary he had deposited in the bank over three decades of living frugally had grown steadily, the Jaguar XK120 he bought on their arrival back in England being a rare extravagance. They went to see two dozen houses – the old vicarage in Stourton, a place by the river outside Britford, a crumbling Georgian manor house – but not one to his satisfaction. "No point moving until we find somewhere better than here," he told her. So they stayed.

Aunt Tessa didn't seem to mind. In fact, she seemed pleased to have the company. Irene liked her. She was well past seventy but hale and hearty, out early every morning to feed the chickens and walk Byron, her geriatric collie. She liked to listen to Irene talking about India. There was part of her that had always longed to travel, she said. But you couldn't do everything.

"Besides, I love it here," she sighed. "I've seen more than fifty autumns in this house, and I'm not tiring of them yet."

Irene was less sure about autumn. The grey days and the drizzle and the prospect of months of darkness ahead. She was surprised how much she missed the tropics. She had intense bouts of yearning that she felt as a physical sensation. The mosquitos and the dirt and the punishing humidity receded in her memory, leaving behind light and warmth, and the chorus of frogs and insects on balmy moonlit nights. Distance makes the heart grow fonder, she told herself. Absence lends enchantment. Still, she wondered sometimes, what if she had been braver? She could have stayed on in India after independence and taught English in a school. She could have taken a boat to Ceylon, Singapore, Mombasa. Even on their way home, she might have disembarked in Suez, slipped off into the bustle of the marketplace and never got back on the ship. People did these things. But not people like her. People like her married men nobody else would marry and found themselves stuck in cold, draughty houses that weren't even their own.

She missed the colonial community life, too; however much she had despised it at the time, at least it kept her from spending too long in her own company. Here, her social contact was limited. When they first arrived, they were an item of some curiosity: Eliza Cotter's boy come back to the village after all these years, a retired colonel no less, and just taken a younger wife. Reginald disliked the attention. "Nosy buggers," he called them, although Irene thought most were just trying to be friendly. Sometimes they lunched with his sister Jenny and her family, who still lived in the village, and there were dinner parties with the Gregsons, an old army colleague and his ghastly wife who lived in Salisbury, and their equally tedious friends. A handful of times, two young friends of Aunt Tessa's had come to stay and the house had lit up with laughter and chatter; it felt sad and silent when Heather and Celia left. Mostly, Irene's social life consisted of church on Sundays and the occasional coffee morning or jumble sale. On a daily basis, her husband, Aunt Tessa and Peggy, the housekeeper and cook, were often the only people she spoke to.

The lack of company suited Reginald. Irene wondered how he had spent three decades in the army: he seemed to care little for comradeship and camaraderie. He preferred his solitary pursuits. Fishing, mainly: two or three times a week he would disappear in the car early in the morning to spend the day by the Test or the Nadder, rarely returning before teatime. Sometimes he would bring back a particularly fine trout that they would eat for supper, but that didn't appear to be the point. Irene thought it might be pleasant to spend a day sitting beside a stream in the sunshine, but when she had asked if she might come along, he'd told her that he couldn't have company, it upset his concentration. There was his shooting too – sometimes he would join a pheasant party with Gregson, but more often he'd take his rifle up to Ashridge and bag some rabbits or pigeons. In winter, when Marshmead became sodden and pools formed on the surface, he would pick off mallards and moorhens, the occasional wigeon and woodcock. It all seemed rather sad and cruel to Irene, but at least it kept him occupied.

She, on the other hand: some days she wondered whether there was any point getting out of bed at all.

And then something did happen. Falling pregnant at thirty-eight was a surprise. She had thought she was too old, and their lovemaking – for want of a better word – too sporadic. The first time had been a few days after their unsatisfactory wedding night. It had hurt a little, but there was a part of her that almost enjoyed it. He seemed faintly disgusted when it was over – with her or himself she wasn't sure – and went to the bathroom to wash. She would have liked to be held for a while. After that, it had happened every month or so, always on his instigation, and always with the same awkwardness afterwards. They slept in separate beds; once they moved to The Lindens, in separate rooms. It wasn't that she didn't want a child. But she had long been resigned to the likelihood that she would never have one, and had spent many long hours convincing herself that this was for the best. That children were mostly an expensive nuisance and that she would be a bad mother anyway, with the bouts of tiredness and sadness that came over her. Well, she was probably right about that.

She knew nothing about being a mother. Shouldn't somebody teach you what to do, before entrusting you with the care of a helpless human child? Shouldn't you have to pass some sort of exam? At least she had Aunt Tessa there. It was Tessa who had chivvied her into decorating the nursery, who had found the lovely old cot in the loft, with the shapes of birds carved into the headboard.

"My father-in-law made it," she said. "Both my boys slept in it. It would make me very happy for another generation to use it."

After the unimaginable pain of Eric's birth, she felt a sense of radiant peace. She felt joy and love. Incredulity. And fear. Fear that this precious, fragile thing could be taken from her at any moment. Fear that all the love she felt wasn't enough, could never be enough. Just like it hadn't been enough for Teddy. All the conflicting emotions fought against each other in the days and weeks that followed until what she felt above all else was numb. An automaton going through the motions of motherhood, feeding and bathing Eric, changing nappies, pushing the pram round and round and round the lawn, settling him to sleep.

One afternoon, after a dozen circuits of the lawn as Eric grizzled and griped into his nap, she slumped down into the arbour by the folly. She broke off a piece of honeysuckle and wound it tightly round her finger till it began to throb.

"You're doing well, you know."

Irene looked up, startled – she hadn't noticed Tessa approaching. Tessa sat down beside her, and placed a hand on her wrist.

"It's hard work, having a baby. Bloody hard work. So don't be hard on yourself."

"I wish he didn't cry so much."

"All babies cry. He looks peaceful now, anyway."

She looked at Eric, sleeping soundly now in the shade of the laburnum tree, yellow flowers drooping over the pram. His wide bald head made him look like his father. Yet he had grown inside her. Had literally been part of her. She felt something stir within her.

He was out there now, underneath the laburnum, playing with the lead knights that had once belonged to Tessa's sons. Sherpa was asleep on his back beside him, all four legs in the air. Eric looked up, smiled and waved when he saw her. She waved back, then turned away from the window.

He was happy here. Was she doing the right thing?

She went into his bedroom and began filling his suitcase. Two pairs of trousers, a pair of shorts, three shirts, two jumpers. Vests, underpants, socks, pyjamas. What else? His piggy bank. A box of keepsakes. His *Eagle* annuals fitted neatly along one side. Which of his soft toys? Raggedy Rabbit of course, and Tiger. Was Cloppy the elephant too big? *Don't get sentimental*, Clara had told her.

She heard a car coming up the drive, and her heart began going haywire. Was that Clara already? Or had he come back? Perhaps he'd forgotten something. What would he do if he saw the suitcase? She stood frozen for a moment, then darted through to the spare room, which afforded a view over the yard. There was a sky blue car, and Clara stepping out of it. Relief lurched through her. She took the stairs two at a time.

Looking back, the next two years seemed like a golden time. Eric learned to smile, learned to laugh, great bubbles of pleasure popping out of him as she tickled his tummy or played peek-a-boo behind a blanket. The miracle of his first words, his first steps, then in no time at all he was talking and walking all over the place. She let herself love him without fear. It was still bloody hard work – shoes and coats and mittens were never where they ought to be, the slightest frustration could throw him into tantrums of extraordinary ferocity, and she continued to lose hours of sleep each week to nightmares and night-time accidents – but she could manage.

Tessa helped. She could anticipate Irene's moods better than Irene herself. "I put the hot water on," she might say. "Why don't I take Eric and you take a nice long bath?" Or she might casually mention that Sherpa could do with a walk, and Irene would put on her coat and wellingtons and stomp up to Ashridge, feeling the wind against her face and watching the dog running figures of eight round the field, and she would feel the clouds lifting. *Perhaps I could be happy here*, she thought.

Sherpa had been Tessa's idea in the first place. After Byron had finally gone to the happy hunting grounds, she had said it would be good to have another dog about the place. He was a daft, devoted springer spaniel, always trying to jump up and lick your face. He doted on Eric, who loved him back to an almost obsessional degree. Reginald loved the dog too. Sherpa brought out an affectionate, humorous side of him that he rarely displayed around people. He would throw scraps from the table for the dog to catch, though he would bawl out Eric in his terrifying colonel's bellow if he ever tried to do the same.

"It's a good thing you're here," Tessa had said as they watched Reginald throwing an old tennis ball for Sherpa to fetch, Eric chasing behind him, squealing with laughter. "I'm too old to get a dog myself – it wouldn't be fair. But it would be a crying shame not to have a dog around during one's final years."

Those final years had been too few. Influenza took her the following winter, a few days before Eric's third birthday. A week earlier she had been up at seven o'clock in the morning, like every morning, to feed the chickens and the ducks. She had come in wheezing and shivering.

"Chilly out this morning. There's ice on the puddles. The ducks are discombobulated."

She made up the fire in the lounge and sat in the armchair wrapped in a blanket, but was still shivery. An hour later she was sweating.

"Should I call the doctor?"

"Oh no, I'm sure it's just a common-or-garden winter cold."

It was a short illness, at least.

"I'm looking forward to being with Roger again," Tessa had said the day before she died.

Irene said something vacuous about going to a better place.

"Heaven and all that? Oh no, I don't think so. But I'll be happy down here, mingling in the same patch of earth."

They buried her in the corner of the churchyard beside

her husband. The church had been packed. After the service and the committal a procession of friends and relatives had descended on The Lindens. It was the last time the house was full. Later, when the people had gone and Irene was drying up in the kitchen, Tessa's favourite tea cup slipped through her fingers and smashed onto the tiles. Peggy came in to find her slumped on the floor of the kitchen, weeping.

"Whatever's the matter, miss?"

"I broke Tessa's cup. The one with the swallows on."

Peggy bent down and rested her hand on Irene's shoulder. "I don't think she'd mind about that now."

"But today of all days!"

"I think Mrs Tessa would laugh about it, miss. She'd say it were perfect timing."

Eric had been too young to understand. Irene had told him Tessa had gone to sleep. For weeks afterwards he asked when she was going to wake up. But the questions gradually tailed off. Now, he could barely remember her.

In her will, Tessa left The Lindens to Reginald and his sisters. Her nephews and nieces on the other side of the family received only some pieces of furniture and a few hundred pounds. Reginald had no trouble buying out his sisters. The day he came back from the solicitors, the deeds in his hand and his name on them, signed and witnessed, was the most elated Irene had ever seen him. He opened a bottle of champagne, and insisted she had a glass even though it was three o'clock in the afternoon.

"It's all mine! My family home! Ha! Think of that, eh? What would they make of it?"

She wondered who he meant by *they*, but didn't ask.

· · ·

She met Clara by the back porch. Sherpa had got there first, barking his greetings and trying to lick her, while Clara, who was not a dog person, did her best to ignore him. She kissed Irene briskly on the cheek.

"All clear?" she asked.

Irene nodded. "He won't be back till late."

"Good. Are you all packed up?"

"Partly. Not really."

"Well. There's no rush. Why don't I put the kettle on while you finish off?"

Eric was watching them from under the laburnum.

"What have you told him?"

"Nothing yet. I haven't even told him you were coming."

Clara shook her head. "Well. At least that means he won't have blabbed to anyone."

"He wouldn't do that."

"Maybe. Still, you can't be too careful."

"What shall I say?"

"Just tell him you're coming to stay with me for a while."

"But we've never done that before."

"No, and it's about time you did." Clara wasn't one for hugs, but she gave Irene's arm a squeeze. "Come on. It's all going to be fine."

Irene took a deep breath. Then she called to Eric. He came trotting over, shy but curious, holding a knight in each hand.

"You remember Auntie Clara, don't you darling?"

He nodded uncertainly.

"Hello Eric. I remember you, though you're much bigger than when I last saw you. And who've you got there?"

Eric held up the two knights. "Sir Lancelot and Sir Gawain."

"Auntie Clara has invited us to come and stay with her. That will be fun, won't it?"

The boy was non-plussed. "Today?"

"That's right. I just need to pack some things, then we'll have a cup of tea and a piece of cake, then we'll be off. Okay?"

"How long are we going for?"

"I'm not sure exactly. A little while."

In the first five years of their marriage, he only hit her twice.

Only.

He drank a lot, but then everybody in India drank a lot. And he had a violent temper. Several times she had seen him beat the servants: thrashing Virat the driver with a riding whip because the car hadn't been cleaned to his satisfaction, hitting Savita the cook around the face with a ladle after she spilt soup on the tablecloth. One evening she heard shouting in his study. Peering round the door, she saw Reginald with Pramod the houseboy – actually a little man in his fifties, five foot tall and always immaculately dressed in the style of an English butler. Reginald had him pinned against the wall, gripping him by the lapels with his left hand, while with his right, he slapped him hard across the face. "That's for being a drunken sot." He slapped him again the other way. "And that's for being a thief."

"I tell you again sahib, I am not touching a drop of it." Pramod sounded close to tears.

Reginald slapped him a third time, harder still. "That's for being a liar. I am going to give you another chance to admit it. You've been drinking my whisky, haven't you?"

"No, sahib."

Reginald slammed the little man against the wall.

Pramod slumped down to the floor. Irene could see the fear in his eyes. Before she knew what she was doing, she cried out "Stop!"

Her husband turned to look at her.

"Pramod hasn't been drinking your whisky. I have."

He walked slowly towards her, and stopped with his face six inches from hers. She could smell the whisky on his breath. "What did you say?"

"I said I drank your whisky." It had started out defiant, but already her voice was shaking. "Just a few times, to calm my nerves. I'm sorry."

She felt a sudden throbbing pain in her left temple and her ear was ringing like a police whistle. It took her a moment to realise what had happened. Then he slapped her again. She collapsed into a chair.

"You'd better say sorry to poor Pramod too, hadn't you? You hurt him. He got punished for what you did."

"I'm sorry Pramod," she sobbed. The houseboy tried to give her a reassuring smile.

"Pramod!" Reginald barked.

"Sahib?"

"How many times did I hit you?"

"Oh no, sahib, it was nothing, nothing of the sort. Just a little pushing and shoving, isn't it?"

"How many times, dammit?"

"Five times, sahib?"

Reginald leered at her. "Then you'd better hit my wife five times, hadn't you?"

"Sahib?"

"Get up!" Pramod got to his feet, smoothing out his shirt and waistcoat.

"Come here." He came uncertainly towards them.

"Now hit her five times. One for each time I hit you."

Pramod looked distraught. "Please, sahib, I cannot be hitting a woman."

For a moment, Reginald looked capable of murdering somebody. Then he turned his back on them and strode over to the drinks cabinet. He picked up the half-empty whisky bottle and hurled it against the opposite wall. It shattered.

"Get out!" he bellowed. "Both of you!"

Pramod fled. Irene followed.

The next day she apologised again for drinking his whisky. He said he forgave her, and that he was sorry if he over-reacted.

The second time was when they were back in England, a few weeks after Eric was born. He was teething and had been griping all day. She had finally settled him in his cot for his afternoon nap, and had gone back to her room. She could feel one of her headaches coming on, so she took three aspirin and lay down on her bed, just for a few minutes. Before she knew it, she was waking up again and Eric was grizzling in the next room. Her head felt heavy. If she waited, perhaps he would settle himself. *Go back to sleep*, she willed him. His crying became louder. She turned onto her front and put a pillow over her head.

Then Reginald burst into the room. "Irene, the baby is crying!" he yelled. He grabbed her by the wrist, crushing it in his grip as he dragged her to her feet.

"Get up! What's the matter with you?"

"I'm sorry... I fell asleep. I was tired."

"You were tired? You don't think I'm tired of hearing him crying all day? Tired of seeing you moping around? What kind of mother are you? You need to pull yourself together."

Slap. The shock was worse than the pain. She staggered backwards.

"You need to snap out of this. Now go and stop him crying."

It didn't occur to her to ask why he couldn't comfort the baby himself. Reginald had little time for babies. On the rare occasions when they had company, he might dandle his son on his lap, acting the proud progenitor. But at the first whimperings or whiff of a dirty nappy, he would be barking orders at her: "Irene! Take the baby away."

And he was right. She needed to snap out of this. What kind of mother was she? Her poor son. With the father and mother he had, what hope was there for him?

She watched him now, showing Clara where the tea was kept and getting out the cups with the bird designs.

"Those are lovely mugs," Clara said. "Which is your favourite?"

Eric pointed to the one with the robin.

"Oh yes, he's lovely, isn't he? Which can I have?"

Eric considered. "What's your favourite colour?"

"Blue."

He smiled, and handed her the mug with the blue tit.

"Perfect! Thank you, Eric."

Eric beamed. "Mummy can have the wren."

Clara looked up at Irene, hovering in the doorway. "Why doesn't Mummy go and finish packing while you help me make the tea, and tell me more about Sir Lancelot and Sir Gawain?"

Clara was better than her with children. Her sister was better than her with most things. With life in general.

"Come and see Gringolet," Eric said.

"Who's Gringolet?"

"My horse."

"His rocking horse," Irene explained.

"Daddy says we can get a real horse when I'm seven," Eric said, taking his aunt by the hand and leading her into the front room.

Had his father really told him that? It was news to her. Even if he had, that didn't necessarily mean it would happen. *Don't think about it.*

Irene didn't believe in ghosts, but it was uncanny how often she seemed to catch sight of Tessa in the months after her death. A shadow in the corner of her eye, coming down the steps behind the folly or emerging from the dairy. She would blink, and there would be nothing there.

After Aunt Tessa's death, their life had contracted further. Irene missed her terribly. Her company, her conversation, her sense of humour. She had run the household so apparently effortlessly that it had come as a shock to Irene to discover how much effort was involved. She had never had to plan the meals, order the groceries, settle the account with the milkman or ask her husband for the money to pay Peggy and Harris, the elderly gardener. The garden! That was another area Irene knew precious little about. From the snowdrops in January to the honeysuckle that flowered in December, the garden had bloomed as if by magic: she had been only half aware of the hours Tessa spent sowing seeds and pricking out seedlings, dividing bulbs, digging out docks and bindweed. Then there were the fruits and vegetables: Harris might do the heavy work, but the rhubarb and the runner beans and the raspberries didn't in fact pick themselves, nor did the peas pop out of their pods or the quinces turn to jelly of their own volition.

To make matters worse, Reginald insisted that now there

were only the three of them in the house, they could cut Peggy's hours. Irene wanted to say that they needed *more* help now, not less, but didn't dare: "It's not like you have anything else to do," he told her. "It wouldn't hurt you to cook sometimes, would it? Wives do, nowadays." Peggy was kept on for four days a week to clean and serve lunch, though she usually stayed longer. She doted on Eric, and often helped prepare the evening meal. Irene had never had to cook a meal in her life. With Peggy's help, she learned a dozen fool-proof recipes. Or nearly fool proof. The temperature of the Aga could be erratic, and she had a tendency to forget about things until the acrid smell of vegetables boiling dry or a burning casserole brought her back to herself. Usually she managed to hide her disasters from her husband: burnt edges were scraped off, lumpy sauces sieved and whisked into something resembling smoothness. But not always.

Like the time with the rabbit pie.

It was supposed to be a treat, one of his favourite meals. He had shot the rabbits that morning in the orchard. He had skinned them himself, but she had needed Peggy to show her how to gut them. Pulling out the sack of intestines, the heart and the tiny kidneys made her queasy. The recipe she picked was too ambitious. She tried to brown the meat and ended up blackening it. The leeks stuck to the pan. When she added the cream, the mixture curdled. The pastry cracked and crumbled. What came out of the oven was a sorry mess, burnt on top, soggy on the bottom and wholly unappetising in between.

He had every right to be angry.

"What do you call this?" His voice was low and deliberate. Dangerous.

"I'm sorry. It didn't go well."

"No. It didn't." He poked at it with his fork. "I wouldn't give this to Sherpa."

He picked up his plate and hurled it at the wall. The plate smashed. Some pieces of rabbit meat stuck to the embossed wallpaper.

"I'm sorry. Let me make you something else. Let me make you an omelette."

She rushed back to the kitchen, frantically cracked eggs into a bowl, trying to fish out the bits of broken shell as she whisked them with a fork. She opened the hot plate on the Aga, melted some butter in a pan. Then she thought she should clean up the mess in the dining room. She grabbed the dustpan and brush and a cloth. Reginald was still sitting in his chair. He didn't say anything, but she felt his eyes on her as she swept up the remains of the plate and the pie and wiped the stains off the wall. He poured himself another glass of wine.

Then she smelt the smoke. *Oh Christ no!* She rushed back to the kitchen. The butter in the pan was the colour of earth, and choking clouds of smoke filled the room. She pulled the pan off the heat, then went to open the back door and ran straight into him. He grabbed her by the wrist.

"My God." He shook his head. "Ruining one meal per night is enough, don't you think?"

He pulled her over to the Aga. The hot plate was still open.

"You see this? This is hot." He spoke slowly, mockingly, like he was speaking to a child, or a servant who didn't speak English.

"You know what happens when you leave things on the hot plate for too long?" He was holding her left hand an inch above the stove. She tried to pull it away, but he clamped her wrist harder. "Well, do you?"

"They – they get burnt."

"Oh, so you do know?"

There was a beat, then he pushed her hand down onto the scalding metal and held it there for one, two, three seconds. Then he let her go.

"Now maybe you'll remember."

The pain was beyond anything.

Irene ran her hand under the tap, biting back the tears. The cold water soothed the stinging, but the moment she took it out, it felt worse than ever. Reginald didn't say another word. He got out a new pan, melted some butter, and calmly cooked himself a perfect omelette, folding it in half, flipping it over to cook both sides. He turned it onto a plate, added a twist of pepper, and walked out of the room.

She told Peggy the next day that she'd burnt her hand on the kettle. *So silly of me.*

The horrible thing was, it worked. Not knowing what he might do next, she cooked every meal with fearful concentration. She stopped burning food. She set timers. She no longer served up undercooked meat and potatoes, over-cooked fish and vegetables. One Saturday night she roasted a pheasant that he had shot in Ashridge, with potatoes and parsnips and leeks that she had dug up herself. Every part was cooked to perfection. It felt like a small miracle. "That was good," he said afterwards. She hated how much that meant to her.

"Can't beat fresh game," he went on. "Tell you what I like even better than roast pheasant, mind. Rabbit pie." She looked down at her plate, but she could feel his eyes on her. "We'll have rabbit pie tomorrow."

When she woke the next morning, she felt the dread before she remembered the reason for it. She hoped he might forget, but no, he was out with the gun before church and came back with a brace of young rabbits. Being Sunday, she didn't have Peggy to help her.

She looked at the skinned rabbits on the chopping board in front of her, their naked pink bodies like unborn babies. She would have to cut them open. Pull out their innards. Follow each step of the recipe, knowing that one stumble would be fatal.

She put her head down on the table and wept.

She didn't hear him come into the kitchen. She found herself aware of his looming presence in the doorway, his eyes on her. She didn't know how long he'd been standing there.

"What's the matter with you?" Not sympathetic: an accusation.

"I'm sorry. I can't."

"Can't?" He laughed scornfully. "Squeamish? Scared of a little blood?"

He pulled up a chair, and stared down at her along the length of the table, over the horrible rabbit babies.

"Battle of the Somme. Came across a body in the middle of No-man's-land. Thought he was dead, then heard him groaning. Had half his leg blown off by a shell, poor sod. I picked him up and dragged him into a shell hole. Had to amputate his leg, with my own bayonet. I was nineteen.

"Honestly, it makes me laugh. Women like you. Complaining about your nerves. Crippled by a headache. Sobbing your little eyes out over a bleeding rabbit pie. If you'd seen one-thousandth part of the horrors I've seen. Thank God we don't let women join the army."

Perhaps he meant to shake or shame her out of the state she was in, but it only made her cry harder. He stood up abruptly, pushing back the chair which clattered onto the floor tiles. He grabbed her by the shoulders and yanked her to her feet, then spun her round to face him.

"You need to stop being such a pathetic wreck. Get a grip, woman."

But how could you do that when a man was shouting into your face, and you knew what cruelties he was capable of? She tried to swallow back the sobs, and found herself gasping.

"Snap out of it, for God's sake." He slapped her across the cheek. Then he pushed her away. Her feet slipped on the tiles and she fell backwards, cracking her head on the table. She pictured the knife on the chopping board. She could make a grab for it. Then she could drive it into him. Cut him open. Pull out his innards.

She let her body slither to the floor. She rolled onto her side and hugged her legs against her chest, pressing her throbbing head into her knees.

He gave her one sharp kick in the ribs. "Get up. Sort yourself out before your son comes in." Then he stomped out of the room.

Irene lay under the table, curled up in her foetal position, till her sobs subsided. She imagined another life, with a husband who wouldn't mind about a burnt rabbit pie. Where her terrible cooking would be a shared joke. A husband who read her moods and could pull her out of the holes she sank into through kindness and understanding. A husband who would make her happy.

But she didn't deserve a husband like that. This was her penance. After what had happened to Teddy. He had needed her. And she had failed him.

She had known him since she was a child. Teddy had been in her brother's platoon during the first war, and was a frequent visitor to the house. He was nearly ten years older, but was always kind and friendly to her. She thought him impossibly handsome, with his gypsy eyes and his nut brown skin – his mother was Spanish, he told her, which seemed exciting and exotic. He played the piano, and sang songs by Schubert and Ivor Gurney in a delicate tenor. As she grew from awkward adolescence into awkward early womanhood, the attention he paid her increased. When she turned twenty-one, he proposed: down on one knee in the garden before Sunday lunch, diamond ring, her father's blessing already secured.

She had been so happy.

He put a bullet through his head a week before the wedding.

In his note, he talked about the shellshock. The madness that could attack him at any moment. How he couldn't put anybody through that. How Irene deserved a man who would make her happy.

"You can't blame yourself," Clara had told her. "It's like an illness. People won't talk about it, but it's common."

But she did blame herself. If she had loved him more, she could have saved him. Everybody could be saved by love.

She didn't believe that anymore.

Irene went back up to Eric's room to finish packing. She picked up his book of King Arthur stories. It had belonged to Tessa's sons, the ones who'd died in the war, and she had wanted Eric to have it. She added his cowboy hat and a handful of notebooks. What else? Three framed photos on his chest of drawers. She packed the one of Aunt Tessa reclining on a garden chair, taken the summer before she died, and the one of Eric and Sherpa under the apple tree on the top lawn. Then she hesitated. The third photo was of Eric and his father on the steps leading up to the folly. The boy, sitting on the step in front, barely came up to Reginald's knees. They were both laughing. Irene couldn't remember why.

When Eric was four, his father had announced that he would be starting prep school in Salisbury. No discussion, no consultation: it was a direct order.

"But he's still so young," Irene protested. "Aunt Tessa used to speak highly of Miss Forrest at the village school."

"No son of mine is going to that place. You want the best for our son, don't you?"

Irene's days became emptier still. Usually, Eric was quiet and uncommunicative when he came home. But sometimes he was happy, babbling on about new things in his life that had nothing to do with her, and that was almost as bad. Either way, she was losing him.

Reginald got to play the model father, driving Eric into town in the Jag at eight o'clock every morning. Irene would wave them off, her son in his absurd little blazer and tie, a miniature businessman with a cap and short trousers. She wished she could drive.

Though he had taken little notice of Eric as a baby, Reginald had grown into fatherhood as the boy grew older. He built a treehouse in one of the giant oaks at the edge of the meadow. He made bows and arrows and catapults and taught Eric to fire them. Sometimes he would take his son fishing, and Eric would come home bubbling with excitement about catching minnows in a jam jar.

Most people thought he was lucky, to have a father like that. A strict father, naturally – any number of minor infractions might be met by a short sharp smack to the wrist or the bottom, but that was hardly unusual, was it? Mostly,

Reginald stuck to verbal punishment. It was enough. He had made grown soldiers cry; a small boy stood little chance.

Then there was the day with the snipe. The three of them had walked up to Marshmead with Sherpa. It was a beautiful March morning, spring in the air, primroses and pussy willow in bloom.

Eric spotted them: a pair of fat brown birds with long beaks skulking among the tussocky grass. "What are they?"

Reginald looked. "Woodcock. No, snipe."

"Snipe," Eric repeated. Then Sherpa spotted them too, and gave chase. The snipe swept away, then circled down to the far end of the field by the hedge.

"Snip, snap, snipe," Eric was chanting to himself. "Snip, snap, snipe."

Later that day, Reginald went out with his gun. He came back with a brace of snipe over his shoulder. He hung them in the porch, tied by the legs, their lifeless beaks pointing at the ground. When Eric saw them, he bawled.

"You killed the snipe! They're dead."

Reginald laughed. "They're only birds. Plenty more of them."

"I liked the snipe," Eric cried. "I don't like you!"

A sharp slap across the face. "What did you say?"

Eric just cried louder. "I DON'T LIKE YOU!"

Reginald's hot anger could scald, but the cold cruelty was worse. That evening, Irene watched helplessly as he led Eric to the end of the garden, his struggling, blubbing son gripped in one hand and his belt in the other. She watched them return five minutes later. Eric wasn't crying anymore, but his eyes were red and his face was white. There was a wet stain spreading down his trousers.

In the days that followed, she could see the fear in Eric's

eyes when his father was near. She recognised the look. She saw it every day in the mirror.

Over the coming months, the beatings became more frequent. It wasn't that Eric was a bad child. He was a sweet, kind boy, though he was off in his own world half the time – reading, drawing, playing knights and cowboys. He liked to dress up too. One afternoon he asked her if he could borrow a dress. "I want to be a damsel," he announced.

"A damsel?"

"The damsel is going to be imprisoned in a tower. The tower's going to be the folly. Then Sir Gawain is going to come along and rescue her."

"Wouldn't you rather be Sir Gawain?" she asked.

"I'm going to be Sir Gawain too. But I want to be the damsel as well."

It seemed harmless enough. And it wasn't easy for him, having no one to play with. Reginald had made no effort to befriend the parents of possible playmates at school. On balance it was a relief that Eric was an only child, but sometimes she thought it sad he never had a brother or sister. She found him an emerald green sari that she'd brought back from India and never worn, and helped tie it round him. They got an old wig out of the dressing up box, and a tiara that she hadn't worn for twenty years. He made a surprisingly pretty damsel.

She should never have encouraged it. Of course Eric came out of her room just as Reginald emerged from his. They both froze when they saw each other. It would have been comical if she hadn't seen the horror in her husband's eyes, and the terror in her son's.

Eric spoke first. "Look Daddy! I'm a damsel!"

She wanted to scoop him up in her arms and run. She stood rooted to the spot.

Reginald strode over and ripped off the wig. He threw the tiara over the banister.

"What the hell do you think you're doing?"

"Please, he's just playing a game," Irene protested, pulling her son towards her, but Reginald wrestled him away. "You! Change out of that thing now," he roared, pushing him down the landing towards his room. Eric tripped on the end of the sari and fell flat on his face. He began to bawl. "I'll deal with you later. Now go."

Eric got to his feet and scuttled to his room, pulling the door behind him.

"It's only a bit of fun. Reg, please."

"No son of mine is going to be a deviant."

"He's six years old, for God's sake! He was playing a game."

"Are you trying to undermine me?"

She could feel his hot breath on her face, the stench of whisky mixed with the mutton they had eaten that lunchtime. She recoiled.

"I'm sorry. I shouldn't have let him."

"No, but you let him do whatever he wants, don't you? You'll ruin the boy, if you haven't already. I think both of you need to learn a lesson."

"No, Reg, please! I won't let it happen again."

"No, you won't. I'm going to make sure of that."

It was the first time he'd used his belt on her. She hoped to God that he was gentler with their son.

Irene picked up the picture and laid it on top of the others. Then she closed the suitcase.

She had thought about leaving him, of course she had. Cruelty was grounds for divorce. But what if he contested it?

He had a reputation to uphold, after all. A colonel with a dozen medals on his uniform. It would be her word against his; his, and an expensive lawyer's. Him, the model father, and her with a history of mental instability. He might even sue for custody of Eric, if not out of love then out of spite. She couldn't risk it. Besides, she didn't have the energy. Perhaps there could be a better future beyond the horizon, but there would be months of hell to pass through before she got there. Better the devil you knew.

Then last Christmas, Clara and her husband Bill had come to stay. It was the first time in several years. Reginald disliked having guests to stay, though he disliked staying with other people even more. Visits to or from her family, never frequent, had become scarce. Irene dreaded the effort she would have to muster to disguise the wreck her life had become. She had tried to dissuade her sister, but Clara insisted.

"You never come to see us anymore. Nor Mum and Dad. We're jolly well coming whether you like it or not."

They had turned up on Boxing Day afternoon. Clara had brought a big tin of turkey sandwiches, cheese and biscuits ("So you don't have to worry about cooking, and I don't have to taste it."). Eric, though he barely knew his aunt and uncle, had been at his most charming. He showed off his Christmas toys (a sword and shield his father had made him, a wooden train with an engine and three carriages), and before he went to bed he sang "Away in a Manger" so sweetly it brought tears to her eyes. Irene was already a little squiffy from the sherry by then, but Reginald remained remarkably abstemious by his standards. He could put on a front when he wanted to. Bill had served in Africa, and they talked together about the war, about army life and their travels. Reginald told an amusing anecdote about the time a camel in Egypt had eaten his hat. It was all perfectly nice and normal.

The next morning was cold but clear and bright. Reginald had wanted to show off the Jaguar, and he and Bill had gone for a drive, taking Eric with them. Irene and Clara walked up to Ashridge with Sherpa. The puddles in the rutted track had frozen into thin slabs of ice full of trapped white air bubbles, and the hedges glistened with tiny jewels of frost.

"So is everything – well?" Clara asked. "With you? I do worry, you know." Irene didn't say anything. Clara went on. "But that was a very jolly evening. And you have such a lovely home here."

They stopped and looked back across the bare orchard towards The Lindens, the square bulk of the house like a child's painting, bright red brick against the blue sky, a whisp of smoke rising from the chimney. So cosy and welcoming. Really, one could not wish for a more perfect home.

A dam burst inside her. Irene began to cry, great gulping heaves passing through her body like contractions.

"Rene? What in the world is the matter?"

It all came pouring out, a torrent of words, inchoate and incoherent for the most part, finally trickling away into a sob. "I don't know what to do."

Clara put an awkward arm around her shoulder. Emotional support had never been her forte. Practical support, though, that was a different matter.

"We have to get you out of here. For Eric's sake as much as yours."

"But it's Eric's home. He loves it here."

"Rene, he's not safe here. It isn't going to get better. If

anything, it will get worse. His father isn't going to change. You're not an angel sent to rescue him."

She wanted so much to acquiesce, to let Clara take control, but a stupid obstinacy in her still resisted. "And you're an angel sent to rescue me, are you?"

"No," Clara sighed. "But I am your sister."

Clara was right. Reginald didn't change over the following months. Eric had started to wet the bed again. You could hardly blame him. And surely anyone with an ounce of understanding could see that shaming him, shouting in his face and beating him for it only made things worse. Reginald blamed her. She mollycoddled the boy, let him get away with anything. Or else she had neglected him, and this was the poor bugger's way of seeking attention. When she pointed out the possible contradiction, he had cuffed her round the jaw for mocking him.

On June 6th, there was a service in the cathedral to commemorate the D-Day anniversary. Ten years! Where did the time go? Although Reginald had been on the other side of the world in 1944, he had been invited to the service and a reception in the White Hart afterwards, hosted by an old regimental comrade who now sat in the House of Lords. He would be wearing his uniform, medals and all. She had suggested he got it dry cleaned, but he said that was a waste of money and she was just being lazy.

She had ironed his frock coat, and turned her attention to the ribbons on his medals. She liked the colours and the different designs – he had told her once what they all meant, though she couldn't remember. It was pleasing to smooth them flat.

A crash, followed a moment later by the sound of Eric

crying. She put the iron down and rushed into the sitting room. Eric had been playing with a ball, and had managed to knock a vase off the mantelpiece – an expensive piece of Jaipur blue they had brought back from India. Shards and delphiniums were scattered across the hearth rug. She scolded Eric then soothed him, grabbed the dustpan and brush from the hall cupboard to sweep up the pieces. Then she smelt burning. She dashed back to the kitchen. The ironing board was smouldering. She half-filled a bucket of water at the sink and threw it over the rising flames. A second bucket put the fire out completely. But the ribbons were ruined.

Reginald devised suitable punishments for both of them. He fetched Eric's ship in a bottle, one of his most treasured possessions: a replica of the *HMS Victory* that had once belonged to Aunt Tessa's late husband.

"Reginald, please! He didn't mean to do it!"

Ignoring their panicked pleading, he strode out onto the porch steps and held it above his head. Then he let it go. The bottle smashed against the bricks. He ground the matchwood ship under his boot.

"He has to learn his lesson," Reginald said, watching Eric on his hands and knees, scrabbling for the broken pieces. "As do you."

He grabbed her arm and dragged her into the kitchen. He walked over to the charred ironing board and flicked the iron on at the socket.

"Those ribbons mean something." He reeled off a list of names: 1914 Star, British War Medal, Victory Medal. Africa Service Medal, India Service Medal. "Serving my country for forty-five years. Two world wars. Don't you think they deserve a little respect? Don't you think *I* deserve a little respect?"

"I'm sorry, Reg, really. I won't do it again, won't do anything like it again."

"No. I'm going to make damn sure of that."

He yanked down her skirt and knickers. Then he pressed the iron against her flesh. She tried to pull away but he held her tight, and she felt the burn coursing through her, blurring her vision and drowning the sound of his voice even as he ranted about how that was the trouble with her, with this whole bloody country, no respect, no thought of the sacrifices he had made, no idea how he suffered.

That night as she lay in a cold bath, pressing a flannel to the iron-shaped blister, the pain hardened her resolve. *I'm not going to take this anymore.*

The next day, she phoned Clara from the phone box in the village and let her make a plan. Irene would find a day when Reginald was out of the house. Clara would drive down the night before and stay in a B&B in Salisbury, ready to whisk her away. A friend of Bill's ran a boarding house a few streets away from their home in Solihull, she and Eric could stay there until they found a place of their own.

"He needs to be gone for several hours."

"He goes fishing a lot," Irene suggested.

"No, that's too risky. We need to be certain he won't come back early for any reason."

"There's a regimental dinner next month," Irene remembered. "He hates them, but he always goes. He drinks too much and doesn't come home till late."

"That sounds promising. What about the maid?"

"Peggy?"

"Will she be around?"

"No. It's a Saturday."

"Good. You mustn't tell a soul, you understand? You're just going to disappear."

Irene had been wanting to do that for twenty years.

Eric followed them out to the car with Sherpa at his heels. "That's a Ford Anglia," he announced. "Daddy has a Jaguar. An XK120. It can go 120 miles per hour."

"Well, this car can't, but it does have more room in the boot," Clara replied, flipping up the hatch and lifting in Irene's trunk.

"Is Sherpa coming with us?"

The dog pricked up his ears. It was the question Irene had been dreading. "No my love. Sherpa's staying here."

"Why can't Sherpa come?"

"Sherpa needs to stay to look after Daddy."

He laughed. "Daddy doesn't need looking after. He's a grown-up. Anyway, Peggy will look after him, won't she? Hello Peggy!"

Irene swung round. Peggy was standing by the gate to the yard, watching them.

"Peggy, we didn't expect you today," she said, trying to keep the rising panic out of her voice.

"Don't mind me. I just popped by to see if I might borrow the Hoover for the afternoon. Only my Elsie's bringing her young man around for Sunday lunch tomorrow, and it does save so much time with the cleaning. If it's not too much of an imposition."

"No, no, of course. Please, help yourself. You can bring it back on Monday."

"That's most kind, thank you," Peggy said. She didn't move, however, taking in the car, Clara, the suitcases in the boot.

"I didn't know your sister was coming. Would you like me to make up the guest room?"

"Oh no, thanks ever so but I'm not staying," Clara said.

"We're going to stay with Aunt Clara," Eric announced. "But Sherpa's staying to look after Daddy."

"Is that so?" Peggy looked sharply at Irene. "If himself happens to ask where you've gone... just in case he's forgotten, like... what should I tell him?"

"Perhaps it would be best if you hadn't seen us?" Clara said.

Irene looked beseechingly at Peggy, who caught her gaze and held it. Then she nodded slowly.

"Well, I'll just get that Hoover then I'll be out of your way. I'll see you when I see you."

"Goodbye, Peggy. And thank you."

Sherpa knew something was up too. He was looking at them with anxious eyes, his ears and tail drooping. Eric scratched him on the top of his head, then put his arms around the dog's neck. "Good dog Sherpa. See you in a few days, boy."

Don't get sentimental, Irene reminded herself. *We can get another dog.*

Five hours after his wife had watched The Lindens disappear over her shoulder from the passenger seat of a sky blue Ford Anglia, Colonel Cotter revved around the corner in his Jaguar XK120, dressed in the regimental uniform that she had ironed immaculately that morning. He had drunk a whisky and ginger ale, three or four glasses of claret and several more of port. There were no lights on in the house. In the darkness he missed the driveway, and turned instead into the track that led to the brickworks. He was dimly aware that this was a mistake, that the trees around him were not the avenue of lindens, but he kept driving straight on, even as the track veered suddenly left. The car careered over a bank, airborne for a moment, then slammed into a tree. His head crashed into the steering wheel. The blow knocked him out.

When he came round again – it might have been two minutes, might have been two hours – the moon, a day or two past full, was shining down through the leaves. Reginald manoeuvred himself across the seats, stretched out as best he could, and sunk into sleep.

THE WELL
1976

T he motorbike chugged up the drive and stopped in the yard. The rider kicked the stand and dismounted. He was a tall man with deep-set eyes that made him look older than his twenty-eight years. His leather trousers and shirt were saturated with sweat. The t-shirt, once white, was spattered with the remains of insects. He wiped his long copper hair away from his face and looked around. After a moment, he walked over to the brick drinking trough outside the stable. He peered in, then turned back disappointed. The trough was dry.

The old woman, who had come out of the house when she heard the engine, now approached him.

"Well now. Eric! Is that really you?"

He held out his hand. "Peggy?"

She took his hand in both of hers, and kissed him on the cheek. "Just look at you! Goodness, but you're all grown up. Well, of course you are. It's been more than twenty years."

Eric had the impression that she hadn't changed at all, though he had little recollection of her appearance, only vague associations – rock cakes and lemonade, sandwiches cut into triangles.

"Did you ride all the way down from London on that? And not even wearing a helmet."

"I have a helmet. Only the visor kept getting covered in insects. I had to stop every few minutes to wipe it clean. And this heat…"

"Oh, tell me about it! Ninety-one it was yesterday, and even hotter today I reckon. Far too hot to stand out here nattering. Come inside and cool off. You'll be wanting something to drink."

"Where is – ?" Eric began, but she cut him off.

"Oh, never mind that for now, sweetheart. Freshen up first. Did you bring a change of clothes?" She laughed. "There I go again, talking to you like you're still six years old."

He took a canvas haversack out of the bike pannier and followed her around the side of the house towards the back door. The scorched grass on the lawn looked like coconut matting, overgrown with plantains and dandelion clocks. Brambles and bindweed choked the flowerbeds, the leaves wilting in the heat. Over the wall, where the old brickworks used to be, the few trees that Eric remembered had grown into a proper wood. The trees had passed straight through the rich green of high summer, and now the parched leaves were just hanging on for autumn. The wisteria that draped the back porch was yellow and withered.

"You go and freshen up, sweetheart," Peggy ordered him. "There's a basin of water in the bathroom upstairs. I'll make you a nice cold drink."

"Leave the plug in," she called after him as he headed up the stairs. "Have to do our bit to save water, don't we?"

Eric emerged a few minutes later, dressed in a clean

shirt, shorts and sandals. The kitchen with its stone floor and tiled walls was mercifully cool. The faintest hint of a breeze fluttered the drawn curtains.

"I finally persuaded himself to put that Aga out a couple of weeks ago," Peggy said. "It was like a furnace in here before. Didn't want to do it 'cause he needs it for cooking, he says, though mostly he just lives on bread and biscuits far as I can see. Anyway, my Christopher found him an electric kettle and a little camping stove. Mind you, I reckon as how you could fry an egg on those paving stones outside."

"Where is he?" Eric asked again.

"He'll be up at his pond, shouldn't wonder. You can go up there in a bit. No rush."

"Does he know I'm coming?"

Peggy shook her head. "I thought it best not to say. Didn't know for sure that you would. And he can get in quite a state, you know, when he's upset about something."

"So you still work here?"

"Not exactly. But I like to keep an eye on the place, like. I've known it more than sixty years, after all. And your father needs someone to look in on him, him being on his own and all. Well, I've got time on my hands – my Charlie died four years ago, God rest him. Might clean up a little while I'm here, make sure he's got enough food in the pantry."

"But he can look after himself?"

"More or less. Still walks to the post office. Manages to feed himself alright. Though he's become more and more what you might call eccentric. Reclusive, if you like. 'Course, this place is far too big for him. Half the rooms in here he never opens. And the garden – well, you've seen it. Mrs Tessa would turn in her grave. But enough of my wittering, what about you, sweetheart? Tell me about yourself. Fancy you living in that London."

Eric wondered what he could possibly tell this woman about his life. How he'd arrived in That London at its swinging height, eighteen years old, naïve and fragile but desperate to leave his home behind and start afresh. How he'd dropped out of the economics degree after six months but had kept up the pretence to his mother for another year. How LSE had given way to LSD, and he'd blown the bloody doors off his mind, seen Hendrix and the Floyd when they were just starting out, hung out at happenings, slept with numerous girls, two boys and one who was something in between. Peggy, no doubt, had read all about his sort in the paper, and considered them a menace to society.

He had crashed hard, a few months after the decade ended. There had been *episodes*, and a crushing darkness that left him unable to leave his flat for weeks at a time. Then a spell in hospital, and a slow, precarious climb back to some sort of equilibrium.

"I work in schools," he told her.

"You're a teacher?" she asked, sounding pleased.

"Well, sort of."

It was probably best to leave it at that. He didn't feel like explaining his theatre-in-education work. It was Raymond's company – a Rada drop-out he'd met in the psychiatric hospital – and he'd been asked to join more through friendship, or pity, than for his acting ability or affinity with children. They performed earnest plays about ecology and nuclear disarmament to bored nine-year-olds, and tried to drum up discussions afterwards. The work was sporadic, but it paid the rent. And he rather enjoyed dressing up and pretending to be other people, even though Raymond said that was not the point and the performances were supposed to be Brechtian.

And then there was Katya. She was the most talented actor in the company, despite her heavily accented English. She had come from Germany as a student and never went back. She had a three-year-old son called Ludo, whose father, an Australian barman on a tourist visa, was unaware of his existence. Eric loved everything about her. The way she said *wegetables*. The infectious enthusiasm she always kept up with the children in their workshops, however sardonic she could be about them afterwards. The intense way she looked him in the eye when they talked, and how her severe face could suddenly melt into a smile. The way her body fitted into his when they spooned together after making love.

She was the only person he'd spoken to about coming here.

He'd shown her Peggy's letter. "My father wants to see me."

"You want to go?"

"I'm not sure. Would you go and see your father, if he asked?"

She frowned. "I don't decide yet."

Katya hadn't spoken to her parents for almost ten years. "They were fucking Nazis," she told him. "Straight from der fucking Hitlerjugend and die fucking Bund Deutscher Mädel into the Party, and true believers to the end. Now they say let's forget about it. And I say, no, let's don't forget about it. Let's remember it every single fucking day. Because you know what's fucked up? People like them run the country. Their fucking generation. They all say now that they weren't part of it, but you know, fuck them. I'm not going to live in a fucking country of people who look the other way when their neighbours are committing a little bit of fucking genocide."

(The way she swore was another of the things he loved about her.)

"My father killed people," he told her. "I just always sort of knew that about him. He was in the army in both wars, and all the time in between. It was his job to kill people. I just can't imagine what that does to you. Taking someone's life from them. How do you live with that knowledge? I don't think I could ever get over it. But there's thousands of people like him. Those war heroes we revere – they killed people."

"At least they beat the fucking Nazis."

"Yeah, I know. But still. I think the world will be a better place when it's not run by people who know what it's like to kill another person."

She'd given him an ironic hippie salute. "Peace out, man."

But she'd said he should go. "Not for his sake. Fuck him. But for you is good, I think. To see him, and to see the house you lived in."

And so here he was, sitting in a kitchen that made him feel oddly anxious.

"It was good of you to come, anyroads," Peggy said. "I didn't know whether I'd be able to find you in the first place, let alone whether you'd want to see him."

"So how did you find me?"

"When your mother left... well, I wasn't altogether surprised. That she'd want to, I mean. Though I was surprised that she actually did it. It fair broke my heart not to be able to say a proper goodbye, but good luck to her, I thought. Figured she wouldn't want me to tell anyone – it wasn't my business, after all. But I copied down her sister's address, just in case. It's a blessing she never moved."

"No. She's still in Birmingham. Mum's still there too, though she's moved a few times."

"And how is your mother?"

"She's fine, thanks."

"Fine? Haven't heard hide nor hair of her for more than twenty years and all I get is 'fine'?"

"Well, I mean, she's very well. She's retired now – she used to work for the council – social services."

"Married again?"

Eric nodded. "Tony. She met him at work. They've been married... coming up for fifteen years."

"And what's he like?"

What was Tony like? Square as anything. Conservative with a capital C and a small one. Dull. Dependable. Patient. Kind. Good.

"He's nice. Solid. He's retired too now. He's into model railways and growing dahlias. He's good to her."

"She's happy?"

Eric nodded again. "As happy as she can be, you know? My mother never has been very good at being happy."

A year or two ago, he had made the mistake of suggesting she might talk to a therapist. Umbrage had been taken.

"You think I should go and see a psychiatrist? I suppose you think I'm crazy, is that it?"

No, he'd insisted, it wasn't like that. "I found it helpful. After that time in the hospital. Just to talk things through with a stranger who doesn't judge, who just listens and helps you to understand your feelings."

"Oh, no doubt everything is your mother's fault. That's what they say, isn't it?"

"That's really just a cliché." In fact, one thing that Caroline, his therapist, had helped him see was that he had blamed his mother for years. Blamed her for wrenching him away from the home he loved to a squat terraced house in an ugly city. For tearing him apart from his beloved, irreplaceable dog. For lying to him.

"You experienced trauma," Caroline told him. "It's normal to feel anger. It's one of the stages of grief."

"What does grief have to do with it?"

"You're grieving for a state of lost innocence, in other words, the time before the trauma. In your case, the idyllic childhood home that you've reconstructed in your mind. Do you think it's an accurate recollection?"

"Parts of it are."

There was a silence. "And parts of it aren't?" the therapist asked eventually.

"I guess not."

"Which parts?"

More silence. "I suppose this is where we talk about my father?"

"Do you want to talk about your father?"

"I don't remember much about him."

There had been three framed photos. Nanny Tessa, whom he barely remembered, sitting in a chair. Him and Sherpa, that wonderful dog. And one of him and his father, laughing. He had left the others on display, but had hidden that one at the back of his underwear drawer. His mother never said anything. Sometimes he would take it out and look at it with a ghastly, guilty fascination. It was the only souvenir he had of his father.

"What do you remember?"

He didn't respond.

"Can you describe what you feel when you think about him?"

Eric thought for a while. "Fear, mostly."

"Can you expand on that?"

"I used to have this recurring dream. After we left... and for years after that. It would always start nicely... we'd be outside, in the garden or in the orchard. Or somewhere around the property that didn't actually exist in real life. Sherpa would be there."

"Your dog."

"Yes. And my father would be in a good mood. Because he could be, actually. I do remember that about him too."

"Then what happens? In your dream."

"Then... Sherpa runs off – after a rabbit or something. And then I see the gun, and I realise I'm in the nightmare, but it doesn't make it any the less real. He picks up the gun. And then he shoots him. Sherpa. And I start screaming because I know Sherpa is dead, but he just laughs and says it doesn't matter. If I'm lucky, that's when I wake up."

"And if you don't?"

"Then there's a second part. It's later that night and we're sitting at the table in the dining room. And my mother brings in a pie she's baked, and I know it's Sherpa in the pie. I refuse to eat, and he tries to force me to, but I don't let him."

"Anything else?"

"Then he beats me."

"Did your father beat you?"

"My mother says he did. I've kind of blanked it out."

"It's very common to suppress these experiences. But they have a habit of seeping out into our subconscious mind. Recurring dreams like yours are one of the ways they manifest themselves."

"When I'm dreaming... when he's beating me... I don't know if that's my imagination or my memory providing the pictures."

"That's an interesting question."

"What's the answer?"

Caroline smiled. "I'm not here to give you answers. But it's good to keep asking questions."

"Ask me a question then."

"You mentioned the gun. Did your father have a gun?"

"Yes. I'm sure that's real."

"And he used to go shooting?"

"Yes. Rabbits, pheasants... other birds."

A picture floated into his mind. Two brown birds with comically long beaks.

"Snipe," he said.

"Is that a type of bird? I'm afraid I'm not very good with birds."

"Yes. Funny little wading birds with long beaks. I'd never seen them before. I really liked them."

"You're recalling a specific occasion?"

The image came to him then of their limp bodies hanging from a hook in the porch. "He shot them."

"Do you remember what you felt?"

"Absolute rage. Hatred. Defiance."

"Defiance?"

"I shouted at him. Screamed my head off."

"What did he do then?"

Eric tried to remember. It felt like staring down into an unfathomable well (though when had he ever done that?), straining for something dropped in the depths.

"That must have been the first time he beat me."

. . .

"Are you sure you won't have anything to eat?" Peggy was asking. "I expect I can find something to rustle up a sandwich."

"No, really, I'm fine. I don't feel much like eating in this heat."

She tutted. "You're thin as a rake, sweetheart. Mind you, you always were a skinny boy."

"I think I'd better bite the bullet," Eric said. "Go and see him."

"I should warn you, he's a little vague sometimes these days. Gets some funny notions into his head. Like I say, he can get in a bit of a state when something happens outside his usual routine."

How would such a man react to meeting the son he hadn't seen in twenty years?

"He's been talking about you, though, like I said in the letter. Keeps asking where you are, when you're getting back and what have you."

"Where did you say he would be?" Eric asked. Hadn't she said something about a pond?

"Up at his pond, shouldn't wonder. Lawks, you don't know about the pond. Dug it himself, not long after you left."

"Where is it?"

"Up in Marshmead. If you walk up through the meadow, you can't miss it. Do you want me to come with you? Introduce you, like?"

Eric shook his head. "I'll be alright."

After the relative cool of the kitchen, the air outside felt hot and heavy. Eric made his way across the desiccated lawn, up the steps by the laburnum tree into the top garden.

There was an apple tree with a large crop of small fruits that in the drought had grown barely bigger than crab apples. A memory came into his head of reaching up on tiptoe to pick a perfect shiny red apple. This must have been where the vegetable patch was, though now it was overrun with nettles and weeds. And there was the wicket gate – he hadn't thought of it in years, but remembered it instantly. He unfastened the catch on the gate and headed up the slope they used to call Jupiter Hill. The bushes overhanging the path were junipers, he noticed, like the hedge outside Aunt Clara's house. Had he remembered the name wrong all these years?

He stopped to look back down on the house, its double gabled roof and four chimneys desert red against the washed out blue of the sky. So it had been here all the time, his half-remembered, half-imagined home, a real place of solid brick. Despite the wilderness of the garden, it all felt weirdly familiar. There was that big tree at the top of the slope: the first thing he used to see when he opened his bedroom curtains each morning. The Ace of Clubs they used to call it, for its shape in silhouette. Only now the tree was a withered skeleton. Eric wondered if it was the drought. Then he remembered reading about Dutch elm disease. Had it been an elm tree? He couldn't remember what an elm tree looked like.

The meadow hadn't been cut, but there was a well-tramped path through the tall grasses, already as dry as last year's hay. The plants were crawling with ladybirds – there had been ladybirds everywhere that summer. There were red admirals, peacocks, other butterflies whose names Eric didn't know.

You couldn't miss the pond. It was far bigger than Eric had expected – more like a small lake. Or a crater: it was almost dry, the red-brown clay cracked and strewn with dried out pondweed and waterlilies. Only on the far side was a small pool of water a few feet across. Near it sat an old man in a folding chair, his back to Eric. He was wearing grey linen trousers streaked with dirt and a vest that might once have been white. Next to the chair were a walking stick and a zinc bucket. Eric walked down the slope towards him. The old man didn't seem to hear him. He was staring straight ahead, at nothing as far as Eric could see. He stopped a few feet away.

"Colonel Cotter?"

Slowly, the man turned to look at him. Eric wasn't sure which came as more of a shock: how different he looked, or how familiar. Everything about him seemed to have shrunk. Eric remembered his father as a huge, hulking presence, impossibly old even then but still a powerful man in the prime of life. The face that looked up at him was that of a frail, elderly man, yet it was instantly recognisable as the face from his photo. Eric felt – he didn't know what he felt. None of the fear he used to feel – he could snap this man in half if he wanted to. Not hatred. Not love. Not much at all.

"It's me, Eric. Your son."

His father stared at him blankly.

"Eric," he repeated slowly. "My son."

The morning after the accident, Colonel Cotter woke to discordant birdsong. It was already light, and his first thought was to wonder why he'd left the curtains open. Then he realised he was still in his uniform, and was lying in the passenger seat of the car. He was used to waking with a dry mouth and a hurting head, but it rarely pounded with such ferocity. His ribs ached, and he had a crick in his neck from the awkward angle at which he'd slept. Fragments of the night before were coming back to him.

He hauled himself upright, catching sight as he did so of his reflection in the cracked wing mirror: a gash across his forehead, dried blood down his face. The windscreen was shattered. Wincing from the pain in his ribs, he opened the car door and climbed out to inspect the rest of the damage. The front of the car had crumpled like a tin can. The tree appeared unharmed.

Reginald clambered up the slope to the track, pushing his way through the nettles and snagging his trousers on a bramble. The stings on his hands and legs produced a buzzing sensation that, set against the pain in his skull and his ribs, was almost pleasurable. He climbed up the bank to the back of the folly and down the steps to the lawn. The back door was unlocked. He let himself in. He heard barking, and Sherpa rushed up to him, squealing with delight. He kicked the dog away, and Sherpa slunk off to his bed at the bottom of the stairs. In the kitchen, Reginald drank two mugs of water and washed the worst of the blood off his face. The house was silent. The grandfather clock in the hall said quarter to six.

It was chiming twelve when he awoke. His hangover had eased somewhat, but the pain in his ribs was worse than ever. He'd broken a rib before, on the battlefield, when he'd fallen against the butt of his rifle. He'd carried on then as if nothing had happened. It was a full week before they finally checked on him in the field hospital. No need to call a doctor now.

At first he thought they must be late getting back from church. When lunchtime came and went, he decided they must have gone out for the day, though he didn't remember Irene mentioning anything. Reginald went up to her room.

The trunk was gone from her wardrobe, and half her clothes were missing. Next he went to Eric's room. A quick recce from the doorway provided confirmation. Reginald went back to the kitchen. He found some cold meat and bread in the pantry. He made two sandwiches, ate one, then gave the other to Sherpa. He took the whisky bottle from the drinks cabinet and went back up to Eric's bedroom. He stretched out on the bed, looking up at the circling Spitfires on the hanging mobile. He drank the whisky to numb the pain in his ribs. At some point he must have fallen asleep.

Peggy came round in the morning. She asked how many they would be for lunch, and he replied "one". She didn't ask any more questions.

That afternoon he went back to the brickworks to look at the car. He made a few attempts to crank the engine, but a glance under what remained of the bonnet showed it was hopeless. Another man might have wept.

Pride prevented him from getting the car towed away. Better to leave it there to rust than to have to explain what had happened. He didn't want people asking questions. He never bought another. The same pride prevented him from looking for his wife and son. If she was going to do something so stupid as to run away, then let her. She'd come crawling back soon enough.

Only she didn't. And by that time, it was far too late to change his mind.

He drank. Wine from lunchtime – there was a cellar full of the stuff – and spirits in the evening. He deserved to drink. Four decades in the army, fighting for his country, watching comrades die beside him. And now his wife had deserted him, taking his son with her. Christ, a man who'd endured what he had, who'd made the sacrifices he had made, had surely earned the right to a drink now and then.

Sometimes, two-thirds of the way down a bottle of wine, he grew maudlin. He missed his wife and son, or at least the idea of them. He'd had a home and a family – what more did a man need? – and now he had lost them. But he rarely stopped to wallow in sadness or regret; better to wade deeper into drunkenness. Sometimes other emotions would bubble up: rage, shame, self-pity. Then he would have to keep drinking until he reached a state of blessed oblivion.

Only the oblivion wore off into the fug of the next morning. He would wake with his head aching and his body feeling older than its fifty-eight years. And if there had been anybody to ask him whether he was glad to see the dawning of another day, he would have laughed in their face. The bleak expanse of winter stretched ahead of him. He began to think a lasting oblivion wouldn't be such a bad idea.

One morning in November he shut Sherpa in the kitchen and took the shotgun from the cupboard in the cloakroom. He walked up Jupiter Hill and through the meadow to the far side of Marshmead – the extreme end of the property, as far from the house as could be. He sat down on a pile of logs, the remains of an elm tree that had fallen in a storm back in the spring. He had meant to cart the wood down to the yard, to saw it and split it and stack it in the back of the stable ready for the following winter's fires. That didn't seem necessary now. He cocked the gun, held the barrel to his lips, and closed his eyes.

He fingered the trigger. And heard barking.

He opened his eyes to see Sherpa bounding towards him, tail wagging madly. Exhilarated to have escaped, somehow, from the kitchen, overcome with delight at finding him. Reginald let the shotgun slip between his knees. The dog darted up to him, planting his muddy paws on Reginald's lap as he tried to lick his face and knocking the gun to the ground.

"Alright, alright. Get down!"

Sherpa obeyed, and sat, tail wagging, ears pricked, eyes expectant.

"Somebody would have looked after you, you know," Reginald told him. "You'd have got fed alright." He sighed, and scratched the dog's head.

He picked up the gun and fired into the sky. Sherpa dashed off in a frenzy of barking, then stopped and looked back at him, head cocked quizzically, wondering why no bird had fallen.

Reginald laughed. "Silly fool. I wasn't aiming for anything, was I?"

He held out his hand. Sherpa trotted over and gave it a lick. Reginald stood up and slung the shotgun over his shoulder. Then he picked up an elm log under each arm and trudged back to the house.

No, it didn't make him fall in love with life again. He didn't greet each breaking morning with a song in his heart and a spring in his step. His soul wasn't filled with joy and wonder by the beauty of a frosted spider's web or a blackbird singing among the bright rowan berries. It didn't make him stop drinking. It didn't make him decide to seek his son. But he took the dog for a walk every morning, and could see there was something to learn from the simple pleasure that Sherpa took in it.

The dog was the only person whose company he cared for. He told Peggy he didn't need her any more, but she kept coming anyway, keeping up a patter of gossip and observations about the news and the weather. At least she didn't ask questions. His sister Jenny would call on him every couple of weeks, but they had never been close. She'd ask him how he was, and he'd say he was fine, and that was about the sum of it. Sometimes he'd run into his nephew, her son Stuart, who grazed his cows down at Marshmead and cut the meadow for hay, and they'd stop to chat for a minute or two. But there were days when the only voice that he heard was his own, talking to the dog.

On the rare occasions that the telephone rang, he ignored it. He ignored the telephone bills too. When the phone was cut off, he didn't miss it. He ignored all invitations to social occasions. It was a relief not to have to face another regimental dinner or evening at the Gregsons, to cast off the role of Colonel Cotter that he had performed for so many years. He even ignored a letter from Macca, who was travelling to his granddaughter's wedding in Winchester and hoped he might call in. Reginald liked Macca, wouldn't have minded jawing about old times. But Macca had been his best man, and that would inevitably mean questions about his wife. He couldn't face the thought of it.

He had little to do with the village. Once a week he would walk up to the post office to collect his pension, but he seldom talked to anyone. Everyone knew what had happened, that his wife had left him and taken the child with her, though there were a dozen different stories about how and why. Everyone knew, too, that the Colonel didn't like people poking their nose into his business. For the most part, they left the Colonel alone. The Colonel – everybody in the village called him that, except for a few old timers who remembered Reginald Cotter as a boy. *That's the Colonel's house*, mothers would tell their children when they passed The Lindens, like a warning. When Mrs Lovejoy at the village school read the story of *The Selfish Giant*, it was the Colonel's garden that the children pictured.

A garden that grew wilder with each passing year. Reginald planted a few vegetables – potatoes, carrots, onions, cabbages – but that was all. Spring and summer brought a riot of flowers, but nobody ever stopped to smell them, let alone pick a bunch and arrange them in a vase on the hallway table. Gooseberries and raspberries ripened in a thorny thicket, and insects and blackbirds feasted. When autumn came, the orchard gave off a cidery smell as apples rotted in the grass. In the old brickworks, birches, ash and sycamores sprang up, their seeds spinning in on the wind – one sycamore sapling growing straight out of the bonnet of the Jaguar. The thrushes planted blackthorn and holly, hawthorn and cherry, and the jays and squirrels added oaks and hazel. One spring morning he looked out of the bedroom window and there was a wood.

Inside, he lived in the kitchen and the sitting room, slept in his bedroom, took a bath every week or two, and continued to make frequent trips to the cellar. The other doors stayed closed. He kept the place tidy – four decades in the military had drummed that into him. But he was oblivious to the cracking paint and the mildew around the sash windows, the thickening layers of dust and the clouds of cobwebs on the ceilings. Whenever an electric light bulb blew, he didn't bother to replace it.

For a while, he continued to collect eggs from the chickens. But the eggs dwindled as the flock became increasingly feral. The foxes picked them off, till eventually none remained.

In the winter, the spring bubbled up at the top of Marshmead. The rain fell and the field flooded. The water drew mallard and tufted duck, coot and moorhen. Reginald went out with the gun. He bagged a brace of mallard. Then he spotted a pair of snipe skulking in the reeds. He lined up the sights. The male snipe lifted its beak and looked straight at him. Reginald let his aim drop. What was the point? He'd done more than enough killing for one lifetime.

He missed fishing though. A handful of times he'd been to a good spot on the Avon, but it was an hour's walk away. When the waters in Marshmead subsided that spring, he embarked upon his grand project. He would drain the boggy ground and carve out the old claypits to make a pond. He would stock it well, then he could fish to his heart's content without having to leave the property.

His tools were a shovel and a wheelbarrow. He worked every day except Sunday, three hours in the morning after he'd walked Sherpa, shovelling the heavy clay. He would stop for lunch when he would drink a glass of cider, and if he stopped at one glass he would do another two hours' digging in the afternoon. He marked out an oval, sixty feet long and forty wide, with a small island in the middle where a willow tree grew. The Marshmead side he kept shallow, but towards the claypits he dug trenches deeper than he was tall until it looked like he was building a replica of the Western Front. He took away the clay in the wheelbarrow and piled it into a mound which slowly became a small hill. He covered the clay mound with turfs, and planted some saplings dug up from other parts of the property – an ash, an oak, a horse chestnut.

It took him seven months. Reginald was proud of the pond. He had made something. In a small way, he had made the world better. It was, he reflected, the greatest achievement of his life. He would have liked to share it with somebody. *My son would have liked this*, he thought.

November came, bringing grim days of heavy rain. Reginald looked forward to them like a child impatient for snow. Every day he would walk to the pond to check the water level. He couldn't remember when he'd last found something so satisfying. The pond filled up nicely over winter and through the spring, and though by August he could walk across to the island in a pair of gumboots it didn't dry out. Reeds and bullrushes began to colonise the edges. The next spring, frogs, toads and newts all came to spawn, and a mallard and a pair of coots nested on the island.

Stuart drove him over to a fishery near Romsey, and they came back with a large tank full of eight-inch carp, perch, tench and rudd. As the years passed, Reginald spent countless hours sitting by the pond, casting his line into the water. When he landed a fish, he would look it in the eye as he pulled the barb from its mouth. Sometimes he would talk to it as he put it back in the water. He began to recognise some of the fish as individuals; there were some he landed on multiple occasions whom he came to look on as old friends. But increasingly, the joy of fishing wasn't so much in catching fish as in sitting beside the water, thinking about nothing. Pond skaters tacked across the surface and water boatmen sculled among the waterlilies. Damselflies flashed in the sun. Yellow irises, willow branches and scudding clouds reflected in the water. The birds went about their business, accustomed to the presence of the old man and his old dog, stretched out on the blanket beside him.

"He was a good dog," the old man said. Eric started. They had been sitting in silence for several minutes.

"What was that?"

"He was a good dog," Reginald repeated. "Sherpa."

"Sherpa?" He had been thinking about the dog that very moment. He hoped his father had looked after him. "Yes. Yes, he was."

"I buried him up here." Reginald gestured towards the

bank behind them. There was a small wooden cross buried in the dry grass.

"I missed him," Eric said.

His father nodded slowly. "I miss him too."

They lapsed into silence again. Eric didn't know what to say. His father didn't seem to need to say anything.

It was then he noticed the fish. Two dozen of them at least, bunched together in the dwindling pool of water, their bodies overlapping, barely moving. The biggest, a silvery carp with drooping whiskers, must have been three feet long. Eric didn't know much about fish, but he figured it couldn't be good for them to be crowded together in there. Did fish run out of oxygen? Was it like having lots of people trapped in an enclosed space? What would happen if it dried up further? The weather didn't look like changing anytime soon.

"The monsoon's late this year," Reginald said suddenly.

Eric began to laugh, thinking it was a joke, then stopped, realising it wasn't.

"You don't think the monsoon is late?"

"No, no, definitely," Eric said hurriedly. "We could do with a monsoon."

"I've been bringing water." Reginald indicated the bucket. "For the fish. But it keeps disappearing."

Abruptly, though slowly, he rose to his feet. He folded the chair and leant it against the trunk of the ash tree. He picked up the bucket.

"Let me take that," Eric offered.

"I can manage."

He set off back towards the meadow. Eric followed. His father didn't say anything. The path that had been trodden through the meadow grass was narrow, and they walked in single file. An image came into Eric's mind: his father striding along a lane with high hedges on either side, Eric half-running to keep up. It must have been a memory, but he couldn't recall the circumstances. Now his father walked ever so slowly. Eric kept a few feet behind, matching his father's pace. It was the best way to walk in this heat anyhow.

When they reached the bank by the dead elm tree, Reginald stopped. Eric took in the view over the garden and the copse that used to be the brickworks. The house was huge. Larger than the house he lived in now, and that was divided into a dozen flats. Incredible to think that he used to live here. In another version of his life, he might have stayed, grown up here. What would that life have been like? He would be a different person altogether. He was a city dweller now, no question. Still, it felt good to be out of London. The heat here felt less oppressive; there was room to breathe. No other people as far as the eye could see. The meadow stretched behind them, backlit by the afternoon sun, blending into the hazy fields in the distance. To the left was the orchard, and beyond that the wood. Ashridge, that was its name. They used to walk there sometimes. Eric remembered Sherpa going crazy around the foxes' earth.

His father spoke. "Got children of your own yet?"

"No."

"Married?"

"No," Eric said again. Then he added, "I have a girlfriend."

His father grunted. "What's her name?"

"Kat," Eric said after a pause.

His father grunted again. "I'm leaving it all to you," he said.

"I'm sorry?" Eric wondered if he'd heard right.

"I said, I'm leaving it all to you. In my will. The house, money, the lot of it."

He stared at his father. The old man appeared entirely lucid. Eric didn't know what to say. It had crossed his mind over the years, the idea that he might inherit a house worth rather a lot of money. He'd tried not to let himself think about it. Then on the ride down he'd played through just this situation in his head, and how he'd look his father in the eye and tell him, cuttingly, that he didn't want anything from him.

"I – uh... Thank you."

That wasn't what he'd meant to say.

"I mean, I hope it will be a long time before..."

His father gave a snort that might have been a laugh. "Oh, I'm ready. It's only the fish keeping me here."

He picked up the bucket and headed down Jupiter Hill. Eric followed. When they reached the yard, instead of turning right towards the house, Reginald turned left into the orchard. He walked along the hedge and stopped by a patch of tall, dusty nettles. On the ground was a slab of stone, and on it a wooden pail attached to a coiled rope. Beside the slab was a black hole. The well! It came back to Eric all at once. He remembered his father lifting the slab out the way so he could drop stones into the depths and listen to the echo. He knelt now and stared down into the nothingness. It felt cool and inviting down there.

Reginald lowered the pail into the well. He must have let out twenty yards of rope before Eric heard the bucket hit water. Methodically, hand over hand, his father pulled the rope back up.

"Let me give you a hand with that," Eric offered.

"I can manage."

"Isn't there a tap in the yard?" Eric asked. "Couldn't you use that?"

Reginald shook his head. "They won't let you," he said darkly. "If they catch you using a hosepipe…"

When the pail appeared, he took hold of the handle and lifted it onto the stone slab. Then he cupped his hands, dipped them into the water and drank.

"Is it okay to drink?" Eric asked.

His father took another mouthful. "Better than what comes out the taps. They put chlorine in that. Same as the gas in the trenches. That stuff kills people. I've seen it."

Eric too cupped his hands and dipped them into the cool water. He brought them to his lips and sipped. The water tasted chalky, but wonderfully refreshing. He drank several gulps.

"It's for the fish."

"Oh, yes. Sorry."

Reginald poured the water into the other, larger bucket, then lowered the pail again.

"Are there any more buckets?" Eric asked. "I could carry some too."

"In the dairy."

The dairy door was once blue, but most of the paint had flaked off. Eric lifted the thumb latch and pushed it open. Inside was shadowy and stuffy, dust motes floating in the sunbeams that slanted down from a window that hadn't been cleaned in decades. Against the wall to his left was a neat stack of logs, with a heap of uncut branches beside an old saw horse. The rest of the building was crammed with assorted stuff – wooden ladders, strawberry nets, coils of chicken wire, packing crates and garden furniture, all shrouded in cobwebs. There were scythes and rakes, a wardrobe and an iron bedstead. A wooden sledge – a memory came to him of tobogganing down Jupiter Hill. In the far corner, sporting a mane of bird shit, was an old rocking horse. His old rocking horse! What was it called? Gawain? No, Sir Gawain's horse. Gringolet, that was it. All these memories rattling around his head. How was it, Eric wondered, that he had carried them round inside him all this time without even knowing they were there? It felt good to have them back. He found two wooden pails in one of the old cow stalls. They must have been used for milking, he supposed, back when there'd been an actual dairy here, when his father was a boy.

Back outside, the sunlight was dazzling. Reginald was still seated beside the well. Eric joined him. "I found these," he said.

His father nodded but didn't say anything.

On his first few attempts Eric couldn't keep the rope steady, and most of the water had spilt before the pail reached the surface. But eventually he managed to fill his two buckets. Too full, it turned out – when he picked them up, a wave of water sloshed over the top of each of them. The look of disapproval from his father felt disconcertingly familiar. He fared better after that though, walking steadily with his arms held out to the sides. They made slow progress. Reginald kept stopping to change hands and to rest. Eric wondered if this sort of physical exertion in this heat was wise for a man pushing eighty.

Eventually, they reached the pond. Reginald poured his bucket into the water. It sent a ripple through the fish, who began thrashing round for half a minute, before settling back into their state of suspended animation. Eric poured in his two buckets. They didn't make any perceptible difference to the water level.

"Shall I get some more?" he asked.

His father considered, then nodded. "I'll stay here." He gestured to the water in the pond. "Make sure nobody takes this."

At Eric's own speed, it was a ten-minute stroll to the well. He fetched two more buckets, then made another trip. By the time he returned with the second load, his father had nodded off on the folding chair in the shade. Eric went back for more water. Despite the heat, it felt good to be doing something physical. His mind was racing. Was it true? Was his father really going to leave everything to him? The old man wasn't always of sound mind, that was clear enough. But he'd sounded sane when he said that, saner than at any other point that afternoon.

The idea of refusing it seemed absurd now. What would that achieve, really? It was easy to think he could do that when it was just a fantasy, but to give up a small fortune in reality... because of what exactly? Pride? A sense of injustice? Loyalty to his mother?

He couldn't live here – could he? It seemed a shame in a way to sell the place. It had been in his family, sort of, for god knows how long. Since the last century? He thought about Nanny Tessa. It was sad that he couldn't remember her. She'd known him as a baby. Had she imagined him living here one day? Walking up Jupiter (Juniper?) Hill with his own children?

But what did he want with a big house in the middle of nowhere, with an overgrown, oversized garden, fields and a pond? Better to sell. Somebody else would care for it more than he ever could.

What was it worth? He had no idea. Tens of thousands probably. It would transform his life utterly. He could buy a place of his own, somewhere nice in southwest London, with a garden even. He could ask Katya to move in with him, be like a proper dad to Ludo. They could even get a dog.

By the time he completed his tenth trip, there was a small but appreciable rise in the water level. The fish seemed to have more room to breathe. Eric lay down on the ground in the shade of a willow tree, a few yards away from his father, who was snoring quietly. He kicked off his sandals and felt the brittle grass between his toes. He smelt the thick scent of dry mud and water mint, and heard insects buzzing in the vegetation. He lay on his back, staring up through the leaves into the depths of the sky.

DULCE DOMUM
1982

Life, Arthur reflected, didn't get any better than this. It was the end of May, and the first properly hot weekend of the year. Half-six in the evening and still warm enough for shorts, shirtsleeves and bare feet on the lawn. A great tit chittered away in the laburnum tree, swifts wheeled in a cornflower-blue sky, and over in Brickwood a cuckoo was calling.

The garden was a triumph, an extravagance of flowers: foxgloves and lupins, snapdragons and marigolds, wallflowers and poppies, sweet-scented stocks, sprawling mallow and red valerian. He took the time to take it in: the echiums still abuzz with bees, an explosion of roses up the wall of the folly. The elder trees stretching over from Brickwood were in full lacey flower, and the wisteria hung heavy around the back door of the house.

Chores were finished. The goat had been milked, the chickens shut up for the night, the boys fed and bathed. He had read them three chapters of *Danny the Champion of the World* out on the swing seat, and now Eleanor was putting them to bed. Supper was laid out ready on the picnic table: a quiche made with fresh peas and baby chard from the garden, eggs from the hens and cheese from the goat, plus the very first infant new potatoes of the season. Arthur set down the two champagne flutes. This was the life they had made together. He couldn't help smiling. He walked over to the herb garden in front of the greenhouse, enjoying the feel of the soft grass between his toes, and picked a sprig of parsley.

Eleanor had made the quiche; Arthur had made the picnic table. That was them: they complemented each other perfectly. Not just in their marriage, but in their professional life too. Arthur and Eleanor Aldridge, celebrated children's authors, creators of the much-loved Brixton Bunnies series. He wrote the words, she drew the pictures. They were a team.

It had started as a joke. Ten years ago in a squat in Streatham. They'd been sleeping together on and off in a free-lovey kind of way, but they weren't a couple as such. Arthur was making just enough to live on as a private tutor while working on his endless novel about a struggling novelist living in a squat in Streatham. Eleanor, recently graduated from St Martin's, worked in a café where she also exhibited, but rarely sold, her paintings: unsettling sketches of urban wildlife – foxes rooting through dustbins, pigeons perched on razor wire, rats on kitchen surfaces. The latter was not an unknown sight in their basement flat. Five of them lived there, middle-class kids pretending that living rent-free was a revolutionary act. Hugh was a Trotskyite playwright (unperformed) who Arthur had known since Cambridge. Jocelyn had trained as a midwife but was now looking after the final member of the household, a young son named Siddhartha, though mercifully known as Sid.

One evening, Jocelyn had been reading Sid some vapid

book about anthropomorphic mice living a conventional suburban existence that had set Arthur off on a rant about how children's books should be a subversive force but were usually reactionary and only served to reinforce the capitalist hegemony, and these mice were Tory vermin. Arthur and Eleanor spent the night cooking up the idea of a kids' book about a group of rabbits living in a squat in 1970s London. And so the Brixton Bunnies were born. Arthur would probably have soon forgotten about it all – they were smoking a lot of pot in those days, and his great ideas usually fizzled out when the haze ascended – but Eleanor sat down the next day and started sketching. When she showed the pictures to him, Arthur could tell they had something, a strange mixture of nursery twee and urban realism that shouldn't have worked but somehow did. That night he sat down and wrote the first story, telling the tale of how, after Brian Bunny is laid off from his job at the factory, his family are evicted by their rich fox landlord and left destitute. Befriended by some hippie hedgehogs, they end up moving into a derelict building and setting up their own egalitarian commune. Arthur found it easier to write than his novel, and more fun.

Hugh, despite decrying the Brixton Bunnies' lack of active support for establishing a workers' state, shared Arthur's manuscript and Eleanor's portfolio with an old friend from Harrow who worked in publishing. And before they knew it they had a five-book deal and an advance that had at least one more zero than Arthur was expecting. Their professional partnership cemented their romantic one. Calling them Arthur and Eleanor Aldridge was their agent's idea – she thought they would be more marketable as a husband-and-wife team. Perhaps it planted a seed, perhaps it would have happened all the same: either way, in the spring of '74 they were married in Lambeth registry office. Their first son, Sebastian, was born the following year. By then, the books were a hit. Kids liked the stories and the exquisite detail in Eleanor's watercolours, but it was the parents they most appealed to: sixties kids now raising kids of their own, who lapped up the knowing humour and the right-on storylines (little Becca Bunny gets lost on the Tube but is helped home by a sympathetic family of reggae-loving Rastafarian raccoons; Bridget Bunny and her friend Sylvia Squirrel lead a successful protest against a greedy badger's attempt to build housing on the common).

When Eleanor was pregnant with Felix, they decided that the flat where they were living in Clapham was no place to bring up two kids. They had both grown up in the countryside, and even though they had left for London at the first opportunity, their childhoods had by now begun to take on a rose-tinted glow.

They knew The Lindens was the one the moment they set eyes upon it. "I swear the house smiled at me," Eleanor said later. She could be whimsical like that. It was an unseasonably spring-like morning in February, the front lawn studded with snowdrops and crocuses. The place was in a terrible state, but then that was what brought it within their budget.

"No chain," the estate agent told them. "The chap who inherited it just wants a quick sale. It needs modernisation," he added, which was quite the understatement. The dusty velvet curtains, the stone tiles and the cracked porcelain in the bathroom, the exposed wires and the rotting sash windows: Arthur doubted any of it had been changed for half a century. No central heating, but working fireplaces and an ancient Aga in the kitchen.

"Who lived here before?" Eleanor asked.

"Some old army chap. Lived on his own for years. You can see it needs a little TLC. But the house is rock solid – they built things to last back then. And as for the garden…"

That was what had attracted them in the first place. Ten acres of land. An orchard, a meadow, a pond, even a small wood. Arthur had ideas about living off the land that were political as much as romantic. He'd read *The Limits to Growth* a couple of years before, and it had made quite an impression. Four billion people on the planet! It was terrifying. Here, they would be self-sufficient, growing their own organic food and harvesting their own fuelwood, with a cellar to retreat to in the event of a nuclear disaster. And yes, property was theft, but if they didn't buy this house, someone else would. An egalitarian earthly paradise was all very well, but it was a long-term project requiring systemic change; in the meantime, they would make their own paradise on this little piece of earth.

They threw themselves into the work. They stripped away layers of peeling wallpaper, ripped out threadbare carpets and coaxed the sun through windows that hadn't been cleaned since before The Beatles. They sanded floorboards, papered walls, primed and painted woodwork. They rolled layers of insulation across the attic, discovering scores of bats hanging from the beams above. They trawled flea markets and car-boot sales for furniture and furnishings. Among the junk left behind in the loft of the old dairy, below a shroud of dusty cobwebs, Arthur found a rickety rocking horse, brought back to life with a coat of paint and some WD40, and an ancient wooden cot. One leg was missing and two of the bars were broken, but it was a lovely old thing, with proper dovetailed joints and silhouettes of birds carved into the headboard. Arthur set about restoring it as a bed for the new baby.

The garden was a wilderness to tame. They hacked back brambles and buddleia, ripped out docks and ragwort, scythed down nettles and towering thistles. At the back of the house they found rose bushes and hydrangeas, and the flowerbeds, released from the choking hold of bindweed, exhaled spring bulbs and perennials, daffodils and tulips, hollyhocks and peonies. In the top garden, they found a forest of raspberries entwined with honeysuckle, rhubarb bursting out from beneath some old chimney pots. A fruit cage collapsing under ivy yielded prickly bushes with the sweetest yellow gooseberries Arthur had ever tasted and currants red, white and black.

It was exhausting and exhilarating, and they shared the toil and the joy of it, each day bringing a sense of achievement in a joint endeavour. The life they were building. Home. Family.

Five years already! It was hard to believe. Arthur remembered Eleanor carrying Felix in the sling while she pottered about in the splendid Victorian greenhouse, the glass replaced and the wrought iron freshly painted. Felix had been a remarkably calm and sweet-tempered baby, resting in his pram under the Bramley tree or crawling around in the grass while they worked. Sebastian was a robust and resourceful boy, happy to play on his own, climbing trees, making dens, getting dirty and generally having exactly the sort of childhood that Arthur had always hoped his children would have. Felix had turned out less boisterous than his brother, but also loved being outdoors. He liked to pick flowers and help out with the garden chores, pushing round a miniature wheelbarrow. He already knew the names of as many birds as Arthur did, and would spend hours absorbed in the *Observer Book of Birds*.

Last year they had given in to Sebastian's pleading and

bought a television, reluctantly deciding that its absence would prove a social handicap to the boys. But viewing hours were strictly rationed. Arthur wanted his sons to spend their time more productively. He built a raft for them to sail on the pond, and a treehouse in the linden tree nearest the road, where the boys would sit and try to get a thumbs-up from the driver when a car went by. They built a den in the laurel hedge by the orchard – there was a pile of ancient bricks that they made into a fireplace and a chimney pot that Seb, as the eldest, claimed as his throne. They played in the hayloft above the old dairy, climbed trees in the little copse known as Brickwood and rolled down the banks and hollows of the sandy field beside it while their dog Collette, the very best of border collies, dug frantically at the rabbit holes.

In the middle of Brickwood was an old car, a sycamore tree growing through the rusty caved-in bonnet. A Jaguar XK120 of all things. God knows how it had got there, but it was better than any toy they could have bought for the boys. Arthur didn't hold with all the plastic crap capitalism expected kids to swallow, and couldn't help feeling a smug satisfaction when he saw the boys sword-fighting with dead cow parsley stalks or launching helicopter seeds from the wall. And who needed sugary junk when you could gorge on damsons and Victoria plums, hedge blackberries and windfall apples?

What a joy to have an orchard! They drove to Brogdale in Kent and brought back two dozen heritage varieties to supplement the lichen-draped trees that must have been as old as the house. The names alone were a delight: Devonshire Quarrenden, Orleans Reinette, King of the Pippins, Ashmead's Kernel, Laxton Epicure. He grafted cuttings from old trees in friends' and neighbours' gardens, inventing names for the ones they couldn't identify: Beauchamp's Old Russet, Schoolhouse Early, Pippa's Pippin.

Planting trees felt important. A way of leaving a legacy. Arthur had read an article about the greenhouse effect, how burning coal and oil was pumping carbon dioxide into the atmosphere and warming the planet. He figured that planting trees would be one way to redress the balance, particularly if the letter-writing campaign to save the rain-forest that he was engaged in proved unsuccessful. The New Forest, as Eleanor christened it, covered half an acre by the pond. He planned it carefully: willows and alders in the marshy ground, light-loving birches and fast-growing sycamores on the slopes, then oak and ash, field maple and sweet chestnut, bird cherry and beech. At its heart stood two trees that must have been planted there decades ago: an oak and a linden, close together, their branches entwining. The Hugging Trees, the boys called them.

The first year, the deer stripped the bark off the saplings and half of them died. Arthur could have wept. He planted new ones, this time in plastic tubes. Today the willows and sycamores were ten feet tall. Between the orchard and the New Forest was the meadow, a long, gently rolling sweep of land flanked by hedges of hawthorn and blackthorn and a procession of grand old oak trees. They had thought about getting a small herd of Jersey cows, but the grass and the wildflowers were so lovely: in the end they settled on a goat. She was a British alpine, black and white, her quizzical face striped like a badger. On the drive home, she snuggled on Eleanor's lap in the back of their Morris Traveller. "She's a darling thing," Eleanor said, and she was, for the first few months. They called her Gaia. Perhaps it wasn't propitious. She turned out to be less nurturing earth-mother, more vengeful primal spirit. The man they had bought her from insisted she had been dehorned. Perhaps she had, but she grew a pair of lethally curved horns anyway, and learnt how to use them. When she was in season, she would rip out her pole and chain and rampage through the village, and they'd receive a phone call from a bemused, irate or terrified neighbour.

Gaia wasn't keen on being milked. Arthur built a milking stand, a wooden contraption with a hole for her head like she was in the stocks, or the guillotine. If she was in a particularly foul mood, she'd let Arthur milk her out, then very deliberately put a dirty hoof in the bucket and give it a kick. She tolerated Eleanor more. Eleanor would sing to her, and she would stand still and calm; or at least, she usually would. The milk, though, was wonderful. Once you got over the initial distaste, the sheer *goatiness* of it, it was the best milk in the world. When they had more than they could use on their muesli, they'd make milkshakes and hot chocolate, or drain it through a dishcloth and make curd cheese. When her milk dropped off in the winter and they had to buy cow's milk from the village shop it tasted thin and bland.

They bought chickens, too, half a dozen Cuckoo Marans, five hens and a cockerel with magnificent drooping scarlet wattles and fierce spurs whom Eleanor named Goliath. She also bought a book of traditional chicken breeds, and it became their hobby to collect the most absurd birds they could get their hands on. They bought eggs from the livestock market or through the surprisingly active local network of poultry fanciers to hatch when the hens went broody: fluffy white Silkie bantams, Salmon Faverolles with their whiskers and feathered pantaloons, spotted Appenzellers and Polands with punky topknots. Today, despite their ongoing war of attrition with the foxes in Ashridge, they had a fine flock of around fifty defiantly free-range chickens roaming the grounds, all mixed up in fantastic combinations. They'd added some ridiculous Indian Runner ducks too, and Beau Brummel, a peacock given to them as a chick, who liked to show off his crown of feathers to his own reflection in the glass of the greenhouse, and display aggressively to watering cans, wheelbarrows and other apparent rivals.

The chickens laid far more eggs than they needed, so they put boxed-up eggs for sale on a table outside the front gate. Arthur liked the feeling of being part of a village community, a friendly, trusting place where you could leave out a tin for the money and people would usually leave the correct change (though after it had been stolen for the second time, they decided to move the egg box to the back porch instead. Arthur blamed Thatcher.) Sometimes they would take a young cockerel for the pot. Arthur had never killed an animal with his own hands before. Ethically, he had no qualms about it: this was a source of healthy, humanely reared protein that couldn't have been more local, and besides, Goliath and the other high-status cockerels could be fiercely aggressive towards those lower in the pecking order. Still, the first time, as he held the madly flapping bird upside-down by its feet in one hand and attempted to wring its neck with the other, he almost lost his nerve. But it got easier. As well as the chickens, he'd sometimes have to dispatch dying rabbits brought as gifts by Engels, their tortoiseshell tabby. It was, he had to remind himself, just part of nature: you shouldn't anthropomorphise rabbits in real life.

Eleanor, who had ridden ponies in her childhood, decided the stable needed a horse. Their first was an Arab mare offered on loan in the local freesheet, euphemistically described in the classified ad as "spirited". Eleanor could manage her, but the first time Arthur took her out, the mare had spooked when a polythene sheet covering some hay bales flapped in the wind. She bolted for home, leaving him on his sore arse. He'd never ridden again, though the horse they had now, a pretty chestnut thoroughbred named Cressida, was a more dependable character. They'd also taken on a New Forest pony, already saddled with the name Dobbin, as Eleanor thought it would be nice for the boys to have a pony to ride. Privately, Arthur wasn't sure if the boys would be especially keen to ride a pony, but as an avowed opponent of gender stereotyping he kept this quiet.

Horses however were a remarkable machine for turning grass into manure, which was an essential raw material for the vegetable garden, Arthur and Eleanor's magnum opus. It was back-breaking, never-ending work: digging the ground, shovelling horse shit and compost into the wheelbarrow to fork into the beds, raking the autumn leaves and storing them in old seed sacks to mix with the potting compost in eighteen months' time, cutting hazel branches for pea sticks, steeping comfrey leaves in barrels to make tomato feed. Then there was the hoeing and the sowing, the planting and the potting on, the weeding and the thinning, slaughtering slugs and squashing caterpillars.

"I don't like doing this," Eleanor confessed. "It feels like murdering butterflies."

These weren't the only pests. The first year, pigeons pecked at the brassicas, deer grazed down the sweetcorn, blackbirds stole strawberries. When Arthur read *Peter Rabbit* to Felix, he had a newfound sympathy for Mr Macgregor.

"Fucking bunnies!" he raged after a particularly destructive raid on some newly transplanted lettuce seedlings. "Why can't they respect private property?"

"If it wasn't for bunnies, we wouldn't be here," Eleanor reminded him.

"In the next book, what if the Brixton Bunnies raid someone's garden..."

"And are unjustly arrested for trespassing?"

"I was thinking get shot."

They had written a couple more books to keep their publisher happy, but urban life seemed a world away. In what turned out to be the last in the series, the Bunnies moved to a derelict farm in the country and set up their own ecologically friendly horticulture cooperative. In real life, Arthur put up a wire fence around the vegetable patch and a net over the fruit cage.

But oh, it was all worth it! The garden was a miracle, repaying their labours in abundance. Summer was a surfeit of salads and soft fruit, autumn was pumpkins and apples and gigantic misshapen carrots, winter meant potatoes and parsnips roasted in the Aga. Even in the hungry gap before the first of the purple sprouting, there were the last of the leeks, celeriac and a few brave endives to supplement the food they'd stored over the previous year: the sacks of spuds and strings of onions in the coal shed, the jars of tomatoes, pickled cucumbers and inventive chutneys in the cellar. When the Red Lion closed down, they bought the deep freeze off the landlord and filled it with bags of beans and peas, strawberries and red currants.

They made wine from the soft fruits, from dandelions and clover and elderberries, though the idea and the process tended to be more enjoyable than the end result. But the sloe gin was good, and the cider was truly special. Arthur built a press using an old car jack, and they juiced windfalls by the barrow load. The thick, sweet brown juice cleared to a deep gold, dry but smooth and deceptively easy to drink until you couldn't find your feet. Eleanor made herbal teas from the water mint growing at the pond, from nettles, lemon verbena and the linden flowers. Just this afternoon, she'd been making elderflower champagne.

Tonight, though, they were having the real thing. Tonight, they were going to celebrate. Arthur filled the ice bucket. Then he went down the cellar to fetch the bottle of Veuve Clicquot.

Eleanor had had a lovely day. It was the Friday of half-term, and she'd made damn sure it was full of quality time with her children. They'd ridden Dobbin in the morning, and even Sebastian, who had so far displayed little enthusiasm for riding, had been coaxed into enjoying the sort of imaginative game he was already growing out of: Dobbin, as unlikely as it seemed, was an elephant who they were riding through the jungles of India on the hunt for a rare white tiger. He was deep into the Willard Price Adventure series at the moment; Arthur was worried that they reinforced colonialist attitudes, but Eleanor thought they provided nourishing food for Seb's imagination. She'd made fresh bread for lunch: it was a simple joy, watching the boys devour hot brown rolls smothered in butter while she and Arthur got gently tipsy on lunchtime cider, because after all, it was the holidays and almost the weekend. In the afternoon, the boys had helped her pick dandelions and clover to make wine and elderflowers for champagne. They would make a dozen bottles each year, but some would inevitably explode down the cellar, making elderflower champagne a rare and precious luxury. The plastic corks would fly thirty feet in the air, and the boys would chase after them. Then they'd act all sophisticated as they drank it out of proper champagne flutes. They even used an ice bucket. It made it special. And wasn't that the point of life, really? To make every moment special, as much as you possibly could.

She'd miss them when they went back to school. It seemed crazy that her younger child was already gone from her for half of the day, half of the days of the year. Still, the school in the village was lovely: just sixty children, half of them living within walking distance, and an ancient head-mistress, the fittingly named Mrs Lovejoy, who considered nature study and drama to be of at least equal importance with maths and English. A couple of months before, the whole school had come down to The Lindens over the course of three days, infants, juniors and seniors, to see the frogs and toads spawning in the pond and go dipping for water boatmen and caddisfly larvae: it had made Eleanor so happy to see the joy and pride the boys took in showing off their home to their peers. One girl in Felix's class, a pretty little blonde thing called Katie, had been so smitten by Dobbin that she'd cried when they had to leave. Felix had told her not to cry, and gallantly said that she could come and visit again anytime. Eleanor could have melted: he was a painfully shy boy away from home soil.

Still, it would be good to have a few uninterrupted hours in the day to get some work done. She had a commission to finish off – some watercolours for a book of rhymes about fairies at the bottom of the garden. It was rather twee stuff, but she'd been taking satisfaction in filling the pictures with authentically rendered plants and birds, and it paid well. She was in demand these days, and could pick projects that interested her. She enjoyed the books she illustrated for other authors, but it made her feel a little guilty too, like she was cheating on Arthur – though of course she would never do that. She hoped they would do another book together soon. She loved the way they bounced ideas around, creating something all their own. They'd stopped smoking pot when the kids were born, but they could still make each other shake with laughter as they cooked up plot ideas and dialogue that would never make the final cut. She'd made a few new sketches of the Brixton Bunnies in their rural retreat, and they'd been idly discussing the idea of bringing in something about the miners' strike, probably involving moles (maybe starlings as literal flying pickets?), but she could tell Arthur's heart wasn't in it. He'd been doing more writing on his own recently, but he was cagey about it. She hoped he hadn't gone back to the dreadful autobiographical novel he'd been writing when they first lived together.

She took off her *Save the Whale* T-shirt and corduroys. At the bedroom sink, she washed away the sweat and grime of the day with the homemade lavender soap. Then she changed into her silk dress with the butterfly print which she loved to wear at this time of year, and went to look in on the boys. Sebastian was sitting up in bed reading. He looked affronted when she came in. "It's not lights-out yet, is it? I've only got two chapters to go."

"No, not yet. But time to go to sleep when you've finished."

He gave a dramatic sigh. "Phew. Anyway, it's not dark."

"That's because it's summer. Less than a month to the longest day."

"Can we get the paddling pool out tomorrow?"

"Maybe."

"That's what you say when you mean *no* but don't want to say it."

She laughed. "Okay. Yes if it's another hot day and you promise to help clean it. Deal?"

"Deal. And can we camp out in the tent?"

"Maybe. By which I mean no."

"But can we another night?"

She had to remind herself that, for the boys at their age, a night camping out in the garden was a great adventure, and the excitement they took from it far outweighed the hassle of putting up the tent and fixing a 9pm midnight feast. It was good to say yes to your children. "You can camp out sometime soon, I promise. But it's still chilly at nights now."

She kissed him goodnight, and he returned to *Whale Adventure*. Sebastian had decided he was definitely going to become a zoologist when he grew up, although these enthusiasms tended to be as short-lived as they were intense: it was only a few weeks ago that he was going to design and build his own houses, while last summer he had wanted to play cricket at every opportunity in the hope of becoming the next Ian Botham. He reminded Eleanor of her husband in that respect. Arthur had always been full of new dreams and schemes. One month he'd be going to meetings about setting up a community currency scheme, the next he was planning to buy up a rundown farm in the Languedoc and start a vineyard. She loved him for it. Still, she was pleased that, here, he seemed to have finally found something that satisfied his restless energy.

In the next room, Felix was still awake. He was kneeling on the bed looking out of the window. "There are swallows and house martins and I think I might have seen a swift but I'm not sure," he announced.

"Wow. But lights-out time now."

"I haven't got my light on," he said, reasonably enough. "It's the sun."

"You know what I mean. Do you want to get the paddling pool out tomorrow?"

"Can we clean it out with the hose?"

"So long as you don't squirt me."

"I won't, I promise." He gave a mischievous look. "I might squirt Arthur though."

"I'll pretend I didn't hear that."

"Eleanor?"

Arthur had insisted the children should address them by their first names. It was more egalitarian. Privately, Eleanor sometimes wished they would call her Mum.

"Yes my darling?"

"Can we go skating on the pond again?"

The previous winter had been a cold one. There'd been snow before Christmas, and the pond had been frozen solid enough to skate on for more than a week. "If it freezes again. But that won't happen till winter. Skating is a winter thing."

"Like snow. And lighting the fire."

"Exactly. And Christmas."

"When will it be winter?"

"Not for ages. Summer's only just starting. You like summer, don't you?"

"Yes." After some thought, he added. "I like all the seasons. I like doing summer things in the summer and winter things in the winter."

"That sounds wise."

"And autumn things in autumn. And spring things in spring."

She tucked him in, kissed him goodnight, and had just reached the door when he called out "Eleanor?"

She sighed inwardly. Here was the inevitable question: "Why is the sky blue?" or "Where do we go when we dream?" or "How is metal made?". She knew it was a ruse to keep her from leaving, but she couldn't help staying to answer. You were meant to encourage your children's curiosity, after all, not to crush it.

"Yes love?"

"What's the bird that sings '*Was that you, cuckoo?*'"

"The cuckoo, you mean?"

"No, not the cuckoo." Shaking his head impatiently. "It says '*Was that you, cuckoo? Was that you, cuckoo? Was it?*'"

"Ah. That's a wood pigeon. I was always told they said '*A proud wood pigeon,*' but I like your version better."

"Why do birds sing?"

"It's just how they talk to each other." It wasn't a great answer, but you had to stop somewhere.

"But why don't they just talk? Why do they sing?"

"That's a good question."

"Why don't we sing instead of talking?"

"Goodnight now," she sang.

He laughed, and sang back. "Goodnight, goodnight."

Eleanor came onto the lawn barefooted, wearing the butterfly dress she wore so often. Arthur liked that. Fashion was superficial and wasteful. Far better to have a few clothes that you loved, and that expressed your own personality. Eleanor hardly ever wore make-up, and he liked that too. She was so pretty without it. If she had aged in the last ten years, it barely showed. You couldn't say the same of most of their contemporaries. Women he knew were losing their bloom, some almost imperceptibly, some suddenly and shockingly. There were mums, and occasional dads, at the school who it was impossible to imagine as anything but somebody's parents, already settling comfortably into middle age. His wife was still in full flower.

She clocked the ice bucket, and looked at him in surprise. "Champagne? Are we celebrating?"

"We are." He filled her glass, and they toasted, exaggerating the eye contact like they always did. If you didn't make eye contact while you clinked glasses, it meant seven years' bad sex. It was something she'd said the night they met, at a party with a load of art students. They'd locked eyes then, laughing and lascivious, and they'd gone to bed together that night. It had been a shared joke and a superstition ever since. It seemed to work.

"Well?"

"I had a call with Nancy today."

"Oh? Did you mention the mole miners' strike?"

"No. We didn't really talk Bunnies."

She was giving him a puzzled look. Arthur paused. The fact was, he hadn't wanted to say anything to her. He'd been embarrassed. It was a constant nagging worry, that she was the talented one. It wasn't hard to turn out a thousand words of undemanding prose when they'd worked out the stories together, but her pictures were works of art in their own right. It was no surprise she was in demand as an illustrator, whereas he wasn't at all sure that people would want to read his writing shorn of her pictures. So that was part of the reason he hadn't shown her what he'd been working on. Besides, he remembered her reaction when he'd let her read his novel when they first got together. It was great, she said, but she thought he could make it funnier. It wasn't meant to be funny, he'd explained.

"But it is supposed to be satire, isn't it?"

He gave up on it soon after that.

Then there was the question of how she'd feel about him taking their own life as his subject. He wasn't sure she'd like it. He'd written the first one for fun, after Gaia had butted Sebastian into the pond. It seemed like too good a story to waste. Eleanor had just unclipped the goat from her pole, and she'd charged up behind the unsuspecting boy standing on the bank and rammed him into the water. *Like she was auditioning for the part of Big Billy Goat Gruff tossing the troll*, Arthur had written. He was pleased with the way it turned out. After that, he'd written a handful of vignettes about their life in the country. The time he'd tried to transfer a swarm of bees into their hive without doing up his visor, and he'd been stung so badly he looked like the Elephant Man. Gaia on heat running amok through the village before finally being meekly led home by old Peggy Morgan, the redoubtable octogenarian church warden. He'd taken a few liberties, exaggerating stories and turning real people into caricatures for comic effect. There was a parody of a Brixton Bunnies story too, in which the bunnies were accused of trespass and vegetable theft and summarily executed.

He'd typed out five of the more fully formed stories and sent them to Nancy, their agent, just to ask her opinion. Might they have commercial appeal? He told himself it didn't matter: he'd written them for his own amusement, not through any great literary ambition. Still, he didn't want to churn out Brixton Bunnies books for the rest of his life. He was delighted that Eleanor's career was thriving, and of course he was a firm supporter of women's lib, but it was something of an affront to his manhood that she was becoming the main breadwinner as well as the bread baker. So it had been a huge boost to his ego when Nancy had written back to say that she *loved* them, and not only that but she was *110% sure* she could sell them. All the same, he hadn't let himself believe it until she'd telephoned this afternoon to say that she had offers from three publishers, and that a Sunday newspaper could be interested in a series.

"Wow," Eleanor said when he'd told her. "That's amazing!"

She seemed genuinely thrilled. Arthur, relieved, topped up their glasses.

"Why didn't you show them to me first?"

"I don't know. I was embarrassed. I wasn't sure if they were any good."

"You can show me. I'm your wife."

"Well. Then you might not be the best person to give me a critical appraisal."

She seemed to accept that. "But can I read them? Now you know you're going to be a bestselling author?"

"I sent Nancy the only typed copy. Anyway, she says I need to write another hundred pages. I'm going to need your help coming up with some more stories."

As they ate the quiche and new potatoes, they chewed over ideas. There was an interesting piece to write, she suggested, on poultry sexuality – some of the drakes showed clear homosexual tendencies, and there'd been the strange case of Binky, a hen who in her fourth year had stopped laying, grown wattles and a comb and started crowing. And what about some of the characters in the village? There were real old country people whose kind were dying out – Tom the farrier, Peggy Morgan's son who still made hazel hurdles by hand, the charcoal burners up in Ashridge, the Gypsies who turned up on the green every few months in a proper horse-drawn caravan. By the time they'd finished the champagne, Arthur had enough ideas to more than fill the book. He was fizzing with enthusiasm. It was a wonderful feeling.

Eleanor fetched a bottle of last year's blackberry wine

from the cellar – a particularly good vintage, she insisted. Arthur wasn't sure he noticed – it had that same chalky tang that most of her homemade wines did – but it was slipping down well now. They sat on the swing-seat cuddled close as the sun slipped away behind the linden trees, till Venus peeped out and bats swept overhead bringing the night in.

Life, Arthur reflected again, didn't get any better than this.

There was something melancholy in that thought.

WAYFARERS ALL!

1987

The journalist was supposed to be arriving at eleven. At twenty past, she called to say they were lost. "I'm in a phone box in a place called Stourton. I can see a duck pond."

"Ah, you must have missed the turning in Elbourne," Arthur told her. "People usually do. I should have warned you, the signpost gets overgrown." He gave her directions. "We're the last house in the village, on the left."

"The Lime Trees?"

"Well... in real life it's called The Lindens. I'll come out and meet you."

He pulled on his suede jacket and checked his hair again in the hall mirror. He had wondered if famous writers had stylists to dress them before photoshoots. Either they didn't, or he hadn't reached that league yet.

"Was that them?" Eleanor called.

"Yes. They're in Stourton?"

"Did they miss the turn-off in Elbourne?"

Eleanor could do with a stylist, Arthur thought. Old jeans and an orange jumper that she'd knitted herself. She might have made a bit of an effort. He went down the drive to open the gate, Collette at his heels, sensing the excitement of new arrivals.

Arthur Aldridge, wearing a vintage suede jacket, and his collie greet us at the bottom of the avenue of lime trees made famous by his bestselling book...

Five minutes later a Ford Sierra drew up. A bearded man of around Arthur's age driving, a dark-haired woman, several years younger, in the passenger seat. He waved them into the yard.

Collette went to greet the driver, so Arthur introduced himself to the passenger.

"You found us then. Back-of-Beyonds-Ville around here I'm afraid."

"Always good to be reminded what the countryside is like. I do have to write about it, after all."

She looked Mediterranean, Arthur thought, but the accent was crisp public schoolgirl English. Not dressed for the countryside at all in her trouser suit and heels. She held out a hand (no wedding ring, he noticed). "Melissa Tamilio. This is Jason, photographer extraordinaire, terrible navigator."

The driver, who was busy tickling Collette's tummy, gave a wave.

"So. Welcome!" Arthur gestured down the drive. "These are the famous Lime Trees."

And didn't they look fine today, their leaves shining bright gold in the October sunlight.

"There's no limes on them," observed Jason.

Arthur wasn't sure if this was a joke. He suspected it wasn't.

"Well, it's probably not the season," Melissa said.

"Ah, common misconception. The European lime tree

has nothing to do with the citrus fruit. Also known as the linden."

"Oh. I see."

"Sacred to Freya in folklore."

Arthur Aldridge clearly has an encyclopaedic knowledge of natural history and Germanic mythology, yet he wears his learning lightly.

Some of the more inquisitive chickens had come to investigate the newcomers. Melissa was eyeing them warily.

"It's quite the menagerie you have here, isn't it? Jason was hoping to photograph you with the goat. The goat is real, isn't it?"

"She is indeed. Though not keen on having her photograph taken."

"Beautiful day for it, anyhow," Jason said. "Lovely light."

They had coffee in the kitchen, where Eleanor joined them. Arthur noticed her casting disapproving looks at Melissa's heels.

"So, how do you want to do this?" Arthur asked. He was used to giving interviews, but this profile was new, elevated territory.

"Well, many of our readers will feel they know you. They've read *Not to Speak of the Goat* and *Digging the Dirt*. Some will have read the Brixton Bunnies to their grandchildren. A few may even have read your columns in the *Observer*, although it's not the *Country Home* reader's paper of choice. And of course they'll be familiar with, er, Mrs Aldridge's work too."

Eleanor arched an eyebrow. Melissa continued: "So, really, we'd just like to help them get to know you better. And your wife of course. At some point we can sit down and do a proper interview on the Dictaphone and you can plug

your new book. And Jason might want to stage some particular photos."

"Like with the goat, for example," Jason added.

"But mostly, we'll just be chatting informally, and he'll
snap away in the background," Melissa continued. "Does
that sound alright?"

"So is everything we say on the record, as it were?"

"Oh, absolutely!" She gave a tinkling laugh. "So try not
to say anything too salacious or controversial, because I'll
most definitely be obliged to print it."

They started with a tour of the house. Jason suggested
they take some pictures of Arthur in his study, as he'd
hoped they might. He'd prepared for it. He wasn't a tidy
person: usually the place was a mess, the desk strewn with
papers, dirty coffee cups and smudged red wine glasses.
He'd had a clear-out that morning, stuffing the papers away
in the bottom drawer, and given the walnut surface of the
desk a rare polish. He'd artfully arranged his old Remington
typewriter (even though he typed most things on his electric
word processor these days), a Moleskin notebook, a well-
thumbed copy of *The Golden Bough* and a framed photo of
Eleanor and the boys from a few years ago, standing by the
chestnut tree up at the pond.

*"Virginia Woolf said a woman must have money and a room
of her own if she is to write. The same applies to men of course,"
quips Arthur Aldridge as he shows us round his elegant study.*

"So you work in separate rooms?" Melissa asked.

"Well, yes... Eleanor has her studio. She takes up more
room than I do, with the paints and all."

"We used to work in the same room," Eleanor added.
"When we wrote the first Brixton Bunnies books we were
literally working together at the kitchen table."

Arthur couldn't imagine doing that now. The study was

his retreat, his private space. Having Eleanor around when he was working made him uncomfortable. He didn't like being watched. And he didn't like being watched during the periods of not-working that were an essential part of his writing routine: staring out the window, reading the Review section from last week's *Observer*, listening to old Fairport Convention and Incredible String Band records and sipping single malt, trying to hear the music the way it used to sound in his pot-smoking days.

"Any plans to collaborate again?" Melissa asked.

"Well, we're both busy on our own things," Arthur said. "And I imagine the Brixton Bunnies are all settled down in the suburbs these days."

"Do you feel you've left children's books behind?"

"Well, I enjoy what I'm doing at the moment. And our own kids are older now, so children's stories aren't really part of our life in the same way."

"They're still part of my life," Eleanor pointed out. "I'd hate to grow out of children's stories."

Arthur's book, *Not To Speak of the Goat*, had been a hit. Reviews were enthusiastic, and it spent several weeks bobbing around the late teens and early twenties in the non-fiction bestsellers list. Extracts were published in the *Observer* magazine, who commissioned him to write a series of columns, and Nancy was soon in discussions about a follow-up. It turned out, too, that he was a good performer: his readings made audiences laugh, and he found he could bullshit convincingly in response to any question they asked him. Invitations began to arrive, signings in bookshops and appearances at arts festivals. Arthur found it intoxicating. They lived a semi-reclusive life at The Lindens. Now here he was surrounded by people who thought he was someone, life suddenly full of all sorts of fascinating opportunities.

And, it had to be admitted, all sorts of fascinating women. He found himself looking more critically at his wife. He tried to picture her in something other than her gardening clothes or the handful of dresses she seemed to have worn for years. The hours outdoors gave her skin a deep hazelnut tan that he'd always loved, but there were liver spots on her arms now and deep lines on her face; it wouldn't hurt to wear a little make-up from time to time, would it?

The first time it happened was the night of his book launch. April '85. He'd been annoyed at her, which didn't help. It was supposed to be a night out together, which god knows were rare enough. A night out in London, surrounded by interesting people with fashionable clothes and exciting urban lifestyles. A night in a West End hotel at the publisher's expense. And a night when he was to be the star of the show. He wanted her to be there to reflect his glory. Or else to hold his hand if the whole thing turned out to be utterly dreadful. Tonia, Eleanor's sixteen-year-old niece whom the boys adored, was primed to stay over at The Lindens to babysit, not to mention dog, cat and goat sit.

So when the launch turned out to be on the same evening that the boys were supposed to be performing in some schools music festival, he'd thought that, for once, she might put him first. Yes, it would be a shame to miss it (though also something of a relief if he knew anything about children's concerts). And yes, it was inconvenient that they lived out in the sticks, but surely there was someone the boys could get a lift with? Instead, Eleanor had made him feel like he was the unreasonable one when he insisted that it wasn't possible to change the date.

"They're both very excited about it. I think at least one of us ought to be there." Besides, it was a lot to ask of Tonia to milk Gaia and get all the chickens in. Arthur wanted to point out that he was excited about his book launch too. It wasn't as if either of the boys was doing a solo or anything. And Tonia liked the chickens.

"You don't want me cramping your style anyway," she told him. And it was true that she'd never enjoyed the parties they'd been to after the first Brixton Bunnies books were published. They stopped going after a while, then stopped getting invited.

If she had been there, nothing ever would have happened. Which didn't mean it was her fault, but still. Of course, the wine didn't help – at least three glasses of champagne at the reception, then goodness know how many bottles their group had got through at the Italian restaurant afterwards. The girl – woman – was called Jacqui. She did something in marketing – they'd spoken on the phone a few times about headshots and blurbs and his author's profile. He'd liked her voice and her laugh and had wondered what she looked like. A stunning redhead, it turned out, in a blue dress that revealed a little more cleavage than strictly necessary. Mid-twenties. Too old to have grown up with the Brixton Bunnies, but only a little. She told him how much she loved the book, laughed at his well-practised lines about writing and country life and political rabbits. He made sure he sat next to her in the restaurant. And at the end of the evening, it was the easiest thing in the world to mention that he had a minibar in his double room in a hotel just off The Strand.

He was racked with guilt the next day. Staring out the train window as the Hampshire countryside slipped by, nursing a rabid dog of a hangover, he tried to tell himself that Eleanor wouldn't mind too much. They had both slept with other people in the early days of their relationship, and although marriage had changed the terms, their self-penned wedding vows hadn't explicitly mentioned sexual fidelity. They were the free-love generation, after all (they used to joke about making this into a Brixton Bunnies plot line). But it wouldn't wash. He confessed to her that night, overflowing with remorse, swearing it was a mistake that would never happen again.

The second time it happened was a Christmas party thrown by the *Observer* for staff and selected contributors. Being invited pleased him more than he would have admitted, and he'd felt resentful when Eleanor told him she'd rather he didn't go. It was a question of trust, she said.

"Actually, I wanted you to be my plus-one."

"Oh gosh. You know how I hate that sort of thing."

"It's interesting people talking and having a good time. What's wrong with that?"

By the end of the conversation, she was apologising for doubting him and insisting he must go – though she herself would rather stay at home.

"Anyway, it's the last episode of *The Box of Delights* that night. The boys wouldn't want me to miss that."

This time it was only kissing, with a columnist who after several glasses of free wine was almost as attractive as her byline photo. Kissing and a bit of touching. She was married too, but apparently that wasn't an issue. "It's a Christmas party," she told him, and went on to point out at least five other people whose illicit liaisons were an open secret. This time, he thought it best not to say anything to Eleanor.

There were others in the months and years that followed. Not many – he didn't pursue women, he told himself, but he did find it hard to say no when the opportunity arose. Amanda, the creative writing MA student who'd come to a reading he did in Norwich. They got chatting afterwards, went on to a bar together, ended up drinking for most of the afternoon. She asked him questions about writing and listened intently to his answers like he was a literary guru, big green eyes fixed on him. Then she asked if he would read some poems she'd written. She'd love his opinion, and her digs were only five minutes' walk away... He didn't remember much of the poems, but he remembered the softness of her body and those big green eyes looking up at him from between his legs. Holly in Edinburgh, who was acting in some risible fringe theatre piece he'd been dragged along to by a friend of Nancy's who knew the director. In the bar after the show, she'd joked about Arthur's Seat being named after him, and a few whiskies later they were walking up there in the moonlight, laughing like students, and it had been so beautiful up on the hill, looking down over the city and watching the lights across the Firth of Forth. Star-struck Anya from Malmo; he hadn't realised how popular the Brixton Bunnies were in Sweden.

They were all one-offs, and he brought no trace of them back into his home life. There were no letters, no suspicious silent phone calls, and no emotional baggage. It was an itch that needed to be scratched, he told himself, ignoring all the times he'd told his children that scratching just makes an itch worse. What if there were another woman he could be happier with? Statistically speaking, there were probably thousands. What if there were another life, richer and more exciting than the one he lived now? Yes, forty was looming and it was easy to say midlife crisis, but surely the halfway stage of your one and only life on Earth was the perfect time to take stock and consider how you wanted to spend what was left of it?

.　.　.

They visited Eleanor's studio next. Studio was a fancy name for one of the spare bedrooms. In the summer she often worked in the folly, where the light poured in through the windows from eight directions, but it was colder and dimmer by this time of year. For years they'd talked about converting the dairy loft into a proper studio, but they'd never got round to it. The loft remained a place to store hay, though they'd made room for a darts board and a ping-pong table. The boys would spend hours up there, particularly when friends or cousins visited, making dens in the haystacks, playing endless games of killer and round-the-table. She was happy enough painting in here, never more so than in the late afternoon when the sun moved round to the west-facing window.

Eleanor was aware that it was her husband *Country Home* really wanted to feature, though Nancy had insisted it was a joint profile. Yet her own career had continued to be quietly successful. She could pick and choose her projects, and had even published a couple of picture books as a writer-illustrator: *The Sundance Kid* (it was about a young goat) and *Chicken Castle.*

"Can you guess what I'm working on?" she asked.

The watercolour pegged to the easel showed an amphibian in driving goggles outside a manor house.

"Oh, that must be Mister Toad," said Jason. "*Wind in the Willows.*"

"Oh, what fun!" trilled Melissa.

"Well, it is in a way," Eleanor said. Her job usually was, and this was a dream commission. She loved *The Wind in the Willows*, and this was going to be a handsome hardback edition. She'd been briefed to produce a title page and at least three colour plates for each chapter, plus smaller ink illustrations to sprinkle throughout the text, but beyond that she had complete creative freedom.

"The thing is, it feels like quite a responsibility. I used to imagine it all so vividly as a child. Spring cleaning and messing about in boats, the terror of the Wild Wood and then how snug and safe it felt in Badger's house, Mole hearing carol singers near his old home, and all that trippy Piper at the Gates of Dawn stuff. So I have to try and do justice to that – to paint the feelings they evoked."

"I only really remember the parts with Toad," Jason said.

"Well that's another challenge. Once he starts meeting washerwomen and policemen he's apparently human-sized, so all sense of scale goes out of the window."

"Still, I don't suppose the children really notice, do they?" Melissa said.

"Do you have children?"

"Goodness no."

Eleanor nodded, but didn't say anything.

"I read *Wind in the Willows* for the first time at university," Melissa went on. "I had a boyfriend who insisted it was one of the greatest works of English literature. I remember him reading aloud from the chapter where Ratty meets the sea rat."

"'Wayfarers All,' put in Arthur. "That's my favourite chapter." He picked up the dog-eared copy from Eleanor's desk, and flicked through it. "Here, listen to this: the Wayfarer's parting words to Ratty: *'And you, you will come too, young brother; for the days pass, and never return, and the South still waits for you. Take the Adventure, heed the call, now ere the irrevocable moment passes!' 'Tis but a banging of the door behind you, a blithesome step forward, and you are out of the old life and into the new!'"*

"And that's a feeling you have?" Melissa asked.

"Well…" Arthur said. "I think we all feel that pull some-times, don't we?"

The sequel, *Digging the Dirt* , had appeared two years later. It too sold well, and the publishers would have taken another, but by then Arthur was restless for a new project. They could go away, he thought. Buy a run-down farmhouse in Andalucía, or Provence maybe – there could be a book in that. Ludicrous as it seemed, there were people who wanted to hear him tell stories about his life, and companies that would give him a good deal of money to do so. Really, they could do anything. Move to New York, or New Zealand, or a cabin on an island in the Gulf of Finland. Eleanor could do her work from anywhere. The boys could go to an international school, or they could home-school them (there'd be material in that…). What a life they could lead! They could spend a year on a tropical island recreating *Swiss Family Robinson*.

"We could be like Hal and Roger in the Adventure stories!" Sebastian enthused when he brought it up at the supper table one evening. "I used to love those books."

Felix, on the other hand, seemed terrified by the very thought of it. "I don't want to leave here!" he protested, his voice catching.

"It wouldn't be forever. We'd come back."

Eleanor humoured him. She let Arthur spin his ideas, waiting until he ran out of thread. She never vetoed his suggestions, but never failed to point out the downsides, chipping away until the latest dream crumbled.

It wasn't that Arthur didn't love The Lindens. But he sometimes wished it weren't so all-consuming, this life they had created. The garden was a machine that needed constant maintenance to keep turning from year to year. The goat had to be milked twice a day, every day. There were always brambles to clear, wood to saw, fences to replace. Was this it now? Was he going to keep repeating these chores year after year for the next forty years?

They had more money now. He'd begun ordering crates of good wine from Laithwaites which, obviously, was vastly superior to the fruit and floral wines Eleanor still made. Yes, it was lovely to eat their free-range eggs and fresh vegetables from the garden, but sometimes Arthur wondered if it was really worth it: the stuff you could buy on the market was almost as good and far less effort. Sometimes, in fact, it was better, though it would be sacrilege to say so in front of Eleanor: proper shiny aubergines and red peppers, thick heads of broccoli that you didn't have to pick the slugs out of, not to mention proper French goat's cheese, not the curdy stuff Eleanor made in an old dishcloth. There were times, too, that Arthur found Eleanor's puritanical devotion to eating seasonally rather tiresome. Like when he'd bought some Spanish strawberries in April as a treat: Eleanor had said they were tasteless and just spoilt the anticipation of eating *proper* strawberries. They were perfectly fine if you added a little sugar.

Perhaps things could have turned out differently. They had begun talking seriously about spending a year on a croft on the Isle of Mull; they'd had a rare holiday there, in a thatched cottage close to the sea with a peat fire and a western horizon serving up sumptuous sunsets. They'd enquired about renting it for the year; the price was afford-able even without a publisher's advance, and Eleanor was starting to talk constructively about how to transport Gaia and which chickens to bring. But then her mother had fallen ill. Breast cancer. Really, there wasn't much Eleanor could do: they lived three hours away, and there was her sister and any number of friends better placed to help. But the stress of it was enough to put further planning on hold. Or perhaps Eleanor used it as an excuse. At any rate, when her mother was given the all-clear, they hadn't taken it up again.

Anyway, he'd had another idea by then, which would turn into his new book: *Like a Rolling Cheese: Weird and wonderful British festivals*. He couldn't believe his luck when the publishers agreed to it. He spent a year travelling the country, following the May Day Obby Oss in Padstow and the Mari Llwyd in Chepstow, meeting Jack-in-the-Green in Hastings and hunting the Earl of Rone into the sea at Combe Martin. He watched a riotous Shrovetide football match in Derbyshire, caber-tossing at the Cowal Highland Games, the pyromaniacal anarchy of the Lewes Fire Festival. He got to stay in country inns and drink real ale while he wrote up wry accounts, weaving in occasional references to *The Golden Bough* and Bakhtin and observations on national identity. Sometimes they went as a family – to Gloucestershire to watch some loons tumbling down a hill in pursuit of a cheese, to Stonehenge for the winter solstice. But Eleanor took less delight in them than he did. "These rituals used to really mean something to people," she complained. "Now they're just tourist attractions."

Arthur took exception to being called a tourist. But then, if you turned your nose up at tourist attractions, you'd never see the Acropolis or Machu Pichu or the Taj Mahal, and Arthur hoped he'd see all of them at least once in his lifetime. Whereas Eleanor would probably complain that they'd miss the strawberry season or the Stourton village fete.

.   .   .

Eleanor took the book from him. "I always preferred 'Dulce Domum', she said. "Where the Mole goes back to his old home." She leafed back through the pages. "Here: *'He saw clearly how plain and simple—how narrow, even—it all was; but clearly, too, how much it all meant to him, and the special value of some such anchorage in one's existence.'*" Anchorage. She liked that image. She read quietly on: "*'... it was good to think he had this to come back to; this place which was all his own, these things which were so glad to see him again and could always be counted upon for the same simple welcome.'*"

That passage Arthur had read out. The call of the South. It worried her that he had those longings. The Mole coaxes Ratty out of his fit with talk of reddening apples and browning nuts, of jams and preserves and the distilling of cordials, and the hearty joys and snug home life of midwinter. But she wasn't sure if that would be enough for Arthur. He had thrown himself into this life with such passion once, but now that had burnt away.

"You love this place more than you love me," he told her once. It had made her cry, but she couldn't say for certain that it wasn't true.

"I feel we're tied down here," he'd complained. But where Arthur saw ropes, Eleanor saw roots. Plants needed strong roots to flourish. People were the same. She was a creature of routine. Arthur found it constricting, she knew that. But routines were the structure you built your life around. From being woken by the cat rubbing against her face to falling asleep with her book, the days were filled with the same chores – ministering to the needs of children and chickens, goat and garden – and the same little rituals: walking up to the pond with Collette before breakfast, skimming the paper with her mid-morning coffee, drinking a mug of linden tea in her bedtime bath. She had a mug for coffee and a mug for tea and another mug for herbal infusions, and Arthur might laugh and say she had an obsessive compulsive disorder, but it wasn't like that: it was just that those were the combinations of drink and receptacle that felt right, that gave her the most pleasure, and why not make the most of all the little moments in life that you could?

She wasn't an especially spiritual person; she liked to go to the village church for the festivals – Christmas, Mothering Sunday, Easter, Harvest – but that was more for the feeling of being part of parish life and centuries of rural tradition than any religious conviction. Still, she'd gone to yoga classes and talked to plenty of would-be Buddhists back in their squatting days, and if she knew anything about enlightenment, it was that you didn't find it by chasing round after novelty. You found it by tuning in to what was around you. Taking time to smell the roses. And the honeysuckle and the crab apple blossom, the compost and steaming horse manure. Feeling the velvet inside a broad bean pod, the warmth of an egg under the fluffed-up feathers of a broody hen. Noticing the daily changes – the palette of a tree, the behaviours of the birds, the sprouting vegetables and the swelling fruits – in the ever-circling seasons, familiar and new every time.

They ate lunch in the kitchen: fresh bread, pumpkin soup – "Pumpkins from the garden, of course" – and the last of last year's cider.

A wholesome, rustic luncheon is served in the charming farmhouse kitchen with ingredients fresh from the garden. It's warm from the heat of the Aga and the autumn sun slanting through the south-facing windows. I take my jacket off, and Arthur Aldridge hopes I don't notice him staring at my breasts...

Arthur looked away quickly.

Jason was talking about the Brixton Bunnies. "I used to read them to my kids, but I have to confess I'd got them a bit confused in my head with the Brambly Hedge books."

"They're completely different from the Brambly Hedge books," Arthur protested. "Brambly Hedge is a feudal society ruled over by Lord and Lady Woodmouse."

"Oh I don't know, they always struck me as quite egalitarian," said Eleanor. "Or collectivist, anyway. Storing all their food in the communal store stump."

"Well, they're nothing like the Brixton Bunnies anyway."

"I realise that now," said Jason. "I had a read of one before we came here. The one where the cow stops giving milk to the little bunnies' school."

"Oh yes. Not exactly subtle, that one," said Eleanor. "Yet somehow it failed to stop her being re-elected."

"Some of the kids who grew up with the Brixton Bunnies would have been old enough to vote at the last election," Arthur said. "Now there's a scary thought."

"You don't keep rabbits here?" Jason asked. Arthur said they didn't.

"Pity. Could have been a nice photo."

"You were going to get a picture of the goat though," Melissa reminded him.

"Do you think that would be possible?" Jason asked.

"Well, we can try," Arthur said. "Though she's not exactly biddable."

Gaia was tethered up by the pond, so they were able to take a tour of the property en route. Arthur still took pleasure in showing the place off to people: the cider press and the beehives; the orchard he'd planted, the branches of the later-ripening varieties heavy with fruit. Arthur talked about the wassailing festival he'd been to when he was researching his book, traipsing around an orchard in Herefordshire on a freezing January night while people drank mulled cider and sang carols.

"It's wonderful, really, that these ancient pagan traditions still persist," he said.

When Eleanor had suggested they could try blessing their own fruit trees, he'd laughed at the idea. She and Felix had tied a ribbon round the Laxton Fortune and drunk a toast to it all the same. It had a bumper crop this year. Eleanor didn't say anything.

Gaia was straining on the end of her chain to try to reach some ivy growing just out of reach, ignoring the much larger clump on the tree next to her pole. She bleated when she saw them.

"Oh, that would make a great shot," Jason said. "The two of you with the goat between you and the pond behind."

Gaia was generally suspicious of strangers, but she seemed placid enough as they approached. Arthur scratched her between the ears and behind her beard and unclipped the chain. Eleanor held her by the collar while Jason arranged them into position. As he snapped away, Gaia began to get restless.

"Just a couple more," Jason said. "Could you move her forward a little? Her face is in shadow."

This was too much for Gaia. She suddenly surged forwards, her collar slipping out of Eleanor's hand, and charged straight at Melissa. Melissa gave a shriek, jumped backwards, lost her footing and – in excruciating slow motion – slipped into the treacle-black mud at the edge of the pond.

Eleanor grabbed the chain and dragged the goat away.

Jason, braying with laughter, took a picture.

"I am so, so sorry," Arthur said. For a moment, Melissa looked as if she was going to cry, but then she laughed gamely.

"It's alright. I just slipped."

"I would say it's not like her, but that would be lying."

He held out his hand. She grasped it gratefully, and he pulled her up. Her shoes were soaking, and her trousers were covered in mud. Later that night, Arthur would replay the scene, allowing himself a little fantasy that began with him saying "Let's get you out of these wet things...".

In reality, it was Eleanor who offered to lend her some clean clothes, which Melissa graciously accepted, even though she was six inches taller and slimmer round the waist. Eleanor found her some purple paisley harem trousers she'd had since the early seventies and a baggy bumblebee-striped jumper knitted by Arthur's mother. Despite this, Arthur thought Melissa looked effortlessly chic.

Jason said he'd like to take a few more photos outside while the light held. Some clouds were moving in from the southwest, and the wind was picking up.

"Perhaps we could have a one-to-one chat with the Dictaphone now?" Melissa suggested. "If you don't mind, Eleanor?"

"Not at all. I need to pick Felix up from school anyway."

This wasn't exactly true. The village school was only a few hundred yards up the road, and Felix was quite old enough to walk home on his own. But she was glad of the excuse. Besides, Collette liked the walk, and saw rounding the children up as part of her job. She'd become very anxious when Sebastian started secondary school, leaving the flock one short. At half-past four, she would go and wait by the front gate till the bus came past, then rush back to the house barking triumphantly to announce Seb's arrival.

There was another reason she wanted to pick Felix up today. It was Friday, and that meant Pete would be there. Pete was the father of Johnny, Felix's best friend. She didn't meet many parents on the school run – half the kids got the bus over from Elbourne, some walked on their own. Pete was one of the few fathers and, as far as she knew, the only one who was single. He and his wife had split up when Johnny and Felix were in the infants, and now he had the kids on alternate weekends.

Had she always found him attractive? She wasn't sure. Perhaps it was just that little frisson of danger his status gave him that set him apart from the other happily or resignedly married fathers. He wasn't devastatingly handsome – a step down from Arthur, without doubt – but he was charming, and funny, and he looked her in the eye when he talked to her. He had nice eyes.

One Sunday back in February, she'd driven over to his house in Romsey to pick Felix up from a playdate. The boys were immersed in a computer game and Felix had begged to stay longer.

"You can have another ten minutes," she told him, "if Johnny's dad doesn't mind?"

"Not at all. Can I offer you a glass of wine while you wait? You'd be doing me a favour, I always feel guilty opening a bottle on my own."

"Well, I suppose we are beyond the yard arm... just a small one."

An hour later, Felix came to ask if it was time to go yet. She'd hardly noticed the time passing, caught up in conversation that was easy and interesting and sometimes skirted close to flirting. Driving home, she felt tipsier than two small glasses of wine should have made her.

Then there was the Mayday bank holiday weekend. Arthur was away visiting one of his festivals – it must have been the Padstow Obby Oss – and Johnny had come over for the day. When Pete arrived to pick him up, the boys were nowhere to be found.

"I'm sorry, they went off after lunch and I haven't seen them since. I think they were building a den somewhere. Up at the pond, maybe."

"That's fine, I'm in no hurry. Lindsay's at a sleepover, so it's just me and Johnny-boy today. It's great that they can just go off and do that kind of thing. Johnny's always raving about Felix's place. You're very lucky."

"I know. We can go and look for them and I'll show you round if you like?"

They walked up through the old orchard, then past the new one that Arthur had planted – decent-sized trees now, heavy with blossom, pale pink and creamy white. The hedges beside the meadow were foaming with May blossom, overflowing into cow parsley. A cuckoo called from Brickwood.

"I love this time of year," Eleanor said. "The blossom, the birdsong. All the profusion of spring."

"The start of the cricket season," Pete added. "Sorry. You're more poetic than me."

Eleanor laughed. "More pretentious, perhaps. Anyway, I happen to love cricket."

"Really? A woman after my own heart."

Eleanor blushed and looked away. "Ah, I think I spy the signs of an encampment," she said. "Looks like they may be having a campfire."

A curl of smoke was rising above the New Forest, where the trees Arthur had planted now stretched out tentative branches to each other, beginning to close into a canopy.

"Good for them," Pete said.

Eleanor was relieved. Some parents would worry, she knew, kids their age starting a fire unsupervised. "You don't mind? Felix is always very careful, and I think Seb is with them too."

"No! A little fire never hurt anyone. I loved having campfires when I was a kid. And I'm sure they're far more sensible than I was."

They found the boys on the far side of the pond. A horse chestnut tree had blown down in a winter storm the previous year, leaving a living climbing frame. They'd built their fire in the sheltered hollow behind the ripped up roots.

"No, go away!" Johnny cried out when he saw his Dad. "I don't want to go yet."

"Lovely to see you too, son. Kids these days!" Pete said to Eleanor in mock indignation.

"We were going to cook," Felix said.

"Oh really? And what's on the menu?" Eleanor asked.

"Crumpets and marshmallows," Seb answered loftily. "That's their idea of a balanced diet."

"You were going to have them too."

"Look, maybe another time we can plan this properly," Eleanor said. "Johnny could stay over, and you could actually cook your supper over a campfire. What do you think?"

"Can't we do it tonight?" Johnny asked.

"Well, I'm sure your dad already has plans for dinner."

"Not exactly," Pete said. "But I'm sure there's something in the freezer."

They ended up all having crumpets and scrambled eggs cooked over the fire, then marshmallows and goat's milk hot chocolate as a red moon rose in the indigo sky. It was a long time since Eleanor had done something so spontaneous.

"Thanks for having me," Pete had said when he and Johnny finally left. "I hope I can come and play again soon."

Nothing more had happened. But since then, she'd made a habit of picking Felix up from school on a Friday. More than once, she'd encouraged Felix to ask Johnny over on a weekend when she knew Pete had the kids. Then there was the cricket season: Pete helped coach the Stourton Colts, and Eleanor now always stayed to watch Seb (the star all-rounder) and Felix (a keen but limited off-spinner) in their Wednesday evening matches. She'd usually find a chair close to Pete's outside the pavilion, and they'd chat companionably about field placements and who should open for England.

"You know a lot about cricket for a woman, if that's not an awful thing to say," Pete told her.

"It is an awful thing to say! But thank you. My father was always listening on the radio. I picked it up from him."

The Stourton cricket ground was especially bucolic, with the churchyard on one side and fields on the other. Eleanor could close her eyes now and picture it: the spire silhouetted against the evening sun, the wheat ripening to gold as the season wore on. She missed it now autumn had come. Seb played rugby for the first XV in his year at school, but she couldn't conjure up the same enthusiasm for watching boys rucking and mauling on a muddy playing field. Though if Pete were there, perhaps she'd feel differently.

Eleanor was owed an affair. She knew the book launch wasn't the only time Arthur had been unfaithful. She'd recognised it three, perhaps four times since: the hangdog look when he got home, the solicitousness, the suspiciously well-rehearsed anecdote about the night before. She put up with it. What choice did she have? Giving up her children, if only for alternate weekends and occasional holidays, was out of the question. And life at The Lindens was a two-person job. If Arthur wasn't there, who'd dig the potato beds, scythe the nettles round the pond, cut up fallen trees with a chainsaw and split the logs? Added to which, he owned half of it, and she couldn't afford to buy him out, and the thought of what that would mean was unbearable. She could have banished him to one of the spare rooms; the house was big enough. But what would be the point of that? If they were going to live together, they might as well be husband and wife. Besides, she loved him. They were happy together. Weren't they?

At least back in their squatting days they'd had an openly open relationship – though she'd been more hurt than she let on each time Arthur spent the night with someone else. Her own few forays into free love had felt forced and never progressed much beyond a bit of kissing. Now though... She wanted to feel desire, and desired. Her sex life with Arthur had become another routine – a pleasurable one, no doubt, but also one they often let slip. Arthur, she suspected, wanted something more. Well, he wasn't the only one! Most nights, it was true, she was happy to drink her linden tea in the bath and read her book. But sometimes, just sometimes, she wanted someone to rip off her bathrobe and take her roughly on the sheepskin rug on the bedroom floor.

Eleanor smiled to herself as she walked up the road. She

was rehearsing the story she'd tell Pete about Gaia butting the stuck-up London journalist into the pond. She imagined them laughing together.

Melissa sat in the armchair in Arthur's study, the Dictaphone resting on the edge of his desk. Part of the reason she looked so good in Eleanor's jumper, he realised, was that she didn't appear to be wearing a bra underneath.

"So," she began. "Your career started, literally and literarily, in a squat in South London. And now here you are, living in a beautiful house in the countryside, writing about English rural life and folk traditions. I'd love to hear a bit about that journey, as it were."

"Well, in actual fact I was brought up in the country myself, so it's not such a journey really."

She looked disappointed. "There goes my story angle."

"Sorry," Arthur said. "I'll admit that in the books I do rather give the impression of being an urban émigré. There! You can write about how I'm a fake and a fraud. That's a much better story for you."

EXPOSED! Arthur Aldridge's fraudulent faux-naif façade!

Melissa was looking at him intently. She had lovely dark eyes. "I don't think you're a fake. But I wonder if this is really you."

"Meaning?"

"That passage you read from *Wind in the Willows*. What was it? The call of the South? That's something you feel deeply, I think."

Mellifluous: that was the word for her voice. Flowing like honey. Mellifluous Melissa.

"Is this really something *Country Home* readers want to know about?"

She gave that tinkling laugh again. "Probably not. But I'm curious. It strikes a chord. For me, it's the Mediterranean. The Amalfi Coast. Or Zante. Olive oil and fresh seafood in beachfront restaurants. You know?"

In fact, Arthur didn't, or only in imagination. He hadn't travelled abroad nearly as much as he wished he had. Before children, he and Eleanor had spent a summer touring Scandinavia in a campervan, and they'd once stayed in a farmhouse in the Languedoc, but a daytrip to Marseille was all the time he'd spent by the Mediterranean. Since the kids, and the house, had come along they'd mainly stayed in the British Isles – Cornwall, the Brecon Beacons, the Norfolk Broads, the Hebrides – apart from a couple of camping trips to Brittany.

"Is that where you hail from?" he asked, wincing as he said the word *hail*. What a pretentious fool. "Somewhere Mediterranean?"

"My father is from Naples. My mother is from Hamburg. I was born in Kent. So I'm an English rose with Latin passion and Teutonic efficiency."

Arthur laughed, though he suspected it was a line she'd used before. Melissa switched briskly back into journalist mode. "So what's next? Can we expect another volume of tales from the Lime Trees?"

"Well, I could write about the time the goat attacked the interviewer and knocked her into the pond. Again, I am so, so sorry."

"Don't you dare! Though who knows, maybe I'll include it in my own piece. I need some sort of hook."

Arthur wondered if he was boring her. He didn't want to bore her.

"Actually, I'm hoping to get into doing more travel writing," he said. "It wasn't really something I could do with a young family – hiking across the Darien Gap, travelling through Yugoslavia in a donkey cart, crossing the Steppes on horseback. I'd like to do something like that."

She raised an eyebrow. "Really?"

"Well... driving along the Amalfi Coast at any rate."

"That sounds like my sort of travel writing. Reviewing luxury hotels, all-expenses-paid trips to five-star resorts. It's all about having the contacts."

"Do you get to travel much for your work?" Arthur asked.

"I see a lot of country roads around the Home Counties. Sometimes I get to stay in a Trusthouse Forte if they send me further afield. And I've done a couple of country house hotel reviews, so that's a perk." She gestured to the Dictaphone on the table. "But we're supposed to be talking about you. What can readers expect from *Like A Rolling Cheese*?"

"Well... Hilarious depictions of English eccentricity in all its glory, fascinating insights into bizarre traditions, profound meditations on the enduring power of ancient rituals in our secular society... that kind of thing."

"That sounds suspiciously like you're quoting the press release."

Arthur waffled for a while about the book. It was a skill he'd practised at university and honed during Q&As after book readings, talking eloquently while saying little of substance. Still, he thought Melissa would be able to extract a few decent quotes.

"What was your favourite, of the festivals you went to?" she asked.

Arthur thought for a while. "That's a difficult one. The Lewes Fire Festival, maybe. Some festivals feel very sanitised these days, but that one still has an edge of danger to it. And of course there's something very primal about fire."

"I've heard of it," she said. "But I've never been."

"Oh, you should. It's coming up in about three weeks."

"Are you going?"

"I think I will, yes." He hadn't thought of it till now. "You should come. You'd love it."

He had no idea whether she'd love it. He didn't know the woman. Still, he rather liked the idea of going with her.

"Maybe I will. I might get an article out of it."

"Well, let me know if you do."

She smiled at him with those big almond eyes. "I'll certainly do that." She tore a page from her spiral-bound notebook. "This is my number. If you wanted to clarify anything we've talked about. Or if you're ever in London…"

"You've got to hear what happened!" babbled Felix when Seb came into the kitchen. Melissa and Jason had driven off a few minutes before, Melissa having changed back into her own clothes, which had been rinsed and dried on the Aga. "Gaia butted the journalist who was interviewing Dad into the pond!" He insisted on Eleanor telling the story again, and asked for it twice more at supper.

"Jason said he'd send a copy of the photo," Eleanor said. "Though he made me promise we wouldn't tell her about it."

Arthur thought about the page from her notebook, folded away in the top drawer of his desk. He didn't say anything.

"Well, it will make a good story if you write another volume," Eleanor said.

"Uh-huh." Arthur wasn't sure there would be another volume.

. . .

That night, the wind began to roar and scream. It hurled tiles from the dairy, tore the roof off the chicken house and flung the corrugated iron sheets across the yard. It ripped off branches and knocked whole trees to the ground: a huge oak at the end of the meadow, an old cooking apple in the orchard, two of the beeches at the top of the bank in Brickwood.

Felix, waking in the early hours, heard a crash outside. The wind rattled the windows. He looked out, but it was too dark to see anything.

When he opened his curtains that morning, it took him a moment to register the difference. Something was missing from the skyline. The last of the linden trees at the end of the drive was lying stretched out across the gateway, a giant struck down in battle. He felt a rush of sadness at the sight. The linden trees had been a permanent fixture of his childhood, comforting and immutable: something he could always depend upon, like the warmth of the kitchen, the cooing of the wood pigeons, the love of his parents.

GATHERING
1995

Birdsong and sunlight slicing through the curtains. Over in Brickwood, a wood pigeon was cooing: *Was that you, cuckoo? Was that you, cuckoo? Was it?*

Today was the day. In a few hours, she would be here.

Felix sat up and drew open the curtains, letting the sun flood in. The most glorious midsummer morning! The leaves on the lindens looked freshly painted. There was no hurry to get up. A-levels were over. A summer of indolence stretched before him, and beyond that, the big blue cloudless skies of the future. He lay back and closed his eyes again, summoning the image of Izzie Martyn: Izzie tossing back her bronze ringlets like a pre-Raphaelite painting, Izzie's vast brown eyes fixing on his, Izzie's dazzling grin. He imagined kissing her, touching her, undressing her... Could those fantasies really come true today?

It seemed wildly too good to be true, but you had to admit there was a possibility. She liked him. She did! And she was coming here.

She lived just three miles up the road in Stourton. They'd taken the same school bus for years, and he'd watched her turn from doll-like eleven-year-old to indie dream-girl, with her purple Doc Martens and canvas satchel, on which she'd drawn convincing copies of band logos in marker pen – Nirvana, The Levellers, Ned's Atomic Dustbin, James – alongside the CND sign and a Greenpeace badge. She would like him, he had thought, if only he could pluck up the courage to talk to her. But they hadn't exchanged more than the occasional shy smile before this year. Then the play happened: *A Midsummer Night's Dream*, the annual joint production between the boys' and girls' grammar schools. Mr Copthorne, the tragically trendy drama teacher, had attempted to give it a modern twist, with the woods of Athens becoming an all-night rave. Felix was Oberon (a DJ), while Izzie had played Puck, her hair in dreadlocks and her usually prohibited nose stud glinting in the stage lights.

The production as a whole had been, truth be told, only a partial success (the boys' headmaster had publicly called it "brave" and privately, rumour had it, a "fucking abomination"), but their scenes had fizzed. And that on-stage bonding had carried over into real life. Instead of feeling awkward and tongue-tied, the way he normally did around girls he liked, he found he could talk to her. She listened. She seemed interested in things he had to say. Sometimes he even made her laugh, a delighted laugh that made the world two shades brighter. They bonded over Shakespeare and theatre, over books and music and a visceral hatred of the Major government. They agreed that Blur were better than Oasis but that Pulp were better than either, and that The Auteurs really ought to be massive. She loved Stevie Smith and Sylvia Plath and admitted to writing poetry herself, but when Felix asked if he could read it, she laughed and said, "You could, but then I'd have to kill you."

He began to orbit her social circle, finding for what seemed like the first time in his teenage years a group of people he felt comfortable with – misfits in brightly coloured baggy clothes and ethnic jewellery who quoted extensively from *Withnail and I*, railed against the Criminal Justice Act, and concocted elaborate theories about the hidden meanings behind TV shows from their childhood. They watched dodgy bands at the Arts Centre, walked miles along country lanes to rumoured parties, skived sports day to drink Strongbow and feed the swans in the park. At one party Felix had got off with her mate Jemma, who'd played a sober Hermia among the loved-up lovers in the play. She was cute, sang Tracy Chapman and Indigo Girls songs with an acoustic guitar and was really into him. It hadn't lasted though: it was Izzie he wanted. She was a generous hugger and they'd once walked arm in arm on the way back from a picnic in the water meadows, but he hadn't the courage to push things any further.

If she came here, she would see who he really was. He wanted to show her around his life, share things that were special to him. She would get it. She would get him.

Perhaps it would have been easier to have just asked her directly. Instead, he had organised a Midsummer's Eve party, inviting her crowd along with some old school friends. He'd not hosted a party before, but Eleanor had been cool about it, and even offered to provide a demijohn of cider. "Why don't you use the hayloft?" she suggested. "You could make it really special. Take up some cushions and lanterns."

It was enough of a pretext. He found her number in the phone book easily enough. He dialled the number, hung up immediately, sat staring at the phone for five minutes, then dialled again. Her mum answered, and when he said who he was, sounded pleased, as if, oh please god, Izzie talked about him? She came on the line quickly.

"Well hello. This is a pleasant surprise. Hold on, I'm going to take the phone onto the stairs." He heard a door closing, then her voice, more intimate now. "Mr Aldridge. What can I do for you, sir?"

He told her about the loft. How he was planning to rig up music and lights, put down some rugs and drape cushions and throws on the hay bales.

"I've got some Chinese lanterns – I could bring those along?" she suggested.

"That'd be great. Hey. I was wondering, do you fancy coming over a bit earlier in the day and helping me set up?"

There was a moment's pause which lasted an age. "Sure, that sounds like random fun! What time?"

"Well..." (Should he risk it?) "You could maybe come for lunch if you wanted, then we'd have the whole afternoon. I mean, if you're not..."

"Yeah, no, I'd like that."

"Really?"

"Really. It's a date!"

That was just an expression. But still. She wanted to come. She was going to spend the afternoon with him. And the evening. And in all likelihood, since sleeping over in a big group was the norm, the night too. Today was going to be life-changing.

It was nearly ten by the time he'd showered, done twenty press-ups and thirty sit-ups as part of his belated campaign to get his body into shape, and got dressed. She could be here in as little as two hours, three at the most, although of course the possibility of her not showing up at all and his whole life ruined couldn't be discounted. He boiled the kettle and made a pot of English Breakfast. Eleanor would be in soon for her mid-morning cuppa. She was probably taking the goat out. He felt a pang of guilt. That was one of the chores he normally did.

Since Seb had left for uni three years ago – he'd just graduated, and was now Interrailing round Europe for the summer – Felix and Eleanor had been the only humans about the place. He had come to realise how much she did: collecting the eggs, milking the goat, taking the laden frames from the beehives and cutting up the honeycomb that he now spread on his toast. Toast made from the bread she had baked two or three times a week every week of his life. Dough was rising in the mixing bowl by the Aga. That meant there'd be fresh rolls for lunch. Izzie was going to love his mum's bread.

Then there was the garden, the product of countless hours of labour. Picking the produce was a mission in itself: the daily harvest was way more than two of them could process before the next crop was ready, soft fruit by the bucket, lettuces like rugby balls, courgettes that doubled in size if you turned your back on them for a moment. She podded and strigged, chopped, topped-and-tailed, filling the deep freeze down the cellar with bags of fruit and veg, jarring and bottling, pickling and preserving. But she must have noticed that they still hadn't finished the jam from two years ago, that there were jars of chutney untouched since 1992, and that come October there would only be one person around.

Felix had an offer from UEA to study Creative Writing and English. Arthur thought it was a ridiculous idea ("You don't need a degree to learn how to write!") but Eleanor told him he should do something he was passionate about, even if he had no idea where it would lead. "Keep following what you love, and it will lead you to where you want to be," was her advice. Izzie had a place to do Creative Arts at Lancaster. Felix tried not to think about how far that was from Norwich. (It was 248 miles. He'd looked it up.)

The back door opened and Colleen burst into the kitchen, tail wagging madly. She rolled onto her back, tongue lolling, and he scratched her tummy with his foot, making her right hind leg vibrate.

Eleanor followed carrying a trug – carrots, radishes, lettuces – that she placed by the sink.

"Morning. There's tea in the pot."

"Oh, you're an angel, thank you."

She poured a mug and sank into her chair at the other end of the table. She was dressed in faded jeans and an old *Save the Whale* t-shirt, her hair – with just a few stray strands of grey – tied back with a spotted headscarf. She didn't look fifty, though just lately she seemed to get tired easily.

"So, all prepared for your Bacchanalian revels this evening?"

"I told you, it's a civilised gathering."

"Yes, well, I remember Seb hosting one of those and somebody having to be taken to casualty to have their stomach pumped."

"Please. Don't judge me by my depraved brother's standards."

"And is your... *friend* still coming for lunch?"

He ignored the emphasis. "Yeah, she should be."

She was waiting for him to say more. He wanted to. He wanted to tell her that Izzie was the most amazing person he'd ever met, that she was warm and funny and smart and so pretty, and that he was wholly in love with her. He wanted to shout it from the rooftops. At the same time, it felt too intimate to mention to anyone.

"Well. There'll be fresh bread for lunch. Maybe you could make a salad?"

"Make a salad?"

"Women like men who can cook."

"She's just a friend."

"A very pretty one. And a very good young actress I thought."

"Salad isn't really cooking, is it?"

Still, he washed the veg, fanned the lettuce leaves around the wooden salad bowl, and arranged the radishes and carrot thinnings among them. Feeling inspired, he went out to pick some parsley and mint. It was warm in the garden, the grass already dry beneath his bare feet. There really wasn't a cloud in the sky. He thought about adding some chives too. But maybe oniony breath wouldn't be a great idea.

He spent longer than strictly necessary adjusting the angles of the lettuce leaves. Then he picked a carrier bag full of peas and podded them in front of the test match on TV. Cricket wasn't really the thing to make the time pass quicker. But eventually the grandfather clock in the hall struck noon. And a couple of minutes after that, Colleen started barking and there was a knock at the back door. Felix's heart sprang into his mouth. Colleen seemed to have picked up his mood, and was wagging her tail furiously.

He opened the door, and there she was, in real life. Looking even lovelier than he'd imagined, wearing a summer dress she'd tie-dyed herself and her purple Docs decorated with Tippex flowers. Her forehead glowed with sweat.

"Hey. You made it."

They hugged. Colleen bounded over and attempted to hump Izzie's leg.

"Down!" Izzie said in an impressively stern voice. Colleen stopped immediately, and lowered her belly onto the ground, stricken with guilt. "That's inappropriate," Izzie told her. "We've only just met."

This wasn't exactly the beginning Felix had been hoping for, but Izzie didn't seem fazed, because Izzie was amazing and wonderful.

"This is Colleen," he said. "She's only a year old. She can be a little forward at times."

"It's fine," Izzie laughed. "Our dog does the same. Good dog," she said to Colleen, who brightened. "I left my bike in the yard. Is that okay?"

"You cycled?"

"Uh huh. It's a beautiful day."

It was. Oh god, it was.

"Your house is amazing! I always used to look out for it from the bus. Why didn't you ever ask me round before? I come past practically every day."

Could it have been that easy? All this time, he could have just casually invited her to tea one day on the school bus and she'd have said yes?

"Well, I don't really like your company, I just needed someone to help set up for the party."

"Oh, I didn't want to spend time with you, I just wanted to nose round the house."

"Touché. So... do you want to come in? Or go out? We could have a wander round the garden? Meet the chickens?"

"I would be delighted to make the acquaintance of the chickens."

"Actually, they probably want feeding." They walked back through the yard. Felix filled up an old zinc bucket with Layers Pellets from the sack in the dairy. Usually he'd make clucking noises to call the hens, but possibly women weren't attracted to men who made clucking noises, so instead he shook the bucket before scattering the contents across the yard. Fifty-odd birds came flapping towards them, pushing and pecking each other to get at the pellets, with Colleen herding the stragglers.

"Wow. That is a veritable flock of chickens. Do they all have names?"

"Of course. I don't remember them all, but my mum does."

A mother hen – a Buff Orpington, all fluffed feathers and protective clucks – appeared from the stable leading eight chirruping balls of golden fluff.

"Oh my days," Izzie exclaimed. "Look at them!"

"This is Susan Sarandon and her chicks." He tried to pick one up, but they were a few days old now and far too quick to be caught.

"Susan Sarandon? Are they all named after film stars?"

"No. My mum chooses a different theme every year. Alliterative actresses was a couple of years ago."

"Random. Where's Marilyn Monroe?"

"I think that's her over there with the topknot. Although that might be Brigitte Bardot. They look alike. The hens, I mean."

"Greta Garbo? Doris Day? Farrah Fawcett?"

They watched the chickens for a while as Izzie thought up more names, then wandered back towards the house, discussing who was coming to the party. Eleanor was putting the lunch things out on the picnic table.

"Hello. You must be Izzie."

"Hi. Nice to meet you Mrs Aldridge."

"Oh, call me Eleanor, please. Mrs Aldridge is my ex-mother-in-law. Will you join me for lunch, or would you prefer to go off and do whatever you young people do nowadays?"

"Are you planning to have any cider with lunch?" Felix asked.

"If you fetch it."

"Okay, deal." He turned to Izzie. "Want to come and get some cider?"

The cellar too seemed to please her. She admired old vases, enquired after the contents of the various demijohns, bottles and Kilner jars.

"So this is the famous homemade scrumpy? Didn't you bring some to Tara's party? By all accounts it's somewhat lethal."

"It is quite strong, yeah," he agreed, opening the tap on the cider barrel and filling a jug. "Tastes good too though."

Izzie liked the cider. She liked the bread, asking for an extra slice so she could try the honeycomb. She even complimented him on his salad. She talked easily with Eleanor, although she claimed to be star-struck. "We had loads of your books when I was growing up. I loved the Brixton Bunnies. Though my dad said they were commie propaganda."

Eleanor laughed. "Oh, I don't think that's right. I always thought of them more as anarcho-syndicalists."

The conversation and the cider flowed. They discussed favourite children's books and the appeal of anthropomorphism. Izzie asked about chicken names, gardening, beekeeping. She was witty and engaging and in every way delightful, and Felix could see his mother was charmed. Izzie offered to help with the washing up too, but Eleanor told her not to be silly, she was a guest.

"Your mum is so cool," Izzie said when they were alone.

Felix smiled. "I think she likes you."

"So it's just the two of you?"

"Basically, yeah. My brother's just finished uni."

"When did your mum and dad split up?"

"When I was eleven."

She gave his hand a squeeze. "That must have been hard."

It had been an earthquake. Perhaps the size of the house had made it easier for Eleanor and Arthur to keep things away from the children. And, with hindsight, there were signs he should have noticed. Arthur's waning enthusiasm for gardening, and his increasing trips away for work. That strange day out at the beach with Johnny and his dad. The framed *Country Home* cover that moved from the living room to Arthur's study after the glass got smashed. But Felix had had no idea that anything was wrong until the day they'd sat him and Seb down at the kitchen table, and explained that from next weekend Arthur would be moving into a house in Salisbury, and that this would be better for everyone. This seemed such an outrageously false statement that Felix didn't even question it.

But life carried on. From Tuesday to Thursday they stayed with Arthur in Salisbury – first in a rented semi on a modern housing estate, then in the handsome town house he moved into a year or two later with Melissa. He and Seb had their own rooms. They could walk to school in five minutes. Felix got to play a different version of himself – his town self, harder edged, more mature. More recently, there'd even been times he'd had the house to himself when Arthur and Melissa had been on one of their trips abroad. But The Lindens was where his true self resided, and the only place that felt like home.

"Has there been anyone since?" Izzie asked. "For your mum?"

"Yeah, well, that was part of the reason. I think she was already seeing him."

Pete came to supper just a few days after Arthur moved out. Before long he was a regular visitor, sometimes on his own, sometimes with Johnny and his sister Lindsay, who was fourteen and had an attitude and a body that made Felix uncomfortable. They began staying for sleepovers. Then after a few months, Pete moved in. It was odd, but okay. Eleanor laughed more than she had for a long time.

Johnny and Lindsay stayed with them every other weekend, not exactly guests but not residents either. The yellow room became Johnny's and the guest room Lindsay's, though they didn't leave much of their stuff behind. It should have been fun, having your best friend living with you, and it was in a way. When Johnny had come to play before, they used to spend most of their time outdoors, hanging out in the den in the laurel hedge, climbing trees in Brickwood, making up adventure games. But while Johnny liked doing that for a couple of hours, he had a much greater capacity for watching TV and playing games on his BBC Micro. Felix had never much cared for computers. He'd get bored just waiting for the tapes to load. Nor was Lindsay an easy housemate, alternating mainly between rows with her father and ostentatious sulks, though seeing her coming out of the bathroom wearing only a towel almost made up for it.

Pete tried. He dug the beds and took an interest in the garden, though he preferred his vegetables alongside a slice of meat to Eleanor's vegetarian creations. He learnt the names of several garden birds and a few of the chickens. He even showed willing with Gaia the goat, though she treated him with a greater than normal degree of contempt, and would try to butt him when Eleanor wasn't watching. DIY was more Pete's thing. He redecorated most of the house, renovating sash windows, putting in designer lighting, hanging the animal wallpaper in Felix's bedroom. It was Pete who had rigged up the electric socket in the hayloft. He'd wanted to convert it into a games room with a full-size snooker table along with a proper floor, heating, maybe a bar, but Eleanor had objected that they still needed to store the hay there.

"You know Johnny?" Felix asked.

"Tara's boyfriend?"

"Yeah. You know we were kind of stepbrothers for a while?"

"No! That's so random! I knew you knew him, but didn't know how you knew him."

It had been strange meeting Johnny again. After Pete moved out, they didn't see much of each other. Felix had gone to the grammar school (though Arthur objected on principle to selective schooling, he had been mightily relieved when the boys both passed their eleven-plus) while Johnny was at the secondary modern, and their paths rarely crossed. But then a few months ago, Johnny had turned up on the arm of Tara, one of Izzie's friends. The geeky boy Felix had known was now studying computer science at the tech college. Johnny had long hair tied back in a ponytail and a piercing through his eyebrow, and clearly didn't play cricket anymore. He smoked bongs and listened to techno and seemed several years older than Felix. But they'd resumed a sort of friendship – Felix was glad that Johnny would be coming tonight.

"His dad lived with us for a couple of years, but it didn't work out in the end."

The final straw came when Pete announced he'd booked a villa in Spain for all six of them for a fortnight in August. Instead of sharing his excitement, Eleanor had asked who'd do the watering and pick all the fruit and veg and look after the goat and might it not have been a good idea to discuss it with her first? Then he'd laughed unkindly and said she loved this fucking house more than she loved him, and that had made her cry.

So then it was just the three of them. Sebastian, aged thirteen, had proudly proclaimed himself the man of the house. But Seb's enthusiasms tended to be short-lived, and it was Felix who let the chickens out in the morning, collected the eggs and even learnt to milk the goat. He chopped kindling, took the hay to the horses, picked up windfall apples. "I don't know what I'd do without you," Eleanor told him, time and time over.

"Hey," he said suddenly. "You want to come and see something?"

Izzie raised an eyebrow. "Um... yes?"

Feeling a little light-headed from the cider, he led her up the steps to the top garden, along the vegetable patch to the fruit cage.

"You wanted to show me some gooseberry bushes?"

"At the back here, look."

"Oh my word. Is that what I think it is?"

"Yup." There were half a dozen hemp plants, each one over a metre tall. Seb had brought the seeds back from a trip to Amsterdam. He'd started growing them in the greenhouse, but they'd soon become conspicuous, so Felix had transplanted them out here.

"Does your mum know?"

"Yeah, she's cool with it. She and Arthur were proper hippies back in the day."

"Which would be why you call them by their first names."

Felix shrugged. "I guess."

"Can we partake? I mean, do you just pick it or what?"

"You're supposed to wait for the buds really. But you can still get a good mellow buzz on from smoking the leaves."

They picked a couple of handfuls of bright green tips. "We need to dry them out," Felix told her. They walked back to the house and up to Felix's room. He put the leaves in a bowl under the bulb of his desk lamp. Izzie drifted round the room. Sizing it up? Judging him? Would she think it the room of a cool sophisticate (the *Wings of Desire* poster, the Indian throw pinned up behind the bed, the print of *The Lady of Shallot* that reminded him of her) or an embarrassing little boy (the back of the door plastered with Panini football stickers, the large framed painting of the Brixton Bunnies which he hadn't taken down for fear of offending Eleanor, the wallpaper with cartoon animals that he'd worried was a bit babyish even when he'd chosen it aged eleven but had somehow never got round to replacing)? *Look at my CDs!* he wanted to tell her. Notice the Nina Simone and the Nick Drake casually resting beside the new Echobelly album. *Look at my books!* Or some of them anyway.

She lifted something off his desk. "Is that from a car?" she asked, holding up a silver pouncing jaguar.

"A Jaguar. Yep."

"You vandal!" she said, in mock shock. "I didn't think you were that sort."

"It came from the wood. There's an old abandoned car there. Me and my brother used to play in it."

"Yeah, we had an old abandoned Rolls-Royce in our garden."

"Did you really... oh, piss off!"

She laughed, and bounced onto the bed, crossing her legs beneath her. Izzie Martyn was sitting on his bed, wearing (holy Christ!) no more than three items of clothing. Her dress had slipped off her right shoulder and a mauve bra strap was showing. Should he try to kiss her?

Then she sprang up and went over to the bookcase. "Oh wow. Is that all your mum and dad's books?"

Brixton fucking Bunnies, ruining the moment. "The Complete Works, yeah."

"*Becca and the Racoons!* I remember this one."

"A classic."

"And are these by your dad too?"

Oh god. She'd pulled out *Not to Speak of the Goat* and *Digging the Dirt.* "Please don't read those."

The books had hung over him throughout his adolescence. That somebody at school should find out about them was a constant dread. There was enough in them for a boy to be ostracised for life: birdwatching, horse riding, a totally gay love of flowers, the plays he'd acted out with his teddy bears. But while his parents' work had provided a source of mild teasing about bunny rabbits, Arthur's memoirs, mercifully, had remained unmined.

She was reading from the back cover of *Digging the Dirt*: "'*In this hilarious follow-up to the bestselling* Not to Speak of the Goat, *Arthur Aldridge treats us to more tales of life in the country. From rampaging goats to broody chickens in the airing cupboard...*' Seriously?"

"Yeah, that actually happened. Cleopatra. She was one of my mum's favourites. She wouldn't have let just any hen sit in the house."

"Obviously." She resumed reading. "'*... there's never a dull moment at The Lime Trees.*' Oh man. Your dad wrote a book about your family? Are you in it?" She was already scanning through the pages. "Yes, you are!" She read for a while, then gave a snort of laughter. "The goat chased you up a tree?"

"Yeah. Gaia. She could be vicious. She had big horns and used to charge at people. One time I climbed a tree to escape from her."

"And you were stuck up there shouting for help for an hour while she prowled around the base?"

"No, Eleanor came and caught her and I climbed down. There's some poetic licence in those books."

It was true, for example, that when Gaia was in season, she used to pull up her pole and chain and go rattling her way through the village, and that most of the neighbours were terrified of her. But she'd never, as the book claimed, eaten other people's washing or been found attempting coitus with a golden retriever in the vicarage garden.

Izzie sat back on the bed and continued reading. Then she began laughing again.

"What now?" Felix asked.

"*The Henhouse Times?*" she inquired.

That was all true. It was a newspaper he'd produced, on an irregular publication schedule, when he was about eight or nine, reporting the news in the chicken world. It usually ran to four sides, from headline stories (*"FOX MASSACRE"*, *"MYSTERY HAYSTACK LAYER IDENTIFIED"*, *"CHICKEN HATCHES DUCKLINGS"*) to profiles of individual chickens, sports reports, quizzes and adverts (*"Dusty's – the garden's finest dust bath"*, *"The Ladder: an exclusive perch for the top of the pecking order"*). He'd done the headlines with stencils, typed the stories on Arthur's old typewriter, put it all together with scissors and Pritt Stick, photocopied it and sold occasional copies to family members.

"Okay, I was quite a strange kid."

But she was smiling at him. "I bet you were really cute. Can I borrow these?"

"Seriously?"

"I am a massive Brixton Bunnies fan, remember."

There was a strong smell coming from the lamp now. Felix crumbled the leaves into two king-size Rizlas.

"You smoke it pure?"

"Yeah. Tobacco's bad for you, man. It can be a little harsh when you inhale though."

They smoked one of the joints out of the bay window, looking out over the yard and the orchard – the gnarled old trees that produced tart apples of unknown varieties, and the newer ones his dad had planted. Beyond, the meadow basked in the haze.

"You're really lucky to have a view," Izzie said. "My room looks out over the neighbours' garden. I get to look at the massive pants on their washing line."

"I try not to take it for granted. But I sometimes forget how lucky I am, living here."

The joint was almost finished. "Do you want a blow back?" he asked.

"Oh, go on then."

He took the lit end into his mouth and sucked in the smoke, then cupped his hands round hers and breathed out. She closed her eyes as she inhaled, her mouth a hand's breadth from his. Then she had a coughing fit. "You're right, it is quite harsh. I feel... nicely mellow though."

"So, do you think maybe we ought to do some stuff to prepare for this party?"

"Ah yes. I forgot I was here to work. I brought those Chinese lanterns."

Truth be told, he'd already done the hard work: sweeping out the dust and the hay, the cobwebs and the bat droppings, shifting furniture, patching in extension leads and rigging up the fairy lights from the Christmas box. They hung Izzie's Chinese lanterns from the roof beams, along with some bunting and Tibetan prayer flags she'd brought. They spread throws, cushions and beanbags on the hay bales. Colleen, who liked the loft and had followed them up there, promptly claimed the largest beanbag. They put a tablecloth over some pallets and set out plates and glasses. Along with the demijohn of cider, Felix had bought half a dozen bottles of Summer Lighting and a bottle of white wine, Chardonnay, because he knew Izzie drank that. He'd turned eighteen only a month before, and was still amazed that you could just go into a supermarket and come out with alcohol. It wasn't considered necessary for party hosts to provide proper food, but he'd got some crisps and Twiglets, and Eleanor had insisted on them taking a big bowl of strawberries from the garden. At Izzie's suggestion, they fetched empty jam jars from the cellar and put tea lights in them. Felix did wonder if having naked flames, dry hay and drunk people might not be the best combination, but she was excited about the idea, so he didn't say anything.

After a couple of hours, the loft was transformed – no longer the dusty, scratchy place he'd played as a child, but soft and seductive, exotic, like something from the Arabian Nights. And it would look even better in the evening with lights and candles lit. They stood admiring their handiwork. Colleen seemed impressed too.

"Hey! Nice work us," Izzie said, and they high-fived.

"Yeah, thanks. You can go now."

She laughed and punched him on the arm. "So... What are we going to do now?"

"Want to walk up to the pond? Maybe smoke the other one?"

"Sounds good. You have a pond?"

They wandered through the orchard and into the meadow. The grasses either side of the path were waist high, bejewelled with buttercups, poppies and all the other flowers Eleanor told him the names of but he could never remember (Eleanor was scrupulous about the accurate botanical detail in her illustrations, even if this was lost on the vast majority of her readership). Bees buzzed in the clover.

"Whooah, what's that?" Something had just landed on the skirt of her dress.

"It's a grasshopper." He bent down and scooped it into his hands. She leant to look at it. "Hello, little fella." The insect regarded her with its beadlike eyes, nodding its antennae thoughtfully, then hopped off over her shoulder. "Huh. Bye then. Oh, but who's this?"

Cressida, Eleanor's thoroughbred mare, had come over to inspect them, nosing at Felix's pocket. "Sorry, I haven't got any Polos," he told the horse as she rubbed her head against him.

"I've got some mint TicTacs," Izzie said. She shook a couple onto her hand and held it out flat. Cressida gently nuzzled the TicTacs into her mouth. Felix and Izzie both reached out to stroke the soft fuzz of her nose. Their fingers brushed against each other, and Felix felt a shiver pass all through his body.

"Do you ride her?" Izzie asked.

"I used to. But I haven't for years."

"Why not?"

"I guess I stopped when I went to secondary school. Riding was definitely considered gay. Which is ironic, because it would probably have been a great way to impress girls."

"Dead right. Nothing sexier than a man in jodhpurs."

They strolled on through the meadow. "You're really lucky you know," she said. "Having all this as your back garden."

"I am, I know."

"Look at all those butterflies! You probably know all their names, don't you?"

"I know some." He pointed out a brimstone, a comma, a large white, a small tortoiseshell.

"What's that one?"

"That's a meadow brown."

"Because it's brown, and you find it in a meadow? They weren't that creative, were they, the butterfly-naming guys?"

"You want to guess what that one with the orange tips on its wings is called."

"An orange tip?"

"Very good. And that blue one – that's a something blue."

"No shit, Darwin."

They walked on into the paddock that Arthur had planted with trees nearly twenty years ago. They called it the New Forest – a joke at first, but now the young trees formed a leafy canopy, and the trunks of the willows had a girth wider than he could wrap his arms around. In the centre were the two old entwined trees that Felix and Sebastian called the Hugging Trees, and in the hollow beyond lay the pond, fringed with bulrushes and yellow iris, rosebay willowherb and meadowsweet. The family of Canada geese that had hatched on the island were slowly gliding round the far side.

"Oh my word. You didn't tell me your pond was in fact a lake."

That's what Johnny had called it, and some of the kids

from primary school. They used to come here every spring when the frogs and toads were spawning. Dozens of them there used to be, the rampant male toads forming great writhing footballs, suffocating the poor solitary female in the middle. You didn't get so many now. The village school had closed a few years ago too.

"The guy who lived here before my parents dug it himself, apparently."

"Bloody hell. That must have taken ages. Can we sit down somewhere?"

He led her over to the fallen sweet chestnut on the far bank. It had blown down in the Great Storm back in '87, but had sprouted extravagant new growth and still kept them supplied with bagfuls of chestnuts every year. The trunk formed a natural bench. He must have sat here a thousand times. He had no doubt at all that this was the best of them. They smoked the other joint, watching the geese.

"What would really make this perfect," he thought aloud, "would be if we saw a kingfisher."

You didn't see them often. Once or twice a year perhaps. And twenty seconds after he said it, there it was: that flash of iridescent blue. It landed on a willow branch on the island, and perched there perfectly still; their smallness always surprised him. They watched in open-mouthed silence for a minute or so. Then it took off, skimming across the water, a last flash of wing before it disappeared beyond the thicket on the opposite bank.

They were silent for a moment longer, then both burst out in delighted laughter.

"I've never seen a kingfisher before. That was like something God would do if he wanted to make it really obvious he existed."

They kissed then. It was impossible to tell who moved

first, but suddenly there they were, just like that, lips exploring then opening. Her mouth tasted of dreams and mint TicTacs. She smiled at him with her eyes, then closed them. *There is nowhere in the world I would rather be*, he thought, *and no one I would rather be here with. Time could stop right now.*

And it seemed like it did. He couldn't say how long they kissed. When they came up for air, she fixed him with the full, dazzling beam of her smile. "I was hoping you might do that," she said.

"I meant to do it months ago. I was just waiting for the right moment."

She laughed. "Well, you picked a pretty good one."

Then they kissed some more.

Hand in hand they floated back through the meadow in the golden light of the late afternoon. In the yard, Eleanor was milking Freya, the placid, hornless daughter of the infamous Gaia. She was singing an old folk song, "The Sweet Nightingale", softly to the goat, but stopped when she saw them. She smiled, just a little knowingly. It must have been obvious. They were both glowing.

"All set?" she asked.

Felix nodded. He was quite stoned, he realised.

"What time are people arriving?"

"From about sixish." Twenty minutes. Far too soon. He'd been looking forward to the party for weeks, but now he just wanted an evening with Izzie alone.

"I'll be out of your hair by then. People are welcome to come in and use the downstairs loo, but I'm planning a long bath with a book and an early night, so I'd appreciate it if they could be quiet. Keep the music down after midnight, and no smoking in the loft."

"Any other rules?"

"Have a wonderful time," she smiled. "Oh, can you shut Susan Sarandon in the stable on your way past? She should have put herself to bed by now."

The Buff Orpington had indeed settled down in the straw with her brood. Felix bolted the bottom half of the stable door, leaving the top ajar so the swallows could fly in and out. Then they climbed the stair ladder up to the dairy loft. The sun cast long shadows through the low windows. They switched on the lanterns and lit some of the tea lights, and Felix put *Dog Man Star* on the stereo. Then they sat down on the bales and started kissing again.

Too soon, they heard a car pulling up. "Guests," Felix said ruefully.

"Shall we pretend we're not here? Or shall we see who it is?"

It was Johnny and Tara, along with Johnny's friend Neil, who Felix didn't know well but who claimed to be a DJ. He'd brought along his decks and two massive speakers, and Felix helped carry them and three crates of vinyl up the ladder. Felix thought he saw some meaningful looks pass between Izzie and Tara, but he might have imagined it.

"This place hasn't changed a bit," Johnny was enthusing. "It's all so weirdly familiar."

Felix found another extension lead so they could plug in the turntable and speakers as well as the lights and the CD player.

"That's quite a load on one socket," Neil pointed out.

"Johnny's dad put that socket in," Felix said.

"Did he?" Johnny laughed. "It'll probably all blow up later then."

By the time they'd got the decks set up and flicked through the records – dub, techno and classic Northern Soul sprinkled with an eclectic selection of random charity shop LPs – other people had begun arriving. And soon it had turned into just the sort of gathering Felix had hoped it would be. Not loads of people – twenty or so. A few solid school friends, some people who'd been involved in *Midsummer Night's Dream*, some of Izzie's circle, but enough overlap between them that it all felt lovely and convivial. Felix, who'd spent most of his adolescence skirting the fringes of different friendship groups, felt like he was in the centre of things. These were his people, and this was his place.

"This is a wicked place for a party!"

"I love these lanterns!"

"Are we all going to sleep on these hay bales? I want the top bale!"

The gallon of cider disappeared within half an hour, but with the amount of booze people had brought there was little danger of running dry. Felix wasn't jealous when Izzie went off to speak to other people: he just missed her already. But she'd given his hand a squeeze when she left, and kept sending him secret smiles from across the room. He sat with Johnny, who was building an elaborate joint with three king skins.

"I remember playing darts and ping pong up here," Johnny said. "And climbing on the haystacks. Except I'm sure it was all about three times bigger back then."

"How's your dad?" Felix asked. If Pete had never exactly felt like a stepfather, he'd still been a major presence in Felix's life for a couple of years. It felt strange not to have anything to do with him anymore.

"He's alright I guess. He's moved to Basingstoke. And

he's getting remarried again. Third time lucky. And your mum?"

"She's good. Not remarrying though."

"What's going to happen when you move out? She going to stay here on her own?"

Felix thought about the jars of jam in the cellar, the freezer full of vegetables. It was hard to imagine Eleanor here on her own. But harder still to imagine her not here.

"Well, I'll be back in the holidays for the foreseeable."

Johnny licked the papers and gave the joint an expert roll between his middle and index fingers. He tapped it down with the poky bit from his Clipper lighter and twisted the end closed. "Can we smoke up here?"

"My mum asked us not to. She's a bit paranoid about fire. With the hay and all."

"Fair enough. Want to join me?" he asked, holding the joint up.

"Sure."

"I'll just go and grab Tara. Did you see where she went?"

"She's over there with Izzie. She might like to come too."

Outside, they were surprised how bright it still was in the evening sunshine. The four of them found a bright patch of grass between the long shadows in the orchard. The joint appeared to be a never-ending one, circulating at least four times, and stronger than the homegrown Felix was used to smoking. When it was finally finished, he lay down on his back looking up at the sky. Izzie laid her head on his chest, and he stroked her hair.

"Are you two...?" Tara asked after a while.

Izzie tilted her head back to look up at him, her face looking just as cute upside-down. "Are we?" she asked.

He smiled back at her. "I think we are."

"Oh my God," shrieked Tara. "Finally!"

"What?"

"Well, it's been bloody obvious you both fancy each other. Ever since the play. You two seemed to be the only ones who hadn't realised."

Izzie scooched up and kissed him on the lips. Tara applauded.

"So anyway," said Johnny. "I don't know if you two are interested, but we brought some mushroom tea."

"As in – magic ones?" Felix asked.

"No, fucking shitake and oyster, you dick."

Felix looked enquiringly at Izzie. "Well, maybe just a bit," she said. "Have you done shrooms before?"

Felix hadn't. He wasn't entirely sure he wanted to, but he wasn't going to say no to anything Izzie suggested.

"I did some with Tara and the girls last autumn," Izzie said. "It was... well. Minds were expanded."

"It was hilarious," Tara added. They both giggled.

Johnny got a thermos from his bag. He unscrewed the lid, and poured a cup of browny grey liquid. He passed it to Felix. "Mine host?"

Felix took a few sips. It tasted rank, like an infusion of old socks, but he swallowed it down. Izzie, seeing him grimace, fed him a TicTac. He passed her the cup.

"So how long before I start feeling something off this?" Felix asked. He was already decidedly caned.

"Half an hour or so," Johnny said. "It comes up on you kind of gradually."

"Are we going to go back inside?" asked Tara. "Or shall we stay out here for a bit?"

"Let's go to the pond," Izzie suggested.

Felix wanted to ask her to marry him right then and there.

"Oh yeah!" said Johnny. "The lake! Let's go to the lake."

"Felix has a lake," Izzie explained to Tara.

"It's a pond really," Felix protested.

"It's a lake!" Izzie and Johnny said together. They all laughed again. They seemed to be laughing a lot.

When they got there, Johnny said it was smaller than he remembered, and Tara said she wasn't sure if it was a pake or a lond, which caused hysterics. They lay on their backs underneath an ash tree, looking up through its branches. Back beyond the house, the solstice sun was setting behind the avenue of linden trees, but the sky above them was still a deep blue.

"What's your favourite type of tree?" Felix asked. It wasn't the sort of conversation he'd usually start with anyone outside his immediate family, but everyone seemed to like the question. Tara said hers was a weeping willow, which wasn't a bad answer, if a little obvious, but then Tara was a townie. Johnny said horse chestnut, and when pressed why started reminiscing about the giant one in the garden of the old vicarage opposite the school, where for a glorious few days in early autumn all the kids in the village used to collect huge, gleaming conkers, fresh from their spiky-silky grenade cases.

Izzie pondered for a long time. "That's an impossible question. Can I do a top five?"

"No, that's cheating."

"Tough. Okay. Oak, obviously, quintessentially English et cetera et cetera, particularly their silhouettes in winter. Beeches – specifically in late spring, when they're just coming into leaf and there's a carpet of bluebells below them."

"I like them in autumn too," Felix put in.

"Me too. Yew, because it's ancient and magical. Holly, because there's something pagan about it, and it's got attitude. Think I'd have to have a weeping willow too, even if it's a bit obvious. Oh, and the helicopter ones. Sycamore. And those straight up poplars in the water meadows. Lombardy poplars."

"That's seven," pointed out Tara.

"You really like trees," Felix said. He wanted to kiss her.

"Trees are awesome. Trees literally give us life. In fact, I've got to go and hug that tree right now." She got to her feet, went and wrapped her arms around the trunk, leaning her cheek against the bark. "This is an ash tree, right? Did I say ash trees? They're definitely in my top five too."

"That's eight now," Tara said.

"What about you?" Johnny asked.

Felix thought. "Lindens, I guess. For the ones along the drive. Particularly now, when they're coming into flower and they smell like honey. They kind of represent my idea of home. They're the first thing I see when I open the curtains in the morning, and the last thing at night."

Felix felt self-conscious, but Izzie smiled at him. "You get to look at your favourite trees, I get to look at my neighbours' pants. On their washing line, I mean," she explained, when Tara gave her a funny look. "Although... I've just realised they've got a cherry tree in their garden, and cherry trees have to be in my top five as well."

"Have you ever noticed the way trees just divide and divide and divide?" Felix asked.

"How do you mean?" Johnny asked.

"Well, right, okay. Everyone start by looking at the bottom of the trunk. Then follow it up till you come to the fork."

"Okay."

"So you can choose to go right or left."

"Okay, I'll go left," Johnny said.

"I'm going right," said Izzie. Tara said she'd go right too.

"Then carry on up that branch till you come to the next fork."

"Going to go right this time."

"And then carry on up that branch. You can keep going straight on, or you can fork off at any branch you come to. And so on. So you keep doing that till you eventually get to a leaf."

They were all into it now, staring up at the tree in silent concentration. After a while, Johnny called out "Made it!" Izzie shushed him, then a few seconds later breathed out a long sigh. "Me too. That was pretty intense."

"Hold on," Tara said. "I got lost. No, okay. I'm there."

"Okay," said Felix. "So we've each done one path. Now you can go back to the beginning and do it again, but choose a different route, till you get to another leaf."

This was met with stunned silence. Eventually Izzie said in an awed tone: "There's as many paths as there are leaves on the tree."

"It's basically a computer program," Johnny said. "It's binary, isn't it? At every junction you choose zero or one, and you just keep doing that over and over. That's basically how computers work."

They digested this for a while. "But isn't it really like life?" Izzie said slowly. "All these pathways you can follow. You make a decision, and it sets you off in one direction, and all these different possibilities open out in front of you. There's an infinite number of possible futures."

"Stop it," cried Tara. "You guys are literally blowing my mind!"

Felix was looking up through the branches, through the shimmering leaves, and he had the sense that the tree was growing before his eyes, pulsing with palpable life. Somehow, he could focus on a leaf way up in the canopy, pull it towards him like a hologram and examine it up close – eleven leaflets, each one a possible future. He was becoming aware that he was now feeling more than stoned.

"I believe those mushrooms are kicking in," Izzie said, reading his thoughts apparently.

The journey back was an adventure. The slope up from the pond – a gentle ten degrees under ordinary circumstances – seemed impossibly steep. Scaling it was an epic feat, and they celebrated with hugs and high fives when they finally reached the top. Tara stung her ankle on a nettle, but insisted it felt amazing, so they all stung themselves too. And it did, a tingling, tickling pain that was almost orgasmic. Then Johnny had such an intense experience blowing a dandelion clock that they all had to try that too. They searched for the grasshopper Izzie had met earlier, but were unsuccessful. The butterflies had been replaced by moths, which Felix and Izzie invented names for: twilight harbinger, speckled darkling, big fuck-off flappy.

The sky was a floodlit cyclorama: in the northwest, beyond the house and the linden trees, magenta bleeding into orange, and above their heads the blue darkening to indigo, Venus and the first stars blinking on. Profound thoughts about the vastness of the universe were trying to coalesce somewhere in Felix's mind, but shaping them into spoken words was proving difficult. The process of converting impulses in his brain into physical movement in his vocal cords appeared impossibly complicated, and the whole idea of his tongue suddenly seemed absurd. Sometimes waves of paranoia would sweep in and he wanted it to stop, to just feel normal again, to be in a safe bubble with Izzie alone, but then somebody would say something, or they'd laugh, or he'd become aware that the colours in the sky had changed, and it was all amazing again.

Drifting back through the orchard, they could hear the bass and beat from Neil's sound system, and occasional shouts and laughter. Suddenly Izzie cried out, "I've got something in my hair!" They all stopped. Something was caught in her curls, struggling to free itself.

"Hold still," Felix said, calm but authoritative, surprising himself. "Bend down a bit." It was a bat, a tiny pipistrelle. He held it firmly between his thumb and index finger, and it immediately went still. Very carefully, he unwound the hair it was tangled in. This seemed to take several hours. Eventually, he released the last tress and held the bat up to her: it peered at them with its little mogwai face.

"Oh my days! That is officially the cutest thing ever."

He opened his hands and it swooped away. "Izabelle Martyn," he said, very seriously. "If you ever need somebody to untangle bats from your hair, I'll be your man."

She laughed and kissed him.

They'd been gone nearly two hours, it transpired, and the party had progressed in their absence. A few people had left early, a few more had arrived late. Apart from a couple of stoically sober drivers, most people were well under way on their journeys into intoxicated adventure. A few couples were making out on the hay bales. Jeremy Tharby, usually the first to fall, was passed out in a corner.

The loft looked magical now, the candles and the lanterns floating in the air. "The fairy lights are actual fairies," Izzie whispered in his ear, and he saw exactly what she meant.

"I did really have a bat in my hair, didn't I?"

"I'm pretty fucked, but I'm pretty sure you really did."

"I'm pretty fucked too, but I'm pretty sure I've had a completely amazing and wonderful day."

"I'm absolutely sure I have."

Her face was changing in front of his eyes, as if he couldn't hold onto all the elements at once. He could see himself reflected in her dilated pupils. If he looked hard enough, could he see her reflection staring back at him, and so on into infinity?

"Shall we dance?" she asked.

"I'm a terrible dancer."

Izzie went over and said something in Neil's ear. He nodded, picked out a record, and soon "Groove is in the Heart" announced itself over the speakers, to a chorus of whoops. Izzie beckoned him, mouthing along: "*You are going to dance.*" And instead of pointing out that the rapper was the guy from A Tribe Called Quest and did she know the bassline was sampled from Herbie Hancock or any of the other nerdy things he'd normally say, he submitted. The music was sounding colossal, the beats pinballing around the rafters, the bass squelchy and wobbly, weird sounds swooping around in all directions in full Technicolor. They jived and jibed and popped, pirouetted under each other's arms and limboed imaginary bars, and their bodies seemed to flow into each other, and it was hilarious and transcendent and the song seemed to go on for ever and was over far too soon.

They collapsed onto a hay bale, kissing, laughing. Felix heard Johnny calling his name, couldn't work out what direction it was coming from. Finally spotted him with Tara and a couple of others over by the window, gesturing with a lit spliff. They went and smoked with them. The weed seemed to take the mushrooms to another level.

"We shouldn't be smoking inside," Felix managed to say.

"Fire. Hay. Whoosh." He mimed a fire, which made everyone laugh.

"We shall be extremely careful," Tara said earnestly.

"Extremely careful," agreed Izzie, stubbing out the end of the joint in an empty bottle, then pouring some water on top of it. "No fire. No whoosh."

And it wasn't a carelessly discarded roach, a lit match or a tipped-over tea light. It was a worn-out extension lead, overloaded with hours of amps and decks and lights, plugged into a socket rigged by an amateur DIYer without a circuit breaker. Nobody noticed when the old wooden floorboard began to smoulder. Then suddenly a hay bale was in flames, the lights and the music cut out, and people were screaming. At first they tried to fight the fire, throwing lemonade and beer at the flames. But they only made the fire angry. It ripped through the loft, gorging on last year's hay, tinder dry, and the floorboards like kindling. People were pushing towards the hatch and down the ladder. A few tried to help Neil rescue his records, but already the smell of melting plastic was mixing with the smoky hay and the acrid tang of the roof felt.

Felix stood mesmerised, uncomprehending. The magnificence of the fire overwhelmed him. He stared as the flames roared through a bale in front of him, leaving behind an intricate skeleton of glowing gold.

"Felix! Felix!"

Izzie's voice. He couldn't see her, but she sounded distressed. There was smoke all around, and he couldn't tell where her voice was coming from. He stared at the curtain of fire in front of him. Was that where she was calling from? He had to rescue her!

"FELIX!"

He plunged forwards (as Tara pulled a screaming Izzie

down the ladder). Where was she? What was happening? He felt dizzy, his bloodstream a whirling torrent of toxins, hallucinogens and catecholamines. He had to get to Izzie. This was all wrong. The phrase *up in smoke* came into his mind, repeating over and over, and then he was going up, up in the smoke, through the tear in the roof and up into the night sky, wheeling in the air like a swallow. Far below him, the flames danced over the roof of the barn, lighting the midsummer night. There was the house and its four chimneys, the avenue of linden trees. *Up, up, up.* He saw the garden and Brickwood, the orchard, the meadow, the pond... his whole life laid out below him. Rising, up, up on these new-fledged wings, up, up and away, the map of southern England unfolding beneath him, the Solent and the Isle of Wight, his home the merest speck on the landscape. But he could feel it still, pulling at him, calling him.

Felix!

Come back, Felix!

Come back!

THE BLAKE MIDWINTER

2008

J ulia missed making up the beds. It used to be a fixed part of her routine, every Monday morning after the children had gone to school. Stripping the mattress, taking the matching sets of crisply ironed linen from the airing cupboard, tugging tight the bottom sheet, inside-outing the duvet cover and shaking it into place with a practised flourish she was secretly rather proud of, tucking the top sheet over, plumping the pillows, draping over the bedspread, and an extra blanket in the winter. The satisfaction of a job well done.

They were skills she had honed nearly forty years ago, fresh from school, when she'd spent a season as a chambermaid in St Moritz: working every morning, skiing in the afternoons, dancing and drinking with wealthy Europeans till late into the night. She had received offers of marriage from a German count and an Italian film actor, but had returned to England and taken a secretarial job in a firm of architects. There she had met Glen Blake – moderately handsome, kind, going places in his career. He proposed, she accepted, and in what really seemed like no time at all, three babies had become three fully-fledged adults, and those memories felt like they belonged to a different person entirely. She still made their own bed punctiliously, and changed the linen once a week, but that didn't go far towards filling a morning.

She began with the small double for Alexandra in her old room, now a plain, neutral guestroom with magnolia walls and a taupe carpet, divested of all her daughter's things. It stung a little, quite how unsentimental Alex had been about it. "I've taken everything I want, you can chuck the rest away or give it to charity," she had said, but Julia couldn't bear to do that: china animals and snow globes had been carefully bubble-wrapped and placed in biscuit tins in the attic, along with boxes of school books, overstuffed photo albums, notebooks branded PRIVATE! Just in case. You shouldn't throw away your memories.

Ruthie's room was in a state of transition. Since graduating last summer, she had been transferring things to the flat she shared in London, carting away a little more with every visit, though only as much as she could carry on the train. Now there was a half-empty wardrobe hung with dresses she no longer wore, a gap-filled bookcase of psychology textbooks and Harry Potter, a forlorn collection of once-loved soft toys, a poster of three pouting black girls that said *Destiny's Child Bootylicious*, which Julia would have liked to take down, though of course she had no intention of changing things as long as Ruthie considered this to be her home.

Robin's room she had reluctantly redecorated the year before, though it still bore traces of his presence: the shelves with the enormous fantasy novels, a cupboard full of Lego that had never been fully put away from childhood, that she supposed he would soon be introducing to his own children. Though they rarely used it as a guestroom, it would do for Ruthie's friend. Marsha. Glen had laughed when she had proposed separate rooms for them, but she preferred to keep at least a semblance of propriety, and besides, neither of the beds was large enough for two. Ruthie had explained to them a couple of years ago that it was girls she would be bringing home with her, but this was the first time she had done so. Julia didn't disapprove, not really, although it wasn't something she cared to think too much about. But she couldn't help silently mourning the imagined grandchildren whose future existence now seemed less likely.

Robin himself would be sleeping in the stable flat, with Kelly and the twins. It would be good for them to have their own space. Particularly after the last visit. Relationships between mothers- and-daughters-in-law were often fraught, everyone said so, though heaven knows she had gone out of her way to make Kelly feel welcome in the family. There was a separate bedroom for the twins, and she had bought matching cots where they could have their strictly regimented naps in peace.

Julia took a cafetière up to the little kitchen, along with two packets of real coffee – she knew Robin couldn't function in the mornings without it. She'd even thought to get some of the redbush tea that Kelly drank. She wanted them to feel at home.

It would be good to have the flat lived in again. They had redone it that summer, returning it to the rustic-yet-modern open-plan living space Glen had originally envisioned, all oak and glass, which her mother had somehow managed to turn into a suburban bungalow, with chintz furniture and lace curtains. It was so much nicer now, Julia thought, then felt guilty for thinking it. This would be Julia's fifty-fourth Christmas, and her first without her mother.

She brought up a white cyclamen, just coming into flower, which she placed on the bedroom windowsill and an exuberant orange amaryllis for the breakfast bar. It really was a lovely flat, so light and airy in summer but cosy in winter with the wood-burning stove – just the place for a young family. It wouldn't do for the long term. Jack and Finn would need more space as they got older, and would probably want their own rooms. But they could always convert the space downstairs next to the studio if they cleared out Glen's clutter, or perhaps build out over the garage.

"If we wanted to enlarge the stable flat, how would we go about it?" she had asked, trying to sound casual, but Glen had seen through her.

"If this is about Robin, my love, you know I don't think it's very likely."

Yet there were so many advantages. That poky flat in Leeds was no place to bring up boys – three floors up and without any sort of garden. Robin could do his work from here just as easily – it was mostly online, he'd told her, developing websites. Web 2.0, whatever that meant. He could even use the studio downstairs – it was far bigger than Glen needed, and he only worked from home a couple of days a week. Besides, it would be good bonding time for them, father and son. As for Kelly, well, surely she'd like to have the chance to spend more time with her little ones without the pressure of having to chase after her career. And when she did decide to go back to work, Julia would be on hand to provide an on-site childcare service. It all made so much sense.

The twins had been an accident. Or rather, the pregnancy had – twins were always an accident, though not one that anybody could be held accountable for. Robin had graduated the year before, and had only been seeing Kelly for a matter of months when she had let herself get pregnant. Kelly was a few years older; she worked in public relations, and had a strong Yorkshire accent, although that wasn't her fault as such. They had married in a registry office. Alex dismissed the wedding as a PR stunt; Julia thought her eldest could be overly cynical, but wasn't sure it was the sort of marriage of true minds that would have taken place absent the twins' imminent arrival. Kelly had returned to work four days a week after half a year's maternity leave. Julia found this baffling: her children had always been everything, and the idea of packing them off to nursery at six months old filled her with horror. Equally, while she thought Robin a marvellous father, his own decision to work flexibly so he could spend more time at home seemed terribly unwise at this stage of his career. These were not views she would express in front of her children, or at least not directly. They thought her old-fashioned. Well, maybe she was, but was that necessarily a bad thing?

The south-facing windows gave a lovely view over the orchard and the garden. She could see Glen coming down from the top lawn, pushing the Christmas tree in a wheelbarrow. They always bought a rooted tree, then transplanted it into the garden to dig up again the following year. This one was on its third Christmas, but Glen had measured it and said it would still just fit. They had a little plantation now, five saplings growing up the hill behind the juniper trees. The oldest must be thirty feet tall now. Ruth would have been ten when it was planted. Where on earth did the time go?

She suspected the people who had lived here before had done the same thing. There was a row of fir trees at the near end of the field in descending height order, like overgrown children. The Aldridges. Their son Felix had been a few years above Robin in school. She remembered him from that preposterous production of *A Midsummer Night's Dream*, where Alex had played Peaseblossom, or possibly Moth.

Awful what had happened, though her gain, she supposed. She could still recall it vividly, seeing the house for the first time. Glen had been made a partner that year. They had three growing children, a puppy and a kitten, and they were finally ready to move to their dream home. To settle. They had looked at elegant Edwardian townhouses, timber-framed cottages with roses round the door, modern barn conversions, and there had been many she could have been happy with, but none she had fallen in love with. Then the agent had suggested they view The Lindens. It could benefit from some modernisation, she explained, and was in need of some repairs. There'd been a fire in the old stable block, but it had great potential.

"It's in the next price bracket, but I think they might take an offer. And you'd be getting an awful lot for your money."

The moment Julia saw The Lindens, her heart was set. She just knew: this was their forever home. Glen was just as keen, already dreaming up designs for the burnt-out stable and landscaping plans for the gardens, most of which they'd never got round to. And the children had been enthusiastic too. Well, not Alex, but then Alex was fifteen and wasn't enthusiastic about anything.

Now they'd planted five Christmas trees. How many more would there be?

They would decorate the tree tomorrow, in the afternoon, while listening to the carols from Kings on the radio. This was family tradition, and Christmas Eve was the right day for decorating the tree. People did it far too early these days. The beginning of December, for heaven's sake! Whatever had happened to Advent? And the lights on their houses: the flashing Santas and snowmen and candy canes. It all seemed rather vulgar and American. The new housing estate at Ashridge Grove was the worst – like Blackpool Illuminations, where there had been nothing but woods and fields when they first moved in. Nevertheless, she had deigned to allow some simple white lights to be hung from the linden trees along the drive this year, and had to admit they looked rather pretty. She had been nonplussed when Glen suggested it; for all his architectural sensibility, he rarely took an interest in the aesthetics of their own home. The children always loved dressing the tree though. The same old decorations year after year, but they all meant something. Some of the glass baubles dated back to her own childhood. There were tin ornaments she'd brought home from St Moritz as a present for her mother, and carved wooden animals she and Glen had bought, tipsy on gluhwein, at a German Christmas market the year they got engaged. The various decorations the children had made – from playschool through to GCSE art – seemed like newcomers by comparison.

She heard the phone ringing, and hurried back to the main house. She reached the phone, somewhat out of breath, on the twenty-fourth ring.

"Hello?"

"I was going to hang up after twenty-five."

"Alexandra, darling! How was the flight?"

"Horrible. But I'm here now. Or on the train. So, I get in at 13.45."

"Quarter to four? No, quarter to two."

"I'll get a taxi from the station."

Julia tried to argue against this. It was an unnecessary

expense. Ruth and her friend were coming by train too, so she or Glen could come and pick them up. Or come to think of it, Annabelle had rung to say she was popping into Waitrose...

"Who?"

"Annabelle, dear. She and her husband moved into the Fletchers' house a few years ago. I suppose you haven't met her. Anyway, she's terribly nice, and she's going to pick up some walnuts and some dates, because would you believe I completely forgot..."

"Mum, it's fine, I can get a taxi. I get taxis all the time. I'll see you soon, okay?"

Alex hadn't slept much. The flight from Shanghai had been full, so there had been no bump up to business class, and she'd had to settle for premium economy. She wasn't in the right state to handle one of her mother's convoluted logistical plans, but Ruth's train got in only twenty minutes after hers, so she bought a latte with an extra two shots and waited in the station café. She hadn't seen her little sister for a year, not since she'd turned twenty-one. All grown up. Alex almost didn't recognise her when she emerged from the 14:05. It was partly the hair: instead of the mousey bob she'd worn for years, it was cut short and dyed blonde, like she was Jean Seberg in *Breathless*. And since when had she worn a stud in her eyebrow?

"Hey sis." They hugged, then Ruth introduced her companion. "This is Marsha. Marsha, this is Alex, my high-flying, jet-setting sister."

Marsha moved in to kiss her but Alex instinctively pulled back and extended a hand. She was out of the habit of kissing strangers. You didn't do that in China. Marsha seemed momentarily taken aback, then shook her hand with exaggerated formality.

"Delighted to meet you, Miss Blake."

Oh great, now she probably thinks I'm homophobic, Alex thought. And/or racist. Now she thought about it, she remembered Ruth telling her Marsha was mixed race. Marsha's skin was the colour of her three-shot latte. She had shortish hair in corn rows, and was wearing suede boots with a heel that made her nearly a foot taller than Ruth. She didn't look dykey, Alex thought, and immediately scolded herself for thinking it. *God, maybe I really am homophobic.*

"Mum had some absurd plan about getting a lift with her walnut courier, but I'm paying for a taxi, okay?"

Taxis were a rare luxury in her childhood. They'd moved to The Lindens when Alex was fifteen – an age when hanging out with her friends in town was infinitely more appealing than being stuck out in the sticks with her family. God, she'd resented it. The last bus was at six, except on Saturday nights, when she would brave the late one to Alderbourne, used primarily by drunk teenagers, and a mile's walk along the unlit country road. Other times she'd stay over with friends in town, and occasionally Dad would come and pick her up. Christmas Eve was the only time she'd ever caught taxis home.

Town had felt like an exciting place back then. It seemed absurdly parochial as they drove through it now. They passed the business park and out-of-town superstores that her Mum laughably thought of as urban sprawl and were soon on the dual carriageway, heading out into the winter countryside. It was one of those misty English December days that never bothers to get properly light, the landscape all browns and greys. The horizontalness of it all was strange to her: the hedgerows, the patches of woodland, the ploughed fields blending into the low ridge of the downs. Alex's apartment in Shanghai was on the eighteenth floor. She lived in a vertical world, among towering cliffs of concrete and glass.

She'd always wanted to get away. Sure, that was what you were supposed to think as a teenager, but she had been strategic about it. She remembered her mum's reaction when she'd announced the degree she was applying for.

"Economics and Mandarin? Are you sure dear? You don't even like Chinese food."

"This is going to be the Chinese century, Mum. Someone needs to understand what's going on."

She'd graduated with a first, and stepped straight into a job as an entry-level financial analyst with one of the big four accountancy firms. Eighteen months later she'd moved to their Shanghai office. She'd been there three years now. Having executed her exit strategy so efficiently, she was less sure what came next.

Alex liked her old home better now. Or rather, she liked the idea of it: an oasis of tranquillity, a bucolic escape from the rat race. Yeah, right. She soon found the space and the quiet oppressive, and besides, more than a few days at a time with her mum did her nut in. She'd been over in London a couple of times during the year, but had been far too busy to make it down for a visit, or at least that's what she told her parents, and herself. And she really had been too busy to fly back for Nanna's funeral. She felt bad about that. She hoped Mum wouldn't try to make her feel worse.

The taxi turned into the driveway, and there it was: the row of lindens, bare branches silhouetted against the misty sky, leading up to the house, satisfyingly square and solid, a welcoming look on its face. Ruth felt that little surge she always felt: she was home.

"That's a lovely house," Marsha said.

Ruth smiled. "That's our house."

"Whoo. Get you."

Mum was waiting at the gate with Barney, their golden Labrador. They'd got him as a puppy the year they moved in: now he was old and fat, but delighted to see them. He waddled over, tongue lolling and tail beating.

"Darlings!" Mum hugged Alex, then Ruth. "And you must be Marsha." She seemed unsure whether to hug her too, but Marsha leant in and kissed her on the cheek. "Lovely to meet you, Mrs Blake."

Mum was smiling a little unnaturally. Ruth wondered if she should have mentioned Marsha was black. Not that it should make any difference, obviously. But as far as she knew, her mum didn't have any black acquaintances, and you didn't have to be a psychology graduate to see she wasn't wholly comfortable. Of course, that could also be the girl thing. She had been terrified by the prospect of coming out to her parents, spent sleepless nights agonising over how best to tell them. In the end, it had all been fine: sure, they were Tories, but it was the twenty-first century, they loved her, it wasn't a problem.

"Besides, perhaps it's just a phase?" her mother had suggested.

"No, Mum. It really isn't."

She'd always had crushes on girls, never had any interest in boys, and it was such a revelation when she went to uni and discovered a whole world of people like her. Bars and clubs where she could meet all sorts of women who wanted to do things with her that she had only ever imagined, and sometimes never even that.

She hadn't met Marsha at one of those places though. They'd known each other since the first week of the first year – Marsha was studying psychology too. She was the most beautiful creature Ruth had ever seen. Not to mention the smartest, funniest, kindest and sexiest. They'd become friends, and there'd been one drunken night just before Christmas when they'd gone to bed together. For Ruth it had been exquisitely, heart-wrenchingly wonderful, but Marsha had laughed about it the next morning.

"I love you to bits, girl, but maybe not those bits, yeah?"

But then one night last summer Marsha had come round to hers after splitting up with her latest total arsehole of a boyfriend. They'd shared a bottle of wine and were well down the second when Marsha said that what she really wanted to do now was relax in a bubble bath with candles, and somehow they'd ended up doing that together. When Marsha had seen the scars on Ruth's inner thighs from where she used to cut herself, she hadn't said anything, but had gently kissed each one. And then...

The day after that Marsha didn't go home. After graduation, they'd moved into a house in Haringey with another couple of girls from college. Ruth was interning with a mental health charity; Marsha was working with special needs kids in some scary city schools. They barely earned enough to pay the rent. And Ruth was happier than she'd ever been.

Julia, in green wellingtons and Barbour jacket, was eyeing Marsha's footwear. Ruth had suggested she bring boots. Marsha, who had never owned a pair of wellies in her life, was wearing knee-length suede boots with vertiginously high heels. Her coat was black PVC. It was weird seeing her here, treading daintily round the puddles in the driveway. Ruth hoped this wasn't going to prove a mistake.

Marsha had invited her to spend Christmas in Hackney with her mum and sister, who were lovely, but then Julia had done her passive-aggressive disappointed act.

"Oh darling. We'd been so looking forward to a proper family Christmas. Alex and Robin will be here, and they have much further to travel. And we're already going to be without Nanna."

"Mum, it's not like I'm dead."

"You should go, if it means so much to your mum," Marsha told her. "Why don't I come with you?"

"But what about your mum? She won't try to guilt trip you about it?"

"Believe it or not, it's not actually compulsory for mums to do that. Anyway, I want to see this famous country house of yours."

She was longing to show Marsha her home. But she was acutely aware that she reverted to a different version of herself when she was back here with her parents and her elder siblings. She was already feeling self-conscious about her eyebrow piercing under Julia's gaze.

"So, this is where I grew up," she said, bashful. "You like it?"

"It's insane! There's just so much space. Is this all yours? That field with all the trees?"

"The orchard, yeah. And there's a meadow and a pond beyond."

"What about the wood? Don't tell me you own the wood."

"It's only a little wood."

Marsha laughed. "Sure, most people have a little wood in their back yard. If this was London, there'd be, like, a thousand houses here."

"If this was Shanghai, you'd have a few dozen thirty-storey apartment blocks," added Alex.

Ruth wasn't sure if this was friendly, or subtle one-upmanship. She didn't really have an adult relationship with Alex. To Ruth, she was still the aloof, achingly cool big sister. She suspected Alex still saw her as the mousey twelve year-old she was when Alex left for university.

As she knew there would be, there was mistletoe over the back doorway. She took the opportunity to give Marsha a short but ostentatious snog. Julia looked away and straightened the boots in the porch.

Alex was surprised how it hit her the moment she stepped through the door: the sense of home. The house smelt of Christmas; cloves, cinnamon, satsumas. A fire blazed in the living room. On the Aga, there was a batch of her mum's Christmas biscuits and a large saucepan of mulled wine.

"It's a bit early for tea," Julia said.

Ah yes. Tea at 4.30pm was sacred. Probably too early to ask for some wine then.

"Alexandra!" Dad appeared from the hallway, carrying holly. "Would hug you, but I'm a tad prickly. I have just been decking the halls with boughs of holly, which is something one often sings about, but rarely actually does."

"Tralala la la," Alex said.

"La la la *la*."

Alex leant into his chest. Dad could be annoying and embarrassing, and one of the co-benefits of never getting married would be that she'd never have to endure him giving a speech or dancing at her wedding, but right now she felt nothing but love.

"I'm also fully intending to roast chestnuts on an open fire," he said. "There was a good crop this year."

Alex had never really seen the point of gathering the chestnuts that grew in the little wood up by the pond. You pricked your hands trying to get them out of their little green hedgehog shells, half of them were too small to use, and half of those they did keep would go rotten. You could buy a bag where they were all good and twice the size in the supermarket for next to nothing. Same with the apples in the orchard. Most of them looked as unappealing as potatoes, their tough khaki skins mottled with blemishes and maggot holes.

She'd been wearing the same clothes since yesterday, so she had a shower and changed into jogging bottoms, a baggy jumper and slippers. Her old room had an en suite now. She'd have killed for that, growing up. The kettle was coming to the boil when she came back down to the kitchen. The others were already there, Ruth and Marsha sitting on the window seat, their legs and arms just touching.

"I bought you some Lapsang Souchong, Mum. Not a Christmas present."

"Oh, thank you, darling. That's very kind. Though I was just about to make some Darjeeling. Or do you drink your tea green now?"

"Darjeeling would be lovely. Although, would it be pushing it to ask for a glass of that mulled wine as well?"

"Really, dear? It is rather early."

No alcohol before six o'clock, except with lunch on high days and holidays. Another unspoken family rule.

"I am still on Chinese time," Alex pointed out. "It's after ten in the evening for me."

"Homemade mulled wine is the best," Marsha piped up. "It smells amazing."

Julia looked taken aback. "Well, I suppose I can warm it up. So how many for mulled wine, how many for tea, and how many for *both*?" The last word was apparently distasteful.

"Both please," Alex said.

Marsha asked for both too. Alex saw Ruth dart a glance at her mother before saying that, well, it was Christmas, maybe she'd have both too.

"Yes, let's live a little dangerously!" cried Dad. "I'll have both as well. And maybe a whisky chaser."

Julia put five cups and the teapot on a tray, then took four goblets down from the Welsh dresser.

"Mum, have some mulled wine," Alex said. "It's Christmas."

"Oh, alright," Julia sighed and lifted down another goblet, her body language clearly conveying that this was a sacrifice she was making for the greater good.

"What time are we expecting Robin and his merry band?" Alex asked.

"Oh, not till very late," Julia said. "They haven't left yet. If they drive in the daytime it interferes with the twins' sleep patterns, according to Kelly. They have to have their supper – sorry, *tea*, then watch *In the Night Garden*."

"What's *In the Night Garden*?"

"It's this kids' TV programme," Ruth explained.

"It's kind of trippy," Marsha added.

After they'd finished tea, Alex ladled herself another glass of wine and took it into the lounge. She settled down on the sofa by the fire. She should probably call Grant to let him know she'd arrived safely. He liked that kind of thing. He was back in

Australia to see his sons over Christmas. What was the time in Perth now? Early hours of the morning. Okay, she'd call later. Maybe Skype him if the broadband here could take it.

Thompson the cat jumped onto her lap, kneading her tummy with his paws and purring. She stroked him under the chin, and he purred harder. Alex felt cosy. Or something more than that. What did they call it in German? *Gemutlich*. It wasn't a feeling she experienced much. Her apartment in Shanghai was stylish, airy, minimalist and calibrated to a fine degree of thermal comfort, but never *gemutlich*. She gazed at the glowing logs in the grate. There was something hypnotic about staring into a fire. She let her eyes lose focus. At some point she must have closed them.

"I'm sorry about the rooms. I really don't know if Mum disapproves of our sinful relationship or is just concerned about everyone getting a good night's sleep."

"It's okay. I get to play with your brother's Lego. And I have a view over the Blake family wood."

They were sitting on Ruth's bed. Marsha being there was weird and wonderful.

"It's an amazing house. You're well posh, innit?"

"Oh shut up. Anyway, your mum's house is probably worth more."

This might have been true. It was an unremarkable three-bedroomed terrace that she'd bought nearly thirty years ago for not very much at all. But it was in part of Hackney that was rapidly gentrifying and now tried to pass itself off as Islington.

"We don't have a wood though. Or fields, or an orchard. Or a lake."

"It's a pond really."

"I can't wait to see it all in the daylight."

Ruth had a sudden idea. "Hey, you want to see something now?" She jumped off the bed. "Come and have a look."

"You want me to admire your floorboards?" Marsha started talking like she was in one of those TV property shows: "The original floorboards have been carefully restored, adding to the period character..."

"Actually, yes, that's exactly what Dad had in mind. But no, look at this." She lifted up a loose floorboard and drew out a notebook with a maroon cover, battered and dusty. She passed it up to Marsha, who read aloud: "'My dairy – crossed out – diary. Henry Cook. 1940.' What is this?"

"It's this kid's diary. He was an evacuee here during the war."

She still remembered the excitement of discovering it. They'd moved in only a few weeks before, and The Lindens was constantly throwing up secrets and surprises. When she'd felt the loose floorboard, she hadn't really expected to find anything beneath it; she'd grown out of stories where that kind of thing happened. Discovering Henry's diary felt like an adventure. She'd read it from start to finish, and it had made her cry. The idea that a child from distant history had lived right here in this room, and left this book for her, seemed profound and significant. Over the years, she'd read it many more times, always returning the book to its hiding place. It had been her secret. She'd never mentioned it to anyone before.

Marsha was flicking through the pages. "Wow. This is gold dust."

"Isn't it? He really loved it here."

"What happened to him?"

"I don't know. At the end he says he'll leave the diary for when he comes back. I guess he never did."

"Did you ever try to trace him?"

She had thought about it often over the years: had imagined tracking down this kindly old man, who would come over to tea and tell her stories of the past, usually in the company of his attractive granddaughter. But she hadn't got beyond googling the name Henry Cook, which didn't turn up any obvious leads.

"He'd be nearly eighty. If he's still alive."

"It's got to be worth a try. Imagine if you met him. It would be one of those heart-warming 'and finally tonight...' stories on the six o'clock news. We should definitely do this."

She would too. That was one of the many great things about Marsha. She had ideas, and she followed them through. If she said she'd find Henry Cook, she'd find him.

"Hey, you don't have your own teenage diary hidden under the floorboards, do you?"

"I actually did for a while. But I burned it in the end."

"No! Some kid a hundred years from now might have discovered it."

"And laughed at my terrible poetry and tortured Sapphic longings? No way."

Marsha laughed. "I'd love to find a diary like that."

They'd just started kissing when Ruth heard footsteps on the stairs. She pulled away. "Sorry. I just feel like Mum's going to walk in on us any minute."

"That's alright." Marsha gave her hand a squeeze. "But I'm going to sneak in here in the middle of the night and ravish you, yeah?"

Half an hour later, they were sitting round the dinner table.

"So where are you from, Marsha?" Julia asked. Ruth winced. She'd been fearing this. Marsha smiled sweetly, and replied that she was from Hackney.

"And your parents?"

"My mother's from Epping and my father's from Lewisham."

Please don't ask where they came from originally, Ruth prayed.

"And where were they from originally?"

"Mum!"

"What, darling? I'm just making conversation."

"Basically Marsha, she wants to know why you have dark skin, but doesn't want to ask directly because that might seem a bit racist," said Alex cheerily. "Right, Mum?"

"Oh dear, I hope I haven't said something wrong?"

"It's alright Mrs Blake..."

"Julia, please."

"Julia. My dad's from Lewisham. His parents came from Jamaica. Their great-something-grandparents probably came from somewhere in West Africa but there's surprisingly little about them on Ancestry.com. But we do know there were slave traders on my mother's side of the family, so I guess that balances things out," she finished brightly. "Could you pass the grits, please?"

Ruth tried not to giggle as she passed the bowl of hummus.

It was nearly midnight when Robin pulled up in the yard. There'd been a contraflow on the M1, and they'd had to stop three times: a nappy change outside Leicester, filling up with petrol and Red Bull near Northampton, and a routine-breaking feed north of Newbury when Finn's screaming became too much to bear. Now both the twins were sleeping like... something that slept well. Like, not babies.

"We're just going straight into the flat, right? We're not going into the house," Kelly said.

Robin wondered if Ruth was still up, and if she might have some weed. Or he could raid Dad's whisky cabinet. He was feeling wrung out from the Red Bull and the motorways. He checked a sigh. "Sure. They're probably all in bed anyway."

With luck, they'd be able to carry the twins in their car seats and put them straight to bed without waking them. Robin fumbled around trying to unclip the seatbelts.

"Can you put the light on?"

"It might wake them up."

"Yeah, but I can't see what I'm doing. Jesus, why do they have to make this so fiddly?"

Eventually he succeeded in extricating Jack. He opened his eyes, gave a beatific smile, and went back to sleep. It was weird how two babies with identical genetics and the same upbringing could be so different. Of course he loved them equally and utterly, but God, life would be so much easier if they were both like this one. He handed the car seat to Kelly.

"Go on ahead if you like. The door should be open."

Inevitably, Finn woke up as soon as he felt the cold night air and began bawling. In the midnight silence it felt even louder than usual. It was startlingly dark. Robin had taken it for granted when he'd lived here, but now the absence of streetlights felt radical. The clouds had lifted: it was crisp and clear. He marvelled at the stars, how many they were and how bright.

"Look at the stars / See how they shine for you," he crooned, but this only enraged Finn further.

"Okay, okay, you don't like Coldplay. Fair enough, actually."

He carried the car seat and its screaming occupant up the stairs to the flat. Inside, Finn quietened down, settling into a breathy sobbing that, frankly, sounded fake. Were eleven-month-olds capable of faking? This one probably was. The challenge now was to get Finn off to sleep without waking Jack. The chances of this were usually about fifty-fifty. When Robin heard new parents complaining about the trials of having only one baby, he wanted to laugh in their faces. Parents with babies were supposed to be tired, he knew that. What he hadn't been prepared for was the chronic relentlessness of it. He'd had, not to exaggerate, maybe half a dozen uninterrupted nights since the twins had been born. It was like having a head cold you could never shake off, a fogginess around the edge of every day.

They had tried to avoid this. Kelly had read a small library of baby books while she was pregnant, and had decided (to Julia's consternation) that they would practise controlled crying. By sacrificing a portion of your soul as you left your tiny helpless babies to cry out their agonies and terrors, you could train them to soothe themselves, winning back precious hours of sleep and creating robust, resilient children who definitely wouldn't suffer psychological trauma in later life. That was the theory. The problem was, for it to work, as Kelly constantly reminded him, you had to be unerringly consistent. And he couldn't do it: his resolve would break, then he'd be patting, bouncing, singing, walking around the flat in the dark with Radio 3 playing its weird late-night stuff in the background. So yeah, it was probably his fault.

Robin checked Finn's nappy, but he seemed dry. He slipped him into his sleeping bag, did up the poppers, then laid him in the cot with an extra blanket. In the other cot, Jack didn't stir. Finn gave a few half-hearted whimpers but then, thankfully, settled. Ready to wake, all being well, in just under six hours. God, he hoped they had digital TV here now. Robin wasn't sure how he'd cope without CBeebies.

The wood burner had gone out, and the flat was cold. It was strange, sleeping up here. All the years that Nanna had lived in the flat, he'd never spent much time there. Occasional errands, moving bits of furniture, that kind of thing. Tea and biscuits sometimes, but mostly she came to them. He was glad she'd got to meet her great-grandchildren, even if she hadn't been all there in those last few months. Against Kelly's wishes, they'd taken the twins to the funeral, and there'd been something life-affirming about that, generations cycling on. Nanna would be glad they were here.

"You know the baby monitor isn't going to work," Kelly announced from the bedroom.

"What?"

"If we put the twins to bed here, we'll be out of range of the baby monitor. If we're supposed to spend the evenings in the main house."

"I'm sure we can work something out."

"Like what? If it's out of range, it's out of range."

"Let's talk about it in the morning, okay?"

Kelly was soon lightly snoring. Robin lay in the dark, shattered but not sleeping, off-white shapes and blinking lights behind his eyelids. His heart was beating too fast from the caffeine and taurine. He contemplated the mother of his children lying beside him. They'd been seeing each other for six months when the pregnancy thing happened. It had never been more than semi-serious. They'd met at some godawful business networking event, where they'd both drunk too much, and had ended up going back to hers. He'd left early the next morning without leaving his number. But they'd already exchanged business cards, and a few days later she emailed him at work, and they'd exchanged some flirty messages, then agreed to meet up for a drink. It was a relationship largely built on sex, facilitated by alcohol – both of which it now lacked. And here they were, two semi-strangers tasked with bringing up their offspring together. It wasn't so unusual, Robin told himself. Arranged marriages were the norm in most cultures and most historical periods, and they were at least a step up from that. In the animal kingdom, that was what it was all about: you found a mate, you raised your young, and it didn't pay to be too picky.

He leant over and kissed Kelly on the cheek. "I love you," he breathed into her sleeping ear. If he repeated it enough times, it might become true.

Christmas Eve: Julia felt it the moment she woke. Fifty-four years old and she still had a flash of the same pure excitement she used to feel when she was a little girl. She had always loved Christmas Eve best: the Day itself was always tainted with anti-climax and the knowledge that it would all soon be over for another year. She got up and opened the curtains. Venus was still out above the oak trees' eerie silhouettes, the twilight sky tinged with tangerine. There'd been a frost in the night – as close to a white Christmas as they could expect. Robin's car was parked in the yard. All her children and grandchildren here under her roof. Or roofs, anyway.

"Good morning. Merry Christmas Eve." Glen was awake.

"Merry Christmas Eve. Tea?"

"That would be lovely."

Tea in bed was sacrosanct. It used to be a weekends and holidays thing, but it had become a daily ritual; one upside of the children leaving home. How many more morning cups of tea would they have together? Quick mental arithmetic suggested a good ten thousand if they were reasonably lucky. That seemed a reassuringly high number. Julia put on her slippers and dressing gown and went downstairs. She heard the beating of Barney's tail from the sitting room, still delighted by her reappearance every morning. There was a light thump above her head as Thompson jumped off a bed – Alex's by the sound of it. She put the kettle on the Aga, then fed the dog and cat. She set a tray with their two special mugs (the last survivors from a set of six depicting garden birds – his a bullfinch, hers a wren – that they'd bought at a village jumble sale) and a milk jug, made a pot of English Breakfast and covered it with the tea cosy that had been one of Nanna's last crochet projects.

Back in bed, they drank their tea in companionable silence. Glen read his Malcolm Gladwell, while Julia walked herself through the day ahead. Breakfast: there was porridge, muesli, crumpets, plenty of bread for toasting, eggs and bacon, a mini Kellogg's variety pack for the twins even though Kelly wouldn't approve, orange juice. Providing a good breakfast was a pleasure and a duty. She worried that her children failed to breakfast properly away from home. Alex had told her they had Chinese food for breakfast in China, which seemed utterly preposterous although she supposed it made sense. Robin seemed to subsist largely on coffee, and Ruth's eating had always been a worry. Anorexia, mercifully, had turned out to be just a phase, but vegetarianism seemed to have stuck. But then so many young people seemed to be vegetarian now, this Marsha girl too. That reminded her: she'd used chicken stock in the parsnip soup for lunch. She should probably make a separate batch. Although would they actually notice? They would have quiches for supper: ham and cheese, leek and mushroom, broccoli and salmon. That would be mostly vegetarian. Some coleslaw on the side, and some jacket potatoes. What else? She would spend plenty of time with the twins, so Robin and Kelly could have a break. Decorating the tree, of course. It would be nice to go for a walk if the day stayed clear. Perhaps some carols round the piano in the evening? There should be enough crumpets left to toast over the fire for teatime – the children loved that. Although they weren't children anymore, she reminded herself.

When she went back downstairs, she found Alex already in the kitchen, drinking tea without milk.

"Good morning darling. Sleep well?"

"Not really. Bit jetlagged. I was awake for ages in the middle of the night."

"Breakfast?"

"Thanks, I might in a bit. You don't have WiFi, do you? Wireless internet?"

"No I don't think so. There's a cable that plugs into the phone thingy. Your father was talking about getting it for the office, but I don't think he has yet."

"Okay, never mind. I'll 'plug into the phone thingy'." That withering tone of voice: Alex had had it since she was about five. "I should check my emails," she added.

"On Christmas Eve?"

Alex shrugged. "It's a normal work day in China. And I wanted to Skype Grant before it gets too late over there."

"That's all still going, is it? Going well, I mean." She didn't want to pry, but she did wish her firstborn would be a little more forthcoming about the man in her life. "You know he would have been very welcome here for Christmas. Or anytime."

"I know. He's spending Christmas with his kids, in Australia."

"Two boys, wasn't it?"

"Yes, two boys. Twelve and ten. No, I haven't met them. No, he doesn't want any more kids, and yes, I'm fine with that."

It felt like a kick in the stomach. Alex had said it before, of course, that she didn't want children. And she had plenty of time to change her mind. But it still hurt. Maybe she really meant it. Or maybe she would waste the prime of her life with this man, only to realise her mistake after it was too late. Or what if they did decide to have a family after all, but stayed out there in China or moved to Australia and only came to visit every few years? "You have to let them live their own lives," Glen would tell her. And of course he was right. But why couldn't those lives be a little more like the ones she'd imagined: nice young men, white weddings, a bevy of cousins playing hide-and-seek in the garden on their frequent extended visits to their beloved grandparents...?

"Oh yes, I know. Mrs Career Woman," she sighed.

"It's *Ms* Career Woman, Mum. I'll be in the study."

It was just like the old days, Alex thought as she plugged the Ethernet cable into her laptop in the study. She used to spend hours in here, spinning on the desk chair talking to her friends, getting shouted at for monopolising the phone line. Just three or four years later and she'd have had her own mobile. Though they'd probably have found a way to argue about that. Dad had bought her a Nokia brick that seemed cutting edge when she left for university. Now her phone took photos. You could even access the internet.

She opened Skype. There was a green dot on Grant's avatar – a smiley with a corked hat, his comedy Aussie shtick. She clicked on the video camera. *Connecting... connecting... ringing...* A fuzzy version of Grant's face flickered onto the screen, then froze.

"Hello? Hello?"

The internet was a remarkable thing. Connecting you, instantly and free, with people all over the world. Unless, apparently, you were in rural Wiltshire. She wondered how Dad could stand it. Maybe it was faster in the office.

Bad line. I'll try calling you.

This time she could hear him, with a slight delay, but the images were like turning the pages of a flick-book very slowly.

"Can you see me?" she asked.

"I've got a frozen close-up of you frowning at the camera, and to be frank, babe, it's not the most flattering. Shall we switch off the video?"

Audio only was better, although Grant sometimes sounded like he was underwater. "You're not actually in a swimming pool, are you?"

"No, but I will be as soon as I'm off this call. Then we're off to the beach."

"Yeah, well, we've got twelve inches of snow."

"Seriously?"

"No."

"Next year, I'm bringing you here for a proper Christmas. Shrimp on the barbie, chilled white wine, perfect."

Next Christmas. Would they be together next Christmas?

"Or Bali," he was saying. "We should do Christmas in Bali."

Alex earned an absurd salary, but Grant's was in another league. If he wanted to book a beachfront villa in Bali over Christmas, that's what he'd do. Although quite possibly he had a friend who owned one. Grant had friends who owned yachts, who spent half their lives in airport Platinum lounges and never had to travel in cattle class. Alex thought she'd like that kind of freedom. She was pretty sure she could do what he did: management consultancy was basically blagging. As she got older, she was realising that most adults were just winging it: she was still the smartest kid in the class.

The line suddenly went dead. She tried calling back, but the connection was cutting out.

> Sorry – shitty broadband here

> OK. Want to keep trying?

> Or shall I just go for a swim now?

Alex heard the back door open. Barney started barking frantically, and at least one baby began crying.

> you go. sounds like my nephews are in da house. speak tomorrow. Happy Christmas!

> You too. Love you xxx

> love you too xxx

Did she? She supposed so. She enjoyed his company.

She liked his life. Sex showed no sign of becoming boring. He was generous, gallant, supremely confident. He cared about her and respected her. Would she miss him if he wasn't part of her life? Of course. Was she missing him at the moment? Not particularly. Was she missing out on something more? Maybe. But then again, maybe not.

Barney burst into the study, tail wagging furiously, thrilled that she was still here and desperate to show her the fascinating new creatures that had just come into the house. *Come on!* he was clearly saying. *This is going to be the best Christmas ever!*

"Okay you ridiculous dog, I'm coming. Let's go and meet us some babies."

Marsha was sitting in the window seat in the lounge, watching the bird table. "You get so many birds here."

It was one of those things Ruth had always taken for granted, but she missed them in London. "Yeah. When Thompson isn't around, anyway. He's the cat," she added.

"Ah. Not the butler?"

"Piss off. And scooch up." Ruth put an arm round her waist, and Marsha leant back into her. "What birds have you seen?"

"Um, a robin. Very Christmassy. And, um... a little blue one."

"A blue tit?"

"Don't ask me. I can do a robin. That's it."

"Oh come on. You must know more birds than that."

"Duck. Swan. Penguin. Flamingo. I haven't seen any of them though. There, that one." She pointed to the birdfeeder.

"Yeah, that's a blue tit. And the larger one is a great tit."

"That greeny one? Hey, there's two of them. I'm going to tell your mum I've seen a pair of great tits!"

"Don't you dare."

"Hey, what's that one? It's feeding upside down."

"Maybe a nuthatch? Ask my dad, he knows this stuff."

"I think I'm going to become a birdwatcher. I'm going to learn the names of all the birds. Like the kid with the diary. Look, there's the robin again."

She kept looking out the window, absorbed.

A stroll up to the pond and back took an adult about fifteen minutes. It took them twice that long just to leave the house. It was cold outside, still below freezing. The twins were wearing at least four layers underneath their matching snowsuits, along with their Thomas the Tank Engine hats and scarves, and mittens that enraged Finn. Kelly had insisted on packing sippy cups with warm water, fruit bars and two packets of mini rice cakes, along with nappies, wipes, change mat, hand sanitiser, muslins, two spare baby grows, Finn's sanity-threatening singing Iggle Piggle, Jack's cloth-eared rabbit, a pair of teething rings and some blankets.

"We should probably take a compass and a tent too," Robin said. Kelly didn't laugh.

Setting Finn onto his shoulders, he caught an unmistakeable whiff. "Oh great. Someone's got a pooey bottom. Great timing, dude."

Finn began wailing as Robin removed his snow suit. "We could play pass-the-parcel?" Robin suggested. "Take it in turns to unwrap a layer. The winner gets a nappy full of baby shit?" Kelly remained unamused.

Finally, babies clean and dry and wrapped up like

papooses, they made their way outside. There was some further delay as a spare pair of wellies was found for Marsha, it being decided that, even though the ground was frozen hard, her suede boots were not appropriate footwear, and the heels would be totally unsuitable if the pond had iced over.

Grandma – it felt weird calling her that – insisted on taking the twins, who seemed keen to walk, though neither could yet do so unsupported. Barney, delighted to find faces at his level, gave both of them a good lick, which made Jack laugh and Finn cry again. Robin saw Kelly recoil in disgust. Thankfully, she restrained herself from getting out the antibacterial wipes. She was walking with Marsha. Ruth's girlfriend. That sounded weird too. It was something his friends used to joke about, when she'd made it clear that she didn't fancy any of them – although as Alex had pointed out at the time, that might simply have been because his friends were dickheads. He felt bad now about the teasing. And fair play to her, Marsha was smoking hot. Kelly seemed pleased to have another outsider to latch onto. Kelly was a good talker: she kept up a continual stream of questions, which made it seem like she was genuinely interested in you and everything you were saying. When he first met her, Robin had thought she found him fascinating. It was only later that he realised that she used the same conversational technique with everybody.

"You look like you've aged about ten years since I saw you last," Alex said.

"Gee thanks, Sis. You don't look so great yourself."

"No, but I shall be over my jetlag by tomorrow, whereas you have years more broken sleep to look forward to."

"Not making you feel broody?"

"Fuck no," Alex said, with an exaggerated shudder.

"That just makes me think of Mum's chickens," Ruth said. "You remember the one that went broody on the shoe rack in the porch?"

They slipped into childhood reminiscence. It was easier than talking about serious things. The guy who'd lived there before, Felix Aldridge's dad, had written a book about all the *Good Life* type stuff he and his family had done. Julia and Glen had had ideas about emulating it when they first moved in, but it didn't last. They'd inherited a load of chickens from the Aldridges, but after a fox got into the run and killed a dozen hens Julia gave the rest away. She kept the flowerbeds beautifully tended, and Glen grew tomatoes and cucumbers in the greenhouse, but the massive vegetable patch in the top garden was mostly a jungle of weeds and brambles. Glen said it was good for the wildlife, though everyone suspected this was because he couldn't be bothered to clear it.

They walked up past the Christmas trees and into the field. Sometimes Mr Brewster grazed his cows there, but for now it was an empty sweep of cracked frosty ground. It was an absurd amount of land to own, Robin thought. They weren't really country people. Still, he missed it when he was in Leeds, in the third floor flat they rented, staring at his iMac all day. Sometimes he'd take his bike on the train out to Ilkley and go pedalling onto the moor. The landscape was different up there though: wider, wilder, belonging to no one.

"When are you heading back?" Alex asked.

"Probably Boxing Day night, so the kids sleep in the car." Where to spend the holidays had been the subject of intense political negotiation. Kelly had eventually agreed to Christmas at The Lindens and New Year with her folks, though not without making it clear that she expected repayment for this concession.

"I'm leaving the next day," Alex said.

"Back to China?"

"No. Some friends from uni have rented a house in Cornwall over New Year's. I haven't told Mum yet."

"I guess Ruthie gets to be the favourite child."

"We were going to leave then too, actually. Although Marsha says she likes it here."

"Give her another day or two with Mum," Alex said.

In the little wood before the pond, frosted leaves crunched underfoot. They could see their breath on the air. "I reckon the pond might be frozen and all," Robin said.

He was right. There was an opaque layer of ice from bank to bank. Holding onto a willow branch for support, Robin set one foot on it, then the other. It held his weight. He gave a couple of small stamps. "It seems solid," he called. He threw a stick out into the middle of the pond. Barney barked with excitement and chased after it, legs skittering. The ice looked at least an inch thick. Robin let go of the branch. It wasn't deep here – the worst that could happen was a wet boot – but there was always something deliciously dangerous about trusting the ice for the first time. He tried a few slides.

"Robin, are you sure that's safe?" Kelly was looking unimpressed.

"It's fine. Come on!"

He slid over to the bank and offered his hand. Kelly was hesitant, but Marsha had already grabbed Ruth and soon they were attempting a skaters' waltz. With surprising elegance, considering they were wearing wellies. Alex followed, more tentatively.

"I think I'll just watch," Kelly said.

"Oh, come on." Really, why would you not skate on a frozen pond on Christmas Eve? And why would you want to be married to someone like that?

But eventually she did. And lo and behold, she enjoyed it. Hand in hand, they circled round the island, disturbing a coot, which flapped away to the far bank, *coot-coot*-ing in annoyance.

"What's that?" Marsha asked Ruth.

"A moorhen. No, a coot."

"Coots are cute. Cute coots."

"They're really not," Robin said. "They peck their weaker chicks to death."

"Oh." Marsha considered this for a moment. "Coots are brutes."

"You'll understand when you have kids of your own," Robin said. He expected Kelly to give him one of her looks, but to his surprise, she laughed. She looked good in a woolly hat. Her cheeks were rosy with the cold, and her eyes were sparkling like frost. They began skating in step, picking up the pace. He gave her hand a squeeze. It felt almost romantic.

Then there was a loud creak like a branch breaking. A crack appeared, a fork of lightning across the pond. The ice held, but the mood was broken. "I knew this wasn't safe," Kelly muttered, letting go of his hand as soon as they were back on solid ground. Still, there'd been something there, fragile and fleeting as it was. Something worth clinging onto.

Barney was sprawled on the hearthrug in front of the merrily crackling fire, a treble voice on the radio was piping "Once in Royal David's City", and the kids were rummaging in the Christmas box. Julia, sat in her favourite armchair with Thompson purring in her lap, felt she should feel a sense of deep contentment. This was the life she had poured everything into: family, little rituals and traditions, moments rich with meaning and memories. Home. Yet it was already diluted with a sense of melancholy. They were rare, now, rare and precious, these times when they were all together. And they were only going to get rarer.

Glen was at the bay window with Marsha, identifying garden birds. She seemed like a nice girl. Ruth was happy, Julia could see that. She'd always been a quiet one, off in her own world half the time, and not without her teenage troubles, though where they came from Julia didn't know; she struggled to see what more she and Glen could have done for their children. But there was a confidence about her youngest this visit that she hadn't seen before, and a maturity. Well, she was a woman now, that was what it was. How had that happened?

As for Robin, he had aged even faster, though not in a good way. He looked shattered, poor thing, and must have lost a stone since she last saw him. He'd always been such a sunny boy, and even now he had that ability to light up the room when he was in the mood, but he seemed to have lost something of his sparkle. Still, he was relaxing at last, now Kelly had taken the twins up to the stable flat for their afternoon nap. She and Kelly had been scrupulously polite with each other, and friendly on the surface. Still, she knew Kelly had cast her in the role of interfering mother-in-law. It wasn't that Julia was deliberately critical or difficult. But she had strong convictions when it came to parenting, and there were unwritten rules, a certain etiquette she expected in her house. And really, it was absurd to be feeding the boys those expensive Ella's Kitchen pouches without even trying them on the soup.

"Mum, why have you kept all this crap?" Alex asked, holding up a cotton wool snowman. He had long lost his felt hat and nose.

"You made that in primary school," Julia told her.

"Nah, it was your G.C.S.E. art project, wasn't it?" teased Robin.

"Haha. I was always shit at arts and crafts though. Unlike you," she added to Ruth, taking out a miniature Christmas tree made of Fimo. "I was really jealous when you made this. I used to try and hide it round the back of the tree."

"I know you did. I'd move it back."

There had, Julia had to acknowledge, always been squabbles. About whose decorations went where, who got to put the angel on top, which setting to have the lights on. They could be quite brutal; tears were not uncommon. But that wasn't what she remembered: she remembered the glow of candlelight, happy faces reflected in baubles, everyone singing the chorus of "Ding Dong Merrily on High".

Alex poured herself another glass of Bailey's. Julia suppressed the urge to tut. Alex was twenty-seven years old, and she'd bought it herself in the duty free. Perhaps Julia was worrying too much, but the amount Alex drank bothered her. Young women drank too much these days: she'd seen the pictures in the papers, scantily clad girls passing out in the high street. More than once when Alex was a teenager, she'd come home from a party hideously drunk, and Julia had looked after her as tenderly and intimately as when she was a baby, wiping vomit from her face, helping her into her nightie. Usually though, a drunken Alex was obnoxious and aggressive. Well, she'd grow out of it. Wouldn't she?

Thompson was watching the decorating of the tree thoughtfully. As a kitten, he couldn't keep away from the toy-dispensing climbing frame, clambering all over it, batting fragile decorations to the floor. And for several years, he had kept up the tradition of undecorating the tree the day it was put up. These days, to Julia's relief, he contented himself with swinging the occasional paw at a low-hanging ornament.

Glen came over and put some more logs on the fire. "Well, Marsha can now identify several birds that she'd never heard of ten minutes ago," he announced.

"I've never seen so many tits," Marsha said. Julia felt herself blushing. "Blue tit, great tit, long-tailed tit, coal tit. Also robin – which I already knew, thank you very much. Nuthatch, house sparrow, chaffinch, greenfinch, goldfinch... pinkfinch."

"Bullfinch," Glen corrected.

"Bullfinch. That's eleven."

"Coot," prompted Ruth.

"Coot. Twelve."

"There must be more. Blackbird."

"Don't call me that."

Ruth laughed and went on before Julia had caught up with the joke. "Pigeon. Magpie. Swan."

"Mallard?" suggested Robin.

"What's a mallard?"

"You know, the ducks. With the green heads?"

"I thought they were just ducks."

Glen laughed. "We've had at least five species of duck just on our pond. Mallard, tufted duck, pochard, wigeon, teal..."

"Stop! My birdbrain is going to break."

"We must show you our bird charts, Marsha," Glen said. "We've been keeping a list of the birds we see here every month since 1998. It was your idea, wasn't it Ruthie? You said it could be a valuable scientific record."

The service from Kings had reached "O Come All Ye Faithful". Alex and Ruth sang along with the "Sing, choirs of angels" descant – Alex was treating it as a joke, but Ruth still hit even the top notes angelically.

"I thought we could have some music tonight," Julia suggested.

Alex groaned. "Mum, couldn't we just watch TV like a normal family?"

"I haven't heard you play the piano for so long."

"I don't have one at home. I've probably forgotten how to play it."

"I'm sure that's not true. You used to play so beautifully."

"Mum, I got to Grade Four."

"How about 'Walking in the Air'? I bet you can still play that."

Alex sighed. "Fine. I'll play 'Walking in the Air'. If Robin sings it."

"Er, my voice has actually broken now?"

He had had such a beautiful treble voice. Julia wished she could hear it again. Robin and Kelly were always filming the twins on their digital camera. They would end up with a permanent record of Jack and Finn's childhood: thousands of photos, moving pictures, the way they talked. If you were always watching through a camera, you weren't really present in the moment, Julia reminded herself. Though she wasn't entirely convinced: she would give anything for a record like that of Alex, Robin and Ruth.

. . .

Kelly had taken the twins back to the stable flat after *In the Night Garden*. It had been awkward. Julia had suggested they might like to hang their stockings up by the fire, but Kelly had insisted they would want to open their stockings in bed first thing on Christmas morning. Ruth doubted whether Jack and Finn would care much either way.

"Will you come back for supper?" Julia asked with icy politeness.

Kelly said the baby monitor wouldn't work over the distance, and she was hardly going to leave her babies alone in a separate building. Ruth suspected she was glad of the excuse.

"I thought you just left them to cry anyway," Julia muttered.

"Pardon me? We don't *just leave them to cry*. You go in, you settle them, you don't say anything. Then you leave them to go to sleep by themselves. It's supposed to create better sleep habits. But you have to be firm and consistent," she added, aiming a look at Robin.

"I'll bring you some supper over," he said. "We can swap later."

So it was just Marsha left with the five Blakes, and it looked like Mum was going to subject her to a full-on Blake Christmas Eve. "We like to do our own little Christmas concert," Julia explained after supper.

"You have to understand," Alex said, "that for Mum, Christmas is basically a competitive sport. We have to do it better than everyone else."

But she consented to play "Away in a Manger" on the piano, and Robin joined in singing "Walking in the Air". Then they sang some favourites from the green *Carols for*

Choirs book. Marsha sat on the hearthrug petting Barney, who was lying on his back, playing dead but for a slowly twitching tail. She applauded as they finished what Ruth had to admit was actually quite an impressive rendition of "Good King Wenceslas", with Dad doing his hammy baritone and Robin singing the page's part in falsetto.

"I feel like I'm spending Christmas with the Von Trapps," Marsha said.

"Ruthie, you must play your flute," Julia announced.

She tried to protest. Since leaving school, she'd only got it out once or twice a year during the holidays. But when Marsha said she'd love to hear her play, Ruth relented.

The silver and velvet smell when she opened the case was instantly familiar. The notes came easily, and she was amazed once more by the magic of this machine that could turn her breath into birdsong. She ad-libbed around "Silent Night", then segued into "The Holly Bears a Berry". Marsha broke into clapping and cheering when she'd finished. Ruth could feel herself beaming.

"Come on Marsha, your turn to do something," said Alex.

"Yeah, come on Marsha," echoed Robin. "Everyone has to perform, it's the law."

"Guests are absolutely not obliged to perform," Ruth said.

"But you'll never be invited back if you don't," Alex added.

"Okay, okay," said Marsha. "I've got something."

She stood up and cleared her throat. "I shall perform a dramatic monologue from one of my first stage appearances," she announced. She did some exaggerated stretches, then declaimed dramatically: "A baby has been born in Bethlehem. He is God's son." She gave a bow. "Second angel,

St Martin's primary school, December 1991. One of my finest roles. Outrageously overlooked in the best supporting actress category that year."

Ruth could tell that her mother wasn't sure how to take this, but the rest of the family applauded with gusto.

Then Julia recited "The Oxen" by Thomas Hardy, and Glen read an extract from "A Child's Christmas in Wales". Ruth sat cuddled up with Marsha on the sofa, her cheek resting against her girlfriend's chest. She felt her mother watching them, but when she caught her eye, Julia didn't look away embarrassed as Ruth had expected but gave her a smile.

The grown-ups retreated to bed at half-nine. "We'll be getting you up at 5am," Glen said. "Revenge for all those Christmas mornings you woke us at stupid o'clock."

The Bailey's was finished, but Alex brought a bottle of port up from the cellar. Robin was looking through a pile of VHS cassettes. He pulled one out triumphantly: "Yes!"

"Is that what I think it is?" Ruth asked.

"What is it?" Marsha asked.

"*The Box of Delights.*"

"I have no idea what that is."

"It's a children's TV series, from when we were kids. It's kind of a family Christmas tradition."

"Another one?"

"I know, I know..."

In fact, they rarely got past the first episode or two, but the theme tune was all it took to set off a Proustian rush of Christmas magic. Robin fell asleep first. Alex dropped off a few minutes later.

"Well, that was ... strange," Marsha said when they reached the end of the episode.

"You mean the programme, or the whole evening?" Ruth

asked. "You're doing amazingly, putting up with all this."

Marsha kissed the top of her head. "No, it's great. And so are you. You know that, right?"

When I'm with you I do, Ruth thought.

Alex woke up with a road drill blaring in her head and fur growing in her mouth. It took her a moment to remember where she was. Ah. Her old room. Boxing Day.

She was glad of the en suite bathroom, and even more so when she found some paracetamol in the cabinet over the sink. She washed them down with two glasses of water. Bits of yesterday were coming back to her.

It had started okay. Julia had done stockings for the three of them – chocolates, bath bombs, socks, the pointless satsuma.

"Thanks, Mum. You didn't have to."

"Oh but of course I do. I know it's not quite as magical as when you believed in Father Christmas, but you must have stockings!"

"We didn't get to believe in Father Christmas," Robin said. "Alex shattered my illusions when I was about five, remember?"

"We kept on pretending for years though," Ruth added. "We didn't want to upset you."

"I've only just about forgiven you," Robin told Alex.

"I didn't do it out of spite. I had very strong moral convictions. I didn't think it was right that our parents were lying to us."

"Well, we're lying to Jack and Finn, so keep your moral convictions to yourself."

The twins were quite cute opening their presents. Julia made some comment about how they were more interested in the wrapping paper than the contents, and Alex had been about to point out that literally every grandparent ever had made that observation, but she'd stopped herself. They'd all gone to the family service at the village church, where Julia went every Sunday and Alex used to allow herself to be dragged no more than twice a year. The female vicar seemed to be aiming most of the service at the under-tens in the congregation, a demographic numbering half a dozen if you included Jack and Finn, but it had been nice to sing carols in a Norman building and try to imagine all those thousands of lives that had gathered there for nine hundred Christmases.

She made bellinis when they got back. You were allowed to drink before noon on Christmas Day if it had bubbles in, and a hair-of-the-dog went down well. Then she offered to help with lunch.

"Oh no, I can manage. You all sit down and relax."

"Mum, you don't have to be a martyr."

"Well, if you insist, you could prep the sprouts."

Alex found some sesame oil and soy sauce at the back of larder. She stir-fried the sprouts with garlic and ginger and a few chilli flakes.

Julia was appalled. "What have you done to them?"

"I just thought it might be nice to have sprouts that taste of something. Since nobody actually likes them."

"Don't be ridiculous. Anyway, not liking Brussels sprouts is part of the tradition."

Pimped-up sprouts aside, it had been a typical Christmas dinner with all the trimmings and trappings, turkey and stuffing and wonderfully crisp roast potatoes, although Mum had lamented not being able to use goose fat. Dad had brought several good bottles of wine up from the cellar – two Bordeaux cru bourgeois, a Chilean red, a

Sancerre – and they'd helped wash down the rich, bland, comforting food. There'd been candles and the silver napkin rings, crackers and paper crowns and terrible jokes.

Dad doused the Christmas pudding in brandy and set it alight, while Mum tried to get them all to sing "Now bring us some figgy pudding," another excruciating family tradition. Alex could sense Ruth's embarrassment, although Marsha joined in gamely enough. Mum tried to give the twins a slice, which Kelly vetoed.

"It's not at all suitable. Besides, it's soaked in alcohol."

"Might help them sleep," Robin suggested. Kelly gave him a withering look.

"But what about the sixpence?"

"If you get the slice with the sixpence in, you win Christmas," Alex explained.

"A choking hazard," Kelly muttered. "Great. Anyway, I need to take them back to the flat. They're already twenty minutes late for their nap."

After she'd gone, they'd settled down to nuts and Quality Streets. And then Mum had taken the opportunity to ambush Robin.

"You know, darling, we've been giving it a lot of thought, and I think you should come and move in here. You and the boys. And Kelly of course. It seems so silly, us having the stable flat all empty while you're working so hard just to pay the rent on that little place of yours. And I'd be able to help you with the children. What do you think?"

Alex could tell Robin thought the idea was a non-starter, but didn't want to say so. "I don't know, Mum. It might be difficult with work and things."

"You can do your work from anywhere, you said so."

"Yeah, but Kelly has her job. And her folks are up there."

Julia went quiet. "I see. Well, at least Kelly's parents get to be near to their grandchildren."

"Oh, Mum, please. Look, it's a really kind idea. I'll mention it to Kelly, okay?"

Good old Robin, trying to keep everyone happy. It only made things worse in the long run.

They'd managed a stroll up to the pond before it got dark, then they'd opened more presents, because apparently they were now grown-ups who didn't devour all their gifts before 9am. Alex had started on the port at this point, and she must have begun picking up her drinking pace when everyone else was slowing down or stopping. For whatever reason, it had seemed like the right time to mention that she'd be leaving the day after Boxing Day to go to Cornwall.

"But you'll come back afterwards?" Mum asked.

"No. I'm getting a lift back to London with Bex, then I fly out a couple of days later."

Then Mum had started actually crying, and instead of being sympathetic, Alex had been infuriated, because obviously it was attention-seeking self-pity.

"It's what you've always done. Always choosing your friends over your family."

"Mum, I'm allowed to have my own life you know."

"It's just a shame you don't seem to value your home and family."

"Of course I value my home and family."

"Oh? And yet you've moved to the other side of the world, and you're in a relationship with a man nearly old enough to be your father, who has two children living on a different continent."

"Well then, what does that say about my upbringing? Honestly Mum, you make out like this place is some sort of ancestral seat. I only lived here for three years before I went to uni, and you know what? I couldn't wait to leave. We're not coming back, you know. Your chicks have flown the nest. Oh, and Robin and Kelly aren't going to move into the stable flat with their kids. You know that, right?"

Kelly looked up from the ottoman, where she was reading *That's Not My Reindeer* with the nicer of the twins. "What's that?"

"Oh, didn't Robin mention it? There's a surprise. And Robin's not going to move in after they get divorced either because he won't want to move far away from his kids, so you can forget that too."

"Excuse me, what?" Robin said. "Who said anything about getting divorced?"

"Sorry, but you obviously will, anyone can see that."

Kelly picked up the nicer twin and stalked out of the room. The other twin started bawling. Robin scooped him up and went out after her.

"Alex, please, just stop now," Ruth pleaded. Then, oh Christ, then she'd said that Ruth wasn't going to have kids because she was a dyke and Mum needed to face up to that. She may also have used the term carpet muncher. Which she'd meant entirely affectionately, but she could see now how that might not have come across. Ruth had fled the room in tears.

"I hate to miss all the drama, but I'd better go with her," Marsha said. Barney, who hated conflict of any kind, slinked out after her.

"And this is why I moved to the other side of the world," Alex said, downing her glass of port. "Merry Christmas, family!"

She'd stomped up to her room and called Grant on her mobile, and he'd been pissed off because it was 4am over there, and she'd shouted at him too. Thinking about it, the only person she hadn't offended was her dad. Then she remembered the way he'd looked at her – sad, concerned, let down.

She got into the shower, letting the icy cold jets rake over her while she waited for the water to warm up; scouring, shriving herself. She had some apologising to do.

The twins had woken at 6.01am. It was cold in the flat. The fire was long out, and the radiators hadn't come on yet. It could have been the middle of the night.

Robin changed them in turn; grouching Finn first while Jack waited, a stoic expression on his face. They had Kelly's eyes, Robin thought. He dressed them in two layers of baby-grows and the matching panda onesies, their Christmas present from Alex. Then he laid them down under their jungle gyms where, God be praised, they both settled, Jack contemplating the ceiling while Finn devoured a chew ring. He made a mug of proper tea for himself and some rooibos for Kelly. He thought she'd still be asleep, but she sat up when he set it down on the bedside cabinet.

"Morning. I made you some tea. Happy Boxing Day."

"Thank you. Are the kids awake?"

"Changed, dressed and chilling out in the jungle, touch wood."

He thought she'd probably tell him off for not giving them a feed, but instead she said: "You're a good dad. And a good husband. I don't want to get divorced."

"What? Oh, that. Don't mind Alex. She gets like that sometimes. She doesn't really mean it."

"Still. I don't like to think that people think that about us."

"I don't want to get divorced either."

He kissed her on the lips and stroked her thigh. She was

wearing trackie bottoms and a thick jumper, so it wasn't exactly sensual, but he still felt a little surge of desire.

"She was right about how we're not going to move in here though. That's just not happening."

"I know, I know."

"Your mother had no right to spring it on us like that."

"She just wants the best for us and the kids."

"Well, she has to realise that she may not be the best person to decide what's best for us and our kids." She paused, challenging him to contradict her; he just nodded. "She is right, though, that we need to get a proper place."

"We can't afford it."

"We'd pay less with a mortgage than we pay in rent."

"And the money for a deposit?"

She wasn't listening. "We could get somewhere with a garden. I mean, not like this one, but. We can make our own home together."

He leant in and kissed her again. "I'd like that," he said.

A bawling arose from the other room. Robin sighed. "If we do get divorced, we'll have fifty-fifty custody, yeah? You can have Finn."

She looked hurt for a moment, then laughed. "No deal!"

"Okay. We'd best stick together then."

Ruth found Marsha already downstairs, sitting in the window seat again with a cup of tea.

"Morning," she smiled. "I just saw seven long-tailed tits in that bush over there. That's made my day already."

Ruth gave her a kiss and sat down beside her. "You're wearing your slippers." That had been part of her present. Slippers were de rigueur in the Blake family; Marsha had never owned a pair in her life.

"I love them! They're actually the comfiest, cosiest thing I've ever worn."

"You're part of the family now. We've got you in our power."

"I can't wait to wear them with the other part of my present."

Ruth felt herself blushing. The other part had been lingerie, sexy Ann Summers stuff of the sort she'd never dared buy before.

"I'm sorry my family are such a nightmare."

"It's fine. Alex already apologised. She assures me that she's not homophobic, and she says I'm the best thing that could have happened to you. So that's nice."

"Well, I guess she's right about some things."

The rest of the day passed in a pleasant Boxing Day fug. Like the table decorations and piles of presents, yesterday's conflicts had been tidied away. In the afternoon, Julia and Glen had gone to drinks at the Fletchers'. The Fletchers didn't live there any longer; it was one of a number of houses in the village still referred to by the name of its previous inhabitants. This seemed to be a village thing. In their early years, people still referred to their house as the Aldridges'. Some older people called it the Colonel's.

The younger generation played Monopoly, with only good-natured quarrelling.

Blake house rules included putting all the money from taxes and fines into the middle of the board, to be collected by whoever landed on Free Parking. On this occasion, after an unusually long run of income and super tax, street repairs and fines for drunkenness, the stash had built up to more than £1,600 when Alex had finally thrown a double-five straight from jail. This led to a building boom from Oxford Street to Mayfair (somehow, Alex always ended up with Mayfair) and the rapid end of the game.

"This game is so true to life," Robin said, sweeping the plastic houses into the box. "A criminal elite using unearned cash, effectively stolen from the taxpayer, to drive up property prices. And widening inequality plays out to its inevitable conclusion."

"Suck it up little brother. I won!"

"Hardly true to life really," Ruth said. "The idea that you can afford to buy a house in London for less than your annual salary."

Robin and family had left at seven. Ruth said she'd come and visit soon and Kelly said yes she must, and Marsha too. It might be easier if Marsha were there, Ruth thought. Most things were.

The house felt instantly quieter without the twins. Julia was quiet too. She appeared deflated.

"Is your mum okay?" Marsha asked her, later.

"She's just sad not to see more of Robin and the kids. And sad that me and Alex are leaving tomorrow. She likes having us here."

"We can stay longer if you want," Marsha said. "If it makes her happy."

"There's nothing to do around here you know."

"We can go for walks to country pubs. Also, do more birdwatching. In fact, why don't we move into the stable flat? We can grow vegetables."

"Get chickens."

"Maybe open a dairy?"

But Ruth was already looking forward to going back to London. There was a house party tomorrow night, and they had tickets for Heaven on New Year's Eve. She wanted to meet up in trendy cafés and drink lattes with wonderful friends who knew nothing of her life before the age of twenty. She wanted to drop a pill and go out dancing. She wanted to spend hours in bed with Marsha in, and out of, her new lingerie without caring if anyone overheard them. She wanted to be the person she was becoming.

Julia stripped all the beds. She put a first load of sheets into the washing machine. She hoovered the bedrooms and cleaned the bathroom. She hung the sheets on the pulley airer above the Aga and put on a second load. She made a pot of tea. It was eleven o'clock. The day stretched before her, bleak and empty. She flicked through the *Sunday Times* magazine. She contemplated the quiz of the year. The only person she recognised in the pictures was Barack Obama. The children would know who the rest of them were.

Barney got up suddenly and waddled to the door, tail wagging: Glen must be back.

"Is there tea in the pot?"

She nodded. He poured himself a mug, gave her a top-up. He gestured to the washing. "Thanks for doing all that."

"Thanks for dropping the girls off. Did you see them onto the train?"

"No, I said goodbye outside. But I think they can manage to get on a train. I'm sure Marsha will look after them."

"She seems a nice girl."

"She does, doesn't she? You know, she went for a walk up to the pond this morning before breakfast. She saw a heron. Or 'a massive grey bird on stilts', anyway. I think she's good for Ruthie. She's brought her out of her shell."

Julia had to agree. Though if only it had been a nice boy.... She pushed the thought down.

"Alex said to tell you she's sorry again," Glen said. "She's going to come back here for a couple of nights after New Year."

"That will be nice."

They drank their tea in silence for a while. Glen put a hand on her knee. "I know Alex has no sense of tact. But she's right. They've all flown the nest now. And they won't be coming back."

"I've been thinking," Glen continued. "I think we should downsize."

She was stunned. She didn't know what to say.

"We don't need a place like this. And I'll be working for the next twelve years to pay off the mortgage. I'll be sixty-seven."

And then they would enjoy a long retirement here, pottering in the garden, eating leisurely lunches, taking tea on the lawn: that was what she'd always imagined. Surrounded by grandchildren.

"If we sold this place, we could be mortgage free and still buy somewhere fantastic – just a more sensible size. I could cut back on work. Just do consultancy."

"But... we have friends here."

"We could stay in the area. Or go anywhere. Move to the seaside. Or closer to Robin. We could even go travelling. Go and visit Alex in Shanghai. Rent a chalet in the Alps over winter."

She tried to picture it. She couldn't.

"Also, if we bought somewhere smaller... We could help Robin out with a deposit. They need a place of their own."

"But they could..." she began, but Glen shook his head.

"You know that's not going to happen. And poor Ruthie. She has a thirty-grand student debt hanging over her, and she's trying to pay London rent on a voluntary sector salary.

I know they don't need our charity, but it was much easier in our day."

"Alex doesn't need money."

"No. She just needs to be allowed to live her own life."

It had all passed by so quickly. It was no time at all ago that they'd moved in: Alex, too young for the make-up and outfits she wore but already able to run rings around Julia in any argument; Robin with his golden curls, his beatific smile and his voice yet to break; silent little Ruthie, off in a world of her own half the time. And look at them now.

Julia didn't know what to say. "You'd miss your birds."

"I'm sure we can find as many birds somewhere else. Or nearly as many."

It was the thing she had wanted above all in life: to make the perfect home for her family. Of course it had always eluded her, but she had done her best. She had done well – hadn't she? And now they didn't need it anymore.

So what was she supposed to do now?

FLOORBOARDS

2016

Veronika got back from the school run at nine. Half an hour to tidy up for the cleaning lady. A cleaner you had to clean for. What was the point in that? Lego and school books on the carpet – Doreen wouldn't vacuum. Stuff left on the kitchen table – kitchen table didn't get wiped. Only the shelves free of clutter got dusted. It was a power thing, Veronika could see that. Doreen was in her fifties at least and had lived in the village all her life. She had a – what was it? – a *chip on her shoulder*. You might live in the big house, she was saying, but you are an outsider, and you will do things the way we like it. She never said this to Veronika's face. But she didn't hide it either: put those UKIP leaflets through every letterbox in the village, theirs included. A Vote Leave sign on her lawn. One of those people who complained about immigrants *coming over here, taking our jobs*. When an immigrant was literally employing her.

Although she had some sympathy with the cleaning issue. Veronika had worked as a cleaner twelve years back when she'd first come to the UK, and my god, the state of some of the places! But she'd taken any work she could. She had an M.Sc. in molecular biology from Comenius University in Bratislava. For all the good it did her. Apparently not a useful qualification in this country.

She loaded the breakfast things into the dishwasher. She collected the piles of books, hoodies and toys from the stairs and dumped them in the boys' rooms. She was always doing that. Putting stuff on the bottom steps, hoping they'd take them upstairs themselves. They never did.

She wiped round the toilet seats. The joys of having two sons. Not to mention a husband who'd probably never cleaned a bathroom in his life.

Veronika didn't work as a cleaner for long. She found a job as a receptionist for Willow Holdings. Property investment. She didn't know the first thing about it, but all she had to do was answer phones and book appointments. That was where Cameron worked. The first person she'd met in England who'd been to Bratislava – only on a stag do, but still. Mostly, people assumed she was Polish. Or Lithuanian. When she told them Slovakia, they'd tell her about their trip to Prague. Several people she thought she knew fairly well had said bad luck about the football after England beat Slovenia in the World Cup.

Veronika knew people who had come to England to find a wealthy husband. That hadn't been her plan. She had hoped for a career. Culture. Interesting people in a cosmopolitan city. Instead, she had drunk too much vodka and kissed Cameron Lambert at the office Christmas party. And now here she was in a big house in the country. Mrs Lambert. Mother of two. Bored out of her mind.

Moving out of London was Cameron's idea. He said they need somewhere bigger. The boys needed a garden. As far as she could see, the boys only needed somewhere with iPads and decent WiFi.

Cameron said The Lindens was a good investment. "You can get more for your money down here. And the land has development potential."

"I thought it was a family home we were looking for."

"Oh, quite. Still, you know what they say. Buy land, they're not making it anymore."

He was always saying things like that. He thought she thought he was amazingly clever.

The commute meant she saw less of him than she used to. Which wasn't necessarily a bad thing. He would leave the house before seven in the morning and get back after seven in the evening. He'd work from home once or twice a week, was the idea. She hardly saw him then either, shut off all day in the office in the barn. Still, Cameron liked the idea of playing the country gentleman. He bought dogs – a pair of springer spaniels. They would act crazy excited whenever he came home from work. She never got that kind of welcome, even though she was the one who fed and walked them and picked up their shit in little plastic bags. He would go shooting with old school friends. Piers and Rupert. She'd gone along with them once. Had to put up with hours of patronising male banter before she'd finally flipped and told them that when she went hunting with her brothers they would shoot stags and boars, not these long-tailed chickens in drag.

"Pheasants," Rupert protested.

"They don't know how even to fly. They are like clockwork toy."

Piers had tried to get her to say a poem about a pheasant plucker. You were supposed to get it wrong and say pleasant fucker. That was what she called Cameron's friends to herself now – the Pleasant Fuckers. Although they weren't especially pleasant.

There was a school in the next village, but Cameron thought Lukas and Milo should go to one you had to pay for instead. Twenty minutes' drive away. Uniform like fancy dress from another century. Shorts in winter. Caps. They sounded as English as Piers and Rupert now and hardly ever spoke Slovak.

People envied her. She knew that. A rich husband who bought her everything she wanted. Plus a lot she didn't. This big house. Two sons. *Strapping lads.* She didn't need to work. Lucky her. It had been a relief when the children were small. But that was in London. Her days filled up easily. Baby groups, soft-play areas, meeting friends for coffee. Now, she had six hours between dropping the boys at school in the morning and picking them up again in the afternoon. Empty as the fields of ploughed mud she drove past four times a day.

"It's the real England," Cameron had said when they'd first come to the village. "Quintessential." London wasn't the real England, apparently. She'd heard the same from a man in the Alderbourne post office just yesterday. "London's a foreign country these days. Half the people don't look English and half the people don't speak it."

Raj the shopkeeper, the only non-white face in a five-mile radius, had nodded politely as he handed over the man's *Daily Express*.

"I've nothing against foreigners. But it's got out of control. No offence, love," the man added, though Veronika hadn't said anything.

This Brexit. People around here made it clear enough she wasn't welcome. Now apparently they needed a referendum to make it official. Cameron was complacent about it, like his ham-faced namesake the prime minister. "People aren't that stupid," he insisted. Veronika wasn't so sure. He lived in his London bubble. Even the Pleasant Fuckers were voting remain, because of the economy. In London, there were lots of foreigners, and people didn't mind them. Here, it was just her, and they were all bloody UKIP. How could she not take it personally?

It had been sunny first thing but now it was raining again. It had been raining for months. The weather was one English stereotype Veronika had found to be true. Winter was the worst. At home, there were winter days that stayed ten degrees below freezing and the washing on the balcony froze stiff. She didn't mind those. Proper winters with snow and ice and hoar frost on the branches. Here it was grey and damp and mud everywhere.

She was sweeping the porch when Doreen arrived. The dogs rushed out to bark at her.

"I can do that you know, my love. That's what you pay me for after all."

"I would like the house to look nice," Veronika said. "There are some people coming later."

"Is that so?"

Doreen clearly wanted to know more, but wouldn't ask directly, so Veronika didn't say anything. She left Doreen tutting over the kitchen floor. She'd swept it earlier, but now the dogs had covered it with muddy pawprints again. Veronika needed a smoke, so she went up to the flat above the office. They'd been letting it out on Airbnb the last couple of years. She hadn't been sure about the idea at first.

"Why do we want strangers coming here?"

"You're always complaining you don't have any company. And we might as well realise the value of our assets."

They had enough money already, she thought. But he'd

gone and transferred the flat into her name. They'd pay less tax that way, he told her. She told him he was very clever.

But the Airbnb was a good idea. It gave her days some purpose. She liked having visitors. Sometimes, there were interesting and friendly people, and she liked the house better when she saw it through their eyes. *Such a beautiful place you have here! Being surrounded by nature like this.* She'd show them the way up through the meadow to the pond. Put out a vase of flowers from the garden or bring them a bowl of plums or apples. She even started serving them tea made from the flowers of the *lipa* trees along the drive, like her mother used to make. But nobody wanted to stay in February. Which was understandable.

She lit a cigarette. Her left hand felt empty, so she went to the little kitchen to see if there was any coffee left. Nicotine and caffeine went together. There wasn't, but there was the remains of a vodka bottle she'd brought over last week. Nicotine and vodka went together also. She poured a small glass. If she was going to have a drink, it was better to do it early. She didn't drink and drive on the school run.

The people were due at eleven. Doreen would have left by then. Would they want lunch? Perhaps they wouldn't stay long. Or perhaps they would stay for hours. It could go either way with old people. She wondered how much had changed since the man had lived here. This flat and the office must have been some kind of barn. Otherwise, it probably wasn't so different from the 1940s. The decade the English were so keen to return to. Veronika lit another cigarette, and poured another vodka. The last one had been very small. She could have coffee when the people arrived.

·   ·   ·

Doreen was still there at 10.45, dusting the mantelpiece in the living room. Doreen never stayed late.

"Please, Doreen. You have been here more than one hour."

"Oh, is that the time?" The clock was right in front of her face. "I suppose your guests are coming soon?"

"Yes."

"Staying for a while, are they?"

Veronika had learned an English idiom that described Doreen: a *nosey parker*, whatever a parker was. Or you could say *nosey cow*. She could see the woman's mind turning over the possibilities. A lover? A lorry full of Kosovan refugees? Albanian gangsters?

Five minutes after she'd finally left, the dogs started up their barking again. The bell went for the security gates. Veronika buzzed them open, and a van pulled up the drive and into the yard. A man of around thirty got out of the driving seat.

"You must be Veronika?" He pronounced it the English way, with the stress on the second syllable. "I'm Laurence. Thanks for having us."

Two young black women had emerged from the back of the van, and one of them was now helping an old man down from the passenger seat. He was dressed in a tweed suit and a flat cap, and moved slowly and stiffly. But his eyes were bright, and he was gazing around with a look of childish delight on his face.

"Let me introduce my granddad," Laurence said. "This is Henry Cook."

Marsha was surprised how familiar it felt. The row of fir trees at the top of the bank, the solid squareness of the house and the walled garden. It brought feelings flooding back. Being young and in love. Being properly in the countryside for the first time ever. She'd felt at home there, though she'd stayed only a handful of times. That first Christmas – she'd loved it, despite Ruth's sister getting drunk and starting rows with everyone. Then they'd come at Easter time – Julia had got them doing an Easter egg hunt round the garden, insisting it was a family tradition. There'd been daffodils everywhere, and birds singing. Then they must have come in the summer too, because she'd made Ruth go skinny-dipping with her in the pond, even though Ruth had protested that they'd smell like a drain for the next few days, correctly as it turned out. Marsha remembered wildflowers and butterflies in the meadow, drinking gin and tonics on the lawn, smoking bongs up in the folly. She'd been too caned to walk down the steps and they just lay in a beanbag, watching the moths circling the old oil lamp. She'd loved the place. In a recurring daydream, she and Ruth would move into the stable flat. Get out of London and start a brand new life here in the country. They'd joke about it sometimes. Ruth had never suspected that she was at least partly serious.

Then Ruth's parents had sold up. Moved to a cottage on the edge of the Peak District. Robin and Kelly were expecting another baby, and the house they'd bought in Sheffield was only a twenty-minute drive away. She and Ruth came down to help them pack and to collect Ruth's remaining stuff. It was October, and the trees in the orchard were laden with apples. It seemed a shame to be leaving them behind. Julia had been brisk and business-like with the packing, but Marsha could see how sad they all were.

She watched Glen unpin the bird chart from the kitchen door.

"You're not going to throw that away, are you?"

"Of course not." He gave her a sad smile. "It's a valuable scientific record."

Before they left, they'd taken a final walk up to the pond, like some kind of funeral rite.

"I must have walked up here hundreds of times," Ruth said. "I can't believe I'll never do this again."

Marsha said she knew how Ruth felt, but her girlfriend looked sceptical.

The best days of their relationship were over by then. They were both working stupidly hard, investing too much of themselves in jobs that barely paid the rent, and having too little left over to give to each other.

It wasn't that she stopped fancying Ruth, or girls in general. Her sexuality wasn't complicated. She fancied people: people she found beautiful and interesting and thirsty for love. Gender didn't come into it. Nor did colour. That wasn't what Ruth thought, though, when Marsha slept with Jermaine, the buff Bajan guy who taught music at the school where she worked. She'd been flattered by the attention, and drunk, and it hadn't meant anything, though the sex was memorable. But it hit Ruth hard. "It's not just that you cheated on me. It's that cheating on me with someone of a different sex and race looks like your subconscious telegraphing its opinion of me pretty fucking clearly." Marsha had said to give the A-level psychology a rest, and Ruth had cried. But if she was honest with herself, when Marsha looked into her future, she didn't see Ruth there beside her. Not forever.

Ruth moved out a few months later. Her parents had given her some money to put down a deposit on a place of her own. They were friends these days, though it had taken a while. Marsha had been out with Ruth and her fiancé a few times. The beautiful Abigail, who played viola in a London orchestra. They made a good couple. Even Julia liked her.

Marsha's own subsequent love life had been less successful. A couple of one-night-stands, some half-hearted forays into online dating, three half-relationships (one woman, two man-children). Marsha had a thing for rescuing people, she didn't need her psychology degree to work that out. Take Ruth herself – timid little church mouse with scars on her limbs and a history of eating disorders, terrified to come out even to herself. And now look at her: getting interviewed on the *Today* programme, speaking fluently and furiously about funding cuts to adolescent mental health services. And getting married next year. Not that Marsha was trying to claim the credit. It turned out she wasn't that great at rescuing people. Some people didn't want to be rescued. They just dragged you down with them.

Jay, for example – the second man-child. Jay, who had an IQ of 140, who drank himself into a stupor three nights a week, who was clearly bipolar and would nod and agree when she told him there was medication that could help. But he never made an appointment with the doctor, and the time she arranged one for him, he'd got aggressive and told her to butt the fuck out of his life. He'd called to apologise the next day, and they'd gone on like that, on and off and on, for two years of her twenties she'd never get back.

Or Camile, who'd beguiled her with tales of the trials and hardships she'd faced, the people who'd hurt her, betrayed her and backstabbed her, the injustices and the terrible luck she'd suffered. Marsha had listened with compassion and indignation, offered support and solidarity, poured her forces into Camile's struggles, until she'd belatedly come to understand that Camile would always blame her problems on others rather than take an honest look at herself. No doubt she had a new sob story now about how that bitch Marsha had let her down.

Anyway, Marsha had enough of other people's problems to deal with at work. She'd moved from counselling into teaching by then, in a tough primary school, and the only way you could cope, along with the planning and the paperwork and the parents emailing in the middle of the evening, was to not let yourself care too much. But she couldn't do that. The counselling continued on top of all the other work, she just didn't get paid for it. All those poor kids and their already fucked-up lives. Sometimes they'd open up to her. Shanice, whose violent resistance to getting changed for PE turned out to be the result of being abused by her foster father. Rakim, who'd been falling asleep in class, and who it transpired was caring for his three younger siblings along with his junkie mother. Tahar, a Syrian refugee who'd experienced enough trauma to keep a therapist occupied for years, so it was hardly surprising he was sometimes disruptive. And at best she might get them a referral to what was left of the council's support services or to some local charity. But it was a sticking plaster on a hacked-off limb, and each small victory just made her think of the many more losing battles going on every single day. All the people she could never rescue.

She didn't like to think of it as a breakdown exactly. Burn-out was more like it. She'd been getting headaches, and back pain, and she'd been taking codeine for that, and sure, you weren't meant to take it for more than three days, and maybe the fact that she was doing the rounds of six different pharmacies to get hold of it should have been a red flag. But it smoothed the rough edges off the day, and mixed seductively with wine and weed to soothe her to sleep at night. Then she'd wake up with a headache, and of course it was obvious there was a vicious circle going on, but it had taken a full-on intervention from her sister to pull her out of it.

On Aleesha's insistence, Marsha had moved back in with their mum. She got signed off sick for the rest of the term, but never went back. She submitted to a strict regime of home-cooked meals, plenty of sleep and evenings watching Scandinavian crime dramas. But it was the birds that helped most. Her mum didn't have a big garden, but it was more than Marsha was used to – a patch of grass, some shrubs and flowers, pots of herbs, a couple of trees. One day she was in Lidl and they were selling bird feeders. She bought two and hung them from a branch outside the kitchen window.

She remembered the birds at The Lindens, Ruth's father pointing them out to her. He'd given her a copy of the *Observer Book of British Birds*, but despite good intentions she hadn't looked at it much. If there were birds in London beyond the pigeons, she hadn't noticed them. But within a few hours of hanging up the feeders, they'd been visited by a blue tit, a great tit, a robin and a pair of what appeared to be parrots. She didn't remember parrots from the *Book of British Birds*. Ring-necked parakeets, it turned out. Unwelcome alien invaders, apparently, but Marsha liked them.

The more she looked, the more she saw. There was a shrub with orange berries that the blackbirds visited. Gangs of sparrows would descend on the lawn to reconnoitre, then flit off again. Magpies landed in a tree across the road. Starlings circled at sunset. Crowds of crows – did that make them rooks? – came to roost in the park at dusk.

It took her out of herself. You could watch the birds doing their thing and not think about anything else. She went for walks across Hackney Marshes and along the River Lea. Mallards and moorhens and brutish coots. She downloaded an app on her phone. She identified a snowy egret, discovered that the black-and-white dudes that wagged their tails were called pied wagtails, and that made her happy. She went along on an organised birdwatching walk with a local ornithology group, but she was the only woman, and the only person of colour, and the only person under fifty, so she didn't go again. But she began looking out Instagram accounts with photos of birds, started following the RSPB on Twitter.

That was where she'd seen the post. A nature presenter she followed had retweeted one @StumpSculpture:

> My amazing granddad Henry Cook has just had his first book published aged 85. #Birdwatching + memoir = beautiful. #proudgrandson

She was only scrolling, but the name jumped out at her. Henry Cook.

The diary Ruth had found under the floorboards. They'd spent several evenings trawling the internet, trying to trace him, but they hadn't got anywhere. Henry Cook was a common name.

Aged eighty-five would have been around nine years old in 1940. That sounded about right.

She added a comment:

> @StumpSculpture random question I know but was your granddad evacuated to a house in Wiltshire during WW2?

The reply came back a few minutes later:

> @HackneyMarsha Yes he was! That's where his book starts. WTF?!

She looked at his profile:

@StumpSculpture *I'm Laurence Wood. Tree surgeon. Maker of chainsaw sculptures. Yes, I've heard the nominative determinism jokes.*

His account was mostly photos of his sculptures: animals and birds carved out of tree stumps. Squirrels, owls, a hare's head, a stooping heron. Marsha liked them. She sent him a message, explaining about how her ex had found a diary in her old house by a boy who'd been evacuated there during the war. How she'd remembered the name Henry Cook, and how he'd kept lists of all the birds he saw.

Laurence Wood replied almost straight away.

> Marsha! That's mad! I love the internet sometimes. Going to tell my granddad. The first chapter is all about him being evacuated and the old lady who he lives with teaching him to recognise the different birds.

A couple of days later, she got another message.

> Hi Marsha, I told my granddad about the diary. He remembered it – apparently he left it behind because he thought he'd go back to the house, and he's regretted it ever since. Anyway, he's thrilled that somebody found it and read it. So here's the thing – does your ex still have it? He says he'd love to read it again.

Marsha called Ruth. "That's mad," Ruth exclaimed when she told her. "It's hard to believe he's a real person."

"Did you hold onto the diary?" Marsha asked.

"No. I wanted to. But in the end I decided it wasn't mine – it belonged to the house. And I liked the idea that somebody else might find it in the future."

> Hey Laurence. Spoke to my ex – she left the diary behind for future generations to find. Sorry 😣

> Nooo! Don't suppose you know who lives there now?

> No but I know the address. We could go hunt for it?

> LOL

> Or are you being serious?

> Maybe...

> Bring your grandad (seriously)

The next day, he messaged her again, asking if she wanted to meet for coffee. Aleesha insisted on coming along as her chaperone.

"You need to be careful meeting up with random men off Twitter. He could be making the whole thing up."

"He isn't. He knew the name of the house."

"Could be next-level stalking. Even so, it doesn't prove he's not a psychopath and/or sexual predator."

It quickly became apparent that Laurence Wood was neither of these things. He was friendly, though less confident in person than he'd been on the other side of a keypad.

He had a hipster beard, because of course he did, and a lumberjack shirt.

"I guess you can be forgiven, since you are a lumberjack of sorts," she told him.

"Yeah, you know I actually looked like this before it was a hipster thing."

"How very hipster of you."

He laughed. "So, I emailed my granddad about visiting the house and seeing if his diary's still there. He said it sounded like an adventure. What do you reckon?"

"It sounds like an adventure to me too," Marsha replied. "Road trip!"

"You don't know the name of the current owners?"

"No. I asked Ruth. Apparently they have two kids and the woman is from Poland or somewhere, but she didn't know their names."

"Could we google them?"

"I already did, but I couldn't find anything."

It was Aleesha who suggested writing a letter. She worked in events management, and was good at problem solving.

"Like, an actual letter? On paper? In an envelope with a stamp in the corner?"

"Yeah, one of those. Like Postman Pat."

They decided Laurence would write, asking whether it would be possible to bring his grandfather for a visit.

"Don't mention the diary," Aleesha told him. "They may not be keen on the idea of you tearing up their floorboards."

"Well?" Aleesha asked when, two flat whites later, Laurence headed off to pollard some plane trees in Highgate Cemetery.

"Well what?"

"Do you like him?"

"What? No. Not like that."

It wasn't that he was bad looking – she even didn't mind the beard. He liked birds and trees, and he seemed like a nice guy. Too nice, maybe. None of the fragility that, for better or worse, she was drawn to in men and women.

"Jesus, lady, you need to lower your standards," Aleesha told her. "He's a catch."

A few days later, Laurence sent her a screenshot of an email:

Dear Laurence Wood

It is OK for your grandfather and you to see the house. Let me know when is convenient. I have school run 8.30 and 15.15.

Veronika Lambert

Seems we're on 😊

😊😊😊

* * *

"Well?" Laurence asked. "Has it changed much?"

Henry looked around at the yard. It had been dirt and gravel then. He remembered jumping in puddles, sliding on them when they froze in the winter. Now it had a shiny coating in dark grey. Resin. It looked recent. The building in front of them must be the dairy, though it was nothing like the picture in his mind: there were tall glass windows, timber cladding, skylights in the roof. Through the glass he could see a desk with a computer monitor. A Range Rover was parked in what used to be the stable. The winter skeletons of the lindens along the drive seemed smaller than he remembered. Had they been pollarded, or was that just how it was with childhood memories? Beyond the house there was a whole wood that he didn't remember at all. That must have been the brickworks. At the top of the bank stood a row of fir trees in descending order of height, where he recalled a regal elm. But the house itself seemed much the same, at least from the outside. His heart had leapt alarmingly when they'd rounded the corner and he'd seen it again for the first time. Something about its symmetrical design had always made him think of a face – the upstairs windows the eyes, the front door the nose, the porch steps its mouth. And it was a silly fancy, but it was as if it had smiled at him. A bird was singing from somewhere in the back garden. A great tit. If in doubt, it was usually a great tit.

"Yes," he said eventually. "And no."

"That's a fine old avenue of lime trees," Laurence said.

"I like these trees," the woman, Veronika, put in. "*Lipa* tree. Is national symbol of Slovakia. But my husband is always wanting to cut the tops off."

"Ah, lindens are quite happy being pollarded," Laurence said. "These must be as old as the house."

Henry nodded. "Well over a century. Mrs Cann said she knew them when they were saplings."

"That one's younger than the rest." Laurence pointed to a tree at the far end.

"It's a replacement," Marsha said. "I remember Ruth's dad saying. One of them came down in the great storm of whenever it was."

Which tree was that? Henry tried to remember. He had given them all names. Lancelot? Luke. Larry. He used to call his grandson that when he was small, and a feeling, a sudden intense sense of The Lindens would come into his mind. Lucy! That was another. It had been the name of his first serious girlfriend, and somehow his brain still connected her with the lime trees. He hadn't thought about Lucy in years.

"You want coffee?" the woman asked. Russian or otherwise Slavic, Henry thought. Had he been told her name? He couldn't remember. These days, he could struggle to recall what had happened yesterday, or five minutes ago, yet there were moments from seventy years past that remained crisp and clear. Brains were strange things. Perhaps his had simply become too full. He pictured it as a dusty library, rows and rows of shelves groaning under the weight of the leatherbound volumes. Parts of it were still neatly filed – the common and Latin names of a thousand species of birds, the kings and queens of England from 1066 to 1952, every Grand National winner from Lovely Cottage in 1946 to Party Politics in 1992, the entire Seven Ages of Man speech – though some volumes were missing (Grand National winners post-1993, the middle stanzas of *Ode to a Nightingale*, the minor prophets in the Old Testament round about Habakkuk). But there was far more lying loose, stuffed into boxes and cupboards in backrooms. You could lose yourself in there, rifling through drawers that hadn't been opened in years searching for some missing piece of information, and stumbling across things you hadn't even remembered you had forgotten. It must be different for Laurence and those girls. Martha – no, Marsha – and Aleesha. Their minds were like the smartphones they were always using, retrieving and processing information instantly.

Long John Silver! One of them had been called Long John Silver. Mrs Cann reading from *Treasure Island*, sitting on the couch by the fire. He could still remember the voices she did for the pirates. The thought of it brought a smile to his face even now. Tessa Cann was one in a million, truly: a million children evacuated during the war, and you heard some horror stories, but it had been his happy fate to end up at The Lindens. How long had it been? Less than two years when he stopped to work it out, but it felt like one of the longest, richest chapters of his life. And it had changed him, shaped him, there was no doubt about that. The birds, for one thing. He remembered ticking off the names of the birds he had spotted in the garden – blackbird, robin, chaffinch – then, almost simultaneously, much the same thing twenty years later in the rainforest in Suriname, carrying out fieldwork for his PhD. *Variations in the composition of mixed-species foraging flocks in the Neotropics.* Fulvous shrike-tanager, Todd's antwren, yellow-margined flycatcher. He had added Tessa's name to the acknowledgements, though she was long dead by then: *Thank you to Tessa Cann, for teaching me the names of the birds.*

He never saw her again, after he left. The greatest regret of his life. He had asked his mother repeatedly if he could visit, but while she never said no, nor did she do anything to make it happen. Some years later, he had decided that she was jealous, that she didn't want to share him with some strange woman; he had seen it as spiteful and selfish, and resented her for it. Later, he had come to accept that she wasn't jealous so much as insecure, and that it came from a place of fear, of fearful love.

But Tessa wrote to him. Long, lively letters about the birds and the chickens and what was out in the garden, asking him what he was reading, sharing amusing and curious things she'd seen or read about. He must have thrown them all away at some point. He didn't remember when. He wished now he hadn't.

He had written back to her. About birds, largely. Back in London, he noticed pigeons and jackdaws on the roofs, sparrows in the bombed-out waste grounds, starlings wheeling at dusk. He sought out parks and gardens, looking for familiar friends. Sometimes he would take his binoculars and his bike on the train out to the Essex marshes, hoping to identify waders and waterfowl in the bird book she had given him. *British Birds in their Haunts* by C.A. Johns. Did he still have that book? He fancied that he did. He couldn't imagine he had got rid of it, though it must be decades since he'd opened it. But the pictures were still imprinted on his mind, Platonic ideals of the birds of Britain. So many birds he had first fallen in love with while poring over the pages of that book! And they had looked so perfectly like their pictures when he finally saw them in the feather – avocet, oystercatcher, great-crested grebe, hoopoe. The kingfisher, of course. He should pass that book on to Laurence.

She had loved him, he had never doubted that. He was all the grandchildren she'd never had. She had lost her own sons in the first war, and her husband had died before Henry was born. So much love dammed up inside her, and she had poured it into him. It occurred to him that he would like to visit her grave. He would ask Laurence if they could go there afterwards.

Her funeral. That must have been the last time he had been here. He'd come back after the church service with... what was his name? Her niece's son, who he had been at school with. Something beginning with S. Tessa's nephew was living in the house with his wife and their son, a boy of four or five. Lucky lad, he'd thought, growing up here. Though he hadn't liked the nephew – hadn't had the courage to ask if he could look for the diary.

Stuart, that was it. Was Stuart still alive? It was possible, though statistically it was more likely that he was not.

Perhaps he, Henry, was the only person alive today who remembered Mrs Cann. Tessa. In a few years, perhaps very few, there would be no one.

"You alright Henry?" It was the girl, Marsha. ""It must be a lot to take in, yeah?"

He nodded. She smiled, and hooked her arm through his. "Come on, let's go and have a cuppa, then you can have a good look around."

She had read the diary he had written when he lived here. What a bizarre thought that was. He had hidden it under the floorboards, and then more than half a century later some girls had discovered it and read it, and then somehow they had got in touch with his grandson. No doubt the diary would be mostly dull, or embarrassing. He wondered if she could see any connection between the boy who had written those pages and this ancient stranger. Yet he felt a strange closeness to her. She at least knew the name of Tessa Cann. The flame of her memory would flicker a little longer.

Laurence and Aleesha had gone on ahead with their host. Henry and Marsha followed more slowly. He couldn't move fast these days, but that was no bad thing. There was, as she said, a lot to take in. They walked past the old coal shed, which held a lawnmower and some fancy-looking bicycles, and into the back garden. There was the wall he used to jump off – now there was a large trampoline with a net on the lawn in front of it. And there was the folly, a basketball hoop bolted to the balcony. The garden looked bare, but then it was February. It was a shame he couldn't be here in April, Henry thought. Or June, or September... Still, there were snowdrops out – perhaps he could pick some snowdrops to take to Tessa's grave – and a few crocuses. In the wood that had grown up from the brickworks, the branches of the willow trees shone golden. There was that great tit singing again. And a nuthatch! He didn't have nuthatches in his garden at home. He'd completed the RSPB Birdwatch last month, as he always did. A respectable seventeen species. It still brought him joy, watching the comings and goings at the bird table as he ate his breakfast. But it was bittersweet, remembering what he was missing. He hadn't seen a bullfinch for months, a greenfinch for even longer. It was several years since the house martins last nested. Did they still nest here at The Lindens? And the swallows too?

Not by the back door they didn't: there was a large porch with wooden beams and glazed sides, but no eaves for nesting.

"That's new since I was here," Marsha said. "And that conservatory wasn't there either – that used to be a green-house, all along the side of the house."

Henry nodded. "There was a tank. With goldfish."

He could almost smell the duckweed and the compost. He probably hadn't thought about those goldfish for more than half a century.

Inside, the house was nothing like he remembered. The entrance hall, the kitchen and the living room had all become one large room with oak floorboards running its length. There was a sleek, spotless kitchen with a breakfast bar, a long dining table with pendant lights hanging over it, a large leather suite with far more seats than one family could possibly fill facing a wood-burning stove and a gigantic television screen.

"This is very swish," Marsha said.

"We make open plan," Veronika explained. "My husband, he likes knocking walls down."

"What does your husband do?" Laurence asked.

"Property investment. He commutes in London."

"And what about yourself?" asked Aleesha.

"Researcher. Molecular biology. Now, mother and wife of the house."

"Well, it's very of kind of you to let us come," Laurence said. "It really means a lot to my granddad – doesn't it, Gramps?"

Henry nodded. "It does. Thank you."

Veronika shrugged. "Is no problem. So, I make coffee?"

"Could I trouble you for a cup of tea?" Henry asked.

"Excuse me, I make terrible English host. You want milk and sugar?"

The last time he drank tea here, the milk came from the Jersey cows. Tea had never tasted quite right ever since. "Just milk, please."

All of a sudden their names came back to him. Jane, Charlotte, Emily, Anne. Austen and the Brontes. He'd never even realised. Mrs Cann liked her literary names. The hens, all heroines from Shakespeare and classic novels. And the dogs, Byron and Shelley. Years later, without even thinking about it, Henry had called his own dog Kipling.

Back then, he had thought Tessa Cann the wisest, most cultured and most knowledgeable person he had ever met. And yet, he had discovered in a conversation with Celia many years after, she had left school at thirteen. A dairy-maid who married into money. It was remarkable how little he knew about her.

Veronika made a mug of tea, and brewed coffee in the cafetiere. Cameron had bought an expensive coffee machine with little foil capsules and a thing that frothed the milk but it annoyed her to make four cups that way.

"So you live here when exactly?" she asked.

"I came here in August 1939 – just before the war broke out. And I must have lived here for almost two years. Two of the best years of my life."

Always with this nostalgia for World War Two, the English. Although at least the old man had been there. Not like some – the man in the shop, or the idiot politician with the messy hair and the Pleasant Fucker voice. So they'd been on the right side, not Nazi collaborators like her own country – good for them. But now they had to keep bringing it up. Like it made them better than everyone else. Cameron's father had been going on about it when they came round for Sunday lunch. About the Blitz and ration books for food. How it forged the English national character. Uniquely stoical and resourceful in the face of adversity, apparently. Try half a century of Soviet communism, Veronika wanted to tell him.

"And you never come back since?"

"Just once, for Mrs Cann's funeral... the woman who lived here. But that was more than half a century ago."

"So why you want to come now?"

"That's a long story. Probably best if these younger ones explain."

It turned out to be a good story. Crazy that the old man had lived here. Had written about living in this house in a book. And crazy that this Marsha had stayed here before. With the Blakes. People in the village still called the house that sometimes.

"You didn't happen to find a diary under the floorboards in one of the bedrooms by any chance?" Marsha asked.

"No," Veronika said. "But we never look."

"Fair enough."

"Which bedroom?"

"At the front, overlooking the drive," Marsha said. "That was your room, right?"

The old man nodded. "That was the one."

That must be the spare room. The one Cameron used to play computer games and his mid-life crisis Stratocaster. And watch porn, probably. His den, he called it. "You want to go look?" she asked.

"You're sure you don't mind us all snooping around your house?" Laurence asked.

Veronika didn't mind. It was the most interesting thing that had happened here in months. She led them into the hall and up the stairs, stopping every few metres as the old man remembered something or other. "Is that the door to the cellar? We sheltered down there when there was an air raid... This is where the grandfather clock must have been... This was Mrs Cann's room... And oh yes, this was mine..."

Veronika opened the door. Doreen had cleaned the room that morning – she didn't seem to mind cleaning up after Cameron. She'd arranged the cushions on the sofa, polished the flatscreen. Hoovered the wall-to-wall carpet.

"Ah," said Marsha. "That's a problem."

Veronika hadn't thought about the carpet. They'd had it refitted only a few months ago.

"Do you remember where the loose floorboard was?" Laurence asked.

The old man thought for a long time. "The bed was over there. I think it must have been on the far side of the room, near where the sofa is. But it all looks so different."

He sounded sad. Veronika felt pity for him. She knelt down by the edge of the carpet and gave it a tug. But it had been fitted well, sitting snugly under the skirting boards, and didn't move.

"Wait a minute," she said. "I come back."

. . .

She left the room, and they heard her heading downstairs.

"What do you think she's doing?" Laurence asked.

Aleesha shook her head. "No idea. This has been a very random day."

Henry was standing by the bay window, looking out over the drive. The view that way had changed remarkably little. The road was tarmac now, of course – it had been a chalky track back then – but the oak trees that ran along it and the fields beyond felt comfortingly familiar. To the west, though, things were deceptive. The strip of trees that marked the beginning of Ashridge was only a façade: a housing estate stood where the wood should have been. He wondered if nightingales sang there anymore. It was unlikely. Turtle doves unlikelier still.

"Hey, Henry!" Marsha called, jolting him out of his thoughts. "Can I take a picture? For my friend who used to live here? The one who found your diary?"

She put one arm around his shoulders, pressing her face close to his, and extended the other out in front of them to take a photo on her phone. Henry knew what a selfie was, but this was his first experience of one. She examined the image on the screen, frowned, and took another. This one seemed to meet her approval.

"I'll email you a copy if you like," she said.

Always taking photos, this generation. They were lucky. He wished he had more photos from the old days to pin down his memories.

"Thank you. I'd like that. In fact, any pictures you take."

She smiled. "Sure thing."

. . .

Marsha perched on the arm of the sofa and WhatsApped the photo to Ruth.

> In your old bedroom with THE REAL LIFE HENRY COOK!
>
> Also, any idea which floorboard you left his diary under?

Ruth replied instantly.

> WTAF! That's mad! I want to meet him!
>
> I can't remember which floorboard! Somewhere by the bed maybe?
>
> Say hi from me. To Henry, and to the house xxx

"My friend says hi and that she wants to meet you," Marsha said. "You're quite the literary celebrity you know."

At that moment, Veronika reappeared, carrying a clawhammer and small crowbar. She held them up triumphantly. "We have a look now."

Henry began to protest. "Oh no, really, you don't have to take up the carpet."

"It may not even be there," Laurence added.

Marsha cut over them: "Veronika, you are a total legend!"

It was the first time she'd seen Veronika smile. It made her look years younger, and a little deranged. Veronika knelt down and used the hammer to wedge the crowbar behind the skirting board and lever it away from the wall. The nails came out easily.

Marsha unplugged the computer, the desk lamp and the guitar amp. "Come on Ali, give me a hand," she said.

Aleesha sighed, and helped her carry the desk to the other side of the room.

Laurence shook his head. "You are all complete mentalists," he said, picking up the amp and the guitar.

Veronika worked her way methodically along the wall until she could pull the whole skirting board free. Then she used the clawhammer to prise the carpet off the sharp metal teeth of the grippers. She gave a triumphant yelp as it came free.

Marsha, having manoeuvred the sofa over to where the desk was, helped her to pull back the end of the carpet, but it stuck firm at the side. Veronika dealt with that skirting board too, then they folded back the carpet from the corner to the centre of the room. They did the same with the underlay.

"Shit, sorry!" Marsha said. The underlay had ripped as she pulled it.

"Pah, is no problem."

"Henry," called Marsha. "Any idea which your floorboard is?"

Henry, who had been watching from the bay window with a bewildered smile on his face, came slowly over.

"I think it was somewhere near this wall."

They tried lifting each floorboard in turn, but none came loose.

"Maybe it was the other wall?" Marsha suggested, but just then Veronika gave an excited shriek.

"Here." She pointed. "These nails are different colour. Newer."

She picked up the crowbar and hammer, and levered up the board. Then she reached down and drew out a thick notebook with a battered red cover. Still kneeling, she held it up to Henry as if she was presenting him with an offering. Marsha clicked a photo.

Wonderingly, Henry took the book. It was instantly familiar, even the smell of it. On the cover, in his neatest joined-up handwriting, *Henry Cook*. Then the word *Dairy* crossed out and replaced with *Diary*. He opened up the first page.

The old woman has given me this dairy to write things down in. She says it must all be a bit overwhelming and she can under-stand I might not want to talk about it but that it would be good for me to write down my thoughts and feelings because it must all be very different. It is all very different. I just want to go home.

He began leafing through the pages. He was amazed to see how much he'd written. Clearly his observations on life became less laconic. Only a few blank sheets remained.

Tucked inside the back of the book were a handful of photos. Small prints, three inches square, in faded sepia. He picked one up. It said "Christmas Day 1940" on the back – himself, Tessa, Heather and Celia by the tree, with the dogs. Celia was staring intently at the camera like a silent movie star, while Heather looked like she was trying not to laugh. How young they looked! Little more than children. They had kept in touch, up to a point. They both came to his wedding, Heather with her husband and two boys, Celia a woman of intimidating elegance, a moderately successful actress by then. An image came to him of her frozen like a statue – Hermione in *The Winter's Tale*. Cambridge Arts Theatre. He had seen her perform several times. But what with careers, children, travel, contact had dwindled to little more than Christmas cards. And eventually those had stopped coming. Oh, if only they were here to see this!

The boy who was him eyed the camera with suspicion;

he wasn't used to having his photo taken. Mrs Cann had one hand resting on his shoulder. The other was stroking Byron's ear. She looked happy.

A larger sheet had been stuck to the inside back cover. He carefully unfolded it. Of course: it was his bird chart. Down the left hand side, a list of birds; across the top, the months of the year. In the carefully ruled columns, he'd put a tick if he spotted the bird that month.

Wood pigeon, he read. He looked out the window. A pigeon took off from the nearest lime tree. The next row: *Robin.* There, right there – a smudge of red on the railing by the front gate. He moved his finger down to the next row: *House sparrow...*

"In the hedge." Marsha had appeared by his shoulder. She pointed. "On the other side of the road."

He looked. His eyes weren't what they were, but he could make out two small brown birds flitting in and out of the branches.

"Does it still count if they're on the other side of the road?"

"Oh yes," he said. "They still count."

"Shall we help you put things back?" Laurence was asking.

Veronika surveyed the room. "No, is okay. Maybe I take up the rest of the carpet. Is nicer with the floorboards, I think."

Laurence bent down to examine the boards. They were blotchy where the varnish had worn away, and patches of grey-green underlay stuck to them in places, but they were smooth and deep grained.

"Oak," he said. "Give these a once over with a sander and some oil and they'd come up lovely."

Henry turned to the last entry.

I asked Mrs Cann if this would still be my room and she said of course, so I'm going to leave this diary in its usual place under the floorboard for when I come back.

OFFERING

2021

itting in the front seat of his car with the door open, Felix looked back at the house once more, as if to make sure it was still there. It seemed to be looking at him. Pleased to see him? Curious?

He checked his phone again. 1:08. They were late. He tapped the Facebook icon. No notifications. He scrolled. People he didn't really care about posting things that didn't really interest him. Sponsored links for cottages in Cornwall, craft beer and bamboo socks. Some woman he hadn't seen since primary school posting antivaxxer bollocks, which at least made a change from the usual rants about Brexit and the Tories that rang round the echo chamber of his newsfeed. Change.org asked him if he'd help Jeremy Farby by signing a petition about nurses' salaries. He'd signed that one already, for what good it would do. The 6 Music page told him that Massive Attack's *Blue Lines* was thirty years old, which was just cruel.

The algorithm wanted him to know that Alexandra Blake had been tagged in a post. "Robin Blake was with Alexandra Blake and Kelly Blake in Sausalito, California."

That was a funny coincidence. She'd come up as one of the People You May Know a few years ago, and had accepted the friend request he sent, though they'd had little other interaction. He remembered her from the school production of *A Midsummer Night's Dream* – she'd been a fairy in rave glasses – but mainly he was curious about her connection with The Lindens. Her parents had sold the house by then though. Felix clicked on the photo. The caption read "Lovely to see my big sis at her amazing home!" Three adults and three children, sitting on an outdoor sofa with an infinity pool and the sun setting into the sea behind them. He recognised Alex, though she didn't post pictures often, but wouldn't have identified the balding man balancing a daughter on his knee as her little brother Robin. The woman beside him was presumably his wife. In front of them were two golden-haired teenage boys, identical except that one was beaming at the camera while the other wore a contemptuous scowl.

Felix Liked the picture. He scrolled down. He was about to click on a link to "30 times Piers Morgan got ROASTED on Twitter" when he saw "Izzie McFarlane updated her profile picture."

He tapped the photo. Twenty-five years on, Izzie still looked remarkably like herself. She still wore her hair long, though there were a few white streaks in it. The nose stud had disappeared from her photos some years ago. You could see the lines on her face, but it was still the same incandescent smile. The picture was a close up of her and her daughter, Maya, with mountain scenery in the background. The Lake District, probably. It didn't seem long ago that she was posting pictures of a Maya as a baby. Now she must be about fourteen. She looked remarkably like his memory of her mother at the same age when he used to see her on the school bus and never plucked up the courage to talk to her.

Twenty-six people had Liked or Loved the photo already. Felix tapped the heart icon, then added a comment: "I didn't know you had a sister..." He hesitated before adding an "x". Izzie scattered kisses over her social media like confetti – it didn't really mean anything.

She had been his girlfriend for three months, and he had spent all but the first few hours of that time in Odstock Hospital. If he was honest with himself, he'd never got over her. Most of that summer she'd perched on the end of his bed or in the chair beside him, first on the intensive care unit where he was treated for smoke inhalation and third degree burns, then during the long weeks of his recovery on the burns unit. She brought punnets of strawberries and cherries and chocolate chip cookies she'd baked. They talked about everything and nothing. They played highly competitive games of draughts and Othello. They listened to tapes together on his Walkman, taking an earphone each. She rubbed emollient on his burns. The nurses loved her and were always telling him what a lucky man he was. He didn't need to be told. Sometimes when it was quiet she'd draw the curtains round the bed and slip in beside him. He still thought about those moments. Looking back, despite the circumstances, it still seemed like a golden time in his life.

But Izzie had her own life to lead. At the beginning of October, she went off to uni in Lancaster. They agreed they'd *just see how it goes*. How it went, of course, was that Izzie met lots of lovely new people, and more than a few of them fell in love with her. By Christmas, she was sort of seeing someone. And by then his own life had fallen apart.

A month after Felix was discharged from hospital, his mother was admitted. A lump on her breast, growing in secret for months. When Eleanor had finally gone to the doctor, it was too late: the cancer had already metastasised. What if they'd caught it sooner? If she hadn't been preoccupied with his afflictions all that summer, she might have had it checked out before, when surgery was still a possibility. Even a month earlier might have made all the difference.

"It's not your fault, Felix," Izzie told him, over and over, but it was a sore that his mind couldn't help picking away at.

He had been with Eleanor when the oncologist laid out the prognosis. It was terminal, and any treatment would be about extending her life by a matter of months. There were sure to be unpleasant side effects. Alternatively, they might think about making the most of her quality of life for as long she had left.

Felix wanted them to treat her. His mother couldn't die. It must be some mistake. Perhaps the doctors were wrong. Perhaps the treatments were more effective than they thought. Perhaps they'd buy enough time for someone to invent a miracle cure. But where he was stuck in denial, Eleanor had already passed through to acceptance.

"I haven't got much time left. I don't want to waste it in hospitals."

She spent the best part of six months at home. Felix, having deferred his university place for a year, took care of her as best he could. He cooked their meals with lots of fresh vegetables from the garden, telling himself that it would help her immune system fight off the cancer for just a little longer, though she didn't have much of an appetite. They played Scrabble and bezique and watched VHS boxsets of *Poldark* and *Monty Python*. Sometimes she painted – a watercolour of the back of the house that she'd completed that winter hung in his living room today. Sometimes she felt energetic enough to walk up to the pond or along the lane to Ashridge. Much of the time she was exhausted, and the painkillers made her woozy. Seb came back for the Christmas holidays, and she rallied as best she could. Arthur even came over on Boxing Day, and they had a strange sort of family Christmas together. They ended up looking at old photo albums, reminiscing about Collette and Gaia the goat, elderflower champagne, the old car in Brickwood, playing cricket on the lawn.

"We were happy, weren't we?" Eleanor said, in that quiet, wistful voice she used more and more those days.

It was late March when he drove her to the hospice. A perfect spring morning, the lawn freshly painted with tulips and daffodils and the wild cherries in flower over the wall in Brickwood. They had stood in silence for several minutes outside the back door, taking it all in.

She died ten days later. Twenty-five years and one week ago. They buried her in the village churchyard, in a cardboard coffin, and planted an apple tree on the grave; it was unconventional but the vicar had agreed to it, along with her request to have "Always Look on the Bright Side of Life" playing when the coffin was carried out. Izzie came back for the funeral. She held Felix's hand during the service, and stayed by his side all afternoon, keeping up bright, gracious conversation with endless well-wishers when he could hardly string three words together. Back at The Lindens, when all the guests had left, she had cradled his head in her lap and he had wept into her black cotton skirt.

By that time she had met Gareth. At the end of her three years in Lancaster she stayed up north. She was a drama teacher for a few years, then she and Gareth had bought a farm together in the Forest of Bowland. Now they grew organic fruits and made a range of cordials and vinegars that they sold in local farmers' markets, though Felix had once seen them on sale in Waitrose. They had two kids,

Maya and Quinn, and a border collie. Gareth seemed like a good bloke – Felix had never met him, but they sometimes interacted on Facebook. They might be friends if they met in real life. Or not, if Gareth ever suspected how much Felix envied his life.

Losing The Lindens was like another bereavement. That spring, the garden went undug. No tomato seedlings germinated in the greenhouse, but the seed potatoes that Eleanor had left to chit sprouted twisting tendrils in the darkness of the cellar. When the swallows returned, when he heard the first cuckoo, Felix had nobody to tell.

There was no question of staying on alone. The Blakes had bought the house. They seemed like a nice family. They were keen to take on the chickens, but Felix had to find homes for Freya the goat and Cressida, his mother's mare. He and Colleen had moved in with Arthur and Melissa.

Although Arthur had owned half the house, and there had been inheritance tax and cuts for lawyers and estate agents, Felix still found himself with a bank balance in the low six figures. Seb used his share as a deposit on a house, in Bristol. Felix fully intended to do the same – but not quite yet. He decided to go travelling. A gap year would do him good, he thought. He would reapply for a place at university when he felt ready for it. He spent a year bumming round Australia, working his way up the east coast from Sydney to Cairns. He drank far too much, he smoked lots of weed, he spent money without thinking about it, moving a few hundred over from his savings to his current account whenever he needed to. Mostly he stayed in backpacker hostels, but sometimes he'd treat himself to a few days in a nice hotel and eat in decent restaurants just because he could. He formed transitory friendships, which wasn't hard when people saw how easy he was with his money. He spent a fortnight snorkelling on the Great Barrier Reef and saw Uluru from a hot-air balloon. He sent frequent aerogrammes to Izzie, covering the thin blue sheets in tiny writing, being sure to find room to include a future poste restante address. She wrote back, though not as often as he checked the post offices.

He didn't want to come home; he didn't have a home to come back to. He thought perhaps he might become a travel writer, and sent two pieces to his dad (a flowery description of sailing round the "icing-sugar beaches" and "aquamarine lagoons" of the Whitsunday Islands, and a would-be humorous account of the latter-day hippies of Byron Bay and Nimbin), but they came back covered with so many crossings-out and comments in red pen that he soon gave up on the idea.

He washed up in Thailand, six months in a hut right on the beach. The rent was next to nothing but the partying took a toll. He discovered a ravenous appetite for coke and E (though he steered clear of mushrooms), made profound connections with strangers when pilled up under the full moon but avoided eye contact the next day. More than once he thought of the parable of the prodigal son. But the moral of that story was that you could waste your inheritance and get away with it, reach rock bottom and still be forgiven and welcomed home. Besides, the money wasn't even close to running out.

He built up his own myth, reinforced through the story he told to so many sympathetic strangers. How he'd almost died in a freak accident – he'd open his shirt to give them a glimpse of the burn marks – and then lost his mother to cancer. And how that made him determined to see the world and to live every day like it was his last. People said he was amazing. An inspiration. "You the Man." He almost believed it.

One night he'd been trotting this out to a Swedish girl named Frida – "So I'm just trying to make the most of every moment, yeah?" – but instead of offering the admiration and affirmation he was seeking, she'd shaken her head sadly.

"And is that what you are doing? When you are spending every night in the bar on this beach?"

He was taken aback, unsure what to say.

"Sorry, but I think you haven't processed things yet. I think this is your way of putting off dealing with the grief. Running away from it, trying to distract yourself from it. You're hoping it will go away on its own one day. But it won't."

She'd taken his hand then. "You think I'm being a bitch. But I'm only saying to you what I wish somebody had said to me." And she told him about how her beloved but strict father had died when she was fifteen, and how she'd become fixated on honouring his memory by doing as well as she possibly could in school, rather than taking the time to grieve, until the inevitable stress-induced breakdown. Of all the conversations with random people in the course of his travels, that was the one he remembered best.

A few days later, he got a letter from Arthur, saying that he and Melissa were moving to Greece. Was Felix coming home anytime soon? He could stay in their house in Salisbury if he wanted until he found his own place; otherwise, they'd put his things into storage and rent it out. Up to him of course, but it would be nice to see him sometime, and Arthur hoped everything was okay. Oh, and if he wasn't coming back, did he know anybody who wanted to look after the dog?

That clinched it. He booked a flight home the following week, landing in Heathrow in the early hours of a grey October morning. His father met him at the airport; they had exactly a week together before Arthur and Melissa left for Kalamata. They talked about his travels, and about Arthur's plans – the dilapidated farmhouse he'd bought in the Peloponnese with its olive grove and orange trees and the book deal already agreed. They didn't talk about emotions, or the fact that, for all he'd spent two years in the southern hemisphere doing his own thing, Felix didn't feel ready to be left to fend for himself.

He reapplied to university, but by the time the new academic year rolled round – by which time most of his contemporaries had already graduated – he'd slipped into a dark hole that he didn't have the strength to climb out of. He didn't take up the place. He had no job, no friends that he could face seeing. He coped, just barely: paid the bills when the red one arrived, cleaned the kitchen before the dirt grew legs, made a weekly trip to the supermarket for wine and dog food, pasta and pesto. If it wasn't for Colleen's sad-collie eyes guilt-tripping him, he might have gone days at a time without leaving the house. When he did venture out, he would feel everyone staring at him and whispering just out of earshot. Or else he felt invisible, like he could step in front of a car and nobody would even notice.

It passed eventually. He would have similar episodes in the years that followed, but at least he learned to recognise them for what they were. Sometimes they were triggered by something identifiable (when Colleen had to be put to sleep; turning thirty; turning forty), sometimes just by the dreadful knowledge that life, which he had supposed to be something full of joy and wonder, love and security, too often wasn't. He went to university eventually – decidedly stale compared to his fellow freshers, yet feeling little affinity for those strange, focused adults known as mature students – and departed three years later with a degree of little value, a debt larger than the dwindling inheritance in his bank account, and no more idea of what to do with his life. A TEFL course, another year in Thailand, two years in a language school in Crete, and suddenly his twenties were over for ever.

His phone bleeped. A little red circle appeared next to the notification icon with the number 1, then 2.

Izzie McFarlane *reacted to your comment "I didn't know you had a sister... x"*

Izzie McFarlane *mentioned you in her comments.*

He tapped the notification. She'd added a Haha emoji, and the comment *"**Felix Aldridge** I think your eyesight's going – it can happen when you're as ancient as we are 😂😂😂 xxx."*

Felix tried to think of a witty reply that would bring another little dopamine hit. He couldn't, so just reacted with a Haha.

He scrolled down. His cousin Tonia had posted a photo of a sourdough loaf she'd baked. He tapped Like. He hadn't seen Tonia in well over a decade, but had a fairly good idea of what food she ate, where she walked with her Yorkshire terrier and what boxsets she'd been watching.

His dad had posted an update – *"Pleased to announce my latest literary offering, **Living La Vida Lockdown,** is out in July. Available to order from your favourite independent bookshop/tax-dodging multinational online retailer."* There was a link to his website. Apparently Arthur couldn't simply enjoy retirement (in Catalonia, where he'd moved five years ago) but had to keep telling stories about it. He'd churned this one out quickly, Felix had to give him that. He clicked Like. Facebook immediately suggested he might like the page "Arthur

Aldridge fans", along with three of his Friends and 6,000 other people. Felix tapped the cross in the top right corner, and a new suggestion appeared for Brixton Bunnies Shit-posting. There was a picture of Brenda Bunny holding a banner which, in the original book, had said "Save our park" but in this version read "Fuck Brexit". Social media had given the Brixton Bunnies a surprisingly active afterlife. Felix sometimes wondered if he should be concerned about copyright, but he liked to think that on the whole Eleanor would approve.

His colleague Matt had posted a link to the agency's latest listings. He did this every day. Felix had never once Liked, shared or commented on any of these posts. Facebook's algorithm appeared convinced that Felix was more interested in his work than he actually was. Of all the things he had wanted to be when he was growing up – explorer, writer, cricketer, musician, farmer, actor, botanist, sheepdog handler – estate agent wouldn't have made the top 200. He had wandered into it fourteen years ago and somehow never found his way out again. He'd returned to England after a depressing epiphany that being a TEFL teacher in your thir-ties was essentially an admission that you'd wasted your twenties. Though the way he'd wasted his twenties was at least more fun than the way he wasted his thirties. He signed up to a temping agency, and found himself doing office admin with Coffey and Cole – it was all he'd felt capable of, following the latest down episode (not so much a black dog as an anxious rescue dog with sharp teeth). But he'd done that efficiently enough, and soon he'd started taking on more responsibilities. There was something soothing about carrying out repetitive tasks competently, and a steady financial reward for it replenishing his bank account. They took him on full time, and before long he began showing houses. He turned out to be surprisingly good at it. He wasn't a pushy salesman, far from it. But he was good at listening to people, understanding their needs and showing them what they were looking for.

It was like matchmaking, matching people with a house. Although it was becoming an obsolete skill: you had apps for that now. Tinder, Zoopla, it was much the same. You put in your filters – three bedrooms, off-road parking, good sense of humour – and let the algorithm do the work. Of course, for most people, what they really wanted was out of their league. And yet they usually found the one eventually – the one they could love, the one they could call home, despite the imperfections, or even because of them. Or maybe they just learnt to settle.

Felix had bought a house seven years ago – a three-bedroom 1950s semi on the edge of town, just the kind of place he'd have recommended to a young family. Larger than he needed. He put in a new kitchen with an island, bifold doors onto the garden, recessed lighting. He built two raised beds in the garden and grew some tomatoes and chilli plants in the conservatory. It was fine. But not the home he wanted. That was partly because he lived alone, of course. There had been people over the years. Not many: though his face had escaped miraculously unscathed from the fire, he was deeply self-conscious about the burns that disfigured most of his body. And not for long: it wasn't fair to put somebody through the tribulations of loving him if he wasn't sure he could love them back. He never was.

Still, his salary funded a comfortable lifestyle for a single person. He wore good clothes, had a wine club membership, went on hiking holidays in the Pyrenees and the Cairngorms. He went to the gym twice a week, had a collection of guitars and a sixty-five-inch TV screen. *A dish-*

washer and a coffee percolator – or, more accurately, a state-of-the-art bean-to-cup machine with inbuilt milk frother.

Some weeks ago, James Coffey had called Felix into his office to say his father was retiring at the end of the year, and there could be an opening for a new partner. Security for the rest of his career, then a healthy pension. As pacts with the devil went, it wasn't a bad one. He'd taken a down payment on his soul years ago.

A few days after that, Coffey had mentioned a new property they'd been instructed with out near Alderbourne. He was confident he could sell it for seven figures – he'd put it on at £1.1 million.

"Old Victorian place, but modernised tastefully, and ten acres of land with it. There's a converted barn on-site, and other outbuildings too – should be possible to get planning permission. Here."

He handed Felix the particulars. And there, staring back at him reproachfully from the glossy A4 print-out, was the face of The Lindens.

He didn't say anything then. And he didn't say anything when, yesterday morning, Coffey had asked him if he could do a couple of viewings.

"I was supposed to be doing them myself but I've got a valuation in the Cathedral Close. Geoff and Harvey at 11. From Land2Build. Could be interested as a potential development opportunity. Then some family from London who called up yesterday. Sandra has the details. They're at 1pm I believe."

Felix checked the time on his phone again. It was nearly quarter past. He'd give them another few minutes before calling. Rich Londoners buying big homes in the country weren't his favourite people, but he hoped he'd like the Wood family better than the Land2Build guys. He'd dealt with Geoff and Harvey a few times, and wasn't sure which of them was the greater wanker: Geoff, an overbearing gammon who laughed at his own jokes, or Harvey, a spiv with a mockney accent, though Felix was pretty sure he'd been to public school. As the name suggested, they bought land, sorted out planning permission and sold it to property developers at an obscene profit. Some surprising planning decisions went in their favour. There'd been a piece in *Private Eye*'s Rotten Boroughs column suggesting that the consultancy fees the company paid to a Tory councillor who happened to sit on the planning committee might have had something to do with it.

He looked up at the house again, empty and unloved. There were tulips in the front garden, red, white and yellow, but the house looked sad. It was the first time he'd been back in twenty-five years. He'd driven past many times, for viewings nearby and to visit his mother's grave to leave flowers and pick the apples every autumn. He would gather the windfalls, then shake the tree and collect the fruits that fell, sometimes on the neighbouring graves (he offered his apologies to the inhabitants, one Roger Arnold Cann and his wife Tessa Mary Cann, before treading on them). There was something of Eleanor in the tree – literally atoms that had once been part of her. He would slow down as he drove past the house – had seen the burnt husk of the dairy converted into a flat, noted that the lime tree they'd planted after the '87 hurricane was now as tall as its harshly pollarded companions – but had never stopped.

That morning, he'd arrived half an hour early to look around. The house had been unoccupied for several months. When he unlocked the back door – a modern yale lock, not the big iron key from his childhood – the house seemed to exhale. There were no furnishings, and his footsteps echoed on the floorboards. It had been done up reasonably tastefully, he had to admit. Downstairs was light and airy. The new kitchen and the décor felt modern while respecting the character of the building, the estate agent's voice in his head was telling him. Classier than when it had been the Aldridge family home. He tried to picture the kitchen as he remembered it: his mother kneading dough at the kitchen table, Collette (or later, Colleen) asleep by the Aga, washing hanging from the pulley maid, his and Seb's drawings stuck to the fridge with magnets, a pinboard with postcards covering half the wall, where now there were white tiles and shelves of sanded scaffolding boards that Coffey's description predictably called rustic. It was all so strange and so familiar. He was almost relieved when Geoff and Harvey turned up ten minutes early, before he'd wandered too far into the quicksand of memory.

"Felix, right?" Geoff held out a hand, then withdrew it. "Oops, sorry, can't do that, can we? Let's not bother with the elbow bollocks. You tell James he's got a nerve standing us up. That's no way to treat his favourite clients." Geoff guffawed at himself. Felix smiled politely.

"He sends his apologies, but he had another appointment he couldn't miss."

"Ha. Tell him he's lucky I didn't just contact Cameron Lambert directly."

"You know the vendor?" Felix asked.

"Lambert's an old mate of my old mate Piers. You know Piers Hunt?"

"I don't believe I've had the pleasure."

"Ah, well, he used to come out shooting with Piers and the boys sometimes. Dragged his wife along one time. Foxy lady from Poland."

"Slovenia," corrected Harvey.

"Well anyway, you tell James he's lucky I'm a gentleman and go through the proper channels."

"I'm sure we're all very grateful."

They were in and out of the house itself in ten minutes.

"Could probably sell it as it is," was Geoff's opinion.

"Or retirement flats," Harvey said. "Depends on the rest of the development. Course there's those geezers from Four Seasons Assisted Living was looking for rural sites."

Geoff turned to Felix. "I keep telling Harv, now's not the time to be getting into care homes – they've all got thousands of vacancies thanks to Covid." He laughed. Harvey joined in, then stopped.

"Joking aside, though, it's still a massive growth market. And the good thing about your Covid is, anyone who's got the money isn't going to want to go near your big care homes now. They're going to want exclusive, quality sites in the countryside."

Felix imagined James Coffey, or any of his colleagues, nodding along. Coffey had told him to talk up the development potential of the outbuildings. He'd mentioned Brickwood too. "Used to be an industrial site, a brickworks – long time ago, but you could probably get away with calling it brownfield."

"It's right at the edge of the village though," Felix pointed out.

"No, there's that Ashridge Grove estate just down the road, so it counts as in-fill. Or it does if you have Geoff and Harvey's contacts."

Harvey was pointing over the wall to Brickwood now, the wild cherry in full flower and the first bright green on the oak and the hawthorn. "That wood's part of the property, right? Know anything about it?"

"That?" asked Felix. "That's ancient woodland, unfortunately. I'm pretty sure there's tree preservation orders."

Geoff grunted. "Ha! I suppose the place is riddled with great crested transgender disabled newts too, eh?" He supplied his own laughter.

"I believe there are great crested newts actually, in the pond," Felix said.

"I fackin' hate newts," spat Harvey. "I'm not shitting you, I've lost thousands of pounds because of those slimy bastards."

"Well, Boris is going to put a stop to that," Geoff said. "And we won't have all that EU red tape either. You know there's a 'Habitats Directive' [he did air quotes] and a 'Birds Directive'."

"Probably a fackin' Amphibians Directive and all," added Harvey.

"Still, we don't even need to worry about the fields and that. It's all land in the bank, isn't it? More than enough with these buildings here to be getting on with."

"Business park," Harvey suggested. "It's only a mile or so off the Southampton Road, innit?"

Geoff nodded. "Distribution centre, even."

They took a lot of photos of the stable flat, the dairy, the garage.

"So, has there been much interest?" Geoff asked.

"I've got another viewing this afternoon. But it's pretty quiet at the moment."

"Really? I thought the market was picking up. Well, anyway, you tell Mr Cappuccino we'll be in touch."

"Coffey, he means," Harvey explained.

"Actually, it's best if you call me directly," Felix said. "If you're thinking of making an offer."

"Whatever you say, boss. Harv, do you have the number

of the gentleman's portable telecommunication device?" (That laugh again.) "His mobile number, you plonker!"

Felix's phone rang. It was a mobile number he didn't recognise.

"Hi, is that Felix? It's Aleesha Wood. I'm so sorry. We're in a place called Stourton, by a duck pond. We may be a little bit lost."

"Ah, you probably missed the turning in Elbourne. Anyway, you're only just up the road." He gave her the directions.

"Oh, thank goodness. We'll see you very shortly."

A toddler started crying in the background, then the call ended. Five minutes later, a green van drew up. It wasn't the sort of vehicle Felix was expecting. He read the stencilled lettering on the side.

Laurence Wood
Tree surgery and stump art
woodwood.co.uk | @StumpSculpture

The man who climbed down from the driving seat was a few years younger than Felix, with more hair and a beard like he was in some American indie-folk band.

"Felix? So sorry we're late. I'm Laurence. This is my wife Aleesha."

The woman smiled. "Nice to meet you. This is Thalia and Zane."

Two small faces eyed him warily. The boy, who wore a Gruffalo jumper, sported the most impressive Afro Felix had ever seen on a three-year-old. His younger sister had strikingly blue eyes and adorable curls.

"And this is Marsha, my sister."

This hardly needed saying: the woman stepping out the back of the van looked very like Aleesha, though while the latter's hair was cut short with a straight fringe, her sister wore hers long and coily, tied back in a purple headscarf.

"It's Marsha's fault we're late. I said we should just use Google Maps, but she insisted she knew the way."

"I did! I just missed a turning, is all."

"Lots of people miss that turning," Felix said.

"Thank you!" She beamed at him. "See? Anyway, it was your husband who wouldn't stop and ask for directions."

"What can I say?" Laurence shrugged. "I'm a bloke."

"You can't expect a bloke to ask for directions," Felix said. "It undermines our masculinity."

"Exactly!"

After half an hour in the company of Geoff and Harvey, it felt good to laugh naturally. Felix liked these people already.

"So you came down from London?" he asked.

"That's right."

"And are you looking at other places in the area?"

"No," Marsha said. "Just this one."

"Okay." After a few years in the job, Felix had found most people conformed to one type or another, but he was finding this party hard to pigeonhole. Generation-rent millennial Londoners, two Black sisters and the tree surgeon hipster husband, plus two kids, looking to buy a big house in the Wiltshire countryside. It didn't compute. "So what drew this place to your attention?" he asked.

"It's kind of a long and convoluted story," Laurence said.

"But a good one," Marsha put in. "For starters, my ex used to live here."

"Whooah. Not Robin Blake, by any chance? He was a few years below me at school."

"No, not Robin. His sister?"

"Alexandra?" That surprised him.

"No. God, no! Ruth."

"Ah, okay. Sorry. I didn't know her at all."

"Well, her parents still know people who live in the village. She mentioned the house was for sale."

"That's not really the interesting part though," Aleesha said.

"I have a kind of family connection too," said Laurence.

"Great-grandpa Henry," the boy Zane piped up.

"That's right," Laurence said. "You explain, Marsha."

So Marsha began explaining how Ruth Blake had found a diary under the floorboards in her bedroom, written by a boy called Henry Cook who had been an evacuee there during the war.

"Well, a few years ago I came across something Lumberjack Larry here had put on Twitter about a book his granddad had written."

"My granddad, Henry Cook."

"And it was all about birds. And this kid Henry Cook was *really* into birds. So long story short, we got chatting, and now he's married to my sister here and has two beautiful children."

"That's only part of it," Laurence said.

"Quite a significant part," Aleesha reminded him.

"We came down here with my granddad to look for the diary. About five years ago."

"Ruth had put it back under the floorboards in her bedroom when she moved out."

"Which bedroom?" Felix asked.

"The one at the front on this side. Why?"

His room. "Oh, just curious. Sorry, carry on. Did you find it?"

"We did. You can tell from reading it how much Gramps loved it here. It just sounded like the most wonderful place to be a kid."

"Absolutely. Is your grandfather still alive?"

"He is. He turned ninety last year."

"We nearly brought him along with us, but he's not so into road trips these days," Marsha said. "Still sharp as a tack though."

Without thinking about it, Felix led them round to the back of the house. Only strangers and the postman used to come to the front door.

"Should we take our shoes off?" Aleesha asked.

"No, it's fine. It's mostly wooden floors. But we are supposed to wear masks."

"Of course."

Felix had grown surprisingly fond of his face mask. It was a deep blue, with silhouettes of swallows flying across it. He'd bought it off Etsy.

"Hey, snap!" Marsha said. "Almost. Same artist. Check out my tits."

He couldn't see her expression because she had mask over her mouth, but her eyes were laughing. The mask's design was a family of long-tailed tits.

"Never gets old. I nearly got the same one as you, but in the end I decided to go for the cheap double entendre. Plus I am particularly fond of long-tailed tits."

"Me too," said Felix, delighted. "So, I could give you the whole estate agent's spiel, but maybe it's best if I just leave you to it?"

"Thank you," Aleesha said. "I think we'd like to just have

a good look around. Try and imagine what it might be like to live here."

"Well, let me know if you have any questions."

Thalia had already toddled off down the hallway and was starting to climb the stairs. Laurence trotted after her, with Zane following.

"Maybe we'll go upstairs first," Aleesha said, going after them. Marsha hung back.

"The kitchen and the living room were separate when Ruth and co lived here," she said. "This is nice though. It feels really light."

"It's south facing, so you get the sun all day," Felix said.

"Is that part of your estate agent's spiel?"

"Sorry. Can't help myself. It is true though."

"You should also point out that it gives a view onto the walled garden. A lawn extending eighty feet, with mature shrubs and flowerbeds."

"And a unique Victorian folly, which could be converted into an iconic home office space. Or where the kids could play hide-and-seek. So, is it your sister and her family who're looking to buy? Or you as well?"

"Well, the idea is that they'd live in the main house and I could live in the stable flat. The maiden aunt." She laughed. "Sounds tragic, doesn't it? But Aleesha and I have always been close, I get on well with Laurence, and I love my nephew and niece. So it makes sense. Financially as well, obviously. I can't quite get my head around the fact that I'm looking round a property that costs over a million pounds."

Felix had been wondering about this. "I had no idea tree surgeons earned so much in London."

Marsha laughed, but then looked serious. "Actually, Aleesha and I came into some property. Our mum died last year."

"Oh God, I'm really sorry. That's awful."

"Yeah. It is."

"I lost my mum too. That was more than twenty years ago, but it still hurts."

"Oh, you were really young. Poor you." She took his hand and gave it a squeeze. It fizzed through him like static electricity. God, he couldn't remember the last time he'd had any kind of physical contact with another person. He couldn't blame it all on lockdown.

There was a call from upstairs. "Sounds like I'm needed," Marsha said, letting go his hand. He followed her up into what he still thought of as Eleanor's bedroom.

"We've lost the children, Auntie Marsha," Aleesha said loudly. "We need you to help us find them."

A giggle came from inside the built-in wardrobe.

"Oh dear. How terribly careless of you. Now where can they possibly be?" She opened the door to the adjacent bathroom – a new addition since Felix's time. "Maybe they're in the spacious en-suite with free-standing bath and walk-in shower..."

Laurence gave Felix an apologetic look. "Sorry. They have been in the van for the last two hours."

"It's fine, really. They can explore as much as they want."

"Do you have kids?" Laurence asked.

"I have two nephews, but they're a bit old for hide-and-seek. They're mostly glued to their phones these days."

Laurence walked over to the window that looked out over Brickwood. "So this wood is all part of the property, right?"

"Yeah. About an acre."

Laurence sighed happily. "I've always dreamed of having my own piece of woodland. I do these sculptures out of tree stumps."

"I saw that on your van."

"I've been starting to get into woodturning too. Bowls and so on. This is just perfect – all these different trees."

"Do you have a favourite tree?" Felix asked. "For the type of wood, I mean."

"That's a good question. I love oak and yew for stumps. Ash and sycamore are great for turning, and cherry's really pretty. But every piece is different, that's one of the things I love about it."

Marsha had found the children, to exuberant giggles. "You hide now," Zane told her.

"How about I hide when we go outside? There's some great places there."

"Can we go outside now?" Zane asked.

"In a minute," Aleesha said. "Mummy just wants to look around downstairs."

They went down to the kitchen. Felix wished he could put the kettle on and make tea for them all. Maybe serve lunch, and eat it out in the sunshine and drink homemade cider. Ask them to stay for supper.

"Can we get into the folly?" Marsha asked.

"It might be locked, but I've got the key somewhere. Do you want to see?"

"We'll be hiding in the folly at the end of the garden," Marsha stage-whispered to the parents.

The folly turned out to be unlocked. "I used to come up here with Ruth," Marsha said. She laughed to herself.

"What's funny?" Felix asked.

"Oh – just remembering. We smoked a bong up here, and I got freaked out about going down the steps. Probably the last time I ever smoked a bong, actually."

He was enjoying this woman's company. "I've smoked many a joint up here, but never a bong as far as I recall."

She looked at him quizzically. "Sorry, what?"

"Okay, full disclosure. Nobody else knows this, including my boss. I grew up here."

"What the – ? In this house?"

"Yeah."

"Seriously? So, what, you lived here before Ruth's family?"

"Uh huh. My parents moved here when my mother was pregnant with me. Then we sold the house after she died. Twenty years later."

"Wait a minute. It was your parents who wrote the Brixton Bunnies books? And your dad wrote a book about your life here?"

"It was kind of fictionalised, but yes."

"That's insane. Mum used to read the Brixton Bunnies to us. This must be a totally surreal experience for you."

"It is kind of weird."

"I hated putting Mum's house up for sale. Seeing it listed on Rightmove and everything. I really resented having people come to see it."

"I know what you mean," Felix said. "Not you," he added quickly, as Marsha raised her eyebrows. "But I was showing round some people this morning. Property developers. Talking about turning it into an exclusive care home, or building a business park."

"Really?" She grimaced. "Do you think they're serious?"

"They reckon there's money to be made one way or another. So you'd better put in an offer quickly, yeah?"

"Oh God, I really hope we can. We've accepted an offer on Mum's place and we talked with a mortgage advisor the other day, but we haven't got a formal contract or whatever it is you need."

"If you have an agreement in principle, that should do the trick."

"I'm not sure. You'll have to talk to Ali, she's the one who knows about all that stuff."

Aleesha and Laurence had appeared at the back door. Zane ran up the lawn, with Thalia trailing after him.

"Was it amazing growing up here?" Marsha asked.

"I didn't know how lucky I was, but yeah. I loved it."

"If I ever have kids..." she began, but left the thought unfinished. Zane had spotted them through the window and was now tearing up the steps.

"Found you!" he cried.

"Good job. What do you think of this place?" Marsha asked.

The boy looked around. "Is it a play house?"

"It could be."

"Look." He pointed to a brick by the door, indented by the footprints of a small animal.

"I'd forgotten about those," Felix said.

"What are they?" Zane asked.

"Those," Felix told him, "are the footprints of a cat, I believe. From more than a hundred years ago. It must have walked over the bricks before they had set."

"What was its name?" Zane asked.

"Mungo Jerry," Marsha said.

"Or possibly Rumple Teaser," Felix added.

The boy seemed happy with this, and headed back out the door. "I've found them," he called.

They joined the others on the lawn.

"Can we look at the stable flat?" Aleesha asked.

"The auntie flat," Marsha added.

"Marsha's told you about her plans to start a commune, I take it?"

"Point of order, I am not planning to start a commune."

"You can start a commune if you like," Felix said. "It worked for the Brixton Bunnies."

She laughed. "Can I tell them?"

"Tell them what?" Aleesha asked.

"Felix's parents created the Brixton Bunnies. You remember?"

Aleesha nodded. "Wow. We loved those books. I need to look them out for Zane."

"Can I tell them the other bit as well?" Marsha asked.

"Well, I'd rather it didn't get back to my boss, but sure."

"That's good 'cos I'd have told them anyway. Felix used to live here."

It felt good having it out in the open. Soon, he was telling them all about growing up there, pointing out where the chicken run used to be, the stone troughs in the yard where Seb had kept goldfish and shubunkins, reminiscing about riding his trike down the hill under the overhanging juniper trees, the wreck of the sports car in Brickwood. He didn't feel like an estate agent showing clients around a property. He felt like himself, showing friends around his home. Younger, cooler friends, but still. He knew it wasn't real, but the feeling was worth holding onto.

"So was this here when you were growing up?" Laurence asked. They were in the flat, standing by the kitchen island. Afternoon light was streaming in: most of the south wall was window, looking out over the yard and the orchard. It must have been around the spot where they were standing that the fire started.

"No. This was just a hay loft." He didn't want to talk about the fire.

They looked around the other outbuildings, the orchard coming into blossom ("Those trees could do with pruning,"

Laurence noted), the top garden, an expanse of overgrown grass where his parents' vast vegetable patch used to be. Marsha asked if they could go and see the pond.

"I'm sorry, we're taking up an awful lot of your time," Aleesha said. "If you need to be getting on..."

"Honestly, it's fine. I don't have any more appointments this afternoon. And I would love to go and see the pond."

So they walked up through the meadow to the pond – it took a long time since Thalia insisted on walking all the way. Felix and Marsha found themselves going on ahead. The grass in the meadow was long, studded with celandines and cowslips. In the hedges, the blackthorn and the hawthorn were in full bud, waiting to burst into flower. Felix loved this time of year.

"So what would you do with all this?" he asked. "Planning to keep cows?"

She smiled. "Maybe. I love this little wood before the pond."

"My dad planted that."

"Seriously? That's quite a legacy, isn't it? I mean, your dad's written books and things too, but imagine creating a wood. I like the thought of having a piece of land to look after. To leave it richer than I found it, you know? That would be a good thing to do with your life, I reckon."

Felix got his phone out. "I should take a picture to send to my dad." He hadn't been able to bring himself to take any photos up to now.

"You mentioned cows," Marsha said. "I was actually thinking of free-range pigs. They're good for rewilding, apparently. I've been getting quite into the idea of rewilding, but there's only a limited amount you can do in a terrace in Hackney."

They talked about books they'd both read. About

bringing nature back, reversing plummeting bird popu-
lations.

"We'll have thickets full of nightingales, and woodpeckers in the old orchard. Woodpeckers, Felix!"

"Tell me more about your commune," Felix said.

She laughed. "It's not a commune. But, okay. The last
few years, I've been working at this urban farm. Organic
vegetables, free-range chickens, a community orchard...
they have a little café and a shop where they sell the
produce. And they run these programmes – for people with
mental health issues, kids at risk of offending, refugees and
so on. I know it all sounds terribly Woke, but it's good, and
it's been good for me. I'd kind of lost my way a bit. I used to
be a teacher, but the stress of that just got too much. I
started volunteering at this place, and now I do some work
with kids there.

"Anyway, I'd love to do something like that. Make it a
residential thing, so people would work here in exchange
for board and lodging. Almost a sort of retreat. And we'd
do weekends for, like, BAME kids who've never been to the
countryside before. Who've never seen a live chicken. This
place would be so perfect. There's the outbuildings that
you could turn into guest accommodation. And I was
thinking we could have some shepherds' huts up here by
the pond."

"Or yurts, maybe."

"Yurts would be cool. And then there's already an
orchard, and a massive garden, and Laurence can do his
lumberjack thing. Forest school type stuff. And we'd have
chickens, and my free-range pigs... possibly cows. Or I was
thinking maybe goats."

"We used to have a goat," Felix said. "If you need any
advice on goats, I'm your man."

"Perfect. You can run goat-milking lessons. You can be our caprine consultant."

"I like that. I might put that on my business card."

She laughed. "So yeah, basically, the plan is for your old home to be overrun with immigrants and crazy people – are you okay with that?"

"As long as there's goats involved, sure. Honestly, I think it sounds amazing." He really did. He wished he could be part of it.

"So is this something you're serious about, or is it still at the daydream stage?" Felix asked.

"Oh, it's serious. I mean, I'm still daydreaming all the time. But Ali's proper organised. She's written a business plan with costings and projections and all that stuff, and she's been looking into grant applications and all sorts."

They had reached the pond now. It was every bit as lovely as Felix remembered, the willow trees reflected immaculately in the water, downy catkins like hairy white caterpillars. On the island, a Canada goose was sitting on a thronelike nest. The gander circled suspiciously in front of them, his neck flat against the water.

"Canada geese. They used to nest here when I was growing up."

"These must be their descendants. They've probably heard stories about you, passed down through the generations. You're like a god to them."

"I don't know. I don't think he likes me very much."

"He's literally bowing down to you."

That was when they heard the cuckoo, calling its name from the thicket beyond the far bank. It was a sound so familiar that for a moment Felix barely registered it. Then it called again, and he realised he hadn't heard a cuckoo for years.

"Did you hear that?" he asked, though from her grin he could see she had.

"I've only ever heard a cuckoo in real life once before, when I was here with Ruth," Marsha said. "I love all the birds here."

"You're quite into birds, aren't you?"

"I bloody love birds."

He wondered for a moment what might happen if a kingfisher appeared.

It was nearly four o'clock by the time they got back to the house. Laurence had wanted to have a close-up look at the trees in Brickwood, tenderly stroking their trunks; Felix tried to find the whereabouts of the old car he used to play in, but couldn't see any sign of it. Zane had been desperate to play more hide-and-seek; a tantrum was averted when Felix showed him a hiding place in the laurel hedge by the yard, close to where the van was parked. His phone had rung twice. He'd recognised Geoff's number, and let it ring through to voicemail.

"I'm sorry we've taken up so much of your time," Aleesha said.

"Really, it's fine. It's been a pleasure."

"And look, obviously we really, really want the place. And we'd like to put in an offer. But it's tricky. I mean, we've got a large deposit from selling Mum's house. But we don't know quite how much we can borrow."

They didn't yet have a mortgage agreement, she explained. They were talking with an advisor, but it was tricky.

"At the moment, I'm basically a full-time mum since being put on furlough, Marsha's a part-time youth worker who'll be leaving her job anyway, so it all has to be based on Laurence's salary."

"And I'm a self-employed tree surgeon who's earnt bugger all for the last twelve months because of bloody Covid."

"Tell us what to do, Felix," Marsha pleaded. "We're counting on you. No pressure."

It wasn't ideal. Felix was pretty sure Geoff and Harvey would make an offer. They'd go in low, but if they were confident of getting planning permission, and they usually were, then Land2Build would easily pay the asking price.

"If the mortgage agreement comes through, what would be your top offer?" he asked.

"In an ideal scenario, we'd be able to stretch to the full amount, just. But I think that's unlikely, frankly."

"We'll pay them whatever they want!" Marsha said. "Please can we live here, Mummy? Please?"

"Well, look. I can tell the vendor you're interested, and sound them out about what they'd consider an acceptable offer. And I can try and forestall any other interest for a while."

"That would be wonderful," Aleesha said. "We really appreciate it."

"I wish I could promise more. Sadly, I don't have much influence in the matter."

"You can tell Veronika it's us," Marsha said.

"Veronika?"

"The woman who used to live here. We met her when we came down with Laurence's granddad."

"Do you think she liked us?" Laurence asked. "I found it hard to tell."

"We did rip up her floor," Aleesha pointed out.

"She did most of it," Marsha said. "Anyway, I liked her. What happened to her and her family anyway?"

"I've never spoken to them myself," Felix said. "All I know is that he lives in London and she lives in Germany. Frankfurt, I think."

"I did get the feeling theirs wasn't a life of domestic bliss. Well, if you do speak to her, say hi from me. Or don't, if you think it would be better not to."

"One more thing," Laurence said. "I know this might sound weird, but do you think it's okay if I pick some flowers before we go? My granddad asked me if I could leave some flowers on the grave of the lady who lived here. She's buried in the churchyard in the village."

"I'm sure that's fine," Felix said. "Actually, if you don't mind, I might come with you."

Felix drove the half-mile to the church, the scent of freshly picked narcissi filling the car. The others followed in Laurence's van. They parked by the yew hedge along the north side of the churchyard.

"Do you remember where the grave is?" Aleesha asked

"It was over the far side, by the field. There was an apple tree beside it."

"What did you say her name was?" Felix asked.

"Tessa. Tessa Cann."

"No way! That's the grave right next to my mother."

They walked through the lychgate and round the far side of the flint church.

"There's a tap over here," Felix said.

Laurence filled a green plastic watering can, and Aleesha found a jam jar for their flowers. Then they headed over to their neighbouring graves.

"It makes you wish there was an afterlife, doesn't it?" Marsha said. "Imagine if they could see this, your mum and Tessa Cann. She sounded like an amazing person, by the way. Your mum couldn't have a better neighbour."

Laurence put the flowers down. "These are from Henry," he explained to the gravestone. They stood in silence for a few moments. Laurence took a photo of the grave.

"Her husband died more than twenty years before she did," Aleesha said. "1930, look. That's sad."

"That's even sadder," Laurence said, pointing to the next cross along.

Felix read the inscription. He'd not noticed it before.

IN LOVING MEMORY OF
THOMAS JOHN CANN (1895-1916)
AND CECIL PETER CANN (1897-1916)
UPON ANOTHER SHORE AND IN A GREATER LIGHT

"Gramps said she lost both her sons in the war," Laurence said. "I can't even imagine."

"And look at that one," Aleesha said. Beside Thomas and Cecil was a small stone cross with the name MARY CANN, 1901.

Marsha turned to Felix. "We should let you have a moment to yourself. Tell your mum I'm a big fan of her work. Look!" she said, picking up Thalia. "Lambs! Come on."

She carried her niece over to the fence to look at the sheep in the next field; the others followed. The lambs were doing their thing, gambolling and frolicking. Thalia was soon laughing with delight.

Eleanor's grave hardly needed flowers. Her tree was covered in blossom, and the bulbs he'd planted on her instruction – bluebells, narcissi, grape hyacinth – had started to colonise that corner of the churchyard. Still, he poked the narcissi and tulips he'd picked from the garden into the holes of the grave vase. He would have liked to say a prayer. He'd long given up on the God he'd longed to believe in during Easter Sundays, harvest festivals and carol services in that little church, but there was something holy about the place: a sense of stillness and contemplation, where you could feel a part of something greater than yourself.

"Hey, Eleanor," he said in his head. "I've just been at the house. These people want to buy it. They're lovely."

He was under no illusion that Eleanor could hear. Still, he thought it best not to mention Geoff and Harvey.

"The Canada geese are nesting. And we heard a cuckoo. Which Marsha was really excited about. She's the woman with the headscarf. You'd like her. She said to tell you she's a big Brixton Bunnies fan. Anyway, I brought some narcissi. The garden looks amazing. I wonder if these came from bulbs you planted? Or maybe your neighbour planted them a hundred years ago. You know Tessa and Roger Cann used to live at The Lindens before us? That's kind of crazy, isn't it? Right, well. Bye. I love you, Mum."

He stood silent for a while, as if expecting a reply. A breath of breeze sighed through the leaves of the apple tree. Aleesha and Laurence picked up their children and wandered back towards the car. Marsha came over to him. "Are you alright?" she asked. She gave his hand another squeeze, and Felix felt the same static charge rush through him. The apple blossom was shining in the late afternoon sunlight. A blackbird poured out its liquid song from the top of the yew tree behind them.

"I'm all right," he said.

"It's sad, isn't it, death? Our mums. Tessa Cann's kids. Dying too soon." She laughed. "That's my hot take. Death is sad. Also, war is bad, children are the future and the best things in life are free."

"I don't know if the last one's even strictly true," Felix said.

"You could have a point. Still, I reckon I'm right about death being sad."

They walked slowly back through the churchyard.

"She didn't do too badly. Look at that." Marsha pointed to a nearby gravestone of polished pink granite.

"Margaret (Peggy) Morgan. 1899 – 2002," Felix read. "Bloody hell. I remember her. Mrs Morgan. She was one of the few people who could manage Gaia, our goat. She used to go rampaging round the village when she was on heat. The goat, I mean. Not Mrs Morgan. Mrs Morgan would bring her back sometimes. Most people were terrified of her. She had sharp horns and a fierce temper."

"Mrs Morgan?"

"Ha ha."

"Three centuries though. She overlapped with Queen Victoria and Billie Eilish. Imagine."

They said goodbye by the cars. Felix agreed he'd ring the vendor and put in an offer just shy of the asking price. It was after five, but he could still try and get things in motion before the weekend.

"I'll chase the mortgage people again on Monday morning," Aleesha promised.

"And I'll be in touch about the caprine consultancy role," Marsha said. "We've got your number."

The faint perfume of narcissi still hung in the car. Felix checked his phone. There was another missed call from Geoff, a text saying "check msgs", and a voicemail.

"Felix mate, it's Geoff, re The Lindens. Give us a bell when you get this. We want to make an offer."

There was an email too. "Haven't heard back from you but want to proceed with Lindens purchase. £1m starting offer."

Felix marked the message as unread and sent it to his spam folder. It was after five on a Friday anyhow. He didn't have to respond out of work hours.

He drove back into town, through the Friday rush hour traffic. Coffey and Cole's was deserted by the time he got there. He let himself in. There were two new messages from Geoff on the office answerphone. Felix deleted them. Then he called Mr Lambert.

"I've got some good news about The Lindens. I think we've found you a buyer. Lovely family, no chain." (This wasn't strictly true, but it sounded like Aleesha and Marsha had a solid buyer for their mum's place.) "They've offered just a fraction below the asking price – one million and five."

Mr Lambert didn't sound impressed by this. "I think we can hold out for the full price. We're not in a hurry to sell. Market's picking up. Have you had any other interest?"

"Nothing solid, no. I can go back to them and see if they'll increase their offer. I'm sure they will. If they do, can I tell them we have a deal?"

"Well, I have to get my soon-to-be-ex-wife's agreement, since legally speaking she's the actual owner. Just a tax arrangement. But if they're serious then yes, I don't see why not."

"Excellent. Well, I'll be in touch early next week."

.   .   .

And now here he was a week later, pulling up outside The Lindens. He switched off the engine. His hands were still shaking. He felt drained, and exhilarated.

He didn't have the key for the ludicrous security gates, so he walked along the road to Brickwood and climbed the barbed wire fence. He tramped through the undergrowth, brambles catching on his suit trousers, and up the bank, then vaulted onto the wall by the folly.

Geoff had phoned the office on Monday morning.

"Felix, you're a hard man to get hold of. Did you get my messages?"

"I did. I was just about to call you," Felix said, untruthfully. "Sorry not to get back to you sooner. My other appointments overran."

"Have you heard back from Cameron Lambert about our offer?"

"Well, I was about to discuss that with you. To confirm the amount."

"I put it in the email. One mil starting offer."

"Email? I didn't get an email, just your voice message."

"I emailed you Friday afternoon."

"I'm really sorry. I guess it must have gone into my junk mail. I'll have a look now."

Geoff grunted. "No need. Just tell him ASAP."

"Of course. I'll let you know when I have an answer."

"Who was that?" asked Matt, the only other agent in that morning.

"Geoff from Land2Build. Just a question about a property I showed him on Friday. I'm going to pop out and grab a coffee, can I get you anything?"

Felix stepped out into the April sunshine. He made his way down the street, past the coffee shop and into Elizabeth

Gardens. He called Aleesha from a bench by the river and explained the situation.

"We should hear back from the mortgage person by Thursday," she said. "Can it wait till then?"

"I'm not sure if it can. These other guys are quite pushy."

"Look, I'll speak to Laurence and Marsha and call you back, okay?"

"Okay, but I'm sort of bunking off work right now. I didn't really want to talk in the office."

"I'll speak to them right away."

It was Marsha who called back.

"Just offer the full price," she said. "If we don't get the full mortgage amount, we'll borrow the rest of the money some other way. We'll sell our kidneys or something. And if it all collapses, it all collapses."

"I'm happy to do that. But they will need paperwork eventually, proof of funds and so on."

"I'll make sure we get a written offer for the kidneys."

Back in the office, he called Cameron Lambert.

"Congratulations! We have ourselves a deal."

"The full one point one mil?"

"Yep. Send me your solicitor's details and we can get straight onto the conveyancing."

Later that afternoon, he called Geoff. "I spoke to the vendor."

"Yeah? About time. What did he say?"

"He needs to discuss it with his wife. Seems she's the one who actually owns the house. Said he'd call her tonight and get back to me tomorrow."

For the next 24 hours, Felix did his best to concentrate on other things. Mercifully, he had viewings on Tuesday morning: a young couple, expecting their first child, who seemed thrilled by a three-bed new build on one of the

London Road estates, and a morose bloke in his forties – a recent divorcee, Felix guessed – whose budget didn't match his need for three bedrooms. They visited two small terraced houses and a flat, and the man seemed to find them all equally depressing. Felix couldn't say he blamed him.

It probably would have been better to speak to Geoff on the phone, but Felix didn't think he could face it. He emailed instead.

Hi Geoff

Sorry to be the bearer of bad news, but I'm afraid we had another buyer come in with an offer on The Lindens, which the vendors have accepted.

If anything changes, you'll of course be the first to know.

He typed *Kind regards*, deleted it, put *Best wishes* then deleted that too and just signed off with his name.

He left early that afternoon, and switched off his phone.

The next morning, James Coffey called him into his office.

"Felix. Would you care to tell me what is going on? Geoff Danton called me last night, and he's spitting feathers. He believes you have, and I quote, 'fucking fucked him over'. I've been trying to call you, but your phone was switched off."

"Is this about The Lindens?" Felix asked.

"Of course it's about the bloody Lindens, Felix, don't play dumb. He says you let somebody gazump him."

"Well... I put his offer to the vendors to consider. But these other buyers, the ones who saw the property just after him, offered the full asking price."

"Really. That's interesting. The funny thing is, I called Cameron Lambert last night after getting off the phone to Geoff, and he tells me you didn't say anything about another offer. Now why would he say that?"

"Okay, I'm sorry. He said they were going to hold out for the full asking price, and Land2Build's offer was lower, so..."

"So you give them the opportunity to increase it. Come on, Felix, you know how these guys operate. Geoff's already told me he thinks they'd go over the asking price if necessary." He'd adopted a more-in-sorrow-than-in-anger tone. "Now, you can appreciate the situation this has put me in. We've got a vendor who thinks we're at best unprofessional, and a client – a *valued* client, somebody our firm does a lot of business with – going around telling people that we are not to be trusted. And trust is our greatest asset. So, I would appreciate an explanation."

I don't want some wanker turning my home into a fucking business park, Felix wanted to say. *I want Zane and Thalia to play hide-and-seek in the garden. I want Laurence to make beautiful things from the trees, and for his granddad to come and visit and leave flowers on the grave next to Mum's. I want Aleesha and Marsha to set up their not-commune and make people's lives better. I want Marsha to hear the cuckoo calling every spring.*

"The Woods really wanted the place," he said simply. "And I liked them."

"Well that's marvellous, but my father didn't build this business by just dealing with people he liked. You need to put this right, Felix. What we're going to do is, we're going to call up Mr and Mrs Lambert, together. You are going to apologise to him, and you are going to explain the situation. We have a Zoom call scheduled for 5pm. I'll see you back in here then."

Cameron Lambert entered the call at five on the dot, but there was no sign of Mrs Lambert.

"Should we give it a few minutes?" James asked.

"Nah, if she doesn't join us, that's her lookout. All she has to do is sign her name on the contract."

432

James explained the situation. How another buyer was also interested, and how his colleague Felix here had unfortunately failed to pass on the message.

"For which he is terribly sorry," James added.

Before Cameron Lambert had a chance to respond, Veronika entered the call. An attractive but severe-looking woman in her forties, blonde hair tied up in a tight bun. She appeared to be wearing a lab coat.

"Nice of you to join us, Veronika," Cameron said. "Still at work I see."

The woman neither confirmed nor denied this.

"And where are the kids?"

"With a friend."

"Oh? What friend?"

"You don't know him."

James broke in before this had a chance to go any further. "Mrs Lambert, I was explaining to your – er, to Mr Lambert, how we have another buyer interested in the house. A cash buyer – which means they already have the money."

Felix thought he detected an eye roll. He tried to catch the woman's eye, but found this wasn't possible via webcam.

"And they're prepared to up their offer," James continued. "I believe you've met them, in fact. Geoff Danton."

"Geoff? I know Geoff. You remember, Veronika? We went shooting with him once. He's a friend of Piers."

There was definitely an eye roll this time.

"Geoff and his company are very interested," James said. "They see a lot of development potential. I'd be confident we can get another ten grand out of them at minimum."

Felix spoke for the first time. "Funnily enough, Mrs Lambert, you've met the other buyers too. Laurence and Aleesha Wood, and her sister Marsha. They came to visit the house with Laurence's grandfather, about five years ago. He'd lived there during the war."

The woman's face softened. "I remember. Laurence and Aleesha are married?"

"They have two kids," Felix said. "A boy and a girl."

"And Marsha? She is living with them?"

"The idea was that she'd live in the stable flat, yes."

The woman started to speak, then the screen froze.

"Sorry, we missed that," James said when she'd finished buffering. "You froze there for a moment."

"I said we sell to Marsha and family. It's nice that they have the house. Is like fate."

"For Christ's sake, Veronika! We're talking ten thousand at least here!"

"I really think you should listen to your husband, Mrs Lambert," James said. "As I say, I'm confident we can push the price up further."

"Pah. I have money. Anyway, Cameron said we made agreement already."

"Well that's very noble, but it is only a verbal agreement...," James began.

"Trust is our greatest asset," Felix reminded him, and received a dirty look.

"Can we at least discuss this before we make any hasty decisions?" Cameron pleaded.

"No. Is decided. I must get back to work now. Please say hello to Marsha and the others from me," she said, directing this at Felix. "I hope they will be very happy in the house." Then her face disappeared from the screen.

He phoned Marsha that evening to pass on Veronika's greetings, to see if there was any news on the mortgage (there wasn't), and to fill her in.

"Are you in trouble?" she asked. "I feel like it's our fault."

"I don't know. Maybe. But it's not your fault. And I'm not sure if I care anyway."

"How do you mean?"

"I don't think I'm going to lose my job. But if I did, maybe that wouldn't be the worst thing in the world. I'm not exactly living the life I always dreamed of."

"And what was that?"

"I don't know. I certainly thought I'd be married with kids by the time I was forty-three. And have a dog. I also didn't think I'd be an estate agent."

"With a caprine consultancy side hustle," she reminded him.

"I remember when I was eighteen, lying under a tree by the pond and looking up at the branches, and thinking how each one of them was like a path you could choose. Endless possibilities, stretching off into the sunlight. Only I seem to have ended up on a dead branch."

"So choose a different one."

They ended up talking for over an hour. Felix couldn't remember the last time he'd enjoyed talking to someone so much.

The next day, Thursday, she messaged him.

> Don't have to sell a kidney! Got the
> mortgage offer 😊 😊 😊

By the afternoon, Aleesha had sent through immaculate and comprehensive paperwork and her solicitor was already in touch with Veronika's. Marsha messaged him again.

> Told you Ali was good at all that stuff. We're
> so grateful for everything you've done.

> Just trying to earn my 1.5%

> You'll have to come and have a glass of champagne with us when we move in.

> Please bring the champagne, we don't have any money left.

Friday morning – this morning – James Coffey had collared him when he got into work. "Felix. My office at 11. My father's coming in. Matt's taking your appointments."

Felix spent the next two hours catching up with emails and admin. Veronika had emailed to confirm that she'd heard from Aleesha's solicitor. The couple who'd viewed the London Road new build had had their offer accepted and were getting adorably excited about conveyancing. He emailed the divorced dad with a few more potential properties.

Coffey and son were waiting for him in the office, along with Nigel Cole, the other partner.

"Come in and take a seat, Felix," Coffey Senior said. "And close the door, there's a good chap."

Felix sat down in the one chair available. The other three were facing him. It felt like an interview. But they were friendly enough.

"Firstly, I hear you brought in a nice big sale yesterday," Julian Coffey continued. "Congratulations. It's no less than we expect of you. Your sales record is excellent."

"Agent of the Month four times in the last year," James added.

"However... there's a however."

They proceeded to relate his crimes and misdemeanours

of the past week. How he'd failed in his duty both to a prospective buyer and to the vendor. Had misled if not in fact lied to both of them, and lied again when questioned about it. How trust was their most important asset.

"You've also managed to royally piss off an important client with a lot of connections," James added. "Frankly, it wouldn't be hard to find grounds to dismiss you."

"However, again, we don't want to do that," Julian Coffey said. "As James has previously informed you, I shall be retiring later this year, and we had discussed the possibility of offering you the opportunity to become a partner. We had thought of you as a safe pair of hands, Felix. We didn't have you down as a loose cannon. But we're prepared to overlook this episode as being out of character, if you can demonstrate that it truly was out of character."

"Thank you," said Felix. "But I don't know if it was."

"I beg your pardon?"

"I don't know if it was out of character. In fact, it felt like exactly the right thing to do. And I'd do the same again."

They were looking at him nonplussed. "In that case, you need to think very carefully about where your future lies," Coffey Senior said.

"You're right. And I don't think it's here. I'd like to hand in my notice."

Felix had never silenced a room before. He felt like he'd grown a foot taller.

And then he'd walked out. Got in the car and, practically on autopilot, driven out to The Lindens. Three months' notice. May, June, end of July. The start of the summer holidays. The big blue cloudless skies of the future.

He felt like he was playing truant. He was trespassing too, he supposed. He walked down the folly steps, then up to the top garden and through an elaborate metal arch –

there used to be a wicket gate there – onto the juniper slope. Past the orchard, through the meadow and the New Forest to the pond.

He found the ash tree and sat down on the grass. He texted Marsha.

> Seriously need to speak to you about that caprine consultancy...

Then he lay down on his back and looked up through the labyrinth of branches. He spotted a dead twig halfway up. He followed it back to the branch, all the way back to the first fork in the trunk. Then he took the other fork, and followed a new path to the top of the canopy where the first green buds were just beginning to open.

In the blue above, a swallow was circling. The first of the year.

EPILOGUE

2035

Marsha stands by the kitchen window, greeting the morning. She loves this time of year. The orchard is a sea of pink and white, Portia the Gloucester old spot sow and her piglets just visible beneath the surface. The first trees they planted are fully grown now – from here, you can't tell where the old orchard ends and the new one begins. In another few years, the trees they planted this winter will be the same. Aleesha says they'll be able to make twice the volume of cider and apple juice when those trees mature, and still have no trouble selling it all in the shop and the café.

Marsha pours two mugs of tea from the pot. She sees Tess coming down Jupiter Hill with Honey. When Tess spots Marsha at the window, she waves. Marsha waves back. She still can't believe she has a twelve-year-old. No doubt there's a tidal wave of teenage hormones set to break any day, but for now she's thankful to have a daughter who gets up early on a Saturday morning to walk the dog up to the pond. Even if she has probably been spying on that group of boys staying in the yurts.

Tess has stopped and is looking up at something. Marsha follows her gaze, and sees a swallow wheeling across the blue. She watches it sweep over the house and the folly, then circle back round over the vegetable garden. Home again, after its twelve thousand mile round trip. Marsha smiles. She finds a pen, ticks 'swallow' off the bird chart on the back of the kitchen door. The first of the year. Then she calls through to the bedroom: "The swallows are back."

ACKNOWLEDGMENTS

Thank you to everyone whose input made this book better: to my early readers Claire Adas, Matthew Bellwood and Dougie Boyd; to Lindy, Ev, Dougal and Zanna; to Mathias Black (mathiasblack.com) for going above and beyond; to Gideon Burrows (gideon-burrows.com) for his feedback, typesetting and support through the publishing process; to James @ GoOnWrite.com for the cover design; to Jennifer Barclay for believing in it; to Rachel and the girls.

And thank you for reading. If you enjoyed the book, I'd be truly grateful if you could leave a review on Amazon, Goodreads or wherever. Also, books make great gifts. Just saying.